HYDE AND SEEK

A. J. SAUNDERS

Acknowledgements

I want to thank my dedicated beta readers, Lisa, Helen and John for taking time to read.

Table of Contents

Chapter 1

What the hell do I do now?

Jaime pushed her trolley around the terminal, waiting to catch a sign with her name on it.

Nothing.

She traipsed up and down for a good ten minutes. Still hadn't found anyone. Okay, so she hadn't rushed off the plane. There was no particular hurry. No bus or train to catch and she'd guessed her contact would wait. A knot tightened in her stomach before she released a short sharp breath, praying someone would show up.

Passengers pushed past her eager to leave Charles de Gaulle Airport for the next leg of their journey. Some smiled at her. Others tapped on their phones. The stranger carrying an attaché looked dodgy, though. Was it the way he kept shooting furtive glances her way? Or could it be the fact he looked familiar? Whatever, he was scary, observing her with a smile that didn't quite reach his eyes. The way a wolf might scrutinise its prey before the fatal pounce.

She closed her eyes and took in deep breaths. No one knew why she was running away. No one knew who she was running from. The problem was…neither did she anymore.

Shit, the wolf was heading her way!

Swallowing hard, Jaime swerved the trolley round like an ice skater with its partner before doubling back to the arrivals sliding doors. She didn't like the look of the man, and wasn't going to hang around.

Don't panic.

Of course she was panicking. She'd arrived in a foreign country, miles away from home with no one to meet. Surely her new employers would have phoned if they'd changed their minds about having a housekeeper. They wouldn't have abandoned her, would they? Thank God she could at least speak the language. She'd have to put her 'A' level French into action earlier than expected.

When the agency had called, asking if she could start three weeks before Christmas, Jaime had jumped at the opportunity. Leaving at such short notice and spending the festive period away from the family wasn't a problem. Desperate to get away, she hadn't even checked if the company existed. It all seemed genuine enough.

Thinking back now, the agency hadn't even asked for specific qualifications. Just as well. She had none. Her mother had explained everything about running a household when Jaime helped out in the guest house at weekends or when they had a full house. Besides, what qualifications did she need to cook and clean for two old priests? Tweedledum and Tweedledee – that's how she imagined them.

Jaime bit the inside of her cheek, repeating what she was going to say to anyone who could help, when a stunning woman waving a card with 'Jaime Sanders' written in big black letters caught her eye. Why hadn't she seen her before? No one could miss that tumble of red hair. The woman looked like a female devil out of a folklore book. At the same time, she was classy and elegant. She wore black right down to her stilettos. Perfect makeup accentuated huge, midnight blue eyes and scarlet varnish tipped long, elegant fingers.

Jaime approached, the corners of her mouth rising in a slow smile.

"So *you're* Jamie?" the woman said, turning up her nose.

Jaime smiled and tried her best French pronunciation. "That's right, but my name's not *Jay-me*, it's *Jaym*."

She held out a hand only to pull it back when the woman ignored it. "And you are?"

"Never mind who I am. I'm only here to drive you."

Jaime raised an eyebrow and turned to follow the escort.

"It's Leonora, if you must know," the woman called over her shoulder and strutted out of the terminal to the car park.

What a welcome.

They arrived in front of a black Porsche. Leonora clicked open the boot, tapping her foot while Jaime crammed her cases into the small space. Then with a huff, Leonora drove them out of the airport and onto the motorway to Rambouillet.

It began to rain, sapping Jaime's humour. A bad omen? The French always boasted about their good climate. She remembered what one French pen pal had said about the English weather: 'Un temps de merde'. Well, it couldn't be shittier than the weather right now.

Jaime gazed through the bleary front window. New country. New language. New job. She hadn't done things by half measures. But then, she never did.

Leonora concentrated on the road and seemed in no mood to make conversation. Once or twice, she gave Jaime sidelong glances, all the while pulling her fingers through her flamboyant locks. On one occasion Jaime caught the woman pulling a snooty smirk.

Lowering the visor, Jaime peered into the small mirror. Two chestnut brown irises stared back. She was no physical match for this beautiful woman. For a start, not as tall, and her shoulder length brown curls were uncontrollable. As for makeup, she'd never been one for overdoing eyeliner or mascara. No boyfriend had ever complained. Why should she worry now?

She flapped the mirror shut. "Nice car."

No comment.

"What do you do for a living?" Jaime tried again.

Leonora placed her iPhone buds into her ears, putting an immediate end to Jaime's questions.

Outside, the dismal motorway matched Jaime's mood. A blurred sound hummed from Leonora's headset. It mingled from time to time with low muffled voices. Leonora focused on the road, tapping now and again on the steering wheel. No doubt in rhythm to the music.

Jaime wondered if she'd done the right thing coming to France. Could Leonora be a sample of what was to come?

Were all the French so bloody rude?

Jaime closed her eyes and leaned her head against the side window. If Leonora refused to make conversation, so be it. At least she could relax and think over the past few weeks. Life had been hectic. Scary even. Yesterday, she'd been laughing with friends. A week earlier, she'd been at her secretarial job working with super colleagues. Now, she was in France.

So much had changed since that fatal night, eighteen months ago when she'd stumbled onto the scene of a crime. What she'd give to turn back the pages. Return to her existence before the trial when she could go partying or spend evenings at the pub with colleagues without suspecting everyone who glanced her way. To jog alone in the countryside. Stay out all night. Even chat with strangers.

The trial had pushed her into a new future. Less freedom, no more wandering on her own, long sleepless nights. No matter what she did, each detail of that night laid anchored in her mind. She used to be a lively, outgoing person. That had changed. She'd become a bundle of nerves ever since the first threatening notes arrived shortly after the beginning of the trial.

Grant was the one to suggest she leave England. At first, she'd taken her brother's idea for a joke. But when a mangled cat lay sprawled on the hood of the car with the last note, she had to admit the only way to escape was to steer clear of the firing line.

A sharp dig in the ribs and a beeping horn brought Jaime to her senses. She sat bolt upright, momentarily dazed. Shit, she must have dropped off.

Ahead of the car, a set of tall gates slowly opened, revealing a beautiful driveway lined with red-tipped photinia shrubs. Jaime took in the beautiful stone façade of the oblong building. With its hue of warm, blonde colours, it looked convivial, conveying a feeling of character and warmth.

Leonora darted out of the car and opened the trunk. Impatient feet tapped once again while Jaime retrieved the cases. Then, without a word, Leonora slid back into the vehicle and revved away.

"Well, au revoir," Jaime muttered, staring after the car. How could anyone be so rude?

The car disappeared out of sight as a woman appeared from behind the house.

"Oh, I see Leonora's too busy to stop again." The woman held out a hand. "You must be Jaime Sanders. I'm Suzanne de Vere, Father de Vere's sister-in-law. Sorry I couldn't meet you at the airport. I had the children to fetch from school, so I sent my friend."

Some friend.

Jaime took the outstretched hand. Although petite, Suzanne had a determined handshake and a friendly smile, showing beautiful white teeth. Jaime took an immediate liking to the pretty, blonde woman. Something about Suzanne made Jaime feel at ease.

"Here, let me help you with your cases." Suzanne grabbed the biggest, and pulling a case each, they walked up the path and into the house. "I'm so glad to have someone to look after the presbytery again. Since the old housekeeper retired a few weeks ago, the place is missing a woman's touch. Then of course, there's the dog to keep an eye on."

Jaime remembered her own parish priest. An old man just about managing to get about with a cane, dressed in a long black robe with a run of buttons all the way down the front and shiny black shoes peeping out from under the hemline. A map of wrinkles set on his face and a smelly old dog hot on his heels. Yet, on seeing Suzanne, she couldn't believe Father de Vere to be as she'd imagined.

She was here now and would help the priests in their day-to-day chores, even though she wasn't too sure if she could cope with a small, yappy dog. She'd never had pets as a child. Didn't feel comfortable with dogs. In her eagerness to get away from England, she'd overlooked the mention of a dog.

"Come on into the kitchen." Suzanne's soft voice brought Jaime out of her thoughts. "I've made fresh coffee. Or would you prefer tea?"

"Coffee's fine."

"Good. I've prepared a room for you tonight. You'll be staying with us here in Rambouillet. Something cropped up unexpectedly, and my husband can't look after the children. I'll drive you up to Montfort-Le-Gesnois tomorrow."

"Oh!"

Suzanne smiled. "It's an hour-and-a-half drive to the presbytery. We'll go after lunch. That'll give us time to chat."

Although impatient to get over her anxiety about meeting her new employers, Jaime could only nod. Did she have a choice?

Suzanne placed two cups onto the kitchen table. "Are you thinking of staying longer than the stipulated time in the ad? I know it mentioned six months."

"I don't know. I'll stay as long as it takes to find..." Jaime bit the inside of her cheek.

"To find who?" Suzanne's lilac eyes widened from beneath long lashes.

"Er…to find a more appropriate housekeeper. I applied for the job to brush up on my French before I search for a secretarial job with an international company." Jaime cringed mentally at the lie.

Suzanne poured the coffee. "Of course; we don't expect you to stay forever. We know it's temporary until the agency finds someone else. Not a lot of people want to be housekeepers in a small, secluded village for such a low salary."

Jaime took the cup from Suzanne. "I don't mind. I only dealt with Italian clients in my last job as a PA. Lost my fluency in French." *And at least, no one will find me here.*

Suzanne took a sip of coffee. "Your French is very good."

"Nowhere near as good as it used to be. When I worked as a chalet girl in Tignes during my studies, it was almost perfect."

"Oh, I'm sure you'll soon be back up to scratch."

Jaime nodded. "I hope so, and I reckon I've acquired enough experience in my ten working years."

Suzanne's eyes widened. "Ten years? I guessed you were only about twenty-five."

Jaime let out a nervous giggle. "I've always looked young for my age. Has its advantages at times. I'm twenty-nine. Big 3 – 0 is next June."

"We'll have to organise a party if you're still around, then."

Jaime grinned, and they continued talking about the job at the presbytery. Suzanne made it clear that if Jaime needed anything whatsoever, she shouldn't hesitate to call.

Over coffee, Suzanne pointed out that her husband, Luc, was Father de Vere's younger brother. They had met at university where they both studied to become architects. After graduating, Luc had set up his own business while Suzanne worked as an interior designer from their house in Rambouillet, looking after their five-year-old twins at the same time. Jaime listened with interest. She liked this bubbly woman with her open friendliness.

The sound of a house phone echoed in the room nearby.

"Must be my husband. I won't be a minute." Suzanne disappeared into the lounge, leaving Jaime to admire the kitchen. Great space. All the latest amenities. Wonderful mixture of antique and contemporary decor. The kind of room where you could enjoy a cup of tea and share secrets.

Suzanne returned a few minutes later, chewing her thumbnail.

"That was Father de Vere. Something important has cropped up and they won't be there until late afternoon."

Already in a state of nerves about meeting her new employers, Jaime groaned inwardly. She knew she shouldn't let anxiety take over. Of course, she wanted to meet them, but they no doubt had a lot on their plates with church affairs. Whatever that was.

Jaime didn't have any experience working with the clergy and had never been much of a churchgoer either. As a teenager, her mother, Roman Catholic from birth, had forced Jaime to go to church every Sunday. That meant sitting on a hard pew, listening to the priest's sermons when she could have been doing other things instead. All that had stopped once she'd become an adult, and no man of the cloth had better try to convert her. It wouldn't work.

With her stomach churning, Jaime gave Suzanne a weak smile. Would she and the priests hit it off?

Chapter 2

Night covered the small town of Easton with cold, eerie darkness. The overcast sky drizzled a fine spray which seeped through her trench coat and trickled inside her collar. The metallic sound of her heels on cobblestones echoed in the deserted street. All her attention focused on the click-clack rather than the shadows thrown by the streetlights.

Relieved to be out of the noise and smoke of the pub, she inhaled lungfuls of fresh air, clutching her trench coat tighter. Once or twice, she raised her head to give a fleeting look at the closed shops and abandoned, graffiti-sprayed buildings. On the other side of the road, redbrick terraced houses lay asleep in the shadows. She didn't have to walk far. As always, her old mini was parked next to the red mail-box. It stood like a sentry, guarding the narrow entrance to a small alleyway.

A strange, high-pitched screech sent shivers down her spine. A cat, maybe. After a quick glance over her shoulder, and then another to make sure, she hurried to the vehicle. No cat shrieked like that.

A nearby flickering streetlight did nothing to help her nerves. Its intermittent orange glow a reminder of amber eyes while he stabbed his victim. The way he'd gazed at her at the trial when she'd given evidence against him as the prime witness to the murder.

After a few more strides, she reached the mini. But before she could climb into the safety of the car, her gaze was captured by a soggy piece of paper wedged under the back windscreen wiper next to the 'I love cats' sticker.

Another note.

She had no clue as to who left them. Whoever did, got his kicks from scaring the shit out of people. With shaky hands, she released the damp piece of paper, and gazed at the ink creeping down in rivulets.

YOU'RE NEXT!

A chill ran through her. Could he be nearby? Waiting for her to freak out? Well, she wouldn't give him the satisfaction. She stuck out her trembling chin while she aimed her key at the lock. It slipped out of her hand and landed with a resonant clang on the ground.

Shit!

She gazed up and down the street before crouching to retrieve the key. After numerous unsuccessful attempts, she finally got the door to open and jumped in, slamming down on the locks, hoping he wouldn't push his face up to the window.

When she looked through the windscreen, an ear-piercing scream escaped from her throat.

A cat lay on the front of the car, its delicate grey fur matted by the drizzle.

Fresh blood oozed from its side and merged with the rain, creating strange coloured streaks to spread across the bonnet.

Shallow, quick breathing turned to frantic gasping. With closed eyes, she took in deep breaths. If she didn't get her act together, she'd lose it. Getting it together was near to impossible when every note brought back memories of that terrible night, the guttural chokes, agonizing screams, and the sound of his knife slashing flesh. Even more so now with the cat glaring at her through its mangled eye.

Despite her shaky hands, she managed to fish the phone out of her bag. Sweaty finger marks appeared on the screen, blurring as tears welled up. She took in a deep breath and tried to comfort herself with happy thoughts. Not easy under the circumstances.

Biting the inside of her cheek, she called the inspector she'd been in contact with during the trial.

"Inspector King," came a deep voice.

"Good evening, Inspector; it's Jaime Sanders. You said I could call any time if I needed support."

"What's up, Jaime?"

She swallowed hard and tried to keep the tremour out of her voice, but failed.

"I've just got another note," she rambled. "It's on my car...dead...the cat's dead...with another note...what am I going to do–?"

"Take it easy, love, I can't make out what you're saying. Where are you?"

Jaime cleared her throat. "I'm near the small alleyway, a few metres away from The Rose and Crown."

The inspector's calm voice sailed down the line. "Right. Lock the car, Jaime. A police car is on its way."

"I thought it would all stop when he was in prison!" she shouted, chewing her thumbnail and tapping her foot on the accelerator. "Unless he's still paying someone to do his dirty work?"

The inspector cleared his throat. "I've got something to tell you. I was going to ring, but...he's been dead for two months. Killed in a brawl by inmates."

His words brought her world crashing to a standstill. If he was dead, then who the hell was stalking her? There couldn't be another lunatic on the loose, could there?

When a first tear escaped, she knew the rest would follow. And they did. In a nonstop torrent, shaking her body.

A siren broke through the silent evening, and flashing blue lights galloped towards her car in the rearview mirror.

"The police are here, now," she said between sobs. "I can see the flashing lights"

"Great. They'll bring you into the station for a chat."

"Th…thank you, inspector."

She flipped her phone shut and wiped her tears on the back of her hand, trying to ignore the cat sprawled on the bonnet.

In the grip of silent panic, her chest tightened, and a nervous laugh escaped her throat. What would the police do? Take another statement to add to her dossier.

Look into things like the other times she'd left statements? She couldn't put up with the waiting. Whoever this bastard was, he was prowling the streets and freaking her out.

Her jaw muscles tensed. She had to make a decision. And there was only one thing to do.

Run for the hills and hide.

Jaime sat bolt upright, coughing and spluttering. Nothing looked familiar. She peered into the semi-darkness, trying to get her bearings; all the while pressing her palms over her thumping chest. Why was it so dark?

She reached under the pillow and flicked on her mobile phone. Its bluish light brought the room to life. Her cases lay open under the window, and her handbag sat on the chair next to the door. Leaning across the mattress, she switched on the bedside lamp and let out a sigh of relief. She was in Rambouillet.

Flinging her legs over the side of the bed, she headed to the window and opened the shutters. A chilly, early morning breeze entered the room, making her shiver. She slammed the window shut and dashed back to her warm bed. Snuggling down under the duvet, she stared at the ceiling. Those awful nightmares were back again. But she was safe here. He wouldn't find her. He couldn't find her. How would he know where to look?

She nodded in agreement with her thoughts, persuading herself she'd done the right thing in leaving. The police had taken her statements along with the folder she'd prepared with all the notes. Even if they'd been a great support, apart from pinning a detective to her heels twenty-four hours a day, what else could they do? Did she even want that?

When all was said and done, she'd had no choice but to leave.

***

By the time she reached the presbytery later that day, Jaime had discovered a lot about Suzanne's family. She'd enjoyed meeting Luc. In spite of him being rather tall and stocky, giving him the air of a Viking with his longish, honey blond hair and cognac eyes, he had a reassuring smile and came over as a gentle giant. From the way he gazed at his wife when she spoke, the man was deeply in love.

As for the five-year-old twins, they were cute and full of life. Sasha and Santine had inherited their mother's blond curls and lilac eyes. They'd taken to Jaime straight away, and she'd spent a large part of the evening playing with them. All in all, the family had made her feel welcome. She regretted she couldn't stay longer.

One question had been bothering Jaime since meeting Luc, though. How old could the man's brother be if he was so young? She'd imagined priests as old and doddery. Unless Luc was born from a second marriage. Those things did happen. Whatever, she'd soon find out.

Jaime and Suzanne got out of the car and walked up to the presbytery. Halfway up the path, she stopped to study the building. Majestic, yet welcoming. Two large French windows on either side of the solid oak front door looked out over a well-kept garden. Large pots of neatly shaped box trees stood on either side of the stone path. On the first floor, four tall windows sat under a grey slate roof with a dignified chimney, giving the impression of a small manoir.

"Oh, that's Petrus, by the way." Suzanne nodded at the dog standing in the doorway.

Christ Almighty!

A gangly Great Dane, as big as a pony, looked up with huge sad eyes. So much for the small yapping dog. She couldn't see herself shoving this dog into a corner if it wouldn't listen.

Suzanne disappeared into the house and the dog stood firm in the entrance, blocking access to the house. Jaime would have her work cut out with this giant if she had to look after the dog too.

With her back against the wall, Jaime nudged past the dog, taking in short, sharp, breaths every time it moved its head.

"Quick tour of the presbytery?" Suzanne called over her shoulder.

"Er...yeah, I'll do any tour once I get past Hulk."

Jaime followed Suzanne down the hallway. Polished oak parquet covered the floor and stretched right up to the main staircase which swept up to a wide corridor on the first floor. Jaime's first impression was one of grandeur. Each room she popped her head into had a large window framed with heavy velvet drapes with rugs of the same colour.

Despite the old-fashioned pieces of furniture, the house radiated cosiness. The previous housekeeper must have been a meticulous cleaner. The floors shone, and a fresh fragrance of lavender bounced in the air.

Jaime was satisfied.

They strolled into the village which wasn't bursting with life. What had she expected? Apart from a few women carrying shopping baskets, the streets were empty. The small shops still displayed signs from the beginning of the last century. A beautiful stone fountain dominated the heart of the village square, releasing a feeling of past life, and half-timbered houses sat proudly around it. Could she have travelled back to the early 1900s?

Walking down the cobbled road lined with well-kept houses, Jaime had to admit something about the picturesque place pleased her. She couldn't quite describe what. Suzanne mentioned that Le Mans was only half an hour's drive away. The city had proper shopping facilities, and Jaime would find everything she needed there.

When they arrived back at the presbytery, Suzanne gave Jaime her mobile number. After a warm hug and a promise to meet up again during the Christmas holidays, Suzanne headed back to Rambouillet.

Jaime climbed the stairs and entered the bedroom Suzanne had shown to be hers during their tour. The spacious bedroom contained antique, hand-painted murals. A double bed with an ornate mahogany headboard dominated the room. Jaime caressed the fluffy duvet and toppled onto it, inhaling the pleasant scent of lavender. The quilt enveloped her with warmth and softness. It reminded Jaime of her mother's guest house. Same fresh laundry smell. Similar soft, bouncy duvets. Whenever Jaime could, she would laze in bed longer than usual. Not because she was tired, but the duvet simply held her down, unwilling to let go.

Dragging herself away from the bed, Jaime set about putting her personal things into the chest of drawers, and hung the rest of her clothes in the oak wardrobe. When finished, she peered out of the window to the back garden. Shallow hills lay peacefully against the sky, broken every so often with hedgerows like a vast patchwork quilt. Faraway footpaths meandered up the slopes, branching around small thickets of trees before disappearing out of sight. Come springtime, long strolls would be number one on her to do list. She might even take the dog if they hit it off. Or the dog would take her.

A movement to the right attracted Jaime's attention. Through the skeleton-bare Albizia, not far from the ancient water pump, a gardener was busy digging a rather deep hole. Jaime frowned. Where had he popped up from? She hadn't seen him earlier on the tour. Of course, they hadn't been to the back of the house.

From what she could make out, he was well-built, and she reckoned over six-foot tall. Although mid-December and with the temperature edging seven degrees, it appeared he didn't notice the cold. His tight t-shirt clung to his back with sweat, showing rippled muscles under the material.

It had been quite a while since she'd had a man in her life. She enjoyed clubbing with her friends. Loud, blaring music helped her to forget about her worries. It also allowed her to let off steam after a hard week's work. Although she'd never been one for pub crawls, going out with the girls had been fun. Most of them had always come away with a new man in tow.

On the few occasions she'd met up with guys, they were either too serious or out for a bit of fun on a short-term basis. Not her cup of tea. What she'd give to find someone who wanted to have a bit of fun on a more permanent basis. To have a laugh and joke at the end of the day. If Mr. Right came along, she'd even be prepared to invest in a long-time relationship.

Thinking back to her old flames, she realised what a queer bunch they'd been. Navy officer Nathan had preferred going out with his mates. Simon the Banker had been a nightmare, always down the pub with the lads. And Architect Angelo hated going out at all; they spent every weekend in his poky flat playing video games. Could this gardener be different? She smiled, remembering her friends' jokes about French men being great lovers. But she was out for more than just a lover.

A few minutes later, wrapped up in her warm duffle coat, Jaime bounced down the stairs ready to meet 'mystery man'. Her eyes scanned the garden. Beautiful. She sailed down the buff sandstone garden path, eager to start up a conversation. Jaime had to admit the moss-free lawn was perfect in the centre of the pretty space. Stray branches from the many shrubs had been cut back. Even the creeping ivy crawled only along the side of the path. The man did a good job.

On approaching, Jaime heard him whistling a tune she didn't know. Had to be something French. Quite enchanting. With butterflies coming to life, Jaime's pulse picked up a quicker tempo. She joined both hands behind her back and stood in front of him. The sight of his body up close set her groaning inwardly. What she'd give to run a hand up the inside of his t-shirt or along the Celtic tattoo half hidden on his upper arm.

Mesmerized, she moved her gaze to his face. A well-trimmed beard, the same colour as his short black hair, covered his square jaw.

The gardener looked up, and dark captivating eyes met hers. Oh, that mouth. The man was pure sex on a stick – just what she needed to brighten up the afternoon. A little bonus while hiding away in this quiet village.

What if she got him a drink? Watching him lick his lips would be a right turn on. Jaime imagined him pulling his head back to grasp the bottle top with his sexy mouth, swallowing the cool refreshing drink. Drops of water would roll down his chest, dripping from the frosted bottle.

Not going to happen. Not on a chilly day in mid-December.

She rubbed her clammy hands on her coat. "I'm Jaime Sanders, the new housekeeper. You must be the gardener?"

"Well observed." He continued digging.

Jaime scanned the environment. "Nice garden."

"Humph."

"Does it take long to look after?"

"Long enough."

"I can see you're happy in your work," she teased. "Are the priests as talkative as you, or am I in for a pleasant surprise?"

"You could say that," he murmured.

Jaime bit her bottom lip. She knew gardeners enjoyed nature and working the earth. Some were also solitary people preferring their own company to that of others. Couldn't the man make an effort to be civilised just this once?

She pushed her hair back. "Are you always so friendly, or am I the lucky one?

The gardener chuckled.

So he does have a sense of humour.

Jaime thought back to her friends in England. They all had chat-up lines to start up conversations which worked most of the time. Maybe she should change tactics and adopt one. She took in a deep breath, uncomfortable about making a first move. But then, there was only her and the gardener. She'd probably never see him again after today anyway.

"What does it take to get noticed around here? Do a Belly Dance?" A nervous giggle bubbled up from deep inside her. On receiving no reply, Jaime blushed. So much for the romantic French Lover. Maybe the French didn't like jokes.

"Bye, then," she said with a quick turn of the heel. No point in hanging around and embarrassing herself further. Besides, she had the meals to prepare. She only hoped the priests would be more talkative than this gardener.

Disappointed, Jaime trudged back to the presbytery. Could the gardener not be interested? What if he was married? Shit! She hadn't suspected that. How embarrassing. Married men weren't her thing.

On hearing a scuffled sound, Jaime looked up. A dignified Petrus plodded down the path. She stepped onto the lawn to let the dog pass. Much to her relief, the dog continued strutting. He ambled up to the gardener and pressed his head into his hand, nudging for a caress.

Lucky Petrus! At least he's getting a bit of the gardener's attention.

***

Jaime pottered about the kitchen, preparing the evening meal. Her flat heels clicked on the terracotta flagstones as she moved non-stop between the work unit and Aga stove. From time to time, she skipped over to the granite sink to drop dirty utensils into the warm suds. The stove had been fed and roared heartily. More logs stacked nearby waited to be devoured.

She liked the room. Something about the warm, rustic atmosphere made it feel like the place to be. The large, rectangular, oak table displayed elegant porcelain crockery with various hunting scenes. Even though most of the plates were chipped, they added a satisfying touch to the eye. The long-stemmed crystal glasses were in perfect condition.

Jaime set about washing the last saucepans. A few moments later, the back door clicked open. She swirled round and caught the gardener peeking into the room. "Decided to come for the Belly Dance, then?" she chuckled.

Heat flared up her cheeks as he entered the kitchen to stand in front of her. She gulped when her gaze fell onto his priest's collar. Her heart beat so fast, she could feel it hammering against her ribcage.

"Well, I can see you're not the gardener," she managed to blurt out.

He closed the door. "No. I'm Father de Vere, the trainee priest."

I should have bloody well known he wouldn't be that old when I saw his young brother. And why does he have to be so good-looking?

Jaime frowned at his broad smile, showing, of course, perfect white teeth. She tossed the pan into the sink, spilling soap suds onto the floor. "You could have at least told me instead of letting me make a complete fool of myself."

"You seemed to be enjoying yourself."

Jaime grabbed the floor cloth to dry the tiles. "Anyone can make a mistake. Besides, who expects a priest to dig in the garden? Unless it's to dig a grave."

His lips curved upwards.

Jaime threw the cloth into a nearby bucket. "Anyway, I imagined you a lot older."

"Likewise."

An uncomfortable silence set in while they held each other's gaze. The priest's eyes were motionless. Now and again, a muscle twitched at the corner of his mouth. His jaw tightened.

"I'm sorry," he said, holding out a hand. "Let me introduce myself in a civilized manner. I'm Father de Vere."

Jaime wiped both hands on her apron and took his. "Jaime Sanders."

"Nice to have you here, Jaime." The priest held her gaze. "Father Grégoire's sorry he can't meet you; he's eating with parishioners."

A surge of heat warmed the air, and Jaime looked away first. She returned to washing the pans, the heat of his eyes on her back. Or was it on her butt? The priest was disconcerting, watching every move in complete silence. What was wrong with the man?

She scrubbed the life out of the cooking utensils, all the while thinking back to the humiliating episode in the garden. The priest had made her feel a right bloody fool. Heat flushed to her head again. Like someone had tossed a whole forest onto the Aga. She wiped her forehead with the apron. Maybe if she wished hard enough, the kitchen flagstones would swallow her up.

"I'll leave you to it," the priest finally said.

Good idea.

***

When time came for the meal to begin, they sat opposite each other in the dining room. Jaime served the cannelloni. The priest served the wine in complete silence. A few moments later, Jaime took her fork and scooped up a little of the pasta.

Father de Vere cleared his throat. "It is the custom to say grace beforehand." His tone was firm.

"Er...of course." Jaime placed the fork on the plate and grimaced. *Shit, that's another Hail Mary for me.*

The priest reached for Jaime's hand across the table. "Bless us, O Lord, and these Thy gifts, which we are about to receive from Thy bounty, through Christ our Lord. Amen."

The baritone of the priest's voice reverberated through Jaime's body, making her blush. Not to mention the hot grip of his fingers and his sexy voice making her toes curl.

"Yeah, Amen."

The priest unfolded his napkin, and Jaime spotted the edge of a grin. Did the man enjoy embarrassing people?

Once or twice, he glanced in her direction, but nothing gave his thoughts away. Hopefully he'd forgotten about the bêtise in the garden. It would take her a little longer to forget. Her stomach still tweaked at the embarrassment.

The priest wiped his mouth on the serviette and broke the silence. "Tell me about yourself."

Jaime held his gaze, and for a brief moment, black eyes observed chestnut brown. Jaime was the first to look away – again. She grabbed a piece of baguette and broke it into smaller pieces. *Don't let him intimidate you.*

"What do you want to know?" She held his dark gaze for a long moment. The priest's lips curled upwards into a cheeky smile.

"Everything."

Jaime raised an eyebrow. No way was she going to tell him why she fled from England. Maybe she could tell him about the time she visited Paris and had to use the pepper spray because a man had decided to flash his zizi under the Eiffel Tower. Or she could even mention catching their local priest hugging one of the female parishioners. Would that bring a smile to his face?

On second thought, she decided to behave.

Apart from giving answers to his questions about her favourite hobbies as reading and jogging and explaining that her older brother worked in a bank and her mother ran a guesthouse, there wasn't a lot she dared divulge. Besides, she was too busy imagining him doing all sorts of unholy things to her.

The priest set aside his napkin and stretched his legs under the table. "Penny for your thoughts? Isn't that what the English say?"

Jaime smiled to herself. *You'll have to pay a lot more than a penny to know what I'm thinking.*

"So how many people live here?"

The priest folded his arms. "About 3,000."

"Is that all? Why would anyone want to bury themselves in a small village like this?"

The priest tilted his head to one side. "You tell me."

Jaime shifted on her chair. No way did she want to chat about why she'd come to this secluded village. She didn't know the man. Didn't want to share her secrets. Besides, what could he do apart from tell her to pray to the Lord?

The priest sat up and examined the wine bottle. "What do you think of the wine?"

Tasting new wines always made Jaime happy. With her nose dropped into the glass, she inhaled deeply, searching for more discrete aromas. She swirled the crimson liquid in a seductive spin of the wrist.

"I'd say it's quite strong given the oily traces." She observed the wine further before taking a slow appreciative sip, pursing her lips as she drew in air. "Excellent bouquet. Just ready to drink. J'adore!"

The priest arched his eyebrows in silent admiration while he stared over the rim of his glass.

Jaime laughed. "My father used to be the president of our local wine club. Given my good *sense*, I became a member too and learnt how to train my nose and taste buds."

The priest observed every gesture she made to emphasize the explanations.

"The smelling and tasting process is very personal. You have to act as if the wine is your lover – smell...breathe...and taste!" Jaime placed the glass on the table and licked her lips, never taking her eyes off his.

The priest shifted awkwardly on his chair.

Making you tingle? Serves you right for making me believe you were the gardener. Jaime gave one of her sweetest smiles and crushed more breadcrumbs.

"So what are my duties, Father?"

The priest dropped his hand into his pocket and pulled out a folded piece of paper. "I've made a note of the most important chores. The rest I'll leave up to you."

He unfolded the paper and began to read. "Please stop me if you have any questions."

Jaime nodded.

"Preparing meals and cleaning the presbytery goes without saying. There's no need to clean the sacristy. It's off-limits."

Jaime raised an eyebrow. Why couldn't she be trusted with the cleaning there? The sacristy in the parish church back home had never been locked.

"There's all the laundry and ironing. Please make sure clean linen and towels are available at all times. Both in the presbytery and for church services."

The priest looked up and gave a slight smile. "I'd like you to report any incidents or strange behaviour either in church or around the presbytery."

Jaime cocked her head to one side. "What do you mean by strange behaviour?"

"Shouting teenagers. Loud music in the square. The church is a holy place, and parishioners need peace and quiet to pray. Also let me know of any people hanging around the church without entering."

Jaime frowned. Why would anyone want to loiter around the church? Didn't they have anything better to do? Unless they were after the collection box.

The priest handed Jaime the note. "Just one other thing. I'd like us to be honest with each other. If there is anything you need to know or you wish to confide, please come to me. My door is always open."

Jaime placed the folded paper on the table. *We'll see about that.*

The priest raised his glass. "I hope you'll be happy here, Jaime."

"I'm sure I will." She raised her own glass and laughed.

Father de Vere's features grew solemn, and Jaime's laugh hiccupped in her throat. *Now what?* The priest took a sip of wine. A second later, his smile returned.

Jaime's forehead crinkled as she took a mouthful of cannelloni. "What about working hours?"

"If the work's done, we're not one to check when you start or finish your day. We'll also leave it up to you to choose your two days off. Or four half days if you prefer."

Jaime wiped her lips. "Sounds good to me."

"So long as you leave us something in the fridge to heat up, we don't need to know in advance which days."

Jaime made a mental note.

The priest set his cutlery on the table. "I hope you'll find something interesting to do around here."

Jaime popped a few breadcrumbs in her mouth. "I'm sure I will. I run. Looks to be a lot of interesting places to discover."

"I used to run with my brother many years ago. We were very close. Still are, in fact. We spent great holidays at the beach in summer and skiing in winter."

Jaime rubbed her backside, thinking back to the last holiday in the Alps. She'd had a great time. Zigzagging down the snowy slopes, drinking the local vin chaud to keep warm. She'd even brought back a permanent tattoo. Smiling, she looked back to him. "Did that all stop when you became a man of the cloth?"

The priest frowned and gazed down at his glass as he swirled the wine round and round. "It happened little by little."

A bolt of curiosity set Jaime alight. She took her last mouthful of wine and blurted out the next question. "Did you always want to be a priest?"

"Not always, no."

"When did you decide?"

The priest placed his glass on the table, his eyebrows drawn together. "That's a long story."

"And?"

"It's a very long story." He folded his napkin and took the dinner plates to the kitchen.

Something puzzled Jaime about this mysterious man. More often than not, she excelled at analyzing people. *He* was hard to predict. Why had he let her believe he was the gardener? Not very priest like. Unless he had a warped sense of humour. For all she knew, he could be a psycho. Or more likely an ex-convict – they often had tattoos. Priests didn't.

The Priest returned a few minutes later. "What are you thinking about?" He took a sip of wine. "Coming to confession?"

Jaime rolled her eyes. "Just things."

"What things?"

Jaime caressed the tiny crack on the plate. Didn't he say they had to be honest? "Why a good-looking man like you became a secluded man of the cloth."

A gush of Châteauneuf-du-Pape spluttered onto the table. "That's not the answer I expected," he said, dabbing the droplets with his napkin.

Jaime's face broke into a devilish grin. "Wasn't the one I expected to give." Her brown eyes danced with mirth as they met his.

The priest pulled on his collar and stood in a rush, knocking his knee against the edge of the table. Swearing like a trooper, he rubbed his leg and hobbled out of the kitchen, mumbling, "Dear Lord, my patience will be tested with this one."

Jaime leaned back in the chair, her thinking cap stuck firmly on. That man was no priest. He'd just given himself away. Priests didn't swear like that. At least not in public. With a puzzled expression, she cleared the table. Could he be hiding like she was?

Placing their glasses on a tray, Jaime glanced at the grandfather clock. Eight-forty. Not late. After taking care of the washing up, she'd grab a book and sit in the lounge. Reading in front of the crackling fire would get her in the perfect mood for bed.

The back door opened, and another priest stepped in.

"Good evening, my dear," he said, holding out a hand. "You must be the new housekeeper. I didn't imagine you to be so young and so pretty."

Jaime put the tray down and shook his bony hand. "Pleased to meet you, Father Grégoire?"

"Yes, sorry, forgot to introduce myself in a proper manner. I hope Father de Vere made you feel welcome."

"Yes, he did." *Made me believe he was the gardener.*

"That's good, my dear. I hope we'll have the opportunity to chat at some time."

***

No more than ten minutes later, Jaime curled up on the leather couch opposite the fireplace with a glass of warm milk, which she often had before bed. Helped her relax when het up.

Flames from the wood-fire swirled, crackling as they burned the dry logs and cast long, amber shadows over the rug. Now and again, Jaime glanced over at Father de Vere who was sunk down in the armchair, engrossed in a book. His expression a mask of concentration. From time to time, a muscle twitched in his left cheek, and his eyes narrowed.

Jaime sipped her milk, peering at him over the rim of the glass. After a few minutes, he scribbled something on a piece of paper, his tongue slowly licking his lower lip. Jaime stared, hypnotised. With great effort, she dragged her eyes away from his lips to his glasses. Christ, he looked sexy with those black-rimmed frames. All goody-goody and hot.

She darted her gaze back to the fire. The glowing embers moved in rhythm with the flames, spellbinding her. They took the form of the priest, reaching out for her with their clutches. A fiery, seductive consumption, sending up whispering sparks.

Father de Vere moving pulled Jaime away from the bewitching fire. With a quick turn of her head, she saw him watching her before he quickly returned to his reading. A nervous cough sounded in his throat, and Jaime hid behind her book to conceal a smile. Was he thinking about their dinner conversation?

She poured herself into the pages but noticed the priest's uneasiness. Twitching feet, tapping fingers on the book cover, crossing and uncrossing his legs. Furtive eye movements in her direction.

One thing was for sure. The man couldn't concentrate.

A loud slam and Jaime's eyes flew open to find the priest smiling a few inches away. She jerked back and gasped. Had she dropped off?

"Your book," Father de Vere said, holding out a ruffled bunch of pages. He rose from his knees and returned to the armchair.

Jaime tried to straighten out the pages. "I think I'll turn in," she said, stifling a yawn.

The priest's eyes never left his book. "Wise idea."

***

A while later, lying in bed, Jaime peered at the time on her phone for the umpteenth time – a little past midnight. She should be fast asleep. But between the misunderstanding with the gardener and the stress of discovering who the gardener actually was, anxiety weighed on her chest.

Then there were all the unsaid exchanges in front of the fire. Not to mention the body language. She wasn't blind. Father de Vere's attitude hid his true self. Mysterious and dark like the presbytery, the priest was intriguing.

A streak of doubt bolted through her when she finally fell into the arms of Morpheus. Did she have the ability to deal with her feelings for this man?

Chapter 3

Heavy boots squeaked on the stone drive while a winter drizzle floated down from the charcoal sky, turning it into a fine mist. He hated cold weather, especially when the damp sank into his clothing and skin like this evening. His long, woollen scarf didn't stop the cold air from driving down his neck.

The large redbrick house lay in complete darkness. No lights came from the windows. No smoke curled from the chimney. All the evidence screamed that the house was empty. He still scanned the surroundings.

He'd seen Jaime leave two weeks ago, but desperation had pushed him to find the bitch. How many hours had he spent crouched in the dark with only the sound of leaves rustling across the road for company? His waiting had paid off, though. As daylight had advanced that morning, he'd caught sight of her hurrying out of the premises to a waiting taxi, forcing him to retreat further into the darkness. Since she was dragging two heavy cases with her, he knew she'd be away for a while.

Fucking Hell! He'd waited too long. Should have sorted her out when he'd cornered the cat. By putting an end to the animal, he'd killed two birds with one stone: scared the shit out of Jaime and no more meowing outside his window. The bloody thing had driven him up the wall.

He sniffed loudly and stopped to pat the trunk of his favourite oak tree. The place with a good enough view of Jaime's bedroom that he could watch without being seen. He fingered the marks where he'd stabbed his knife into the bark when he'd seen her kiss her mother goodbye and jump into the taxi. But he'd find her.

He continued walking to the house, certain his next plan would work. Surely she'd ask her mother to forward the post. It was a long shot, but what if he could get to Jaime that way? With a bit of luck, she may have written. With both hands shoved into his pockets, he darted forward, impatient to sniff through the mail and leave his note.

At the front door, his face cracked into a wide grin. The letter box was crammed with mail and the daily paper. The old woman had obviously been out for the day. *Thanks for not pushing the mail through, Postie.*

He pulled both hands out of his warm pockets and opened the slot wider, retrieving the obstructive post. His fingers glided across a variety of envelopes – a couple of business-like window envelopes and one or two padded mailers. Thick, bright Christmas cards made up the main batch.

One particular envelope made adrenaline flood his body. He recognized the writing. Clasping onto it, he let out the breath he'd been holding all the while straining for sounds around him or from inside the house. Satisfied no danger prevailed, he carefully opened the seal, and tossed the envelope aside.

A fat Father Christmas gazed up at him from the glittering card.

Happy Christmas Mum!
I know it's my first Christmas away,
but don't worry, the de Vere family
have given me a great welcome.
Hope you like the card.
Jaime

His heart rate soared while he ran cold, clammy fingers over the card. After losing track of her, the hunt could resume.

He loved this sport. Had a long successful experience in the chase and had never once got caught. But that was for fun. *This* was serious. He had a mission to complete. The voices in his head told him what to do. He knew it was his brother's voice. He often spoke to him and knew he could count on him. Weren't they Jekyll and Hyde at their best?

With the light from his phone, he stooped to pick up the envelope. A French stamp peered back at him. What the fuck was she doing in France? Looking closer, he could just make out the post mark. Rambouillet. He turned the envelope to find a scribbled postscript on the back.

P.S. Don't forget to forward my post.

He used his phone to take a photo of the message along with the envelope – he'd study that later.

Satisfied, he slipped the card back into its envelope, and with a hearty push, shoved the bundle of post through the slot, followed by Jaime's card and his own.

"And a Merry Christmas to you, my love!"

Chapter 4

Jaime stared out the window and sighed. The dreary winter scene with its low gravel-grey sky resembled home. It was the start of another week in France, and she was adjusting nicely to the routine. Mornings were for cleaning and shopping, and she spent afternoons pottering outside or walking the dog. Jaime enjoyed the daily trip into town. There wasn't much to explore, but it gave the opportunity to meet people. Besides, none of the locals knew her. Since arriving in France, she'd become her usual carefree, happy self. So unlike the frightened wreck she'd turned into with the arrival of the notes.

When the priests were around, she served lunch at twelve-thirty on the older man's demand. It didn't bother her. So long as the chores were completed and the meal served on time, the old priest let her do her own thing. Besides, he hardly came out of his office; Father Grégoire lived like a hermit. On one occasion he even remained in his office all day. She had to admit he kept to himself and rarely spoke with his trainee priest. Not surprising. The old man was definitely reserved.

Suzanne had just left after another quick visit. Father de Vere needed something particular from Paris, and her visit had given Jaime the opportunity to say thank you once again. With the tobacconist only selling stamps for France, and the local post office out of European ones, Suzanne had done her a great favour a week ago by posting her mother's Christmas card from Rambouillet. It avoided phoning.

Sorting through a cardboard box, Jaime hummed the light melodic tune she'd recorded on her phone. The song the 'gardener' had whistled when she'd first walked down the garden. She loved the tune and played it in a continuous loop.

Christmas Eve had arrived, and she was busy decorating the tree in the living room. A few more jobs needed doing around the house, and then she'd be free to prepare for the next day. It wouldn't take long to sort out the laundry so the priests would have their clean hand towels for the services.

Suzanne had invited her and Father de Vere for the Christmas Day meal. As the older priest would be celebrating Christmas with his family, Suzanne had refused that Jaime spend the day on her own. Jaime couldn't wait, curious to see if Father de Vere would be more talkative in the company of relatives. Unless miserable Father

Grégoire's attitude was wearing off on him. She tried imagining the young priest's parents, but didn't know what to expect. After mistaking him for the gardener, his parents could be anybody. Nothing surprised her anymore.

All stretched out in a tight-fitting grey tracksuit, Jaime balanced on the top rung of the step ladder, and reached up to place the last bauble onto the tree when a noise from the hallway caught her attention. Gazing up into the huge, gold-framed mirror set above the fireplace, she caught Father de Vere's reflection half hidden in the doorway.

Dressed in an anthracite coat with a thick, woollen scarf of the same colour, the priest had clearly just come in from the garden. His tousled black hair was still damp with the mist, his eyes shining from the cold.

Without turning, she called out. "Everything all right, Father?"

He cleared his throat and took a slow step into the room. "I...er...was admiring the tree."

Jaime chuckled. She couldn't tell if the man was blushing, his beard hid most of his cheeks, but the way he shifted his weight from one foot to another was an indicator of embarrassment.

He took a few strides forward and reached for the ladder. "You shouldn't climb up there on your own. You could fall." His mouth curved up into half a smile, and Jaime's hormones rocketed.

"I can manage," she replied.

"Look, I'd feel a lot better if you came down and let me do that."

Jaime rolled her eyes. "I've finished."

She reached for his outstretched hand and took a sharp intake of breath as his cold fingers wrapped around hers. His touch sent tingles vibrating up her arm. With her gaze fixed on his hand, Jaime stubbed a toe on the last rung and tumbled onto his chest.

The priest's hot breath fell onto Jaime's flushed face, and she caught the twitch in his right eye. Fire seared through her cheeks as she pulled her hips back from his. "I didn't mean to stumble."

Father de Vere released her hand and cleared his throat while Jaime distracted herself with the rest of the decorations, listening to his rapid footsteps echoing down the corridor.

A second hot flush raced through her body. That was close. She rubbed her clammy hands down her tracksuit bottoms and tried to shake off her uncomfortable emotions. Time for a run. A jog in the fresh air would clear her mind. The other jobs could wait.

She dashed up to her room and slipped into her fleece tracksuit top. With her woolly scarf wound several times around her neck, she pulled on her gloves and headed out into the beautiful countryside.

Acres of land stretched ahead as Jaime jogged down the quiet road, soaking in the wonderful scenery. It reminded her of Easton back in England with its endless fields and dispersed farms. She loved running.

Alone in the vast silence, each determined stride proved how far she was prepared to push. It also provided the means to think.

Exactly what she needed right now. Calm. Just her with the road. To think about Father de Vere.

She'd always been attracted to tall, mysterious men. Despite being a man of the cloth, the priest fell into that category. Problem was, she could no longer look him in the eye without imagining him doing sacrilegious things. And there were a lot of unholy practices she wouldn't mind exploring with him. Yet, she couldn't afford to do anything stupid. Heaven forbid if she lost her job. No way could she go back to England with a madman on the prowl.

Her tracksuit hood fell back, allowing the wind to sweep around her head. The breeze was cool and crisp like a refreshing drink on a hot summer day. Jaime breathed in the fragrance of the damp woodland while conjuring up the priest's visage, wondering what his first name could be.

He didn't look like a Henri. What about Pierre? That was a typical French name. Or maybe André? Surely not Grégoire. What were the odds of two priests working in the same parish with the same name? She chuckled. Whatever his name...there was something between them. Although he kept to himself, apart from the meals they shared when he didn't have to visit other parishes, the chemistry was there. In their gaze. She couldn't get him out of her head and hated the way he messed up her mind.

Twenty minutes later, serene after the exercise, Jaime stepped into the presbytery gateway only to be knocked into from behind.

"Don't apologise, will you?" she shouted, standing in a hurry.

Wiping her gloves on her sweatshirt, Jaime watched the runner sprint out of sight. Navy blue tracksuit, hood pushed well down over his head, yet something was off-centre. Despite his long confident strides, his feet hit the concrete too hard. Not a regular runner.

In the past, her irrational thoughts had become so fixed, she had great difficulties in convincing herself it was all her imagination. Well, she hadn't imagined the runner, had she?

Bent forward with both hands on her hips, she exhaled, reassuring herself it was a rude jogger so out of breath, he couldn't apologise. People were in such a hurry these days.

Standing upright, she spotted the drapes twitching in Father de Vere's bedroom. Again. Each time Jaime left the house, even to take the rubbish out to the bins, the curtains wavered. Did the man have secret radar? A bell that rang whenever she stepped outside? And why was he spying? Something to hide? Checking on her on the old man's orders? Or did he secretly fancy her?

Confused, she reached the front door and closed it hard behind her, rubbing her sore back.

***

Father de Vere uncurled his sweaty fingers from the thick curtains and ran a hand through his hair. Mustiness from the rough fabric spiraled up his nose as he drifted back into the room.

Shit!

Had she seen him? Watching and waiting had never been his strong point. Frayed his nerves to the quick. There he stood, heart in mouth, as still as a statue, spying on his housekeeper. How on earth had things got to this?

With long strides he marched up and down the room, rubbing his knuckles across his mouth. How long had Jaime been gone? Fifteen? Twenty minutes? That same jogger had been running up and down in front of the presbytery since early afternoon. As if there were no other quiet places to run in Montfort-Le-Gesnois. And to top it all off, he seemed familiar, even though the tracksuit hood covered most of his features.

Had the man bumped into Jaime on purpose?

He didn't like the look of this. Nothing was going as planned. Hated when he wasn't in control.

Since this new housekeeper had stepped onto the scene, all he seemed to do was check her every move. But Christ, she was a sight for hungry eyes. Those tight-fitting running pants hugged her backside, all but shouting *grab me!* And that ponytail she'd tied high, swished like a seductive metronome while she jogged. What he'd give to feel the texture of her hair.

The first time he'd set eyes on Jaime in the garden, he knew she smelt trouble. She perturbed him with her furtive glances, and whenever she shot him one of her smiles, his body ached.

He remembered their meal on her arrival. He'd never been so flustered in all his life. Polite chit-chat had slowly gotten out of control and began to take on subtle undertones which had cost him knocking his knee on the kitchen table when he made his getaway. And that was exactly what it had been. A quick getaway. He hadn't trusted himself in the woman's presence. Not when she started flirting. And she did a lot of that. He was no fool. He'd been around long enough to know her little game. She was testing the waters, and he'd almost drowned.

Jaime was getting to him. Breaking down his defences. More than he cared to admit. The woman filled his every thought. Not wise at the moment. Disappearing had meant a new game of hide and seek. In this particular game, though, *he* was the person being hunted. He'd made the sacrifice to live secluded in this village with no one to distract or worry him. Where had things gone wrong?

Father *Grégoire* knew about his past and had begrudgingly accepted to take him under his wing. But the old priest kept out of his way and that suited him fine.

Shaking his head, he recalled a time when he used to be calm. Relaxed even. That had changed since he'd gone into hiding. He'd become twitchy and irritable, waiting for the inevitable clash.

He had to play it cool. Avoid attracting attention.

Not easy with this new sassy housekeeper.

Chapter 5

"We're going to be late, Jaime." Father de Vere tapped his foot on the bottom step as he shouted up the stairs.

"I'm coming, I'm coming." *What the hell's wrong with you? You've been in a shitty mood all morning.*

Okay, so she hadn't folded the laundry how he liked it. Was that a reason to be in a strop?

She clung onto the handrail. Her new six-inch stilettos looked fantastic even if they were far from practical to walk in. She crossed her fingers, hoping she wouldn't break her neck. Every stair in the old presbytery was a different height, adding to the difficulty of judging when to put your foot down. What on earth had possessed her to buy them?

Suzanne had mentioned that Christmas lunch would be a small gathering with eight people and Leonora would be one of them. Jaime wanted to look attractive. She'd chosen a simple but elegant black dress with a long string of pearls. The shoes had been an afterthought. Not a good idea after all.

"I'll see to Petrus and wait for you outside," the priest called, clicking his fingernails on the handrail.

"Yeah, you do that," she muttered, wondering what seeing to Petrus meant. "Just leave me alone to get down these bloody stairs in one piece."

After a great deal of wobbling, Jaime reached the bottom. Without wasting more time, she grabbed her bag. Then, like a baby taking its first steps, tottered out to Father de Vere's Citroen 2CV. She opened the passenger door and climbed in as gracefully as her shoes would allow. Petrus panted from the back seat. The priest hadn't said anything about bringing the dog with them. She only hoped he would behave.

No sooner had she closed the door than the priest shoved the gear stick into the dashboard and pulled away in a rattling squeak.

You're still in a foul mood, aren't you?

Jaime closed her eyes, enjoying the swaying movements of the car. She loved it when the car tilted as it curved round the bends. It reminded her of the times when her father used to take her to the fair. What fun she used to have, screaming with every bend the mad rollercoaster would take. Those were the good old days, before her dad's car accident, when they'd been a close, solid family.

A little peek now and again at the priest confirmed he wasn't going to talk. His face was straighter than a poker player's. Serious all the way up from his mouth to his eyes. No way did she want to have her head snapped off by asking questions, or worse still, have them answered with grunts.

Apart from the speedy getaway, Father de Vere proved to be a careful driver. Each time Jaime stole a look, his gaze never pulled away from the road ahead. He'd put on his dark-rimmed glasses, the sort one associated with a banker or a lawyer. They gave him a mysterious air. One she liked. A side to him she wouldn't mind getting to know better.

In a nutshell, the priest was a total enigma. She never knew what he was thinking or what his motives for doing things were. Did the man mean to be mysterious or was his standoffishness all for show?

Although he'd said his door was open if she wanted to confide, his body language said the opposite. He was cold, distant. Did he honestly think his attitude inspired confidence? She wondered what his parishioners thought. Maybe she'd ask some of them one day.

An hour later, at a little after twelve-thirty, the car pulled up in front of Suzanne's house. A wreath of ivy and holly with blood-red berries hung from the front door. The upper floor of the house had been decorated with multi-coloured flashing Christmas lights. No doubt to please the twins.

The priest stepped out of the car and walked around to Jaime's side. "Thought you could do with a little help?" he smirked.

"I'm fine." A tint of annoyance edged her words. She pushed his hand away only to grab it a few seconds later when both heels sunk into the gravel of the driveway, scraping the leather of her heels.

Shit!

Once off the pathway, Jaime released the priest's arm and tagged along up the steps and across the patio. She eyed him up from behind as he entered the house, followed by an excited Petrus. Those black designer jeans did wonders for the man's butt. Made a change from his dull, grey, everyday trousers. A casual jacket was the only garment over his open-necked white shirt. She couldn't understand how the man didn't feel the cold. That said, hadn't she found him in a thin t-shirt on her arrival?

"Dante!"

So that's his name.

Like a model on the catwalk, Leonora glided up to them in a stunning coral, above-the-knee, frilly dress. Ignoring Jaime, she slipped a hand into the crook of the priest's arm. With the other on his chest, she brought ruby-red lips down in a loud kiss on his cheek. Dante removed Leonora's hand before greeting the rest of his family.

Crikey, Cruella's friendly. Is this an updated version of 'Thorn Birds'?

"Jaime! Jaime!" The twins came running to her.

Jaime hadn't believed the children would have remembered her. They'd only met briefly when she first arrived.

"Look what Father Christmas brought me." Sasha rattled the box of a dinosaur jigsaw.

"Wow, aren't you a lucky boy? And here's another present for you and one for Santine," Jaime replied, pulling two gift-wrapped books from her handbag. "Père Noël got confused and left them with Petrus."

"How about a kiss for your old uncle?" Dante said, opening his arms.

The twins dropped their presents and rushed up to him.

"Can we have a ride on your back?" Santine asked.

Dante let out a throaty laugh and Jaime's insides melted. She liked that sound. Wished he'd laugh more often. Life stuck in the presbytery couldn't be fun. No wonder the man never laughed. She'd have to change that.

"Please, Tonton," Sasha pleaded.

"Leave your uncle alone," Luc said.

Dante ruffled the little boy's hair. "Just this once then."

He went down on all fours and let the twins climb onto his broad back. They screamed with delight as Dante crawled up and down the room. Jaime couldn't believe it. She hadn't imagined the priest as anything other than the quiet, intimidating type. He obviously had different facets to his character. And this one she liked.

"Come on, children, it's time for the grown-ups to have their lunch." Suzanne led the children to the far end of the room where a mountain of toys laid spread out on the rug.

Luc introduced Jaime to Vadim de Vere, an older version of Dante. His tall, proud figure showed a definite air of authority. Sophia, Dante's mother, was an elegant lady with silver-grey hair tied up in an elaborate chignon. Sharp, bluish-grey eyes circled by dark-rimmed glasses stood out bright and alert. Jaime found the woman beautiful.

"Xavier!" Suzanne called to the attractive man who'd just strolled into the room. "I'm so glad you could make it, little brother."

Xavier bounded up to his sister and fell into an affectionate hug.

"This is Jaime, Dante's new housekeeper," Suzanne said.

Jaime held out her hand. "Hi!"

A wide grin spread across Xavier's face. He took Jaime's hand and lifted it to his lips. "Enchanté."

Jaime swallowed hard as she held his gaze. "Er...enchantée too."

"Sorry if I'm making you nervous."

"Why should I be nervous? I've just never had a baise-main

before."

Xavier burst out laughing. "You look fabulous."

A red flush spread across Jaime's cheeks. He didn't mince his words.

"I'm Xavier, Suzanne's younger brother," he said, releasing her hand. "I work as a trader for the Paris Stock Exchange."

Jaime nodded.

"Suzanne said you're Dante's housekeeper? Can't be much fun. Dante can be a right stick in the mud."

Jaime grinned. She found Xavier pleasant enough. Calm, good-looking, sandy-blond hair, the body of an athlete, and his clothes hung like a dream on his fit figure. His direct, steel-grey eyes were without a doubt his best feature. Thank God she'd worn heels. At least their eyes were at the same level. In general, everyone looked down at her five-foot-three inches. Even stretching her neck made no difference.

For the entire time they spoke, Xavier never left Jaime's side, brushing her arm now again and winking when their eyes met. Jaime's sixth sense came forth. The way he reacted around her meant this wouldn't be the last time she'd see him.

Each time Jaime observed the other guests, she picked up on Father de Vere's expressionless gaze. His eyes tracked her every move, paying very little attention to his family's comments and grunting a few replies to questions asked. What was wrong with the man? It was Christmas Day for crying out loud. Apart from his quick, joyous outburst with the twins upon arriving, he hadn't stopped pulling a gloomy Monday morning face.

"Are you all right, Dante?" Luc asked. "You've gone quiet all of a sudden."

So, she wasn't the only one to notice.

Dante cleared his throat and pasted on a happy face. "I'm fine. One or two things on my mind, that's all."

Holding their glasses of pink champagne, the guests accompanied Luc and Suzanne into the dining room. Canapés lay in the centre of the table, waiting for the traditional toast.

Once Luc made his Christmas speech, and the guests had finished their aperitif, Suzanne served the truffled foie gras with a dab of fig chutney. Jaime popped a small piece of toast covered with the foie gras into her mouth. The rich, butter-like texture set her stomach lurching. She placed the cutlery on either side of the plate and kept her head low, forcing down the mouthful.

Since her arrival, Jaime's appetite had diminished. Not yet accustomed to the French cuisine, some of the dishes were too rich. Apart from a few parishioners who brought meals for their 'Dear Fathers,' Jaime did the cooking. She prepared simpler meals, leaving out the crème fraiche that the French used a lot of in their dishes. The priests didn't seem to mind, or if they did, they never let on. Once or twice, she'd seen Father de Vere frown when she'd served boiled potatoes with ham or minestrone soup. Father Grégoire ate whatever she prepared so long as she served it in his office.

Suzanne stared at Jaime's plate. "Are you all right?"

Jaime looked up. "Sorry, Suzanne, I can't eat all this pâté."

All heads turned.

"Oh, how common," Leonora muttered. "Fancy calling foie gras 'pâté.' I bet the next thing she'll ask for is butter."

Jaime clenched her fists under the table. Why did Leonora make such nasty comments? Did she keep a string of them ready to use?

"Don't worry, Jaime, I'll have your 'pâté'."

With a look of relief, Jaime exchanged plates with Xavier, hoping not to attract more attention. She could do without Leonora's snark, especially on top of the priest's sullen looks.

Suzanne had chosen a typical French main course. From the exquisite smell, the boeuf en croûte was going to be divine. The wild-mushroom stuffing seeped out from the thin layer of puff pastry. Absolutely mouth-watering.

When Luc served red wine, Jaime smiled. Holding her glass in the way of a professional wine taster, she dropped her nose in and inhaled.

Leonora raised her eyebrows. "Worried it won't be up to your standards?"

"Oh, it'll be up to my standards all right. What about you? I reckoned all French people knew how to appreciate good wines."

Jaime took an appreciative sip. She let the liquid glide around her mouth and tongue before swallowing.

"Well, well, we have a connoisseur here," Luc exclaimed.

Jaime cast her eyes in Leonora's direction and smiled serenely.

"And?" Luc questioned.

"Perfect. Beautiful, ruby-red colour. Good bouquet. Consistent notes, intense on the nose and palate."

Luc nodded and served the others.

"So, Mademoiselle Housekeeper, are you going to do that all your life?" Leonora gave one of her best smiles.

"You mean, wine-tasting? I'd love to."

Poised to perfection, Leonora inspected her manicured fingernails. "I can't understand why anyone would want to live in Montfort-Le-Gesnois."

Jaime fidgeted on her chair. "Because of my job, of course."

"Aren't there other jobs? Seems a bit crazy to me."

"Leave it, Leonora." There was a clear warning in the priest's voice.

Leonora reddened. "I can give my opinion, can't I?"

Luc reached for the wine bottle, frowning at Leonora's comments.

"More wine, Jaime?"

Jaime pasted on a forced smile. "Thank you. I could do with another glass." *Then if I slap that smirk off her face, I can blame it on the alcohol.*

Leonora ran a hand up Dante's arm. "I can't stand doing housework. I'm too busy doing volunteer work."

Vadim turned to Jaime. "It can't be easy coming to live in a foreign country, leaving friends and family. I hope you are happy at the presbytery."

Jaime blushed and caught the priest's weird look. Her heart missed a beat. Was that anger etching the fine lines around his eyes? He couldn't have heard their conversation. Vadim had kept his voice low. She turned her attention to the older man. "Yes, I am. Suzanne's a great help too."

Dante's father looked over at his daughter-in-law. "Yes, she's a wonderful person. Luc is a lucky man. They're happy together."

Jaime gave the old man a slight nod.

"I hope Dante is happy with his new life." Vadim tilted his head to the end of the table. "We were all shocked when he told us about his desire to become a priest."

Jaime couldn't help giving the old man a curious look.

"Up until then, he was dating Leonora."

Bloody hell! That's why she's so friendly. Must have come as a huge shock.

"Then about six months ago, Dante phoned from Italy to say he'd be coming to Montfort-Le-Gesnois for the last part of his training before being ordained. We were all astounded."

"I can imagine."

"He told us his desire for priesthood was stronger than his desire for marriage. We of course, accepted his wishes."

Jaime stole a glance at Father de Vere and slipped on her thinking cap. Did he have the 'calling of God'? She was no expert, but didn't it take a while to become a priest? How mysterious. He must have organised everything in secret. That wouldn't surprise her. Choosing between a snarky cow and the house of God, the church would win hands down any day.

The next hour went by without Jaime noticing. She found herself speaking easily with Dante's father. His charismatic voice had a soothing effect.

"We understand you've already met Leonora," Vadim said.

Jaime took a sip of wine. "She met me at the airport when I arrived."

"Of course. Suzanne is one of her best friends."

Jaime hesitated before speaking, "She doesn't like me."

The old man chuckled. "I shouldn't worry about that, my dear.

Leonora doesn't like any woman who she considers a threat."

"She's very beautiful."

Vadim patted Jaime's hand. "Don't judge a book by its cover. And don't forget that beauty is only skin deep."

While the guests continued their conversations, Jaime sipped the wine and scrutinised Dante. Luc said something, and a huge grin cracked the priest's face, giving him that youthful look she liked so much. It suited him. Made him look years younger. Less pasty-faced. A huge change from the straight-laced side of him.

"So, how's life at the presbytery, Dante?" Leonora pushed a few ringlets back and leaned forward to rub a hand up his forearm.

The priest took a sip of his drink and glanced at Jaime. "Fine."

Heat ran up Jaime's face, and she took a huge gulp of wine before settling her gaze on Leonora. The woman was visibly frustrated. She played with her napkin constantly and did everything possible to attract attention. Especially Dante's. Every movement betrayed the woman's inner emotions. Anyone could see, she still had affection for Dante.

Suzanne appeared from the kitchen with dessert. The traditional Bûche de Noël. A butter cream cake in the shape of a log, topped with colourful Christmas figurines. Leonora clapped her hands like a child. "Looks lovely. I'm sure Jaime would like double helpings."

"I'll leave the second slice for you. Appears to be your favourite."

"So how's your French coming along, Jaime? Have you picked up any new vocabulary?" Leonora asked.

Yep, enough to give you a piece of my mind any day!

"I have, thank you," Jaime replied sweetly. "What about your English, Leonora? I hear you're having private tutoring. Apparently, it's a difficult language to learn. Makes people frustrated and antsy."

Leonora turned an unbecoming shade of crimson, followed by an awkward silence, broken only by the light clatter of cutlery on plates. Jaime peeked at the priest and then at Leonora. Who would have guessed those two had once been an item?

Luc broke the uncomfortable hush by praising his wife.

"The meal was a great success." Sophia confirmed her son's compliment. "Thank you, my dear."

"My pleasure," Suzanne replied as they all walked to the lounge for coffee. "I'm glad you all enjoyed it."

Jaime jolted when two strong hands came down on both shoulders. Xavier turned her gently around. "I'd like to get to know you better."

She gasped, cheeks burning. Where had this come from? No beating about the bush with this Frenchman.

"Xavier," Suzanne called, "can you give me a hand?"

With a cheeky wink, Xavier caressed the side of her neck and headed into the kitchen.

Desperate to get out into the cool afternoon air to appease the fire in her cheeks, Jaime took advantage of Xavier's absence to step outside. The breeze hit her face, reviving her mind and blowing away her uneasiness.

From the patio, she spotted a robin with its bright red plumage amongst the evergreen shrubs. It moved its head from side to side, no doubt listening for worms. Jaime wrapped both arms around her body and gazed out across the garden.

Her heart pinched as she recalled Christmas time back home in England, when family and friends got together to share the festive spirit. Office parties would be in full swing, frantic last minute shopping number one on the list. Memorable childhood scenes also rushed to mind. Piles of presents under the Christmas tree begging to be ripped open, carol singers ambling from house to house, looking forward to a warm drink.

Everything was different this year. What sort of Christmas could she have expected back home with a nutter on the loose?

"Jaime?"

She turned to have Xavier take her hand and bring it to his lips. "I'd like to take you out."

Jaime was flattered, but did she want things to go further? He seemed to be a nice enough person, and she wouldn't mind having him as a friend if he'd accept. But no more. There was spark.

Over Xavier's shoulder, Jaime caught sight of Father de Vere with his back against the doorway, arms folded across his chest. Like a sleek panther gazing at his prey through narrowed black eyes, the priest scrutinised Jaime's every move with an ugly twist to his mouth.

"Time to leave," he said in a cold voice.

Xavier put an arm around Jaime's shoulders. "I'll drive her back."

Dante stormed up to the couple, brushed Xavier's arm away, and placed Jaime's jacket around her shoulders. "We are leaving right now." His voice came out in a growl.

Jaime couldn't figure the man out. Often sulky for no reason, condescending when he put on his priest's hat, amused when she put her smart mouth into action, and now furious because she'd been speaking to Xavier. The man needed a huge kick up the arse. She had to admit that his concern about the cold was pleasing though. He'd even brought her jacket out to her.

"Come on, Jaime," the priest pressed.

Reluctant yet not daring to protest, Jaime headed after Dante into the house, rolling her eyes in Xavier's direction. The priest sure was a strange piece of work. Okay, so she'd been acting familiar way with a person she'd only just met. But it was none of the priest's business how she behaved. She wasn't a nun.

They returned into the house to say their goodbyes. Suzanne invited

Jaime and Dante for the New Year, but the priest refused. Jaime couldn't believe it. What on earth was going on in that mind of his?

After gathering their belongings, Jaime climbed into the car and shoved her iPhone buds deep into her ears. No way did she want a sermon from the 'High Priest.'

Neither of them spoke during the first part of the journey home. Even Petrus kept to himself. No more happy panting. Yet, despite Father de Vere's stone-cold mood, Jaime was happy. She'd left worries and fears back in England. With a New Year about to start, she hoped her fear of the last eighteen months would be replaced by happiness and serenity.

Staring absently out of the car window, a warm smile stretched across her face. She wanted to share this sudden happiness. Turning a little toward the priest, she picked up on his stern features – pinched lips, narrowed eyes, and white knuckles on the steering wheel. Why couldn't the man relax? Let his hair down for Christ's sake? Did he know the meaning of the word?

The idea of cracking a corny joke came to mind. Anything to get him to snap out of his sulky mood.

She pulled the buds from her ears, took a deep breath and broke the silence, "What do you call a priest who's also a lawyer?"

Without waiting for a reply, she gave the answer. "A father-in-law."

Dante's lips curved up into a faint smile as he relaxed his grip, and Jaime fought back a grin herself. The priest just needed someone to loosen him up. Treat him like a normal person, not the uptight man of the cloth he liked to pretend his was. Maybe he was trying to prove to Father Grégoire that he was worthy of being a full-fledged priest. Besides, something in the way his expression lit up brought butterflies to life in the pit of her stomach.

And that feeling, she liked.

***

Dante pulled up in front of the dark presbytery, glad to be away from the chaos and mostly from Xavier drooling over Jaime. The man had gone over the line. Way too far over.

He knew Suzanne's brother well enough to know the man was trying to get into his housekeeper's pants. He recognised the look in Xavier's eye. Another notch to add to his bedpost. On cloud nine about the idea of bedding an English girl.

The bastard!

Jaime slammed the car door shut, bringing him back to his senses. A quick draft of air blew past, and he caught the peachy scent of her perfume. Fresh and light. He gazed after her silhouette while she stormed up to the house before letting herself in. Lights came on one after the other as she moved from room to room. She seemed in a hurry to get to bed.

He slipped out of the 2CV and headed into the house, stroking the dog's neck. Father Grégoire's car was nowhere in sight. The man had probably decided to spend the night with his sister's family. Petrus dived straight for his basket while Dante locked the door. Too annoyed to sleep, he strode into the study for a nightcap. He needed something strong. A long drink to calm his nerves. To numb his head.

Pouring himself a whisky, he wondered if Jaime had noticed his foul mood. Of course she had. The woman was no fool. He'd woken up in a bad mood and didn't know why. And Leonora had done nothing to appease him. In fact, it seemed her only interest was to belittle Jaime. His housekeeper had stood her ground with her smart mouth, though. He liked that.

He sank into his armchair and examined the changing colour of the alcohol in the dim light glowing from the desk-lamp. The colour of Jaime's eyes. His housekeeper had been a breath of fresh air today. As every day. Apart from Leonora, everyone had fallen under her bubbly charm. His father the first. And Vadim was a good judge of women. Hadn't his father been right about his disastrous relationship with Leonora?

Dante downed the rest of the drink and winced as the fiery liquid burned a hot trail down the back of his throat. Jaime needed to be protected. He hadn't let her out of his sight all day, watching her every move. Until Xavier disappeared after her into the garden. An unexplainable force had pushed him to rescue her from Xavier's claws. He'd only done his duty as her employer. Coming up with the idea of handing Jaime her coat was a great alibi. Well, *he* believed it was.

He feared she must hate him. He'd caught the look of disappointment on her face when he'd refused the New Year's Eve meal. There was no other choice. He couldn't face Xavier sniffing around his housekeeper again especially when the clock would strike midnight and everyone would kiss to celebrate. Knowing Xavier, he'd shove his tongue down Jaime's throat and choke her.

Dante let out a frustrated groan, got to his feet, and switched off the lights. He'd drunk enough to send him to sleep – that was if he managed to make it to bed. Half-way up the stairs, the joke Jaime had made in the car came to mind. He stopped and chuckled. She couldn't have hit the nail straighter on the head.

Did she know his initial career path was as a lawyer?

He had to be careful with this clever woman. She might suss out more than he was prepared to divulge. More than was good for her. More than was good for them both.

Chapter 6

It was coming up to nine-thirty the next morning when Jaime ambled into the kitchen and set about making the coffee. After the priest's foul mood the night before, she hoped he'd be in a better frame of mind this morning. Apart from her joke, not one word had been spoken during the journey back. On arriving home, she'd wished him goodnight and headed straight upstairs.

Other things had been on her mind too. In particular Leonora.

The woman had behaved like a spoilt brat for the whole meal. She hadn't stopped throwing snide remarks her way, and Jaime wasn't going to stand for that. If Leonora insisted on antagonising her, maybe she'd have to bend the rules and fight a little dirty. In a witty way though. She didn't want to appear bitchy in front of the priest or his family.

One thing was for sure: she'd have to watch her back.

"Good morning, Jaime. You have post." The old priest shuffled into the kitchen and placed a large brown envelope in front of her.

Jaime raised an eyebrow. *So the old hermit has ventured out of his cavern.* "But it's Boxing Day."

Dante entered and reached across the table for his cup of coffee, catching the last part of the conversation. "It's not a public holiday in France."

She gazed at the large envelope, recognizing the familiar handwriting. "It's from my mum."

Father Grégoire turned and headed out of the kitchen. "I'll take my coffee in my office. I've got important work to do."

Jaime waited for the younger priest to leave too before she opened the envelope. After reading her mother's note with a quick rundown of life back at the Guest House, and a short message from Grant hoping life was treating her well, Jaime set about reading the rest of the mail which turned out to be Christmas cards.

And then one card brought Jaime's world crashing to a standstill.

I SAW YOU LEAVE ....
BUT I'LL FIND YOU!

NOOOOOO!

Jaime forced the eruption to stay inside, but a strangled whine managed to escape. The bastard had spied on her while she'd said goodbye. Every muscle froze. She couldn't believe this was happening.

Calm down before you get hysterical. He doesn't know where you are.

Frantic breathing came back in short, painful gasps as she rocked back and forth on the chair. A few tears escaped. She should have guessed the card wasn't from a close friend. Didn't recognise the writing. With shaky hands, she put the card back into its envelope.

A noise from the doorway drew her attention. She jerked her head up and caught Father de Vere staring at her. Had he been there long? His piercing eyes made her stomach churn.

A deep furrow appeared between the priest's eyes. For a second, anger flashed across his features. "Everything okay?" he asked.

"Everything's fine." She forced a tight smile.

"Don't forget the offer still stands. If you need to talk, you know where to find me."

Jaime bit her lower lip. She'd been frightened, shadowed, and spied on. The sheer idea that she'd fled England to land in France and still had this following her, had her wondering if she'd ever see the end to all this. Without a word, she dropped her gaze, and Father de Vere hurried out of the kitchen. His footsteps scurried down the corridor, fading as he disappeared into the study.

An uneasy atmosphere fell over the room. What a strange man. Lonely. Lost even. Jaime didn't know what to make of the odd expression that flashed across his face or the times when he'd turn up out of the blue to watch her every move. She couldn't fathom the man.

Brushing away her tears, she replaced the card in the envelope, and dealt with it as best she could. Out of sight – out of mind.

***

Alone in his cold study, Dante's thoughts went to the housekeeper. Again.

Something in him had cracked on hearing Jaime's pitiful whining. Cautious eyes had met his when he'd returned to the kitchen. Eyes like those of a petrified animal. What could be tormenting her so? He wanted to comfort the woman. Wrap his arms around Jaime's body. Brush those tears away and see her gaze at him with gratitude. And those sexy lips. He couldn't take his eyes off them. He'd had to swallow down the need to kiss them and had fled from the kitchen.

He'd sworn no one would get to him. Not under the present circumstances. It wouldn't be fair. So why was Jaime different? Try as he might, he couldn't pinpoint what it was about her that pushed him to think of her nonstop.

There was something about Jaime that pulled at him. She was

breaking down barriers; she even knew how to make him smile. Not to mention the way she hummed his song while carrying out the household chores. Little by little, Jaime was getting under his skin.

But he had to put more distance between them. Not let on his attraction. She believed he was a priest for Christ's sake. He'd better behave like one. If he dropped his guard and let his body rule his mind, he'd pass the point of no return. He couldn't afford that. Not now.

For the past six months, he hadn't been able to form a bond with anyone and not only because of the priest disguise. It wouldn't be fair to drag anyone into his world. If *they* ever discovered his fondness for Jaime, they'd stop at nothing.

Anger surged like a rolling tide.

"What more can I do?" His voice echoed in the room.

He avoided his housekeeper as much as possible, often skipping breakfast. When he could, lunch was taken in a small bistrot between parishes. That left the evening meal where he made civilised conversation before retiring early. He even avoided reading in front of the living room fire. And he resented her for that. Well, not her. His emotions.

The crackling of logs in the fireplace while the flames radiated their warm glow around the room was long gone. Instead, he shut himself away, trying to get her out of his mind.

Would he ever be able to resume the quiet life he'd known before Jaime had stepped onto the scene? A glass of wine and a good book in front of a warm fire wasn't much to ask.

It didn't look as if that would be on the agenda for a long while.

Maybe never again.

Chapter 7

"It's me, Marcel. Merry Christmas!" The man's excited voice bellowed down the phone.

"Hey, where are you, mon ami?"

"I'm around home –"

Marcel cut him off. "When are you coming?"

"Whenever you want."

"Good. I've got tons of work lined up for you."

He blew a bubble from his gum. "Can't wait. I'm a bit short of cash. Could do with some extra dough. I've got a bit of a...how should I put it? A bit of hunting to do."

A dirty chuckle echoed in the phone. "No problem. Take your time."

"Give me a couple of days to get things sorted here. I'll be with you as soon as I can."

"Okay, mon ami. Let me know when you arrive, and I'll make the necessary arrangements."

"Great."

He hung up and adjusted his fedora, placing it at an angle on the back of his head. Things were going to plan. Ever since he'd run into Marcel, things looked rosy. They'd hit it off as soon as they'd been introduced in one of the down town bars. Well almost.

At first, Marcel had come over as a cold ogre. Normal under the circumstances. New recruits had to be trusted. Although one of his mates had put in a good word for him, he had to prove he was worthy to hook up with Marcel. He had to be tested. One false move and the nick lay in wait with open arms.

Prior to his meeting with the Frenchman, things had gotten out of hand in his neighbourhood.

The drug trade had become harsh and dangerous. With the arrival of a new, bigger gang in town, business plummeted. His superiors were on his back to make money, and he had to be more on guard, watching out for both the police and rivals.

The odds of surviving weren't in his favour. Not only was he making less, he was gradually losing his freedom. All in all, things had to change before *he* got changed into minced meat. Besides, he'd had enough of working around the clock for low wages enforced by the threat of violence. Competition was tough. Brutal even. He had to get out. And quick.

His life was set up to end in one of two ways: jail or death. He didn't fancy either. Time had come to move on. Move away to another neighbourhood or to a new city. He'd chosen a new country. Jaime had crossed the channel. He would do the same. Especially now that he was assured of work.

Chewing on his gum, he hitched up his baggy tracksuit bottoms and bounced away on his trainers. He was prepared to take the risk.

The final reward would be worth it.

Chapter 8

Jaime lay back and concentrated on the day ahead. Sexy Father de Vere sprang to mind as first and foremost.

It was 10 a.m. on New Year's Day, and she allowed herself a lie-in after arriving home late last night.

After declining Suzanne's invitation for the New Year's Eve dinner, the priest had changed his mind. The man was a pain in the backside. Did he know what he wanted? In any case, they'd gone, and she'd enjoyed every minute of it.

The priest had finally let his hair down, cracking jokes and playing with the twins. Jaime could have banked on them having a good time. Xavier hadn't been around. Suzanne mentioned her brother had an important meeting with stockbrokers in London and would be away for a week. That news had brought a smile to the priest's face. Not to Suzanne's, though. Her brother never went abroad for work.

Jaime rolled out of bed with a sudden urge to speak to her own brother. With an hour to kill before preparing lunch, now was perfect. In spite of her being a great deal younger than him, Jaime was close to Grant in part due to their father's frequent business trips. All the more after his sudden death.

She grabbed the phone, searched for his number and let it ring. "Happy New Year, Grant!"

"Jaime! How are things?"

"Great."

"Nice to hear from you. Did you do anything special last night?"

Jaime leaned against the wall and grinned. "We went to Suzanne's. She cooked a super meal, and Father de Vere was charming. All smiles. Made a change from his usual serious self."

Grant laughed. "He seems a right moody bugger."

"He has his moments."

"Nothing you can't deal with, right?"

"Right. At least the older priest keeps to himself and out of my way."

Father de Vere *was* a moody bugger. She recalled the number of times his eyes flicked between her and Suzanne's brother at Christmas. Yesterday had been perfect. With no Xavier, the priest had been a different man.

Deep down, she bet Dante was jealous. Something in the way he reacted made her believe so. Sullen looks, clenched teeth, muttering under his breath whenever Xavier was around...

"How long did you stay? I know how much you enjoy partying." Grant's voice pulled her back into the conversation.

Jaime chuckled. "We left a little after midnight. Father de Vere had to be back to help Father Grégoire with the New Year's Day mass." She took a quick glance at her watch. "That's in about three quarters of an hour."

Jaime chewed on her thumbnail before daring to admit, "I received another letter, Grant."

"What!"

"It arrived in the post Mum forwarded. I got it on Boxing Day."

A moment of silence set in before Grant exploded. "Who the hell is this bastard? I imagined you'd be safe in France."

Grant had done everything possible to protect her – driving her back and forth from work when he could, escorting her home after partying with friends. The notes had still turned up. Everything possible hadn't been enough, and she knew Grant blamed himself for letting her down. It seemed the notes popped up when she had no escort. As if the stalker had access to every surveillance camera in town.

"Please don't tell Mum. She'd worry. It could be a one-off. It's not as if he knows where I am."

After another short silence, Grant said, "Speaking of Mum, have you wished her a Happy New Year?"

"I sent a quick text message."

"She misses you, Jaime. More than you think."

Jaime chewed her thumbnail again. "You know it's complicated, Grant."

"It doesn't have to be."

Jaime sighed. Despite her mum being around when needed, not once had they had a heart-to-heart talk. They didn't have a strong bond, but they got by. Jaime couldn't say her mother hated her. Hate was a strong word. It was more like indifference...and that hurt.

She was sure they both had mutual deep feelings for each other. Her mother simply didn't show them. At times, the family was even ignored. Well, not so much Grant. He was the lucky one.

Over the years, Jaime had come to accept her mother's cold ways, and they'd managed to get on rather well. Could being away for a while bring them closer? She remembered her father saying something about absence making the heart grow fonder. She hoped so.

Jaime fiddled with a strand of hair. "I'll write more often."

Apart from the Christmas card and a few lines she'd texted for the New Year, Jaime hadn't contacted her mother since moving to France.

The more she thought about the long silence, the guiltier she felt.

"How about if you phoned?" Grant asked.

"I'll think about it."

There was a pause.

"We both love you, Jaime."

She beamed. "I know you do. Look I have to go."

"Take care, little sister."

"I will. Love you."

Jaime flipped the phone shut and gazed outside. The distant, rolling hills were like those of home. Same winding footpaths, same gradual slopes. She clicked her fingernails against the window-pane, wondering when she would she be able to go back. Back to a normal life. If that existed.

With a sniff, she left the bedroom. There was no point in bringing up the past. She had to look to the future. Be patient. Sit tight. See what the New Year would bring.

***

A familiar buzz vibrated in Leonora's open bag. She glanced down and fished out the phone. A quick look at the screen showed it was Maxime. What the bloody hell did he want?

She'd started New Year's Day with a splitting migraine. Too much to drink the night before. New Year's Eve had been at home. Alone. That didn't bother her, and didn't stop her from celebrating. Being alone meant she didn't have to share the booze. But she now regretted drinking so much. A percolator of extra strong coffee had done nothing to subdue the thumping headache. She didn't need Maxime's smarm on top of that.

Since they'd split up a few months back, Leonora hadn't heard a word from him. That had suited her fine. Why was he ringing out of the blue?

Her finger hesitated in mid-air before it swished across the screen. "Yes?"

"Leonora, darling."

"What do you want?" Her tone was clipped and direct.

"You don't seem happy to hear from me."

She rolled her eyes. "Should I be?"

"Hey, it's a new year. Why not bury the hatchet? I'm sure this year is going to bring us together."

Christ, she hated his smug voice. "Not if I can help it."

"You haven't changed a bit. My same old Leonora."

"Cut out the chit-chat. I'm not in the mood. What do you want?" she repeated.

"I have something which I'm sure will interest you," his sadistic whisper clipped her ear.

"Which is?"

"Photos."

His chuckling was getting on her nerves. "I don't know what you're talking about."

"Oh, I think you do." His voice took on a tone of playful menace. "Don't you remember a special night in Rome?"

Leonora swallowed hard and closed her eyes, bringing back the images of that night when he'd coaxed her into letting him take shots during their lovemaking.

"Photos of you in very original positions with very original toys."

"And?" Impatience etched her voice.

"And I assumed you might like to have them back."

"So send them. You know my address."

Maxime cackled. "Steady on. I'd like to know what you're going to give me in return."

Leonora couldn't believe she was having this conversation. "I'll give you what you deserve. NOTHING."

Maxime's voice took on a harsh tone. "Not that easy, Darling. I want something or –"

"Or what?" she butted in.

"Or other people might like to see these."

Leonora's head pounded with renewed vigour. Was this bastard going to make her pay for one pathetic night?

"That's blackmail." She couldn't manage more than a whisper.

A scary laugh echoed down the phone. "Call it what you like, honey."

In a grip of silent panic, Leonora was ready to throw up. Saliva thickened in her mouth. It took a few long seconds to regain her wits. "Okay. How much do you want?"

"They're not up for sale, but thanks for the offer."

"Then what *do* you want?"

Maxime cleared his throat. "I want to regain my rightful place in your bed and all that comes with it."

Leonora saw red. She hadn't expected that. "You must be out of your mind. It's over between us. Can't you get it into your thick skull?" She hung up, swearing under her breath.

Christ Almighty! What the hell had she seen in him?

They'd met in a casino on the Côte d'Azur. Her eyes had immediately fallen on him, a man who she believed was rich enough to fall for. She needed someone to get over the breakup with Dante. Maxime wasn't good looking with his receding hairline and pale-blue eyes, but she wasn't out for looks. She was in it for money.

Maxime had looked up, hooked onto her gaze and grinned. He'd offered a drink, bought dinner, and before she knew it, they were making love in his hotel room. She'd never been one to hesitate. If she wanted something, what was the point of waiting?

When she thought about the messy situation she was in now, she'd been too hasty. Maxime had made out to be rich, but after a few months, certain signs gave him away. To her horror, he'd turned out to be an imposter, also looking for a rich partner. Today, she was no better off from a financial standpoint, still alone, and being blackmailed by the swine.

The phone rang again.

Let it ring.

But she knew he wouldn't give up. Taking a deep breath, she answered it.

"Mmm. I'm looking at the photos now. Delicious."

"Get to the point," she snapped.

"I've changed my mind. I'll take the money. I'm going through a rough patch. A bit of cash will come in handy."

Leonora paced the room. "What if I refuse?"

"I don't think you can afford to refuse, chérie. These photos would look great on the Web."

Her eyes widened. "You're bluffing."

"Wanna bet?"

Leonora couldn't afford to take the risk. "How do I know you have them?"

"You'll know soon enough. I'll bring them to the family estate Saturday morning around ten."

Leonora didn't like the sound of this. "What if I'm not free next Saturday?"

His laugh blasted through the phone. "Believe me, if you don't want people to see these pieces of art, you'll be free."

Leonora clenched the phone. "How much?"

"5,000 Euros."

She pinched the skin at her throat. If she got the photos back for 5,000, it wouldn't be that bad. 5,000 Euros wasn't going to break the bank. "Okay, bring them over Saturday morning."

"I don't think you got it. It's 5,000 for *each* photo."

Her hand nearly crushed the phone. "What? 5,000 Euros for one photo? You must be off your rocker."

"By the way...I've got about a dozen of them."

Speechless, Leonora stared at the phone and let out an ear-piercing scream.

What a shitty start to the year.

Chapter 9

The 'Pink Panther' tune blaring out of the phone shattered the silence in the café. Marcel dragged his eyes away from the newspaper. He relaxed when he saw the number and swished his finger across the screen.

"Marcel, I'm in the street, but I can't find the café."

"No sweat, mon ami, where exactly are you?"

"Hang on a minute...I'm on the corner of rue La Vieuville and rue des Martyrs."

"You're not far. I'll be there in a sec."

***

A few minutes later, the two men greeted each other with a hand slap and a tap on the back. Marcel still had that sparkle in his dark eyes, but his physical appearance had changed – and not for the best. Middle-aged folk had a tendency to put on weight, and Marcel was no exception. Dressed in a black leather jacket and scruffy jeans, he appeared bloated. Puffy even. His dyed black hair was tied back in a short ponytail. And it suited his friend. Maybe he should let his hair grow. Make a new start in life. New Year. New country. New look. Something to think about.

Following Marcel, he headed across the street and down a tiny side road. The sour odour of urine mixed with putrid litter spiralled up his nose. The stale air made him sneeze. Weird shrieking from the flats, louder for the absence of the main street traffic, added to his momentary unease.

After fifty metres or so, they came to a halt in front of a grim, 19th century Parisian apartment block. The building had seen better days. A few of the first-floor windows were boarded up. Most of the persienne shutters needed a fresh coat of paint.

Marcel took a long gasp of his cigarillo and turned to him. "I live on the top floor. Sorry, no lift."

By the time they entered the flat on the sixth floor, they were both ready for a drink. Marcel showed him the room that would be his. Although rather small, it was big enough for a double bed and a round table for his precious laptop. The toilet and bathroom were across the narrow corridor. He didn't mind sharing. He'd done worse.

After a cool beer and a hot shower, Marcel explained what his job would entail.

Two days later, his first mission came through.

***

He entered the bar and strode straight to a window seat. From there, he had an excellent view of the entrance. No way could he miss his contact. Thank God he'd arrived early; the place was now packed solid. Not that it bothered him. He'd have less chance of being spotted. Even so, his nerves were stripped to the bone.

The waitress arrived with the menu, bright red lipstick amplifying her pouty mouth. Her skirt, or should he say large belt, only just covered her backside. Trollop. Was she looking for a man to give her a ride? Or was she simply a cock-teaser who needed to be taught a lesson?

"Just a beer." He waved the menu away and focused on the door again.

Shady dealings were nerve-racking to say the least, but Marcel was a genius. They had to be cautious, and his friend had come up with a well set out plan. A smart strategy. He'd attached a red grosgrain ribbon around his black felt fedora hat. If he didn't recognise his contact, the contact would recognise him.

The waitress returned with the beer. He paid and took a sip, all the while eyeing up her long legs while she searched in her pouch for his change. The hussy made his groin itch. She'd better be good at quenching his lust. The trollop owed him that for strutting around like a hooker.

"Chanel Number 5, isn't it?" he said, taking the change she handed him.

"Yes...it is." Her eyes widened and a small smile played on her lips. "A present for Christmas. I can't afford to buy perfume myself."

He handed her a tip. "What time do you knock off?"

She rolled a stray hair around her finger. "Why? Wanna take me out for dinner?"

Yeah, and the rest.

"I'm new in town," he said, taking a long look around. "Maybe you could show me around before we choose a nice restaurant to finish off the evening?"

The young woman's lips pulled back into a broad smile showing a set of teeth held prisoner in braces. "Could do. I finish at six-thirty. I'm on the early shift."

What the fuck do I care? "Great." He gazed down at his watch. Five-thirty. "I'll wait for you outside in an hour then."

"Cool."

He made a grab for her wrist and caressed it with his thumb. The young waitress let out a quick yelp of surprise.

"Hey, honey, calm down. No one's going to harm you." *Not yet.* He gazed down at her hand and smirked.

"Bonjour," came a low voice.

His eyes darted up to see a young chap slip into the chair opposite him. After a few more seconds, he released the waitress's hand and watched her skip lightly away.

He turned his full attention to his client, acknowledging him with a nod. The man pulled out an envelope and slid it under the table. With a steady hand, he grabbed the envelope and stuffed it inside his jacket before handing over a black pouch, his mind bouncing between excitement and adrenaline pumping hard.

Pleased with the purchase, the young man winked and left.

Quick and efficient.

He downed his beer in one gulp, happy with the transaction. A good job done. He could now relax and dream about his date.

Rising from his seat, he headed towards the exit, his eyes searching for the waitress. No sign of her. Ten to one, she'd gone to get ready for their rendez-vous. He stepped outside, whistling into the brisk air. Another hour to kill before he led Snow White into the woods.

Chapter 10

He woke the next morning to the pitter-patter of light rain tapping on the tiny skylight. Everything had gone to plan with the delivery, and Marcel had given him a healthy cut. Which was more than he could say for his date. When he'd returned to the bistrot to pick her up, she'd been nowhere in sight. A fellow waiter told him she'd knocked off early and vaguely mentioned something about a sudden migraine leaving her nauseous.

Lying bitch!

Dragging his gaze away from the window, he looked on the bright side of things. He was lucky to have come across Marcel. The man had promised to make him a partner and had kept to his word. Had even put him up free of charge.

An ugly, thin line defined his mouth as he glanced around the room. The place lacked something. He needed to create the same cosy atmosphere he'd had at home where he'd pasted hundreds of photos of Jaime on the walls.

He lit up a joint. The room grew heavy with the lingering scent of pungent sweet smoke and stale coffee. Inhaling slowly, he propped up onto an elbow and reached for his cup. A thick skin of milk plastered the top.

Shit, he'd forgotten to clean it? He turned his nose up in disgust. What he needed was a reward. Yet the reward in mind wasn't going to walk up to his flat and knock on the door.

Loneliness crept over him. Apart from Marcel, no one talked to him. Friends had deserted him, calling him crazy. They weren't on the same wavelength. They didn't understand that his brother could talk to him in his head.

"I'm normal! They're the crazy ones," he shouted to the room.

He grabbed his flick-knife and carved a deep groove in the bedside table, the tip moving deeper into the soft wood as his frustration mounted. He still couldn't get over the fact that his date with the waitress hadn't pulled through. He needed a woman. A girl who would please him after his 'rounds,' or even new friends. Someone to communicate with. He headed over to his laptop. How about a girlfriend?

He stabbed the table with the knife and put out the joint, abandoning it with the other butts lying in the ash-filled plate used as an excuse for an ashtray. With a push of a finger, he switched on the computer and surfed various different chat groups.

It would have to be a teenager-chat group. A French one. No point in belonging to an international group if he wanted a girl to keep him warm in Paris. His bedroom French would at last be put to good use.

Young women were favourites, but he'd always been careful with their age. He didn't want to be ranked in the league of paedophiles. They were monsters, and he wasn't. He simply wanted to be loved.

He gazed down at the screen. Using his real name wouldn't be a good idea under the circumstances. His eyes scanned the room while he racked his brains. When they fell onto the small poster of crocodiles Marcel had pinned on the back of the door, he'd found it.

They were good at hunting.

He'd have to lie about his age. That didn't bother him.

At twenty-six, he was still young and attractive enough to begin a new life, confident he could achieve anything he set his crafty mind to. He'd studied law in London, enabling him to get away from the heavy atmosphere at home. His dad had been a hard-working, self-made man. Yet, despite a decent income, he'd refused to pay the extras needed for his son to live a cushy life at university. Meaning he had to find a part-time job.

He looked gazed at the Graduation Day photo next to his bed, one of the few personal belongings he'd brought with him from England. His father had hugged him, saying how proud he was. One big lie. Things had become clear the day his mother passed away. He'd gone through bits and pieces to find letters written before his father's death. The two-timing bastard!

Why did his father have to spoil the image he had of him? He'd loved the man. Thought the world of him, even though he feared him at times. As he'd grown older, his father had spent less time at home. His business, or maybe other women, had kept him away from his family. He no doubt preferred his hussies. No strings, no wife to care for, no son to look after.

Adrenaline rushed through his body and his chest tightened as he grabbed the frame and threw it across the room. Why had his parents passed away with so many unanswered questions? He wiped away a stray tear and plodded over to the smashed frame. Pulling the photo out of the broken glass, his fingers brushed against a small piece of paper tucked between the photo and backing. Hello...how come he hadn't found this before? He unfolded the sheet.

"The lying cow!" Spittle fell onto the paper and his vision blurred while a flame curled in the pit of his gut.

Red. Everything went red. Why had his mother told him the man in the photo was his father? Memories of the man he'd loved weighed on his chest.

Grinding his teeth, he cleaned up the glass. Shards pierced the skin of his fingers, but he hardly felt the pain. It would take time for the incredible news to sink in. Later, with some investigating, he'd find answers to his questions. For the moment, all that mattered was finding Jaime.

***

The scrunch of tyres on the gravel outside brought Leonora out of her reading. A quick glance at the grandfather clock showed 10 a.m. She flung the magazine onto the gueridon and stepped out of the vestibule onto the patio. It hadn't taken Maxime long to drive up the two-hundred metre avenue of lime trees leading up from the gates.

Already out of the car, he bounced up the half a dozen stone steps in fast easy strides, a large brown envelope clutched under one arm. Leonora noted he hadn't changed much. Same pale eyes. Same pathetic grin. Two minor things had turned for the worse, though. The once well-kept beard was now a grubby stubble, and he'd shaven his head.

Maxime's face split into a malicious grin. "Hi, gorgeous." He handed her the brown envelope and brushed some fluff from his jacket lapel.

With trembling hands, Leonora opened it and stared at the content. Bile swept up to the back of her throat.

"Nice, isn't it?" Maxime sidled closer, hand open for payment.

With a huff, Leonora slid the photo back into the envelope and marched into the house, all the while listening to Maxime's casual footsteps in the tiled hallway.

"You could have waited outside." Her tone was condescending.

"Why? I like it here. Don't you remember our aperitifs on the front terrace under the beautiful cedar trees?"

Leonora huffed. "I'm trying hard to forget."

Maxime chuckled and followed her into the grey-walled study. A bag lay open in the centre of the large mahogany desk. Leonora took out a wad of notes and dropped the money into his outstretched hand.

Maxime clasped the notes. "That's better, darling. Oh, by the way, that photo is one of my favourites."

Leonora closed her fist around the envelope, crushing it with rage.

With a cocky grin, Maxime licked his thumb and counted the notes one by one.

Leonora let out a disgusted snort. "Don't you trust me?"

Maxime rocked back on his heels. "Oh, I trust you all right, baby. I just love the feel of money."

Pathetic fool. The sheer sight of him made Leonora gag.

The counting over, Maxime rolled the notes before sliding them into his inside jacket pocket. "I'll be off then...unless you want to come for a walk? Remember what we used to get up to in the woods on the far end of the property?"

"Goodbye!"

Maxime chortled and blew a kiss. "See you soon."

Rot in hell, you bastard!

Chapter 11

Dante was settled in his favourite armchair in the lounge, the parish magazine in one hand, a cup of coffee in the other. Father Grégoire had left a few minutes earlier for a meeting in the village of Saint-Corneille, and Jaime had gone shopping in Le Mans eager to get bargains in the January sales and wouldn't be back until late afternoon. Great. He could take it easy.

It was impossible to relax in the housekeeper's presence. Christ, she had a firm arse and slim, muscled legs. Something stirred deep inside, but now wasn't the time to think of bedding the woman – even though his groin tightened at the simple prospect of Jaime naked against him. He'd been thinking of that on and off ever since she tumbled off the ladder.

All this time without a woman was driving him nuts. But he didn't want any woman. He wanted Jaime. And not just her sexy body. He wanted the whole package. Her easy-going manner, bright spirit, and continual quick wit. Not to mention the outspokenness which often drove him around the bend.

The revving of a car engine brought Dante out of his sensual reverie. He got to his feet, swearing. Who the hell was accelerating like a prat? The vehicle sounded as if it would take off any minute and land in the front room. Peeking out of the window, he snorted on seeing the sports car. Xavier. What the bloody hell did he want?

A few moments later, Xavier brought the vehicle to a halt in front of the presbytery. He jumped out with a box of chocolates tucked under his arm.

Dante returned to the armchair and continued reading, lips pinched together in a thin line.

"Hey, Father," Xavier called, entering the presbytery without knocking or ringing. "I've come to take Jaime out."

Dante looked up in silent prayer. "There's not much to do around here. You'll get bored."

Xavier chuckled. "Not with what I've got in mind."

Dante's fists whitened. "She's out. You should have called. It would have saved you the trip over."

Xavier's expression sank like a soufflé removed from the oven. He dropped the chocolates onto the table and raked a hand through his hair. "When will she be back?"

"No idea." Dante didn't bother looking up from the newspaper.

Xavier shuffled from one foot to the other. "I'll wait."

"Please yourself. She's gone to Le Mans."

Xavier paced up and down the lounge while Dante turned a page of the magazine, his lips bearing the resemblance of a hidden smile.

"Can you give her these chocolates?" Xavier said, letting out a long sigh. "And tell her I was sorry to have missed her."

Dante grunted, and Xavier left in a huff.

No sooner had the door slammed shut than Dante headed to the window and peeled back the net curtains. The day had started out great. A quiet time on his own, no one to distract or annoy him... His good mood had since evaporated.

He tapped a finger on the window ledge. Xavier was getting on his wick. It was a long drive from Paris, but that hadn't stopped him from coming to see Jaime. He'd have to put an end to all this. Why couldn't he be the one giving Jaime chocolates? The one to go sightseeing or nightclubbing? What he'd give to be able to share jokes with her, hear her lovely laugh, take her places and watch her face light up.

Dante hated his present life. Unable to reveal his true identity. Obliged to keep this pathetic disguise and remain in hiding while the other jerk was allowed to take Jaime out. He'd have to sort Xavier out once and for all.

A couple of hours later, on hearing Jaime return, Dante swiped the chocolates off the table and buried them at the bottom of the rubbish bin.

***

A few days later, Xavier phoned Jaime. He wanted to take her sightseeing in Angers. At first, Jaime was reluctant. After their first meeting, she worried Xavier would come on quick again. With a throaty chuckle, Xavier had promised to behave, and Jaime had eventually agreed. Had he been able to sense her hesitance?

Angers was a beautiful place awash with renaissance architecture. Jaime had strolled up the cobblestone path to the medieval castle and shuddered in front of the two high, black-stone bulk towers which loomed over her. She'd been transported back in time.

Xavier had found a super place to eat on the Place Sainte-Croix. Jaime loved the small bistrot with its warm decor and pleasant atmosphere. It faced a fifteenth century renaissance timber building called La Maison d'Adam, and Jaime couldn't have wished for a better view.

After a quick lunch, they only had time for a short tour of the cathedral. Jaime hadn't been fond of its mish-mash styles. The sixteenth century gothic carvings hadn't appealed to her. Neither had the more modern parts.

By the time the afternoon drew to an end, Jaime was drained. Christ, how her feet ached. She flopped down in the car seat and slipped off her boots. Xavier pulled away, and they chatted about their day during the drive back to Montfort-le-Gesnois. Jaime enjoyed the conversation until Xavier brought up a subject that puzzled her.

"I forgot to ask," he said, tapping his fingers to the lively tempo drumming from the radio. "Did you like the chocolates?"

Jaime turned to him, mouth slightly open and loose.

Xavier paled and his hands clasped the steering wheel tighter. "It's just a small gift from a friend. Doesn't mean you have to give me anything in return."

Jaime managed to paste a confident smile on her face. "They were...er...they were delicious."

"I guessed you'd like them." Xavier released the tension in his fingers. "They're from one of the best chocolatiers in Paris."

Jaime turned and gazed out the window. What had become of the chocolates? They couldn't have disappeared into thin air. Maybe Xavier hadn't bought them at all, but then, why should he lie? Something to look into.

All smiles as the car pulled up in front of the presbytery a little after six-thirty, Jaime and Xavier strolled into the lounge. Jaime settled herself in Dante's favourite armchair. Xavier pulled up a stool and grabbed one of her feet. "Let's take these boots off. Your poor little feet must be aching."

"They're fine," Jaime said, a little nervous. The priest had already shown displeasure when he'd observed the two of them at the Christmas lunch. She didn't want to have to put up with another bout of sulking.

As if on cue, a flared-nostril, curled-lipped, Father de Vere appeared in the doorway. Jaime tugged her foot out of Xavier's hand, positive the priest had been spying. He was good at that.

"I'm going to church." Dante's voice was harsh. "People are coming to confess with Father Grégoire before Mass. Would you like to join them, Jaime?"

Jaime choked back her surprise. How dare the priest patronise them? They weren't kids. Besides, there was no written notice to say she couldn't sit with Xavier in the lounge. Who the hell did the priest think he was, insinuating she should confess?

Dante turned to Xavier. "As for you, I would appreciate it if you didn't distract our housekeeper in the presbytery."

Xavier pulled a sweet smile and got to his feet. "Okay, okay, no need to get shirty. You're taking after the old crusty. I was just about to leave anyway." He fished his car keys out of his pocket and headed out of the door, not forgetting to blow a kiss in Jaime's direction.

Determined not to let the priest have the last word, Jaime waited for Xavier to be out of earshot before she leapt up. "Hang on a minute, *Father*. Xavier said he brought a box of chocolates the last time he stopped by."

"That is correct."

"So where are they?" Jaime stood hands on hips.

A muscle twitched in the priest's left cheek. "Unfortunately, Petrus ate them, so there was no point in bringing up the matter." And he stalked out of the room.

"Yeah, I bet," Jaime muttered, stunned by the priest's shameless lie. "So why wasn't the dog ill, you lying frog?"

***

Leonora sat on the front pew in the church, crossing and uncrossing her legs as she stared at the stone slabs on the floor. It was time to talk to someone about her ordeal. Glancing repeatedly behind her, waiting for Dante to appear, she dug her nails into her leather handbag.

After a while, she recognised his determined footsteps echoing down the aisle and turned to meet his gaze.

"What the hell are you doing here?" His voice was almost a shriek.

"I need to speak to you about something important."

Dante rubbed a hand over his beard. "You could have phoned."

"But you refuse to talk to me," she snapped.

"Keep your voice down and get into the confessional."

Leonora settled down and peered through the screen to where Dante was sitting in the adjacent booth.

"You have to accept I'm a priest, Leonora. I don't want you coming here again. Have I made myself clear?"

Leonora weaved her fingers through the intricate latticed opening. "But we were good together. Why for Christ's sake did you put an end to our relationship to become a bloody priest?"

Dante eased the door open to peek out. "You're in a church. So stop swearing and keep your voice down."

Leonora giggled. "If you don't want me to shout, let me into your booth."

"Stop it." Dante's voice held a harsh warning.

"Oh, stop being such a stick in the mud."

After a few seconds, Leonora divulged her problem in a low voice. "My grandmother has left a Will with a rather unusual pre-condition to my legacy."

"What would that be?"

Leonora bit her lower lip. "I hate to own up, and I've managed to hide it pretty well. That is...up until now."

Dante leaned in closer. "What are you talking about?"

"I'm being blackmailed."

"Are you serious?"

"Of course, I'm bloody serious!" Leonora's voice echoed in the quiet atmosphere of the church.

"Keep your voice down," Dante hissed.

"There's no one here!" she shouted even louder.

Dante cracked his knuckles and took on a calmer tone. "Have you got proof?"

Leonora nodded. "There's proof in the car. I'll show you." Without waiting for a reply, she swished the crimson velvet curtain aside and sat on a pew, tapping impatient fingers on her bag.

***

When Dante emerged, she shot up and led him outside. "How the hell am I going to get out of all this shit? I don't deserve this."

Dante took in a deep breath as they walked side by side out of the church.

"Why does bad luck always have to come my way?" Leonora said, opening the car. "First, *you* end our relationship, I get mucked about by a string of worthless boyfriends, then Maxime blackmails me. Can any more bad luck fall onto my plate?"

Dante lifted his eyes and mumbled a quick prayer for patience. Leonora never stopped talking. What on earth had he seen in the woman? At least in becoming a priest, he'd brought an end to their pointless relationship.

He examined his ex a little closer. Too artificial. Her smooth expressionless complexion had no wrinkles. She must have gone strong on the Botox. Did she need it? Although four years older than him, thirty-nine was far too young to go hard on the jabs.

Settled in the car, Dante opened the envelope she handed him. One glance was enough. "What on earth possessed you to do this?"

"When you ended our relationship, I was devastated. I loved you."

Dante replaced the photo into its envelope. "Did you? Or was it my social position?"

"Same thing, isn't it? When I met Maxime, he made me feel alive again."

"Or rather his money. Are you feeling any remorse?"

Leonora gave him a weak smile before grabbing his arm. "Please don't reject me. We were lovers, after all."

Dante remained silent.

"I need your help. My inheritance is contingent on my godfather,

Tancrède Mérignac being content that I have not brought the Saint Clair family name into disgrace with any 'immoral or outrageous behaviour.'" She quoted the latter part in a sarcastic voice.

The priest gazed straight ahead. "Your grandmother knew you well."

Dante had met Portia de Moncade, several times during their relationship. He remembered a small, pale-complexioned woman with a haughty expression. Leonora had inherited the old lady's manners.

Leonora's father, Augustin Saint Clair, had been Portia's only child. He'd led a life of celibacy until the age of forty, when he'd become smitten with Valentine Mercier, a young waitress. Valentine had become pregnant and married Augustin at the age of eighteen. Portia never liked Valentine. She was convinced the waitress was after the family riches.

A few years after Leonora's birth, Valentine could no longer bear Portia's sarcasm. One day, she packed her bags and left. With Augustin often away from home, the little girl stayed with Grandmamma.

Augustin had never been close to his daughter, even less after Leonora's mother died in a car accident. Not long after Valentine's death, Augustin realised he'd made a complete mess of his life. He'd gone to bed one night after drinking a whole bottle of whisky along with a couple of packets of sleeping tablets and had drifted off into eternal sleep.

"And this ridiculous stipulation is to run for a year after her death." Leonora brought Dante back to the present.

The priest tapped the envelope on the dashboard. "If I remember rightly, Portia passed away about seven months ago, which means…"

"Which means, if I don't deal with this bastard right away, I'm not going to inherit a single penny."

Dante recalled the magnificent Saint Clair estate tucked away in the quiet outskirts of Paris. Set on three acres of picturesque grounds, he'd been captivated by the grandiose landscape designs. What a pity if Leonora lost the property.

"Why are you here, Leonora?"

"I need your help."

"But why now and not before?"

"Because I thought I could deal with it, but it's gone too far." She leaned closer. "I know Maxime thinks I'm stupid to pay, but I don't have a choice. Some photos show my face. I also know he can print off as many photos as he likes. Blackmail me for the rest of my life. But I'm only playing along with him until I inherit my money. After that he can do what he wants with the damned photos."

Dante felt sorry for the woman. She'd landed herself in a huge mess and even more so now that she'd started paying the man. Maybe if she'd sought advice before giving in to the threat, things could have been different. If only she'd used her head for once.

Dante stared out of the window. "I'm afraid only you can take the decision, Leonora."

***

Jaime spotted the priest with Leonora in the Porsche.

Coming closer, she saw Leonora gaze at the priest's mouth with parted lips. She couldn't miss Leonora's long looks. The woman was still in love.

Jaime frowned. They could do what they wanted. She couldn't give a toss. Yet, how could she justify the stab of envy at the familiarity between them? She tried to swallow her disappointment. It stuck in her throat like an aspirin struggling to go down without water.

She tugged her coat around her and flounced up to the car before tapping on the window. "Want anything special for dinner, *Father*?"

Dante flung the envelope he'd been holding under the seat before scrambling out of the car. Jaime tilted her head to one side, enjoying his disarray.

"Shall I prepare an extra plate for your lady friend?"

Dante turned an unflattering shade of red. "You're getting the wrong end of the stick."

Jaime held both hands up in mock surrender. "Ooh la la! I'm not getting any end of any stick. You do what you want with your life, Father-not-so-goody-goody-after-all."

She turned and headed to the presbytery, the priest's rapid footsteps and loud muttering following her. No sooner had she put a foot in the door than Petrus knocked her flat to the floor.

Stifling a groan, Jaime managed to get the dog's snout off her mouth and pushed up onto both elbows. The mutt was impossible. She'd been out for no more than ten minutes. He couldn't have missed her already.

Turning to one side, Jaime spotted Dante chuckling. "What's so bloody funny?"

The priest's lips curled upwards at the sight of Jaime's wet face and ruffled clothes. He held out a hand and hauled her up.

"I'm not much good with dogs."

Dante brushed a damp stray hair from her cheek. "I can see that."

Jaime gazed into his eyes and took a few steps back. The hot touch of the man's fingers sent an electric current through her body. Jaime's insides were going haywire. The chemistry between them was unbalancing. Could he feel it too?

"Er...I'd better change out of these clothes before preparing dinner," she said, and raced up the stairs.

Once in the bedroom, she leaned back against the closed door and placed both hands on her burning cheeks.

Shit, she was falling for a man of the cloth.

***

Dante clasped the dog's collar and dragged Petrus back into the kitchen before getting himself a drink.

What had come over him? Since when had he taken such liberties? He had to pull himself together. Get a grip on things. In a moment of inattention, he'd slipped out of his priestly disguise when he'd removed a stray hair from her face in an intimate way. Not permitted.

The dog stepped into his basket, turned several times like an elephant in a paddling pool and settled down with a satisfied growl. With his head hung over the side, the dog looked up with pitiful eyes.

Dante crouched to stroke his cheeks. "Hey, buddy. Did she taste good?"

Petrus gazed up and sighed with doggy contentment.

Chapter 12

Father de Vere woke to the sound of heavy breathing.

After months of hiding, anything unexpected was a threat. In a split second, his eyes flew wide open.

Feeling a presence in the dark to the left, the priest dropped a hand to the side of his bed, ready to retrieve the crowbar. He didn't have the opportunity to use it. Jaime's voice broke the silence.

"Father, there's someone in the house."

Dante's heart missed a beat. There couldn't be anyone in the house. Petrus would have alerted them...unless they'd dealt with the dog first. Fear spread through him. The same fear he'd felt once before when they'd paid him a visit in Italy.

He switched on the bedside lamp and slid out of bed. He pressed a finger to his lips before pointing to the space between the bed and the wall. He motioned Jaime to get down, mouthing *don't move!*

Jaime gaped wide-eyed at Father de Vere's half-naked body. Annoyed, Dante clicked his fingers and once again pointed to the other side of the bed. Jaime nodded.

While Jaime crouched behind the bed, Dante quickly slipped on his shoes. With the crowbar held tightly, he crept downstairs and straight to the kitchen. The dog lifted his head and snorted.

"Good boy," he whispered.

Dante moved around the house, checking every door and window. Moonlight enabled him to make his way about. He knew the house by heart. Lights weren't necessary. Nothing was out of place.

A shuffle to the right brought him to an abrupt standstill. Dante held his breath and ice grew in the pit of his gut. Without a sound, he took a few steps back in an attempt to make out the whereabouts of the noise. His heart tried to escape from his chest as he crept along the corridor.

Another muffled squeak.

Dante came to a halt, resisting the urge to look over his shoulder. A cold sweat broke out across his brow as he gripped the weapon tighter. Someone was breathing nearby.

With the crowbar raised high, Dante spun around, ready to strike.

"Father!"

The priest let out a huge breath. "You scared the shit out of me! I thought I told you to stay behind the bed." His voice came out in an angry whisper.

"I was frightened."

Dante's body was like a live-wire, but he couldn't tell if that was because of Jaime scaring him or of the woman's nearness? Since his housekeeper's arrival, his feelings which had remained dormant for so long were now coming to life.

The sharp ring of the house phone brought him back to his senses. He switched on the light and rushed into the study.

"Hello."

No answer.

Dante stared at the phone for a brief second. What was going on? Luckily, Father Grégoire's room was at the far end of the presbytery, and the old man always slept well. Dante had heard his snores echoing down the corridor many a time. Besides, he always took his hearing aid out.

He hurried back to the lounge to find Jaime perched on the edge of the sofa, clasping the fire poker as if her life depended on it. With her top teeth biting onto her lower lip, Jaime focused on the rug.

He was about to speak when the intercom at the front door buzzed like an angry rattlesnake. Jaime jumped, her knuckles whitening around the poker. Dante shook his head in disbelief and rushed to the door. With a finger on the intercom, he waited for the caller to speak.

No one.

"Hello?"

Still no answer.

His finger sprang off the buzzer. "Who the bloody hell is this?"

Throwing on his coat, Dante surged out of the house to the gate, his breath forming thin clouds in the sharp January air. With a pull, he yanked the gate open, hoping to catch the culprit. His eyes fell onto the back of a man jogging down the road. Who the hell would jog in the middle of the night? He slammed the gate shut and raced back to the house.

After having been threatened, beaten up, and left for dead, he knew how easy it would be for them to track him down. But this small, secluded village had been the perfect place to hide. To be forgotten. To be left alone.

Up until now, everything had run to plan. So why was all this happening since his housekeeper had arrived? Coincidence?

"Who was it?" Jaime stood in the doorway.

"No one."

Her eyes narrowed. "I heard the buzzer."

Dante bolted the front door. "Whoever it was has gone."

"So there was someone?"

The priest turned to her. "Yes, but there's no need to worry."

Jaime's left hand worked back and forth over her leg while the right hand held firm onto the makeshift weapon.

"Jaime?"

Dante approached, and one by one, slowly prised each finger away from the fire poker all the while whispering words of reassurance. He'd guessed right. Something was wrong.

"There's no one in the house," he murmured softly. "You're safe here."

Jaime took a quick glance at the door. "I'll see you in the morning, then."

"Are you sure you'll be all right?"

Jaime nodded.

"Come on, I'll take you up." He accompanied her to her room before coming back down to check the house again.

Someone was snooping. He had to make sure no one could get in. The more he considered the situation, the more his brain spun with unanswered questions.

He rubbed a hand over his face. What if they'd tracked him down? Could it be one of the parishioners? They all seemed genuine folk from the village, but how would he know? Didn't they all believe him to be a genuine priest? He'd have to be careful, more alert, keep a close eye on everyone. Another thing to watch for.

On his way upstairs, gentle sobbing brought him to a standstill. He opened the door to Jaime's bedroom and peered in. Her small body lay curled up on the edge of the bed. His heart twanged with something he hadn't felt since his days in the courtroom: the overwhelming need to protect.

"Are you okay?" he asked.

Jaime bolted upright, her eyes wide with fear. "I'm scared," she said in a strangled whisper.

Dante stepped up to the bed and lay on top of the duvet, facing Jaime's back. He put a comforting arm around her frail body, and felt her relax in his embrace while he listened to her sob in the semi-darkness. It pulled at his gut.

When there were no more tears left to cry, she huddled deeper under the duvet.

"Why can't you be the gardener?" she muttered into her hanky. "I can't fall for a priest."

Dante muscles twitched. He was falling for her too, but had to hide his feelings for the time being. In the dim light drifting through the slits of the shutters, Dante listened to Jaime's breathing slowly calm. Her body relaxed in sleep while the old presbytery settled around them.

***

Dawn had yet to break when Jaime opened her eyes. The room was silent apart from a few birds chirping from the treetops. Despite the commotion in the middle of the night, she'd slept well. A lazy butterfly came to life in her chest as she remembered the priest's strong arm holding her tight.

She stretched and turned to find herself alone. When had he left? The spot next to her was cold so it must have been a while. Had he gone to church after spending the night in a room with a woman? She wondered if this conduct would cost him a couple of pater nosters. Or worse still, a flagellation in front of the cross. What would Father Grégoire think if he ever found out? Would Dante be excommunicated?

Jaime recalled the night before. It wasn't so much the fear that disturbed her; it was what she'd seen under the priest's bed. Something else to add to her belief that this man was no true priest.

Those weapons weren't offerings from the parishioners, and they hadn't been there before, or she would have noticed when she'd vacuumed. She contemplated plausible answers to his stock of munitions. Nothing logical came to mind. At least not for the time being.

Sometime later, Jaime came downstairs and set about her chores. A lazy melody floated out of the radio. The same tune the gardener – or should she say – the priest had hummed when she'd first met him in the garden. The edges of her mouth curled upwards as she gazed through the living-room window.

Puffy white clouds swirled and twisted, changing shapes. Shapes that developed into the priest's features. Warm imaginary arms slid around her like the night before. She closed her eyes and relished in the delight of it.

Her eyes flew open when something wet brushed her hand. With a startled squeal, she pulled it back in a flash. Petrus's sad eyes gazed up, shattering the daydream.

"You scared me," she said, ruffling the fur on the dog's neck. "I assumed you were in the garden."

Petrus let out a sorry whine.

"Hungry, are you? Come on, then. Let me get you back to the kitchen."

***

When it was time to prepare lunch, Jaime remembered to set an extra place. Xavier had invited himself for the meal. He wanted her to accompany him to Le Mans. Suzanne was having a birthday party for the twins later that evening, Xavier needed to buy gifts, and Jaime needed to get out of the presbytery's oppressive atmosphere. As usual, she'd prepared a tray with Father Grégoire's lunch and had taken it to his office.

While she placed the glasses, she wondered if Father de Vere would honour them with his presence. She hadn't seen him since their nocturnal disturbance. He'd disappeared into thin air. The man of the cloth was good at that. He'd wander off for hours on end, either barricaded in his cold study or locked up in the secret vestry. The two priests made a right pair.

"Bonjour, Jaime." Xavier entered the kitchen and gave her a quick peck on the cheek.

"Hi!" Jaime placed the last napkin under a knife, and they both sat to wait for Father de Vere.

"So what's new?"

Xavier sat back in the chair with both hands behind his head. "I've been given a pay rise."

"Wow. Congratulations."

Xavier thrust out his chest and cracked a smug smile. "Thanks. My boss said I'm so good at my job that I deserved it."

Xavier liked blowing his own trumpet, and loved talking nonstop about himself.

After draining his work repertoire, he leaned forward and rested both elbows on the table. "Where's grumpy Father de Vere? I'm starving."

Jaime chuckled. "Let's start. Doesn't look as if we'll have the pleasure of his company."

Xavier reached across the table and covered Jaime's hand. She jolted and made an attempt to pull it free, but Xavier tightened his grip. Jaime looked up and stiffened. Over Xavier's shoulders, a tall, familiar figure headed down the corridor towards them.

"Jaime?"

As always, her heart missed a beat on hearing Father de Vere's voice. She had to stop reacting like this. After the way he'd held her close the night before, she didn't want her body betraying her emotions. What if she ended up losing control and doing something stupid? Like running a hand up the inside of his shirt or crushing her mouth against his in a passionate kiss. He'd need a huge whip for self-flagellation.

She swallowed hard as she looked into the priest's gaze.

His expression darkened on seeing Xavier's hand covering hers. Behind the priest's furious eyes, Jaime detected a tinge of hurt. His fists tightened.

Xavier followed Jaime's eyes. "Dante! We didn't think you'd join us."

Dante's lips pressed into a white slash. "I'm not. I have to finish my work since Suzanne has invited us to spend the night. I also need to prepare a night bag as well as Petrus' gear. She knows the dog can't stay on its own."

Xavier stroked the back of Jaime's hand. "I've asked Jaime to help me choose presents for the twins. I'm so grateful to her."

Dante came to the table and grabbed a piece of baguette.

"You carry on with your work," Xavier said. "When we finish in Le Mans, I'll drive Jaime straight to Rambouillet."

Dante grunted, took another piece of bread with some cheese, and left without another word.

***

When Dante entered Luc's living room that evening, the twins were ready to open their presents. Sasha ripped the paper off the fire engine and examined the flashing lights.

"It's just what I wanted, Oncle Xavier!" He squealed with excitement.

Suzanne thanked Xavier and helped Santine open the present from Dante. A beautiful Corolle doll. Santine stood gob-smacked.

Suzanne rubbed her daughter's arm. "Well, say something, honey."

"Tonton," was all the little girl managed to say as she ran up to her uncle. Dante swung her in his arms and held her close. Jaime looked on, swallowing hard. God, he loved the children. She'd seen that at Christmas.

"Happy birthday, my darlings." Suzanne smothered the twins with kisses.

Jaime laughed. She loved the little six-year-olds with their high pitch chatter and carefree ways. In truth, she felt more at home at Rambouillet than at the presbytery.

Luc turned to Dante. "I'm so glad you could come. You always turn down our invitations. But we've seen you twice since Christmas."

Dante rubbed the back of his neck. "They're special occasions."

Bizarre thoughts drifted through Jaime's mind. Why did he avoid his family? What was he hiding? If the arsenal he kept at the presbytery was anything to go by, the man could be a terrorist for all they knew.

She chanced a glance his way. Dante's face, once again, was straighter than a poker player's. Only his dark, piercing eyes moved.

As usual, they revealed nothing of his thoughts.

Dinner was pleasant enough. Suzanne chatted away, all the while keeping the twins under control. Dante kept to himself, raising his head now and again to answer Luc's questions. Xavier sat at the opposite end of the table, making eyes at Jaime throughout the meal.

When it was time to turn in, Jaime headed to her room and into the en-suite bathroom. She needed a hot bath to relieve the stress of the past days. Lavender bath salts would help unwind.

Sinking into the steaming water, Jaime let out an exhalation of pent-up frustration before sliding under the surface. She did that when she was a child, concentrating on holding her breath rather than on worries.

Droplets trickled down her forehead when she emerged. She wiped away a stray hair and rested against the rim of the bath. Various ideas came to mind. The jogger to begin with. Coincidence that he'd run into her? Or purposely done? And what about the arsenal in the priest's room? The weapons hadn't been out on display for all to see, but they were still there. Why would a priest need an arms cache? She slid down under the water again.

Twenty minutes later, after a much-needed pampering, she left the bathroom, feeling refreshed. The bedside lamp dropped softened shadows across the bed. The organza flowered curtains blocked out the sharp night air. Jaime drew back the heavy fabric and peered out into the night. The wind had ceased, and the fog had dissipated.

Was Dante looking out into the night too?

She let the curtain fall back and turned into the room. Why did her mind always come back to the priest? She'd often found him staring while she went about household chores. Each time she'd met his gaze, he looked away. Did that mean anything? Or was she reading into something that didn't exist?

She slumped down on the bed, and for no reason, broke into tears. During the last few months, she'd been scared and unable to confide in anyone. From pride? Fear of making a fool of herself? Or from having no one she could trust. Tears trickled out along with the worry that her past might spurt forward into the present and destroy any semblance of sanity.

A light tap sounded on the door, and with a swish of her hand, Jaime wrapped the bath robe tighter around her body.

"Yes?" she called, clutching the damp hanky.

Xavier poked his head around the door. "You okay?"

Jaime stood in a flash. "What are you doing here?"

"You've been crying," he said, ignoring her question.

Jaime's gaze dropped to where Xavier's eyes focused on her body, and a slight flush heated her cheeks. The bathrobe had gaped, showing her breasts. Xavier's eyes gleamed as they took in the cleavage. Jaime tugged the clothing more firmly into place.

Xavier took determined strides and pulled Jaime into his arms. At first, she stiffened but soon conceded; his arms were comforting. She relaxed a little, enjoying the warm hug. Xavier placed a kiss on the top of her head. Jaime guessed where things could be heading.

"I'm not sure I want this, Xavier."

He rubbed his hands up and down her arms. "I'm falling for you, Jaime."

Oh hell! She hadn't believed she'd been leading him on. "Look, Xavier, I enjoy your company, and I'm fond of you..."

"But?" He released her and ran a hand through his hair several times.

"I can't let this go any further. I like you as a friend, but that's as far as it goes." Her voice took on an apologetic tone.

Xavier looked away to conceal the disappointment in his eyes. "Are you seeing someone else?"

Jaime didn't answer.

A muscle twitched in his left eye, and his mouth set into a harsh grimace. "Do I know him?"

"Does it make any difference?"

"It makes a difference to me." His features fell into cold anger, and both hands closed into tight fists.

Jaime took a step back.

"At least have the decency to tell me who he is."

Jaime headed to the window. What could she say? She had a crush on the priest? He'd take her for a bloody fool. It wouldn't change anything if she told him anyway; could even make things worse.

She turned to him. "I'm sorry, Xavier. I really am."

Xavier weaved his hands through his hair, offering a bitter smile before his expression turned to stone. After staring for longer than necessary, he left without another word.

***

Haunted by images of Jaime with Xavier, Dante couldn't sleep. He'd observed them during the meal. It was blatant Xavier was after Jaime and looked to be on the right track to getting there. The man had been after Jaime for two whole months, but Dante wouldn't put up with it for much longer. His housekeeper needed protection. As her employer, he had to make sure of that. He shook his head. Who was he trying to kid? More like he was jealous of her being with Xavier.

Holding Jaime close during a good part of the previous night had brought back feelings he hadn't felt for a long time and was trying hard to hide. He couldn't afford to start a relationship. Least of all now. It wouldn't be fair. Besides, she believed he was a priest.

He had to get into his head that nothing had happened between them – which was true. Their relationship had to get back to professional. An employer/employee attitude would keep his hands from reaching out for her. When she spoke to him, he'd keep his answers short. Small-talk had never been a strong point anyway. No problems on that front.

Dante punched his pillow. He had to get some sleep. But no matter how hard he tried, his body refused to relax. He tossed back the duvet, swung his legs out of bed, and padded barefoot to the chair. He needed a drink. A stiff drink. It would make his head numb, but it would be easier to sleep. He stepped into his jeans and eased open the door.

At the far end of the corridor, a thin strip of light widened into a beam before Xavier stepped out of Jaime's bedroom. *The sneaky bastard!*

Dante's cold gaze trailed Xavier as the man returned to his room. They hadn't wasted any time. No sooner had they met up than they were already at it. Unless they weren't? But then, what was Xavier doing in Jaime's room? Dante's jaw tightened. Maybe his jealousy was making him imagine things that didn't' exist.

He crept to Jaime's room. With his forehead against the cold wooden panel, he held the door handle. He felt like a stalker. A pathetic peeping tom. He hadn't done anything like this since his teens. What was up with him? He withdrew his hand and hesitated.

Flat out frustrated, he returned to his bed. The luminous hands on his watch showed a little before eleven. He had to get some sleep, yet the more he tried to drop off, the more he kept thinking of Jaime. Why did he have to find this sassy English girl so irritably attractive? His obsession had to stop.

He gazed up at the dark ceiling, thinking of Jaime stretched out on top of him. His body ached for hers, and no quantity of tension release would appease his needs. He missed a woman's body and good sex.

Eleven o'clock moved into twelve, and then into one.

Go down for that bloody drink! At least you can quench your thirst.

He left his room for the second time, creeping downstairs where a sleepy Petrus greeted him. With the dog trudging behind, Dante headed for the fridge. A glass of milk would be better. He sipped the cool drink and gazed at the dog who stared back, his head cocked to one side.

Dante sighed. "Just the two of us on our own, buddy."

***

The next morning, Jaime was sat at the breakfast table with the family. There was no sign of Dante, and Xavier had left early. He'd mentioned something the night before about an important meeting that would go on until late evening.

Jaime was helping the children pour cereal into their bowls when Dante entered the kitchen without a greeting.

"Are you okay?" Luc asked.

Dante frowned. "Do I look okay?"

"Not particularly."

"Well then you've got your answer, haven't you?" Dante banged his cup on the table before reaching for the coffee pot. Luc winced as he glanced at Suzanne.

After drinking two coffees in silence, Dante informed Jaime they would be leaving shortly. He said a curt goodbye to the family and told Jaime he'd wait in the car.

What's up with misery guts? I wasn't the only one who had a bad night.

Luc turned to Jaime. "We're used to his sulky moods; he never could hide his feelings."

Jaime had never seen the priest like this before. Dark sunken eyes, drawn appearance...the man was scary.

Luc rubbed her arm. "Trust me, he'll get over it. Everything will be back to normal soon."

Jaime pushed back her chair and headed out to the car. She was welcomed with a cold glare. God, how she hated sulky people. You never knew where you stood with mood swingers. Why couldn't the priest be the affectionate person she'd seen with the twins? She liked that warm side of him. Laughing, showing love, playing around without any worries.

Deep down, Jaime was sure he had a sensitive heart and would make a great partner. If he hadn't married the church maybe she would have found out. But that wasn't to be. The priest was out of bounds. She had to accept that fact.

Yet, what she'd give for him to be affectionate with her.

Chapter 13

Leonora woke up sick with worry. It was the end of the month, and Maxime was due for another payment. A glance at the clock on the wall showed almost 10 a.m. He'd be here any minute.

Her slender fingers pressed into her forearms, colouring the skin with four red nail marks. She hated that Maxime believed she was easy to control. When all this ended, she'd make the bastard pay.

Leonora's footsteps echoed on the marble tiles of the living room as she paced the room. She gazed at the clock again. Not quite ten. Why couldn't the bloody thing tick faster so she could get this over with?

Her future looked grim. Yet what could she do? Her inheritance depended on playing along. She turned her attention to the clock again. Only one minute had passed.

A familiar tap on the door made her frown. Strange. She hadn't heard a car pull up.

"Hi, darling!" Maxime slipped into the house.

She raised an eyebrow. He hadn't shaven and his clothes had seen better days. The collar on his designer jean jacket was ripped. Not to mention the stitching which had faded to a horrid rust colour.

Leonora handed him the cash envelope. "I didn't hear you drive up."

"That's because I didn't. I left the car off the estate. Remember how I enjoyed walking through the gardens?" He breathed into her face, licking his lips.

Leonora gave him a sneering huff before pulling the print out of his hands. "Get out!"

Maxime put the envelope in his pocket and grinned as he sauntered away. "I'll be back for another instalment same time next month."

Leonora slammed the door behind him and headed over to the fireplace. Taking a lighter, she put the photo into the flame. It charred as she blew onto it, eager to speed up the burning. The photo lit up into a yellow and blue blaze before disintegrating into black ashen flakes. Holding tightly to the edge until forced to let go for fear of burning her fingers, she dropped the last tiny corner into the grate.

And you reckoned this would hold you to me, you scum? Only another four months to pay, and I'll be rid of you for good.

And as far as scums went, he could qualify for the top step of the podium. She'd never loved him anyway. Maxime had been another gap-filler until she could figure out how to get Dante back. His decision to become a priest had brought all her childhood insecurities to the surface. Abandoned as a toddler when her mother walked out on the family, her father had committed suicide a few years after her mother's car accident, and then Dante had married the church. No one wanted her.

But *she* wanted Dante, and no priest's habit would get in the way. She always got what she wanted – and would do anything and everything to get him. Before securing her future with Dante though, she had to deal with a few other things. Maxime to start with.

From somewhere in the room, her mobile rang. She hurried to the small coffee table. *Not again!*

"It's me, darling." Maxime's voice took on a chirpy tone.

"I've given you the money. We had a deal."

"I've changed my mind. Again."

Leonora didn't like the sound of this. "So?"

"I've come back to my initial idea. I want us to get back together."

She clenched her fists. "I made myself clear on that point."

"Still got some photos. I'm sure people would love to see them. Might teach them a thing or two."

Christ, how she loathed that smarmy voice.

"What will everyone think of Leonora with her arse in all sorts of provocative positions with those sex toys?"

Leonora almost exploded. "Like I said, forget me."

Maxime's voice turned dry. "I can't. I can't forget your hot mouth on mine, all over my body. Your hot mouth when you take me in it."

"Shut it!" Bile rose to the back of her throat.

In the beginning, it had been a bit of fun. When Maxime turned out to be an imposter with no money, she came to the sad conclusion that she'd been tricked. He hadn't even been good in bed.

"Look, I'll call later when you're calmer." His voice snaked through the phone. "We're good together, and you know it. We're meant for each other."

Who was he trying to kid? Men and their egos.

Before Leonora could answer, the line went dead. She stared at the phone, fear creeping through her.

***

"PING!"

"Holy shit! I've got a hit. I'm a member of 'Angel Ados.'"

A huge smile spread across his features as he rubbed his sweaty palms together. His hands were poised over the keyboard ready to explore the site when his fingers stopped in mid-air.

Another idea came to mind.

Les Pages Blanches. The French telephone directory was what he needed.

He grabbed the phone and searched for the photo he'd taken of the card Jaime had sent her mother.

Happy Christmas Mum!
I know it's my first Christmas away,
but don't worry, the de Vere's
have given me a great welcome.
Hope you like the card.
Jaime

How could he have missed that? He had the family name. What easier way to track the bitch down?

He typed in de Vere, Paris, and hit 'enter.'

Two results showed. His luck was in. Taking his phone, he took a shot of the screen. He'd check those out when he got a car, which looked to be pretty soon; he was making good money with Marcel.

Coming out of Les Pages Blanches, he howled with mocking laughter. What a pathetic first name one of the de Vere's had. Who on earth called their kid that?

Pleased with the findings, he slipped his phone into his pocket. With that sorted, he could now spend the rest of the evening hunting on the chat group.

Chapter 14

Jaime came down the next morning, uncertain of the atmosphere. The one-and-a-half-hour drive back to the presbytery had been in complete silence – apart from a panting Petrus. With fingers crossed behind her back, she entered the kitchen, hoping she wouldn't get the same gloomy mask from the day before.

"Morning, Father."

Dante looked up from his parish gazette. "Bonjour."

Well at least I got a 'hello'.

Jaime examined the circles under his eyes and the way his eyebrows drew together while she poured herself a coffee.

"I'm going into the village to buy some groceries this afternoon," she said.

Dante folded the magazine. "Would you mind going to the bureau de tabac? Father Grégoire needs stamps." He pushed back his chair and grabbed his briefcase. One after the other, he slid his documents and magazine into his attaché. All neatly placed. Jaime watched his methodical and precise movements, his gestures calculated and slow. Did he ever loosen up?

"There's no hurry for the stamps. It's our weekly visit to the nursing homes. We'll be away for the whole afternoon."

A long silence set in, and Jaime's tension rocketed. She carried her empty cup to the dishwasher, placed it inside, and slammed the door shut.

Dante jumped and pressed his fingers to his temples. With slow but steady steps, he headed to the medicine cabinet and grabbed a box of painkillers. Taking the last gulp of coffee, he swallowed a couple of tablets.

"I'm sorry, Jaime, I'm going through a bad patch at the moment." His voice was barely audible.

Jaime folded her arms. *So am I, but I'm not sulking about it.*

Dante scratched his beard. "Things are a bit complicated."

"Is that complication me? You've been uptight for weeks."

The priest gave her a sideways glance, his features washed with confusion.

Yes, Father de Vere, women do have a sixth sense.

In a fraction of a second, Dante grabbed his bag.

"Could you prepare a small snack? I'll eat in my study."

She hated when he answered a question with a question. He'd have made a great lawyer; they never gave anything away.

As always when confronted with a situation he couldn't cope with, the priest preferred solitude. Was this the 'in thing' with priests? Did the man have to get away before he slipped up and showed his true feelings? Or was that wishful thinking?

***

At a little before two, Dante observed Jaime leaving the presbytery from his bedroom window. She shut the gate behind her and marched up the road with a shopping bag held firmly in her hand.

The way her hips swayed made him feel like a horny teenager. He couldn't keep his eyes off her butt. His heart quickened. Mustn't let that distract him. He had a little investigating to do before the trip to the nursing home.

The woman had problems. She clammed up when pushed to talk and shot out mouthy comments when she felt intimidated. He'd seen the way she'd reacted on receiving post from England. She did her best to hide her emotions and believed no one found her vulnerable.

He did.

Why didn't she confide? Priests inspired confidence, didn't they? Had he given the impression she couldn't trust him? He admitted he found it difficult to talk to her. Too worried she'd ferret out his secrets or stir up his feelings. In truth, Dante was falling for this little English housekeeper.

The moment their eyes had locked in the garden, he knew he wanted more than an employee/employer relationship. Being close to Jaime on a daily basis was bringing old feelings to the surface. Something in the way Jaime laughed reminded him of his better self before all this hiding. From time to time though, apprehension appeared in her eyes. More than just worry. He couldn't quite pinpoint what. But he knew something was wrong, and he wanted to help.

A moment of guilt tweaked Dante's insides as he turned the handle to Jaime's room, but only for a moment. He had to concentrate on the issue at hand and not waste time dreaming up different scenarios or go down the 'if only' lane. He had to find what bugged the woman. It had nothing to do with the fact he wanted to get to know her better or smell that peachy fragrance she wore.

The jogger who'd bumped into her could be a threat. Or was that sheer coincidence? Jaime needed to be kept safe. If things got sticky, he'd send her away. Losing her would bring him great unhappiness, but he couldn't take the risk. There was no other choice.

Grateful that Father Grégoire had left for his nursing homes earlier, Dante opened the door, taking in that wonderful clean, fruity scent.

The room was tidy with everything set in a precise way. He'd have to be careful. Jaime would know if anyone misplaced anything.

Closing the door behind him, he began his meticulous search.

***

It wasn't only the priest who feasted his eyes on Jaime heading up the street. Half hidden in the nearby bushes, a dark silhouette stared after her until she disappeared from sight. Without a sound, he turned and sauntered away.

***

Jaime entered the tobacconist's.

A pungent aroma of sweat, stale garlic and alcohol, blended with fresh coffee hit her in the nose. Rough, grimy paintwork coated the walls, scattered now and again with posters of winning lottery numbers. Behind the bar, photos of petanque players holding trophies hung lopsided and curling at the corners. Incoherent mumbling droned in the background, broken now and again with dirty laughter.

An embarrassing silence set in as she approached the counter where a few men were enjoying their drinks. The hairs on the back of her neck thrust upwards. Jaime hated these places. Not only did they smell musty, but she despised the way the men ogled women. Heavy tension hung in the air.

Ignoring the strong urge to leave, Jaime forced a smile. Every head turned in her direction. Jaime's stomach muscles tightened. *Right. Take them by surprise.*

"Bonjour, tout le monde." Jaime's cheerful voice rang out loud and clear. A few men returned the greeting before they returned to their drinks.

Jaime stepped up to the counter, elbowing herself some space to put her bag down. She asked for the stamps and paid the tobacconist, all the while shoving away the muscled arm on the right that was determined on rubbing hers.

Fighting back the impulse to slam a heel onto the man's foot, Jaime turned to leave only to bump into a hard chest.

Beautiful, angel-white teeth gleamed from a well-kept black goatee. With long dark hair and black eyes shining with lust, he could have been the devil. Especially dressed from head to toe in black leather.

Is Lucifer a biker?

"Excuse me," she said, pushing him to get by.

"You're the new housekeeper, aren't you?" His voice was deep, almost captivating. "A little young, aren't you?"

Jaime's chest tightened. "Who are you?"

"Me? I'm the mistake you're dying to make."

Jaime gave him a who-do-you-think-you-are look and muttered a quick, "Sod off, Lucifer." They were attracting attention. A few men had turned to lean against the counter, enjoying the show.

"So, what's your name?" he asked.

Adrenaline pounded through Jaime's system, making her mind move faster. She looked him straight in the eye. "What's it to you?"

"I'm only being friendly."

"Well go and be friendly with somebody else." Her patience had hit its limit.

Before she knew it, Lucifer grabbed her hand and brought it to his mouth. Jaime gasped when he licked her palm. She whipped her hand back and shoved it hard against his chest. What was his game?

Unaffected by the rebuff, he took a step nearer. "I know what you need."

A couple of wolf whistles flew through the air followed by suggestive grunts. Lucifer looked round and bowed at his audience. Jaime's palms grew clammy. Who the hell was this cocky git? And how did he know she was the priests' housekeeper? She'd only met a few of the shopkeepers in town, and he hadn't been one of them. Nor one of the parishioners either.

Jaime pushed past him and stepped out of the tobacconist's. She wasn't in the mood for fooling around. Not in the village tobacconists with over-excited men for spectators. With a last glance over her shoulder, she saw Lucifer in the doorway, blowing a kiss. A weak smile played across her face despite her irritation. She had to admit the man had charm. Hitching the shopping bag higher on her shoulder, she lengthened her strides to the grocery store.

***

Twenty minutes later, Jaime let herself into the presbytery garden. Busy rummaging through her bag for the house keys, she didn't look up until she reached the front door. A gasp escaped from her throat.

Ti osservo!

Il tuo tempo è finito

Cas

With eyes agape, she stared at a handwritten note pinned to the presbytery door, its curled corners fluttered gently in the breeze. Jaime's insides clenched. Had her past caught up with her?

She'd panicked on receiving the anonymous Christmas card, but the stalker had been in England. This note, nailed to the wooden panel, meant he'd followed her. The bastard had found her in France.

Was he lurking somewhere close?

Jaime swallowed hard. It could be anyone. The innocent-looking postman on his rounds. The sturdy tobacconist. Why not the rude jogger from the other day? Or even the hand-licking devil. One thing was for sure: he knew where she lived.

Snatching the note from the door, she stepped into the house with that familiar hollow pit in her stomach. In escaping to the continent, she'd expected no more notes. She was wrong.

With trembling legs, she hurried into the kitchen and read the note again, translating it to herself in English.

I'm watching you!

Your time's up.

Cas.

Her heart thumped in fits and starts. He'd left a note. In Italian. How did he know she understood the language? Why had he signed it? He'd never done so before. And why did the priests have to be away?

Footsteps crunched on the gravel before the front door handle rattled. Jaime's eyes widened. As much as she tried to calm her breathing, air entered her lungs painfully slow.

After a brief silence, the door opened, and heavy footsteps echoed in the hallway.

Shit! I forgot to lock it!

In an instinctive reflex, Jaime stretched a hand across the kitchen work surface and grabbed a heavy saucepan. Beads of sweat trickled down the back of her neck. She had to catch him off guard. She gripped the pan tighter and surged out into the corridor, ready to pounce on the intruder.

An arm shot out and grabbed her wrist. Jaime let out an ear-piercing scream as the saucepan crashed to the floor with a resonant clang.

"What the hell's going on?"

Jaime's hands flew to her chest. "You scared the shit out of me, Father!"

Dante out a relieved sigh. "I can assure you, it's mutual." He ushered Jaime into the lounge and took in a deep breath. "Care to explain yourself?"

"I found a note." Panic laced her voice.

Jaime sank onto the settee, the note in her hand screwed into a damp tiny ball. A moment's silence stretched out between them.

"What's wrong, Jaime?" he asked in a calmer tone.

Clouds floated in front of the sun. The lounge grew dark. Dante knelt and took the small piece of crumpled paper. Unfolding it, his expression changed to one of astonishment.

"Christ Almighty!"

Jaime bit the inside of her cheek. *Oh, my God! Please don't tell me you know him.*

The priest gripped her wrist, preventing her from getting away.

Jaime's eyes darted around the room. Why was he reacting like this? She'd had doubts all along about him being a priest.

Beads of sweat formed on her upper lip.

"You know I wouldn't harm you, don't you?" Dante spoke in a calm voice.

Jaime gazed from his expressionless face to his strong hand around her wrist.

"I thought you trusted me?" he said.

So did I.

"You're hurting me," she said, trying to pull free.

Dante loosened his grip but didn't let go. "I know who wrote the note, Jaime."

She screamed deep inside. Those instincts had been right. He was no priest. She tugged at her wrist once again, but to no avail. He wasn't going to release it.

"I'll let go of you if you promise not to do anything stupid."

She took a deep breath and nodded. Dante removed his hand.

Jaime threw all her weight onto the priest, pushing him over, and shot out into the corridor toward the front door. Pounding footsteps and blasphemous swearing echoed in the hallway. Language so unlike that used by a pious priest.

A hand slammed onto the panel as Jaime tried to pull open the door. She let out a shrill scream. Her ribs heaved as if bound by strong ropes, tightening her lungs. Saliva thickened in her throat. She had to get away. The man could be capable of anything.

With his arms wrapped around her, Dante dragged Jaime back to the lounge despite her thrashing legs. "Will you hold still?" His voice bellowed in the hallway.

"Like hell, I will!"

The priest strengthened his pressure, squashing all the air out of her.

"You're hurting me, you bastard!" The man was as strong as an ox.

Dante growled in Jaime's ear. "I. Am. Not. Going to hurt you."

Could she trust him? Tears of fear escaped. So many signs made her believe she couldn't. Then again, if he'd wanted to get at her, he'd have done so before. But why wasn't he at the nursing home?

"I'm just as scared as you are," he said on a gentler note.

Jaime sniffed loudly and relaxed. "What are you doing here? You shouldn't be back until this evening."

Dante waited a moment more before he released his hold. "The nursing home called when I was about half-way there. Most of the elderly have come down with flu. They told me to stay away."

Jaime rubbed her sore arms. There were times when her brain couldn't cope. Now was one of them. That note had triggered all sorts of wild emotions. She'd mistrusted and suspected the priest, bringing on a feeling of anger and even betrayal.

The priest pulled the crumpled paper out of his pocket. "This note is from a friend of mine."

Jaime slumped on the sofa. "Do all your friends leave notes pinned to the front door telling you your time's up?"

A muscle in Dante's cheek twitched. "This one does."

He came to sit beside her, his brow wrinkled with worry. "Why were you frantic after seeing the note?"

Jaime shook her head.

"Was it something that happened in the past?"

"Yes, that's it." Her reply came a little too quick.

"Humph."

"I got a nasty note from a boy in college."

Dante looked at Jaime with a 'why-won't-you-confide' expression but remained silent.

"You can always talk to me, you know?"

"Okay, I will. So who is Cas?"

Dante rubbed the back of his neck. "It's nothing for you to worry about. I need a drink."

Why was he struck on her confiding in him when he wouldn't confide himself? Whenever the opportunity arose, or she dipped into his world, he'd change the subject.

She took in a deep breath and headed to the kitchen. She could do with a drink too. "By the way, when I went to buy the stamps, I bumped into someone strange." The words shot out from over her shoulder as she headed for the kitchen.

Dante tagged close behind. "Go on."

"He knew I was the housekeeper." Jaime grabbed the half bottle of red wine next to the cupboard and poured a generous glass. Sitting on the edge of a chair, she sipped the wine in short, quick gulps and caught confusion in the priest's eyes. Anger even.

Wild, uncontrolled ideas shot through her mind. Had she fled England to land straight into more trouble?

The priest crumpled the note between his fingers and cleared his throat. "I'm sorry, Jaime, your trial period's finished. We have to let you go."

Jaime choked on the wine. "WHAT?"

"I think it's best if you found another employer. Someone who is less demanding. Your work is a bit sloppy at times. We've both noticed that."

For a moment, Jaime remained too shocked to move. His words stung like salt on an open wound. Fighting back tears, she let out her rage. "You, bastard. And I don't care if you are a priest. You are a bloody, low scum, bastard. And lying doesn't suit you."

She slammed the wine glass on the table and jumped to her feet, sending the chair skidding across the flagstones. It fell to the floor with an echoing clang as she shot out of the kitchen.

A moment later, she banged the front door shut.

***

Dante grabbed a glass and poured himself a drink. Sitting heavily on the chair, he unfolded the note.

Had they already caught up with him? It seemed they had spies everywhere.

Anger surged through him. He had no choice but to send Jaime away. He was a walking target. Too many things depended on his silence, and if they ever got their hands on her, God only knew what the outcome would be. She wasn't safe here. The note confirmed it.

Visions of Jaime came galloping back as he took another long gulp of wine. The pain and astonishment in his housekeeper's eyes when he'd fired her stabbed him in the heart. She didn't deserve this. The desire to comfort her had pulled at his gut. He felt like a despicable rat at the lies which had slipped over his tongue. The way Jaime's eyes had narrowed before she'd lashed out at him, hurt. He deserved every single word she said.

What he'd give to wrap her in his arms and caress her pretty face until that horrid frown disappeared. Tell her it was all a lie. An excuse to keep her alive. He couldn't burden anyone with his worries, though. Jaime had her own demons to deal with and he had Satan to send back to hell.

It was hard enough staying out of sight himself; he couldn't keep another person safe. Not with someone already out to get her. Hadn't he discovered that when he'd snooped in her bedroom?

***

Furious with Dante's pathetic excuse, Jaime had run out of the driveway. She hadn't noticed the cold, damp air until the fine drizzle seeped into the inside of her jacket collar. Now, half an hour later, she couldn't stop shivering.

The creeping up of an old transit van caught her attention. A gruff voice called from the passenger window. "Need a lift, lady?"

The hairs on her nape rose. "No, thanks."

"Where are you going?"

Jaime waved a finger at the horizon. "Over there. It's not far. I'm fine."

"There's nothing over there. No houses, no people, no nothing. So get in."

"I said, I'm fine."

"And I said get in the van!"

Jaime cringed at the menacing voice and the stench of alcohol seeping from the vehicle. She tried to pick up speed, but the driver kept the van level with her, enabling his passenger to converse.

Without warning, the man made a grab for her arm. Jaime took a step back, but the man was quick. His strong hand squeezed around her muscles, making her cry out. Absorbed in releasing the man's fat, dirty fingers, Jaime hadn't heard a car pull up in the opposite direction.

A young chap popped his head out of the Mercedes window. "Everything all right?"

Jaime let out a huge breath. "It would be if you could give me a lift?"

"Jump in then."

Jaime wrenched her arm free, dashed to the other side of the road, and jumped into the Mercedes. With the seatbelt fastened, she relaxed, her heartbeat regaining its steady drum. Until a horrid idea crossed her mind. What if this stranger was the van driver's mate?

She turned to see him wiggle his eyebrows. "Where are we going, darling?"

Oh no. Out of the frying pan, into the fire.

"I don't want to put you out of your way," she stammered.

"No risk of that, cutie."

Jaime gazed straight ahead, biting her lower lip. "If you could drop me off at the end of the road, my friend should be along any time."

The young chap gave Jaime his full attention. "Sure you don't want me to take you somewhere nicer?"

Jaime swallowed hard. *Make it sound convincing.* "Another time. How about giving me a number?"

With a huge grin, the young chap opened the glove compartment, unnecessarily brushing Jaime's thigh. Taking out a couple of business cards, he handed her one and tossed the rest on the dashboard.

Jaime examined the card. "I'll ring you up some time...*Jerome*." She made sure he saw her fondle the card before slipping it into her pocket.

The chap ran a hand through his hair. "I'll be waiting for your call."

Jaime gave one of her sweetest smiles. "You can count on it."

With a delighted look, he dropped her off at the end of the road, blew a kiss, and drove away.

Jaime watched the car's headlights dance across the trees as it moved off before she darted away. She didn't want to hang around in case the van returned. There was only the one road. If it did come back, it had to come this way. She took longer strides.

The watery sun had gone down. Shadows stretched across the pale February sky, and the fog was seeping through the trees. With darkness descending, she soon wouldn't be able to make out where she was going. The temperature had dropped too. Jaime's warm breath made puffs in the air.

Heavy legs and aching feet broke her morale. The lingering light dulled as twilight prepared to step onto the scene. Absolute stillness filled the countryside. Nothing stirred. No rustling. No movement. Not a sound. She was easy prey for a predator.

Jaime stopped walking, straining her ears. The only noise she picked up was her heart thumping. She stopped again, and this time she heard something else. An engine in the distance. Someone was coming. The fog made it impossible to see but a vehicle was moving slowly. Too slowly. As if the driver was looking for something – or someone.

Jaime let out a tiny whine. The van? Prickles crept up the back of her neck.

Screaming inwardly, she crawled behind the sparse bushes at the side of the road and sat back on both heels, cursing the priest for putting her in this situation. Something ran over her hand, making her jerk. Pulling her hand back, she scratched it on some brambles and swore at the priest again.

Twigs snapped on the left. Two shining marbles appeared through the thin bush. Jaime shooed whatever it was away before sinking back to the hiding place.

An approaching engine set her heart racing. A few seconds later, a vehicle appeared out of the fog and came to a halt. The driver's door swung open, and a dark figure got out. The engine continued to run.

Paralysed with fear, Jaime's chin and lips began to tremble. *Please don't let them find me.*

The silhouette came to the edge of the road a few feet away from where she huddled amongst the brambles. How long would it be before he found her? Her heart raced when the shadow shed by the car's lights loomed over her. Jaime kept her head down, pressing it deeper between both knees. She squeezed her eyes tighter and bit deeper into her hand.

Anxious heavy breathing and a shoe scuffing the ground as it kicked into the shrubs made Jaime shrink further into the dark. Her legs ached from the crouching position, but she refused to move. Unable to hold back a minute longer, she eased back onto the damp ground. The moisture seeped into her jeans. Tears burst forward as the footsteps came nearer.

The figure remained stationary for a long while.

"Jaime?"

She froze. *He's found me!*

"Jaime?"

Headlights prevented her from seeing who it was, but she knew that voice.

"Are you there, Jaime?"

She didn't know whether to laugh, scream, or cry. What were the odds he'd find her? She bit the back of her hand. Fear had her stomach locked up tight like a ball of tangled wool. Lost and confused, yet happy and relieved.

Jaime scrambled out of the bushes, feet skidding on the damp ground. She couldn't afford to let him leave. He was the only person she knew.

"Father!"

The priest jumped and turned to face her, a slow smile forming across his face.

"You can't imagine how worried I've been. I've searched everywhere for you," he said.

Trembling, Jaime let the priest guide her to the passenger side of the car. Shaking with cold and emotions, she slid in and waited for Dante to join her.

"How did you find me?"

"I've been stopping at random for a while now, hoping to spot you," he said, rubbing her cold hands.

Jaime shivered again.

"Let me get you back to the presbytery." His voice held concern.

Jaime snuggled back into the seat, savouring the welcoming heat. The heavy fog had seeped through her thin jacket. She folded both hands under her armpits and gazed straight ahead. The silence lengthened.

"Say something, Jaime. Please."

Too shook up, Jaime's voice died in her throat.

"I can see you're still upset."

"Too true, I am. Don't you think I know you're keeping something from me? Why don't you just tell me what's going on?"

The priest put the car into first and pulled away. Jaime took in the beam of the headlights picking up the twists and turns in the quiet country road. They'd soon be home. But home to what? More lies? More pretending?

Jaime broke the silence. "I'll have my bags packed by tomorrow."

"You don't have to go right away."

"I'm going tomorrow." Jaime turned away before fresh tears

escaped.

"Do what you think is best."

A paralysing hurt spread through Jaime's body. He didn't want her.

Chapter 15

Unable to sleep, Father de Vere stepped out into the chilly early morning. Petrus yawned and plodded behind his master. High above the trees the moon seduced the dark grey, swollen clouds, rubbing them with its pearly glow. Dante loved this time of day when silence was heavy and the cool air invigorating.

On the other side of the garden wall, the solitary whistle of a blackbird broke the morning hush. Dante pulled both hands out of his pockets and sat on the top step of the presbytery. The cold stone filtered through the denim material of his trousers, numbing his backside. Petrus plopped down beside him, laying his head on the priest's knees. Dante curved a hand around the dog's ears, and a sound halfway between a whine and a bark escaped the dog's snout.

Dante gazed up into the magenta streaked sky. His mind wandered to Jaime. How was he going to cope without her? He'd kept his feelings in check and had played this new role quite well. There had been no outside world to tempt him until the bubbly housekeeper had stepped onto the scene. That wouldn't be a problem anymore though. She was leaving. The snag was that he couldn't get her out of his mind.

Falling under Jaime's charm wasn't the only issue. He had to keep the woman safe even if it meant finding her a new employer elsewhere. But he'd miss her. That was undeniable. He'd mentioned his fears to Father Grégoire and the old man had gone along with Dante's plan. At one point, he'd sensed that the old man was sad to see her go.

Dante eased the dog's head off his knees and stood. "Come on, boy. Let me get you back into the warm."

He entered the kitchen with Petrus close behind. Jaime stood at the sink, her back to him. He loved the swell of her butt in her tight tracksuit bottoms. Showed all the curves. This morning, she'd even pulled her hair back into a strict ponytail. What he'd give to run his tongue up the back of that slim neck.

He cleared his throat. "Bonjour, Jaime."

Jaime turned to face him but remained silent.

"About yesterday..."

Jaime let out an exaggerated sigh and headed to the percolator. "You're in my way, Father. I don't want to do my job wrong and get another black mark." She dodged around him and poured a coffee. "For your information, I've packed my bags. I'm leaving this afternoon."

"I'll drive you."

Jaime pushed past him. "I said you're in my way. Why can't you stay in your study like the other oldie?"

"Look–"

"There's nothing to look at!" She slammed her mug onto the table and swore as the contents swilled over the rim.

He took a step back as she threw the kitchen cloth onto the splattered coffee. "My job is up to scratch, and you know it. If you two want to get rid of me, at least have the decency to be honest. Making poor excuses doesn't suit you, *Father de Vere.*"

Dante winced. Why did she always have to emphasize the 'Father' part? Okay, he'd lied. He didn't want her to leave, but did he have a choice? How could he explain the mess? The living nightmare he was in?

"Have you found a replacement?" Jaime's angry words brought him out of his thoughts. "Don't forget to tell the new housekeeper she'll only be here for a couple of weeks. No point in unpacking her bags even." Jaime flung the soggy cloth into the sink and stormed off.

He ground his teeth. She'd taken the decision to leave right away. Perhaps it was for the best. If the man in the tobacconists was who he suspected, she'd be safer away from the village. Nevertheless, he should have handled the situation better.

He retreated to the study with long, slow strides. He hadn't been himself since he'd got up. Shaky and cold, he hoped he wasn't coming down with flu. He had parishes to visit.

With both elbows propped on the desk, he dropped a heavy head into his hands, thinking of the past nine months. His sudden return from Italy. The new life at Montfort-Le-Gesnois. His cheeky housekeeper. And now, her imminent departure.

Damn her!

Dante shoved some documents into his file, too exhausted to think. He pushed back his chair and went to stand in front of the window.

If he were honest with himself, Jaime was a breath of fresh air. She amused him with her smart mouth. She tried to make out to be a tough cookie, but beneath that hard outer shell, the woman was vulnerable. She'd only been at the presbytery for a short time, but he'd figured her out. Jaime's sharp tongue was a way of hiding vulnerability, and he wanted to help. To love her. Bury himself deep inside her.

Damn her a second time!

He couldn't change the past. It looked as if he couldn't choose his future either.

***

Exhausted, Jaime leaned back against the old wooden bench at the train station. The walk had begun downhill, but the road leading out of the village had been never-ending. Why had she refused Father de Vere's lift? Especially with her two heavy cases to pull. She now had over an hour's journey to Chartres before changing trains for the final trip to Paris. That would be another hour.

Tears gathered at the back of her eyes. If she'd told him about the problems in England, he wouldn't have sent her away. She'd only been in Montfort-le-Gesnois for three months and was going to miss it...well, at least the priest.

Why did she have to fall for the so-called man of the cloth?

With her chin dropped onto her chest, Jaime wept in silence, rocking back and forth. Every time the priest popped to mind, more tears escaped. She'd never been so humiliated. And had never, ever lost a job.

Sod him!

"Penny for your thoughts," a strong voice called from a car window.

Jaime wiped her tears and looked up at Lucifer. Couldn't be. What were the odds of them meeting again?

"You okay?" he asked, coming to sit beside her.

Jaime put the damp hanky away. "What are you doing here?"

"I was passing and..."

"Just like that?"

He put out a hand to caress her cheek. "Yeah, just like that."

She jerked out of his reach. "Don't touch me."

"What's wrong?" he asked, pulling his hand back.

"What's it to you?"

"I'm only trying to be friendly."

Jaime sneered. "You've used that catch line before. Can't you change your tune?"

He smiled at the catty comment. "I think we got off to a wrong start. Let me introduce myself. I'm Corentin."

"And what's that going to change?"

He tilted his head to one side. "I live in hope."

Jaime let out a deep sigh. He was being pleasant enough, and she was taking her anger out on him, when in fact, it was the priest who needed to be brought down a peg or two.

"Sorry, I'm having a bad day."

Corentin jerked his head toward the cases. "Is running away going to help?"

Jaime gave him a sidelong glance. "Who said I was running away?"

"Do you always go shopping with your suitcases?"

Jaime burst out laughing. The man had a sense of humour. In the past, she'd believed only the English to have that particular wit. To tell the truth, she was beginning to warm to him. He brought a smile to her face, and she needed that right now.

He leaned back on the bench and stretched both legs out in front of him. "All finished with your men of the cloth?"

"You could say that."

"Didn't last long." He placed an arm across the back of the bench, his fingers only a few inches from her shoulder.

Jaime sat up straight. "Too long if you ask Father de Vere."

A muffled buzz vibrated from inside Corentin's coat. He brought the phone out and stood.

"All okay?" he asked, talking into the phone.

Jaime examined his back. Broad – like the priest's. Nice square shoulders – like the priest's. A little hunched as he spoke into the phone. Not bad on the eyes. Like the sodding priest. Why did her thoughts always come back to Dante? He was becoming an obsession.

After a few seconds, Corentin turned and pinched the bridge of his nose. "Yeah, sure," he said into the phone. His eyes scanned the scenery before narrowing into slits. "Give me a sec, and I'll be there. Ciao!"

He slapped the phone shut and took a step toward the bench. "I have to go. Pity we couldn't get to know each other better. We could have hit it off." He gave a quick salute and wandered off.

"Probably," Jaime muttered to herself.

Her tote bag slid off her knees, and Jaime swore as a few belongings toppled to the ground. She stooped and retrieved the purse and train ticket.

"How about putting a man out of his misery by giving me your phone number?" Corentin had returned and was looming over her with a cheeky glint in his eye.

The corner of Jaime's mouth twitched into a smile. "What's the point? I'm leaving this place." She stuffed the things into her bag.

"I've got a car, and distance isn't a problem."

Jaime grinned inwardly at his quick wit. It wouldn't hurt to give him her phone number, would it? She gazed up into his eyes.

He seemed harmless enough. Besides, she'd left the stalker back in England and was feeling stonger by the day. She had to admit he made her laugh and boosted her morale, especially after she'd been kicked out of her job. And he made her feel attractive again which she hadn't felt since being stalked in England.

After a brief hesitation, she handed over her phone.

Corentin took it, tapped in his number and returned the phone with a wink. After blowing her kiss, he climbed back into his car and drove off.

The train came into view, and Jaime hurried around the small building onto the platform. The few raindrops which had started to bounce on the concrete were now pelting down her cheeks despite the sheltering hood.

"Jaime!"

The voice set her heart thumping. She turned to see Father de Vere marching towards her, inky-black hair stuck to his face, dark eyes full of hurt. There was no mistaking the set of his shoulders. The man was forlorn.

"Ooh la la! Come to help me put my cases on the train, have you?" Jaime snapped.

Dante flicked a few droplets from his wet hair. "No. I've come to take you back."

"Have you now? No one to cook for you two anymore?"

They stared into each other's eyes for a long moment before Jaime looked away as tears blurred her vision. Or was it the rain?

The priest's warm, reassuring hand encircled hers.

"Please, Jaime." His voice was no more than a whisper. "I didn't mean what I said back there."

Jaime gazed up to the longing in his eyes.

"We need to talk," he said, seizing one of the cases.

Rooted to the spot, Jaime stared at him.

"Come on," he coaxed.

Jaime sighed and grabbed the second case. Was he going to confide after all? She was eager to hear what he had to say. It had to be serious.

Serious enough for him to send her away.

***

Driving back to the presbytery, Dante kept gazing across at Jaime huddled in a little ball on the passenger seat. The poor woman was shivering. Now and again she let out a loud sniff and wiped her nose on the back of her hand. What a bastard he'd been. Her mind had to be in turmoil, trying to figure out what the hell was going on. He'd sent her away in a brusque manner and now was bringing her back.

Okay, so he'd panicked on seeing the note and had acted rashly. It was only on reading the message with a cool head that he realised he was being watched over and that 'time up' meant he'd soon be able to come out of hiding.

He'd also realised that the only place Jaime could take refuge was back home in England. He couldn't have that. It wouldn't be fair on her. After the Christmas card he'd discovered in her room, he'd be throwing her back to the wolves.

His eyes shifted sideways as Jaime moved awkwardly and turned her back on him. She no doubt hated him, and he no doubt deserved it. Yet, if she'd spoken to him about her problems, he wouldn't have sent her packing like that.

He didn't know much about her stalker or how dangerous the jerk was. That said, could the man be more dangerous than the Albanians? He figured it would be better if she stayed with him at the presbytery where he could care for her. After all, he did have someone watching over him.

In all honesty, he'd fallen for the woman and didn't want to let her go. He now knew he wanted to make a go of their relationship. Get to know Jaime better. Do all the normal things couples did when courting.

With a bit of luck, this fiasco would soon draw to a close and he'd be able to reveal his true identity to her.

***

Back at the presbytery, Jaime took the cases upstairs. Her bedroom had never been more welcoming. Cosy and tranquil, she was happy to be back. And ready for answers.

What had brought on Dante's change of heart? Had Father Grégoire told him off? Was he aware he'd been unfair? He had to apologise. She might even get him down on his knees. Now that was a nice vision.

She changed into dry clothes and rushed down to the lounge.

"Well?" she asked, head held high.

The priest slipped both hands into his pockets and cleared his throat. "I know I made a rash decision by sending you away..."

He avoided eye contact. Jaime caught the wrinkle on his brow. Something serious was going on. She wrapped both arms around her body and spoke in a calmer tone. "Has this got anything to do with that note on the door?"

A heavy silence settled in. Worse than a hospital waiting room. The only sound audible was their heavy breathing.

After a short moment, he nodded. "Probably."

Jaime had gathered that much. "What are you hiding?"

The priest remained motionless, eyes focused on the small crucifix above the fireplace as if searching for inspiration. "The less you know, the safer you'll be."

Jaime rolled her eyes. "That's a bit melodramatic. I mean, people say that sort of thing in films."

A muscle flickered in the priest's cheek. "Believe me. This is no film."

Jaime chewed on her fingernail.

"Sometimes people need to get away or bury their heads in the sand. But I promise you won't be sent away again," he said.

Jaime met his gaze and toyed with the idea of pushing for more, but refrained. He always kept his business close to his chest. That much she'd learnt while living at the presbytery. He wouldn't divulge anything if she didn't. She wasn't ready to do that. Not quite yet. Not quite ever.

After examining the priest's expression for a few seconds more, Jaime turned and left the room. There was something weird in the way he'd stared at her. Why would an alleged man of the cloth go into hiding? Did Father Grégoire know how his trainee behaved? Or did he conceal facts from the old man too? And why was he set on sending her away? Because of his so-called perilous past? Or could he be worried about breaking his vows?

There was a mutual pull. She'd seen his look. Yet, the more time she spent in the priest's company, the more difficult he was to figure out. What had she gotten herself into?

The man was dangerously close to falling into temptation.

And so was she.

Chapter 16

Leonora entered the house after a brisk, morning walk. She hadn't taken any sleeping pills and hadn't slept much. The crisp March air had woken up her numb head.

Entering the lounge, she froze. *What the bloody hell's he doing here? It's not the end of the month yet.*

Maxime grinned, arms opened wide. She hurried past, but he grabbed hold of her hand. "How about a kiss? I dreamt about you all night."

Leonora tried to yank free. "How about giving me back my photos?"

"Kiss first – photos after. I've come to talk about our new start."

In a barely concealed sign of revulsion, Leonora's nose shrivelled up. She couldn't bear to look at him, let alone touch him. And what was all this about a new start?

"Do you want the photos or not?" He pulled a small envelope out of his jacket pocket. "Look at me, baby. It's your Maxou."

Inch by inch, Leonora's head rose until their eyes met. What she'd give to slap that pathetic grin off his face.

Maxime came up close, and Leonora let him trail kisses down her neck. With determined fingers, she released the envelope from his hold, but Maxime gripped the escaping envelope. "Easy, Baby. Maxou's got an SD card."

Leonora took a step back. *Shit!*

"You didn't think I'd give you all the photos without keeping some kind of insurance, did you?"

Before she knew it, Maxime crushed his strong mouth onto hers. His powerful tongue probed her lips open. The stale taste of tobacco flavoured her mouth. Leonora drew back.

Bastard! You are going to regret that night in Rome.

Maxime threw the envelope on the table and unbuttoned his trousers. "How about being a bit nicer?"

Leonora gritted her teeth and turned to leave. The reminder of the photos and the SD card brought her to a halt.

Maxime grinned. "Yes, darling, we fuck first, and then we'll discuss the SD card."

In one quick movement, he swished up her flimsy pleated skirt, pulled down her lacy thong, and leaned Leonora forward over the table, her eyes only a short distance from the envelope. In a few minutes, or maybe less, the contents would be hers. A couple of thrusts, and she'd be through with the jerk.

The rip of a condom wrapper broke the ugly silence. Leonora waited, drumming her fingers on the table, counting the seconds. After a short moment, his heavy body fell onto her back as he climaxed.

"Well, that was something," he whispered.

Leonora rolled her eyes. He had to be kidding.

"Mmm, really nice. I'd love to hang around, darling, but I've got a few things to deal with." He pulled up his trousers and left.

With the envelope in her shaky hand, Leonora fell to the ground in a heavy mass. No need for panic. The envelope and photos were in her possession. She took in strong long breaths. What the hell would she have to do to get the SD card?

She headed upstairs to the bathroom and into the shower, turning the water on full blast. She needed to talk to someone. A good friend who wouldn't judge. Someone with a reassuring voice.

That person was Dante.

***

Jaime was about to head upstairs to clean Father Grégoire's bedroom when a bold knock echoed in the corridor. Her heart pounded. Another parishioner bringing a cake? She couldn't stand any more French patisseries.

Pulling swift fingers through her hair, she went to the door, wondering why the person hadn't rung the bell. Looking through the peephole, an impatient Leonora glared at the door. What the hell was she doing here?

"Where's Dante?" Leonora stood on the presbytery porch, hands on hips. Her tight-belted red coat with knee-length boots of the same colour accentuated Leonora's flamboyant auburn curls.

"He's not here, so there's no point in wasting your time." Jaime began to shut the door, but Leonora's hand shot out and banged it open.

"Just because you're sleeping with him, doesn't mean you've come up in the world, Mademoiselle Housekeeper." Leonora's words were spat out, cold and clear.

Jaime staggered back, sucking in a quick breath. "I am *not* sleeping with him," she shouted. "Don't put me in the same league as you."

Leonora pulled a hand through her bouncy locks. "We're not in the same league, chérie. I've had something you'll never have. And Christ Almighty, was he good."

Jaime clenched her fists.

"Why don't you go back to England? There's nothing for you here." Leonora's midnight blue eyes were full of hostility.

Jaime took in a deep breath, checking her temper. "Look, Leonora, just because you don't need to work for a living doesn't give you the right to insult me. Why are you aggressive with everybody all the time? Or are you making an exception for me?"

Somewhere in the house, the phone rang.

"I have to answer that, so go back to Paris and stay there. Goodbye Leonora." Jaime slammed the door on the woman.

The phone kept ringing. Jaime let it.

So many contradictory feelings fought inside her. Jealousy, anger, and irritation to mention a few. The one that bugged the most was frustration.

Why was she attracted to such a mysterious and off-limits man?

***

Warm air whirled upwards from the gutters and hit the early morning breeze. The draught teased his ankles, making him shiver. His head throbbed, and he was about to heave again. Too many Morito cocktails. Looking down at his clothes, he glimpsed tiny specks of what he'd splattered on the pavement in an overflow of vomit. He felt like shit.

In a foul mood, he staggered along the street in search of a pharmacy. He needed to lash out and hurt someone – or something. That would make him feel better.

A smoky grey cat came out of a small side road and wandered up to him, tail high in the air, nose sniffing around his calves. He eyed the animal, pulled his foot back, and kicked it hard in the side. The cat yelped and scampered out of sight over a low brick wall.

Christ, that felt good.

Across the road, a rich looking idiot pulled up in his BMW, jumped out, and darted into the tobacconist's, the car engine still running. Prat! Offering his car to any thief. He ambled over to the vehicle and scanned the surroundings.

Wonder if I've lost my touch?

He opened the passenger door and whipped open the glove compartment. Nothing apart from a couple of CDs, some chewing gum, and a brown A4-sized envelope.

Any money in there?

He didn't have time to find out. In the side view mirror, he spotted the prat stepping out of the tobacconist's again. In a flash, he grabbed the envelope and slapped the glove compartment shut. With the booty held tight against his chest, he slammed the door and disappeared down a side road.

***

Back in his room, he collapsed onto the bed, clutching his thumping head. The aspirin was taking longer than usual to ease the pain. Closing his eyes, he waited for the room to stop spinning.

He rolled onto his back. Christ, he felt awful. Rubbing some life back into his eyes, he looked at his watch. Shit! Almost eleven forty-five. What a waste of a morning.

With heavy legs, he stumbled towards the door, avoiding shambles of discarded clothes and empty bottles. Dragging his feet to the bathroom, he stripped off and stepped into the shower. Hot water cascaded onto his head, fading the dullness until he came back to life.

Towelling himself dry, his mind wandered to the envelope he'd stolen on his way home earlier that morning. Eager to inspect the contents, he kicked his dirty clothes into a corner and sauntered back to the room to dress. Ten minutes later, he was at the table, staring at his prize.

He peeled open the seal and tipped the contents onto the table. Pushing a hand deeper inside, he verified the bottom – something he'd learnt from experience. Always double check. His fingers latched onto a small, folded piece of paper. He grabbed it and tossed it next to the photos, the SD card, and a visiting card.

An impulsive wolf whistle escaped from between his teeth. "Not bad at all," he said, rubbing his crotch.

He slid the SD card into the computer and grinned. Explicit images appeared on the screen. He turned his head from side to side. "Bloody hell, how did she manage that?"

The prat who'd taken them had to be a right psycho. Who'd print photos like this? Did he plan to plaster his bedroom wall with them?

Dragging his eyes away from the screen, he opened the note.

How to get Leonora back

1) *Call her*
2) *Mention photos (5,000 Euros each – 12 in all)*
3) *Organise meeting for exchanges*
4) *Keep SD card – guarantee*

If she says no

- *Post pictures on the Web*
- *Silly bitch won't refuse*

His face pulled into a broad smile. Thanks to this meticulous arsehole, whoever the twit may be, he'd found another way of topping up his income.

This was *his* little find. Marcel didn't need to know.

Chapter 17

Slouched on the couch with a good book, Dante rolled a large glass of whisky between his hands. Petrus lay nearby, the dog's sad face mirroring his master's.

Jaime entered the lounge, fluttering long eyelashes like butterfly wings. She wore a short, open-backed, black dress which moulded to her body well. A pair of peep-toe black patent court shoes finished off the attire.

Dante's eyes widened, and a splutter of whisky sprayed down the front of his shirt. Christ Almighty! The woman was close to naked. Thank God Father Grégoire had retired early for the night. The poor man would have had a heart attack.

Clad in heels a little lower than those she'd worn to the Christmas lunch, Dante had to admit they did wonders for her legs. He wondered how she'd look stark naked in the four-inchers. Dumbstruck, he wiped his chin. The urge to kiss Jaime was overpowering. What he'd give to pull her down on the settee with him. Show her he wasn't as holy as she believed him to be.

Concealing the bulge forming in his trousers with a magazine, he repeated to himself that she was his housekeeper. His employee. Off-limits. He had to leave the room. Otherwise, she'd end up in her panties before she could slip off her stilettos.

Jaime coughed, and Dante dragged his eyes away from the sexy shoes.

"Got a problem?" She toyed with her hair. Shiny chestnut strands slipped through her fingers.

Dante sat upright and the dog jumped to his feet. How could anyone playing with hair make it look so sexy?

"Are you meeting someone?"

Jaime rolled her eyes. "I'm going on a date. Need to see something other than aprons and dusters."

Dante squeezed his glass tighter. "And does this date have a name?"

Jaime ignored the comment. "Your dinner's ready to heat up." She fiddled for the house keys in her pouch bag.

Petrus ambled up to Jaime and sniffed the tops of her legs before disappearing into the kitchen.

"Who's the lucky man?" Dante tried again.

"I don't think you know him."

Dante jumped up in a flash and sailed a hand through his jet black hair. He stood tall and cold like a marble statue. "I don't think it's wise for you to go out with strangers. It's best if you stay at home."

Jaime's amusement evaporated. Angry hands clasped her bag tighter and her eyes narrowed into slits. She pulled on her coat and tightened the belt in one sharp pull. "Unlike you, *Father*, I am *not* married to the church, and I refuse to become a nun."

Dante's lips twitched. There she was, emphasizing the 'Father' part again. She seemed to love winding him up. He took a long gulp of his fiery drink and caught the strong burn in his chest. "It could be dangerous."

Jaime's lips curled up into a sly grin. "There's danger everywhere, Father de Vere."

A succession of melodic notes cut the awkward silence.

"Aren't you going to answer your phone?" Jaime asked.

Dante swore and stormed out of the room, unhappy at the idea of Jaime with another man. Who the hell could the jerk be? Not Xavier, surely?

Taking the phone from his pocket, every muscle froze. The number flashed through him, a phantom from the past.

Christ Almighty!

Dante shut his eyes for a few seconds, his mind sailing back to a year ago when each time the number showed, his heart had drummed, waiting for the voice to deliver its instructions. This could only mean something had cropped up. Trouble.

The phone slid around his clammy hand as he held it to his ear. "Yes?"

A familiar voice blasted down the phone. "Enjoying priesthood, Dante? We assumed you couldn't wait to get back to your normal life. Marriage to the church seems to suit you."

Dante heard a group of men guffawing in the background. No doubt the team who'd watched over his security in Italy before he'd gone into hiding. He also picked up comments about wearing a dress, turning gay, and not needing a woman to warm his bed.

"What the fuck are you talking about?" Fury edged Dante's words.

"Didn't Casanova tell you?"

"Tell me what?" Dante hissed. Was this one of Casanova's jokes?

"We've captured the Drug Baron. He's now waiting for trial. Why are you still hiding?"

Dante took in long breaths as a spark of anger ignited deep inside. "When?"

"About a month ago. On Valentine's Day, to be exact. At first, Casanova came to watch over you. He was then told to inform you."

Biting down uncontrolled rage, Dante spat through gritted teeth.

"Where is he?"

"I've just said he's been sent to watch over you."

Dante gripped the phone tighter. "His address?"

"I'll send it by text message."

He thrust the phone into his pocket, grabbed the car keys and stormed out of the study. A little drive to Casanova's place was what he needed. That, and a few flying fists to teach the bastard a lesson. He could drink himself senseless later.

He bolted down the driveway and froze.

Corentin's lips grazed Jaime's cheek in a welcoming kiss. A muscle twitched at the corner of Dante's left eye, his mouth in a rigid grimace. While he'd been unnecessarily undercover, Corentin had stepped in and stolen his girl.

Unnecessarily undercover. He couldn't get over it.

Watching Corentin's hand wander close to Jaime's butt, Dante lost it. Anger swirled like a red tide, rising to choke him. His breath sharpened and his hands curled into fists, itching to swing out and put a dent in Corentin's kisser. Eyes flashing with fury, Dante charged forward like a bull heading for a red cape.

Corentin looked up to see Dante's flaring nostrils. "Sorry, Dante," he smirked "I didn't get the opportunity to–"

He had no time to finish the sentence. Dante's fist collided with Corentin's nose, cracking the cartilage.

Jaime let out an uncontrolled scream.

"You bloody bastard," Dante growled.

Jaime took a step back, shocked by the priest's explosive reaction. "What the hell is going on?"

Without a word, Dante rushed off, rubbing his sore fist. He had to leave before he killed the man.

***

Jaime gaped, her fingers pressed onto her parted lips. "What's going on?" she repeated.

Smirking, Corentin held a bloody hanky to his nose. "I should have known better."

Jaime let out an exasperated sigh. "Will someone please tell me what's going on?"

"Dante should be the one. Or maybe you already know, seeing as you're sharing his bed."

Jaime's mouth froze wide open.

Corentin caressed the side of his swollen nose and winked. "Don't worry, sweetheart, I sussed you out a while back. If you're not sleeping with him yet, you soon will be."

Unable to string two words together, Jaime walked away, heart thumping with every hurried step. She stormed into the house and made a beeline for the priest's study. "Father?"

She turned the door handle.

Locked.

"Father," she called again, knocking on the wooden panel. "Open this door. We need to talk."

No answer.

She banged louder. "Open this bloody door now! Haven't you done enough hiding?"

Silence filled the air.

"Why can't someone answer my simple question?" she bellowed. "With you hiding in your study and Corentin taking care of his bloody nose, you both make a right pathetic pair!"

She marched into the kitchen. A strong drink was called for.

***

Dante sat at his desk, head in hand, fuming. Every time he conjured up visions of Jaime with Corentin, heat flushed through him. He loosened his collar. He had to talk to Jaime. Explain. Yet, he'd just ignored her. He clenched his teeth.

"One whole month wasted!" he yelled.

Corentin had crossed the limits. The swine wanted Jaime, but she was his property, damn it. *His* housekeeper. If he played his cards right, she'd soon be his. Full stop.

Dante pulled his head out of his hands. Had he actually thought that? The idea scared the shit out of him. Claiming someone like that wasn't like him.

He stood and marched around the desk. Jaime needed to be protected. He was only doing this to save her from Corentin's claws. And yet, by disregarding Jaime's pleas, he'd cleared the way for the arsehole to have his way with her. He knew Corentin too well. Hadn't they always shared the same girls? Competing had been their way of life.

He slammed a fist on the desk. Alone in the study, he regretted ignoring Jaime. Corentin would no doubt end up strapping the woman to his bed.

He wasn't called Casanova for nothing.

***

Jaime slipped her coat off and gazed out the kitchen window. A few faraway anthracite clouds crawled towards the presbytery across the almost dark sky. Silence covered the garden like a protective blanket. It was soothing. Light. More than could be said for the atmosphere in the house.

She shook her head. What on earth had pushed the priest to act like a street fighter? He obviously knew Corentin. He wouldn't hit a complete stranger, would he?

Familiar footsteps resonated in the corridor and stopped in the doorway. Jaime wrapped her arms around her body, ready for the showdown. Without turning, she asked, "Ready to tell me what's going on?"

"Corentin deserved it."

"You're a priest. What were you thinking? No one deserves a smack in the teeth."

"Well, *he* did. Believe me, we go back a long way."

Jaime took in a deep breath. "He must have done something really mean to deserve a broken nose."

Dante grunted. "He did."

Jaime continued staring outside, heart thumping against her ribcage. She caught Dante's silhouette in the reflection of the window. His eyes roamed over her bare back while his tongue rolled over his upper lip.

She swallowed hard. The man desired her. No mistaking that. A shudder ran through her body while she imagined his sexy mouth over hers.

She took in a deep breath. "So, are you going to tell me?"

Dante stalked up to Jaime and put his mouth to one ear, his hard chest warming her naked back while hot lips grazed down her neck.

"God, Jaime, I want you so much, I can scarcely breathe." Dante's voice came out in a provocative whisper.

"Father!" Jaime's breath jolted in her throat as she reached behind to caress his cheek. "I didn't think *priests* spoke like that."

Dante chuckled and trailed tiny kisses across her shoulder. "This one's been defrocked."

Jaime let out a gasp and turned to face him. Their eyes locked, chestnut brown into almost black. Dante looked at her in a way she'd never been looked at before. There was more than desire in those eyes.

A teasing smile crept across Dante's face and goosebumps broke out over Jaime's skin. Nothing like the ones that appeared in the cold. These made knees go weak and breasts grow fuller.

"I hope defrocked means what I think it means?" she whispered.

"And more."

With his fingers on either side of Jaime's neck, Dante contoured her cheeks with his thumbs. Jaime's lips parted. She brushed her tongue from one side of her mouth to the other, licking both thumbs.

Dante shuddered, and Jaime felt the bulge in his jeans. His mouth moved to hers, and the few inches between them disappeared. Jaime's teeth pulled on his lower lip before a hungry mouth covered hers with a kiss that blended skill, patience, and power.

Unable to move, Jaime's senses spun. She tried to concentrate on Dante's mouth, but other parts of her anatomy were firing up. Christ Almighty. The man's kiss was pure sex. She slid both hands around Dante's neck and twisted hungry fingers in his hair.

Dante responded with an approving groan and moved his hands under Jaime's dress, tracing a determined line across her smooth stomach. He curved both thumbs into her hipsters and lowered them until they cruised past her thighs and dropped to the floor.

Jaime's blood raced when Dante's hand ventured upward to a breast, murmuring her name as he continued kissing.

"I've had an itch for you since I believed you were the gardener," she whispered between kisses.

He flashed another teasing smile. "I know."

She tugged at the zip of his jeans while Dante removed his shirt in quick, precise movements. With one swift move of the hand, he cleared the top of the kitchen work surface and lifted Jaime onto the edge of the countertop without breaking off their kiss.

"Yes, please," she whispered into his mouth.

Dante withdrew the condom from the back pocket of his jean and sheathed himself. They were both more than ready. No foreplay needed. Hadn't they been mentally touching each other since they'd met? Dante slid into Jaime with short meaningful pushes.

Jaime's whimpers and the soft humming of the fridge were the only sounds audible in the silent kitchen. Over and over again, Dante kissed Jaime's swollen lips, gliding his tongue into her mouth, copying the slow tantalizing movements down below.

He moved with powerful thrusts as Jaime's legs grasped him tighter around the waist. Erotic whispering mingled with groans in perfect rhythm with every push. Dante probed deeper and deeper and Jaime climbed higher and higher until she finally came. Waves of bliss galloped through her. Every nerve screamed out in release, welcoming that familiar, shivering cascade of pleasure. She cried out his name, a sound so gripping, it kept ringing in the room. With a stifled groan, Dante shuddered as he too climaxed, unchaining all the tension built up over the past months.

Jaime's head fell onto his chest. "Wow."

Dante pressed a kiss on the top of her head. "Glad you could cope with the hungry animal I'd become."

Jaime fluttered her eyelashes. "Glad I could oblige." She pulled her head back and gazed into his burning eyes. "How long have you had that condom in your back pocket?"

Dante chuckled.

"I mean, do all priests carry them around? A reminder of their vow of chastity?"

With a cheeky smile, Dante hauled her off the work surface and into his arms. "I wouldn't know, but this condom has had your name on it for quite a while. Now let me get you to bed. I'll clear this mess tomorrow."

He carried Jaime to her room and dropped her gently onto the bed, both eager for another make-up-for-lost-time love session.

***

An hour later, Dante woke with a start.

Releasing Jaime's arm from across his chest, Dante twisted a leg free from her thighs and slipped out of bed. He pulled on his boxers and crept out of the room.

In his study, he grabbed the half bottle of whisky and paced the room, downing large gulps of the burning liquid. He hadn't bothered with a glass.

His thoughts returned to their hot lovemaking. He hadn't regretted any of it.

With a few problems solved, his future seemed brighter. At least for now. But what about Jaime's tomorrow? When would she confide?

For the first time in years, he believed he had a future with someone. But he had to wait until the trial was completely over. For the moment, with the Drug Baron behind bars and waiting for his sentence which hopefully would be for life, Dante knew he was no longer in danger. He only hoped the judge didn't figure on the bastard's payroll.

Snapping out of his reverie, Dante took another swig of drink. He needed to get back to his room – if his legs could carry him. Besides, he could no longer think straight.

He clasped the bottle tighter and left.

Chapter 18

The door gave a faint squeak. In the mid-morning light, Dante's body lay sprawled on his bed, one arm over his forehead.

"Dante?" Jaime headed to the bed, almost tripping over the empty whisky bottle.

No movement.

"Dante?" she called again, kicking the bottle under the bed.

He grumbled and rolled over. Jaime took a step back when a breath of stale alcohol hit her nose.

"Jaime?" Dante clutched the sheet against his bare chest.

"Yes, Jaime! Who did you think it was? The Pope?"

Dante clasped both ears. "Stop yelling and leave me alone."

"I'm not going anywhere until I get an explanation. You left my bed to get drunk. Was I that bad?"

Dante let out a loud cackle and clasped his head.

Jaime marched to the windows, yanked open the curtains, and pushed the windows open wide. A sharp March breeze carried the fragrance of fresh earth into the room. A comforting delight compared to the strong overpowering reek of drink. "You ought to be ashamed of yourself. A respectable grown man getting yourself into this state. You need a shower."

Dante eased himself up slowly onto an elbow and winked. "Would be even better if you came with me."

"Is that so? Well, you burnt your boat when you left my bed."

Dante chuckled and grasped his head in his hands.

"I'll wait for you downstairs. Don't forget we're celebrating Luc and Suzanne's wedding anniversary. Everyone will be waiting." Jaime stepped into the corridor slammed the door and bumped straight into Father Grégoire.

"Do you have a problem, my child? Is Father de Vere ill? Not very ladylike coming out of a priest's bedroom, is it?" The old man chuckled and gave her a wink.

Jaime rolled her eyes and without answering, stormed down the stairs. *The old swine is in cahoots with Dante. He knew all along.*

***

Dante fell out of bed and hit the floor with a hard thud. Shit, that hurt. Rolling over, he gripped his head in both hands and released a bestial grunt, trying to swallow down the urge to vomit.

Serves you right, you bloody fool.

On unsteady legs, he headed for the bathroom, ignoring the swaying room. With his mind in a dull blur, he slipped into the shower unit and set the spray on full force. The hot water drilled down onto his aching shoulders. A hot shower was the best way to bring his brain back to life. Get rid of the cobwebs.

He remained face turned to the sharp drumming of the water for a long moment. How had he got back to his room? When did he leave Jaime's bed? He adjusted the water temperature to almost cold, hoping it would jog his memory.

He remembered hitting Corentin and marching to the study in a rage. He remembered making love to Jaime in the kitchen and then in the bedroom before returning to the study again. He'd grabbed a bottle of whisky and downed the alcohol in quick gulps. He still felt the blaze of the fiery spirit.

What a bastard he was leaving Jaime's bed like that. Apologies would be in order. If she'd let him. Knowing Jaime, she wouldn't let the matter drop without some kind of payback. A few ideas came to mind. He'd trust her to come up with something colourful.

"God, I feel like shit!"

The ringing of his phone broke through the sound of the running water. Dante let it ring. Any quick movement would send his head throbbing.

When he finally felt human, he wrapped a large towel around his hips and stepped into the bedroom. A trail of wet footprints smudged the parquet behind him.

He dressed as quickly as his pounding head would allow. Waves of nausea added to his misery as he looked around the room, checking he hadn't forgotten anything. With a shrug, he grabbed a jacket and closed the door, cringing under his migraine.

What he needed was a couple of boxes of aspirin and a whole percolator of strong coffee.

***

The car pulled up in front of Luc's house, and Dante took in long deep breaths. Much to his despair, Jaime had driven. She'd shot round the bends at sixty on purpose. The movements caused the windows of the 2CV to flap on each swerve, making his stomach heave. Her cackles of laughter hadn't helped. To top it all off, Petrus had decided to show deep affection by panting doggy breath into his face. Damn dog.

They entered the lounge, and every eye in the room turned.

"Bonjour tout le monde," he mumbled, taking a seat next to his mother on the couch. "Sorry for being late."

Luc grinned. "Let me guess. Heavy traffic?" Dante glared at his brother and accepted the glass of Perrier he held out. "Reckoned you could do with a soft drink," he said, winking at Jaime.

Leonora's gaze shot to the ceiling. "You all right, Dante? You're not drinking."

Dante ignored her. The last thing he needed was Leonora grating on his nerves.

Luc's gaze shifted from Dante to Jaime. "Are you two not speaking to each other?"

Dante took a long sip of his drink. "We had a minor disagreement."

"And?"

"And nothing."

Luc peered at Dante's sunken features and gave him a tap on the shoulder.

When they moved to the dinner table, Dante sat with slumped shoulders, trying to ignore the pain that twisted his head. He felt like a wet weekend. Everyone talked and laughed during the meal. Even Jaime was in deep discussion with his father.

Dante kept to himself, struggling to survive through an endless meal with a fuzzy hangover. Nausea swirled deep inside him. The prospect of what he was about to divulge wasn't helping his thumping head either. He glimpsed down at the floor. Petrus lay flat on the ground, his sad eyes cast up to the table.

"I know how you feel, buddy," he muttered to the dog.

"Another aspirin, Dante?" Suzanne asked.

Dante held up his hand. It was too painful to talk.

He managed to make it through the meal without heaving. Once or twice he'd come close to embarrassing himself, swearing on his mother's life he'd never drink again.

The meal finally came to an end – much to his relief. He pushed back his chair and cleared his throat. "I have something important to say."

Every head pivoted in his direction.

"I'll cut it short because my head's splitting." He took a gulp of fizzy Perrier. "I was involved in a drug trafficking case in the south of Italy. Something to do with money laundering for the Albanians."

Jaime's glass fell out of her hand, splattering the last of the champagne onto the tablecloth. Dante's words hung in the air while Jaime scanned the family for any reaction. None came. An awkward silence stretched for what seemed an eternity. Luc whistled through clenched teeth and poured himself another drink.

Dante gazed at Jaime's forlorn features and gave a weak smile. "It's a long story, and I can't apologise enough for deceiving you all. Believe me, if I could have done otherwise, I would have. I was acting under strong advice."

Luc ran a hand through his hair. "Well, that's come as a bombshell. We've only just got over the one you dropped when you came back from Italy as a trainee priest."

Vadim coughed, his expression pained. "You could have trusted us."

Dante brought both hands to his pounding temples. "It wasn't a matter of trust, Father. I was keeping you all from harm."

Sophia folded her serviette. "Well I suppose ignorance is bliss."

"Exactly, Mother."

Vadim gazed at his son, worry etched across the old man's features. "Why are you telling us now? Aren't you scared they'll find you?"

"No, even though there are a few other loose ends to tie up, the main drug dealer is behind bars. They aren't that professional. Just mean Albanian buggers with no great reach into rural France. Besides, a secret agent has been watching over me."

Before anyone could say a word, Dante gave a curt nod of the head and turned to leave.

"Hang on a minute. No more explanations?" Luc's tone revealed a streak of annoyance.

"Not for the moment. I have a headache, and it's a long drive back."

Luc slammed his glass on the table. "Headache or no headache, you can't leave it at that!"

Dante raised a questioning eyebrow. "What more do you need to know?"

Luc clenched both fists. "Oh, come on, Dante. So many things for us to take in with no precise details."

Dante's eyes reached the ceiling searching for patience. "I'll explain later."

"How about explaining now?" The tone of Luc's voice hardened.

Dante gazed at the faces staring back at him and realised how unfair he was being. If he'd been in their shoes, he'd have wanted to know more too. Had going into hiding made him an inconsiderate bugger? Indifferent to people's feelings? Especially his close family?

He rubbed a hand across his chin. "I can't tell you everything in detail until I have the official okay. I've been sworn to secrecy because of the sensitivity of the case."

"How did you get involved in all this?" Luc asked.

Dante reached for his glass and downed the Perrier before clearing his throat.

"I was asked by a good friend who works with the French

authorities to help out with a sticky drug case because of my good Italian. We discovered the Albanian gang wasn't only dealing with drugs, they were also trafficking Eastern European young women to be sold into sex slavery through the Italian port of Brindisi."

Jaime placed a hesitant hand over her mouth.

"I was flown out to the south of Italy and introduced to the top members of the Italian team. However, they underestimated the Albanian Drug Baron, and things took an unexpected turn when a few dealers turned up in my hotel room."

A yelp escaped Jaime's mouth as she reached for Dante's arm. "Don't tell me they beat you up?"

"Beaten up and left for dead. Concerned for my life, the Franco-Italian authorities arranged for me to go into hiding. I needed a profile that the drug gang would least suspect."

"A priest," Dante's mother said.

"Yes. Pretending to be a priest was the best they could come up with. Not only to protect me but also my family."

Luc scratched his jaw. "Not everyone can pretend to be a priest."

Dante turned to his brother. "You're right. During my convalescence, I went into hiding in a monastery somewhere in Italy where Padre Angelo looked after me and helped the police organise my return to France with a safe place to hide. I was put into contact with Father Grégoire. He was happy to take me under his wing, and we negotiated how I could be undercover as a priest without offending the church."

"Is that why you rarely visited?" Suzanne asked.

Dante smiled at his sister-in-law. "The authorities allowed me limited contact with my family. They knew if I didn't pay any visits, you'd guess something was up."

Suzanne nodded and clasped her husband's hand.

Dante pushed his chair under the table. "As soon as I get the go ahead, I promise to let you all know exactly what's going on. Until then, it's time to head back to the presbytery where I won't be staying for long. I'll soon be able to return to Paris once some loose ends have been tied up."

"Dante, darling." Leonora escorted him into the hallway. "You never fooled me with your priest's regalia."

"I'm not in the mood, Leonora."

Leonora ignored the rebuff. She placed a hand in the crook of Dante's arm and spoke to him in a low voice.

"Are you coming, Jaime?" Dante removed himself from Leonora's grip and held a hand out to her.

Jaime slid past Leonora and squeezed his fingers tight. Dante put her palm to his mouth and winked. "I'm afraid you're driving again. Promise me you'll keep the four wheels on the road this time."

He walked round to the passenger side and climbed slowly into the car.

***

Jaime took in long breaths, her emotions running wild. With Leonora making it clear she was out to reclaim Dante, Jaime had to place her stake – and quick.

She jumped back in surprise when a furious Leonora grabbed her arm and dug her sharp nails in hard.

"This is not finished by a long chalk, you trollop. You may have won this little battle, but no way will you win the war." Daggers shot out from Leonora's narrowed gaze.

Jaime wrenched her arm free and moved up close. "Think what you like, but I'm the one warming his bed."

***

Dante and Jaime were in the kitchen, enjoying a pizza. Jaime had put together a quick green salad and Dante had opened a bottle of red wine. He poured out large glasses.

Jaime's eyebrows shot up. "Are you sure you should be drinking?"

Dante chuckled. "This is a pick-me-up. But I promise no more whisky."

Jaime raised her glass and tilted it towards his, thinking back to what he'd divulged at Luc's place. Visions of young women tied to beds waiting for their persecutors to strip any virtue they had came to mind. Not to mention Dante in a mess on the floor, eyes swollen and bloody spit drooling from his slack mouth. He must have gone through hell.

"Want to explain the rest of what's going on? There are still a few things puzzling me. Like the guns under your bed."

Dante twiddled the stem of the glass in his hand before answering, "Corentin's on it. They won't be there much longer."

"Oh!"

"Corentin's my contact. An agent bodyguard to protect me should anything unforeseen arise. His undercover name is Casanova – or Cas for short. Sorry, I couldn't tell you all this before."

Jaime sat upright in her chair. "So the note pinned to the presbytery door was from him? Why would he want to do that?"

"To tell me things were progressing. It was written in code."

Jaime fiddled with her serviette. Corentin had even worried *her* with his note. The man was a jerk. No wonder Dante had given him a smack in the face. Corentin or Casanova or whatever he was called had led Dante to believe things were progressing when in fact the case had been wrapped up a month before.

Jaime took a bite of the margherita and wiped her lips on the paper serviette. "So Father Grégoire was in on this all along."

Dante grinned. "That's right. He was a bit reluctant at first, but when he found out what I'd been through, he accepted. Despite his harsh behaviour, the man has a heart of gold."

It was Jaime's turn to grin.

"What about the priestly side of things?"

Dante paused and poured them another glass of wine. "Not a lot to say, really. I never wrote any sermons or took any confessions."

Jaime took a sip of her wine. Dante was right. She'd never seen him in the confessional, but he spent a hell a lot time in his study. "So what were you doing all that time, locked away in your private room?"

Dante winked at her. "Staying out of your way."

She took in a deep breath. There was another important question bugging her. "What happens now you're no longer in hiding?"

Dante sat back and ran a finger up and down the smooth crystal stem of the glass. "You mean now I'm no longer a priest?"

Jaime nodded.

"Like I said to my family over lunch, after tying up a few loose ends, I'll go back to my job and home in Paris."

"What about me? I can't go back to England." Jaime's tears welled up, ready to flow. Where did she fit in? Was there room for her in his life? Now that she was no longer the housekeeper and Dante no longer a man of the cloth, did their romance end there?

Dante placed a hand over hers. "I want you to come with me. To be part of my future."

Jaime tried to blink back her tears but they managed to trickle down her cheeks. He wanted her with him.

Dante came to crouch beside her. "Jaime, I've told you my story. Why don't you tell me yours? I want you to trust me as I've trusted you. I want you to confide in me."

Tenderness and concern filled Dante's voice, urging Jaime to say more. She gazed into his eyes. This wasn't the moment to bring those inner demons out of the closet. Right now, she'd rather share something more than the weight of her past. Something physical.

Dante caressed her cheek, and Jaime leaned into his warm, loving touch. Could he guess what she needed?

Without breaking eye contact, Dante came closer, his smile widening into a seductive grin. "Confide in me," he repeated.

She'd never been good at confiding or asking for help. Maybe now was the time to divulge a little. Show she was prepared to share.

Taking in a deep breath, she spoke, "Someone's stalking me. I got threatening letters in England. My brother encouraged me to go abroad to get away from the bastard."

Dante frowned. "So that's why you were scared when you saw that note. He has to be more than a pathetic stalker for you to leave your family and friends. Your country even."

Jaime debated whether to say more. Get the burden off her chest. Truly confide. But convinced telling him the whole story wouldn't change her life apart from bringing more worries onto his plate, Jaime remained silent.

"Jaime?"

"Right now, I need you to love me." She dragged his lips between her teeth. "I promise, I'll confide later."

A lot later.

***

Half-conscious, Jaime slowly stretched as she surfaced from a lovely night's sleep. Visions of their love-making came to mind, bringing a slow smile to her face.

One after the other, she peeled open her eyes to find Dante propped on an elbow and gazing down at her. He pulled a stray hair away from her face and tucked it behind her ear. "Bonjour, beauté."

"Hi, gorgeous yourself." She took his hand and kissed his palm.

A set of frown lines creased Dante's forehead, and Jaime's grin disappeared. "What's up?"

Dante hesitated before whispering, "I have to go to Italy for a few days."

Jaime turned her head away from him.

"Jaime?"

She hadn't forgotten about what he'd said to his family about a few loose ends to tie up, she simply didn't want to remember. "I heard you, Dante."

He held her chin and turned it gently towards him. "Talk to me."

"What happens now?"

"Nothing's changed. I have to go to Italy. Father Grégoire will still do the services and look after the church. You can stay here until I return. I know you'll be safe here with him and Petrus.

"So Father Greg knows you've come out of hiding?"

"I told him everything yesterday before we left for Luc's place." Dante caressed her cheek. "I need to get this mess out of the way once and for all. When I return from Italy, we'll make plans."

Dante rubbed her knitted brow. "I can see your mind ticking. I can only take one step at a time, but I want to take those steps with *you*."

Jaime bit back her tears. She had to go with the flow and stop her questions. Questions to which she might not like the answers. Dante was right. They should enjoy each other's company and take things in their stride. Besides, it wasn't a holiday. He had business to deal with.

She reached out and caressed his cheek before bringing his head down to hers. Dante slid an arm around her waist and pulled her to him. "I want to delve into every single inch of that sexy body of yours," he murmured into her neck. "Something to remember while I'm away."

Jaime shuddered. Even more so when he swept his tongue across her nipples. The effect was immediate. A deep quiver fluttered in her womb while she gazed up into his eyes. She wanted him inside. Taking her.

"Love me," she whispered as his mouth moved onto hers.

Dante's hand moved up and down her body while she whimpered his name. After a few more tantalizing caresses, Dante grabbed a condom and slid into her, inch by inch.

"Mmm, that feels so good, Dante."

He continued rocking, his body tensing and tightening, looking for a way to seal their bond. Each thrust intensified in power, and Jaime found herself mounting. With half closed eyes, she waited to tumble into sweet release.

"Come for me," he whispered.

Jaime's head hummed in a cloud. The only liberation would be for that cloud to burst and for the rain to fall. Pleasure drummed up, eager to reach the top of the wave. Jaime cried out his name, hitting climax as he did. Their bodies arched and convulsed, exploding in silent wonder.

Jaime savoured the feel of his body over hers. She rubbed both hands up and down his muscled back, feeling him gradually withdraw. He'd proven once again how much he cared for her. Their lovemaking had been intense and meaningful. Perfect even. It hadn't stopped a horrible thought sinking into her mind, though.

What if something happened in Italy and he never returned?

Chapter 19

With narrowed eyes, he stared out the small window in his room. A few pigeons cooed on the glistening rooftops, their silhouettes dark against the streaked evening sky. Not a great view of the city's cornices, but he wasn't admiring the panorama. He was thinking about Jaime. The bitch was out there somewhere.

Taking a long drag from his joint, he sucked the smoke deep into his lungs, recalling Jaime's chestnut brown eyes and clear complexion. She'd better make the most of her pretty appearance. When he finished with her – and if he was in a good mood – he'd slit that slim throat to end the pain. Not that she deserved the favour. Hadn't she made him suffer?

How could he find her though? He didn't have enough money. Didn't have transport either.

He tapped the small card with Leonora's number against his chin and grinned. That could soon change. Patience had never been one of his strong points. How many times had his mother scolded him for doing as he pleased? If he wanted something bad enough, he made sure he got it. Nothing ever stood in the way when he put his crafty mind to it. Why should that change now?

He shuffled to the bed and dropped down heavily on the mattress. Jaime shouldn't have done that to his brother. The pain would never go away. Because of what she'd done, he couldn't get on with his life.

With an arm thrown over his forehead, he imagined caressing Jaime's soft breasts. Excitement tickled the pit of his gut. He closed his eyes ready to slip away into the land of dreams. A place where Jaime was tied up and gagged while inch by inch, the razor blade sliced layers of skin.

And should she fight back, he'd slice deeper.

Chapter 20

The slamming of a car door pulled Jaime away from her chores. She'd just spent a good hour cleaning Father Grégoire's office. How could anyone be so untidy? It was clear why the old priest needed a housekeeper. Thank God he'd be away until the next morning. It would give her the opportunity to clean up and spend the evening alone with Dante.

She headed to the living-room window in time to see Leonora march up the presbytery steps and disappear into the house.

What was she doing here? Dante had only moments ago arrived back from his ten-day trip to Italy. Apart from a quick kiss, they hadn't even had a chance to talk. Dante said he still had a few things to tie up. Jaime's fingers gripped the feather duster tighter. How did Leonora know Dante would be back? Unless he'd told her?

Leonora's footsteps echoed in the corridor until they disappeared into Dante's study. Jaime pursed her lips and returned to the dusting.

***

"Thanks for letting me come," Leonora said once Dante closed the study door.

"Look, Leonora, I only agreed to see you because I can imagine what you're going through. I've just got back from Italy, and I want to unwind."

"I won't take up any more time than necessary, chéri."

Dante sat at his desk. "Did you bring your grandmother's Will, like I asked?"

Leonora handed him the document, and Dante set about reading, nodding and huffing with every page turned.

"Well?" Leonora asked after a while.

"I'll ask a colleague for confirmation, but for the moment, either you report Maxime to the police, or you get an injunction."

Leonora grumbled.

"If you opt for the injunction, we could do it for a period of three months, bringing us up to mid-June. That's when the stipulation clause in your grandmother's Will draws to an end."

"What do you mean by injunction?"

"It's a judicial order restraining Maxime from continuing his blackmailing. If he breaches the injunction, he could end up in prison."

"How much would that cost?"

Dante whistled through his teeth. "We're looking at something around 30,000 Euros."

"Bloody hell! That's a bit steep."

"Stop shouting." Dante placed the document back into the file.

Leonora smiled sweetly. "There's no one here. Just me and you."

"There's Jaime," he said in a harsh voice.

"Who gives a shit?" Leonora mumbled.

Dante stood and handed the file back. "Your best bet is to keep stringing Maxime along. It'll cost you less to pay 5,000 Euros a month than to get an injunction."

"But you haven't heard the latest. I've got all the photos, Dante. Maxime is now threatening me with an SD card. He doesn't want money anymore. He wants *me*." A vein pulsed in Leonora's slender neck.

"Emotional blackmail as well, then," Dante said more to himself.

Leonora slipped the file into her bag. "Maxime's an imposter after my social status. He's a leech. A lying, loathsome leech!"

If the situation hadn't been so dramatic, Dante would have laughed. A lying, loathsome leech fitted Leonora's ex down to a tee.

"Look, Leonora, I can't snap my fingers and put everything right. I'm no magician. These things take time."

Leonora's lips pinched together.

"Why don't you go to the police?" Dante asked.

Leonora jerked her head back. "I value my privacy too much."

Dante's eyes widened and he shook his head.

Leonora came to stand in front of him and glided a hand into the inside of his jacket lapel. "We were so good together."

Dante gripped Leonora's wrist and pulled it away. "It's over, Leonora. Practice your charms on Maxime."

Leonora rubbed her wrist. "Stringing Max along with promises is one thing. Sleeping with him is another."

Dante shrugged. "Like I said, there's no way out for the moment."

***

Jaime crept down the corridor and placed an ear to the study door. She heard movements. Not a lot of talking. Were they kissing? She rubbed her stomach, soothing the contortion of muscles. Her breathing changed from erratic to shallow. There had to be a plausible explanation for the sudden and secretive meeting.

A chair scraped the floor and footsteps approached. Before Jaime could dive out of sight, the door swung open, and she came face to face with Dante's angry stare. Her heart accelerated.

She swished the feather duster. "Er...I didn't realise the door was so dusty."

Dante's eyes narrowed. "Good-bye, Leonora," he said without turning to the woman.

Jaime stepped aside as a mumbling Leonora stormed past. She couldn't make out what the woman said, but the few words she did catch, set her heart thumping.

"...bloody...kill you."

A sudden coldness crept over Jaime's body. Was that accusation aimed at her? Jaime shook her head. Couldn't be, could it?

Dante held out his arms and Jaime threw her duster onto the floor and dived into them.

"I missed you," she said as his mouth came down on hers.

"Not as much as I missed you."

His warm lips covered hers, making her toes curl – as always.

Pulling back, Dante gave her a tiny peck on the nose. "Let's eat out. We need to talk."

"I'd like that."

"Okay, you get ready. I'll say hello to Petrus and feed him."

A short while later, they strolled arm in arm to the village and to Le Blé Noir a quiet crêperie where the sarrasin pancakes were delicious.

The place had a cosy atmosphere with heavy oak furniture and lime-washed beams stretching across the ceiling. The perfect place for a chat. Dante asked for a quiet table in the corner and ordered two Forestière pancakes with cider. It was the tradition to drink cider with savoury pancakes.

Jaime sat opposite Dante, happy yet apprehensive.

"I've something important to say," Dante said, taking her hand. "I've had time to think during my trip to Italy, and I still want you to come and live with me in Paris."

Was she ready for this? She slipped her hand out of his and was about to say something when the waiter arrived with their order.

"You've already been my housekeeper," Dante continued once they were alone.

Jaime popped a cherry tomato into her mouth. "It takes more than being a housekeeper to live together."

Dante tilted his head to one side. "You can share my bed this time."

Jaime giggled and took a sip of her cider. "What about Petrus? How will he cope being confined in a flat? No more garden to wander around?"

"Petrus is Luc's dog. My brother left him with me for company. He'll go back to his true home."

Jaime's face relaxed into a smile.

"Of course being a couple means no secrets between us," he added.

Jaime's smile transformed into a frown. That wouldn't be easy. Did he need to know her problems? Would it change anything if he did? Probably not. She pushed the food around her plate.

"You didn't finish telling me about your stalker."

Jaime's fork made a dive for the plate, splattering the mushroom garniture onto the table. *Shit, can he read my mind?* Despite her thundering heart, she gave a weak smile. "There's nothing to say. He stopped stalking when I came to France."

Dante gave her a questioning look. "Really?"

"Well, apart from a Christmas card in my forwarded post."

"What did it say?"

Jaime raised an eyebrow. Was he testing her? "He said he saw me leave."

Dante gave a knowing nod. "You'll be safer with me in Paris."

Jaime relaxed and picked up a few more tomatoes. On looking up, she caught Dante's determined gaze.

"I'd like you to work for me as my personal assistant."

Jaime opened her mouth to speak, but Dante held up a hand. "I've been thinking about this since I left for Italy. I need a person with a good level of English and someone I can trust. More and more foreign clients expect me to write in English. You would correct my work when necessary." He stopped to take a sip of wine. "The company has an assistant who prepares our files and helps with research. You would work with her when English cropped up."

Jaime took another long sip of her drink, unsure of what to answer.

"This will save me subcontracting and wasting time. It could work for both of us."

"Seems like a favour."

Dante chuckled. "I'm putting myself in your shoes. If you accept, you'll be self-sufficient. If things don't work out, even though I know they will, you won't be financially bound to me. And I am in need. My written English is nowhere near as good as my Italian."

Jaime over-chewed the food, playing for time. Could she see herself living with this person?

Dante took in a deep breath. "I'm not going back home without you. Is that clear?"

A slow glow swept through her. She felt special. Maybe because she knew he'd never lived with Leonora. This was a first for him.

"Don't you want more time to think about this? I mean it's a big step for you too," she said.

"I've had enough time to think. I know what I want – I want you with me."

Jaime gave a delighted squeal, leaned across the table and kissed him. Dante moved his mouth in an affectionate, decisive way, as if they were signing a contract. Breathless, Jaime pulled back, wholly convinced of his feelings. "If we make our relationship official, Leonora will stay away."

Dante tilted his head to one side. "So I'm not the only one with a little jealousy problem."

Jaime blushed and raised her glass. "Touché!"

***

Jaime gazed out of the bathroom window the next morning. Dew spread its fine layer of beads across the lawn, and the sun had started its ascension. This awakening magic of a new day added to her good mood.

Dante had made things up to her in a way she hadn't experienced before. As always, their lovemaking had been intense, but his time it had been more meaningful. They'd even spoken long into the night. Maybe it was time to speak to her mother. Four and a half months had passed since her arrival in France. Time to reveal what she intended to do.

She grabbed her phone and tapped in her mother's number, chewing her thumbnail while her heart picked up a quicker tempo.

"Hello!"

"Morning, Mum."

"Jaime! What a surprise. Everything all right, love?"

"Everything's fine. Just thought I'd touch base and put you in the picture."

"What's happened?" Antonia's voice was laced with worry.

"Have you got five minutes?"

"I've got lots of time, honey. Fire away."

Jaime explained the situation. About Dante being an undercover priest and his coming out of hiding. His true job as a lawyer. And how she'd fallen hard for him.

"I'm going to settle down in France," Jaime said, waiting for the interrogation to begin.

And it did.

"Where exactly? In some pokey flat in Paris? How will you pay the rent? May I remind you that you no longer have a job? The so-called *priest* doesn't need a housekeeper anymore."

"Dante wants me to work as his PA."

Antonia huffed into the phone. "Is that so? And will you earn enough to pay the rent? I hear prices are high in Paris."

Jaime took in a deep breath. "He's asked me to move in with him. He's got a beautiful flat in rue Lecourbe."

"Have you seen it?"

"Not yet."

"Then how do you know what it's like?"

Jaime rolled her eyes. "If he's a lawyer, I can imagine what it's like."

Another silence set in. "Are you sure this is a good idea?" her mother asked. "What do you know about the man? One minute he's a priest, the next he's a lawyer. What will he be tomorrow?"

"Oh, Mum."

Her mother sighed. "I never imagined you'd settle there for good. You went to France to get away from the letters. They've stopped. You can come back."

Jaime flopped down on one of the chairs, wondering if she should confide. After taking a deep breath, she confessed. "I got a Christmas card from the stalker in the first post you forwarded. He said he saw me leave."

A gasp echoed in Jaime's ear. "He's still around then."

Jaime bit her bottom lip. "That was about four months ago. I've had nothing since."

"He may be biding his time." Antonia sounded tired. Jaime imagined her mother struggling with her emotions. "Do you know enough about Dante to move in with him?"

"I've been living with him all this time as a housekeeper. This is what I want, Mum. Please be happy for me."

Jaime heard her mother sniff, and her eyes widened. Antonia never cried. The last time her mother had shed a tear was at her father's funeral. Even then, the mourning had been brief. That had puzzled Jaime. Although her mother never showed a lot of emotion, Jaime had expected her to show a bit more grief. At one time, Jaime even wondered if her mother really cared for her father. That said, people reacted differently in certain situations.

"Mum? Are you still there?"

"Yes, love. Maybe it's for the best. But remember, darling, I'll always be here. No matter what."

Chapter 21

Rapid breathing sounded in Leonora's ear before an excited voice broke the stillness.

"Good afternoon, Leonora. You don't know me, but I've got something that belongs to you and–"

"Who are you and how did you get my number?" She cut the speaker short.

"Don't interrupt, you silly bitch."

Leonora took in a sharp breath.

"I've got kinky photos you may want to get back."

The words hit her like a thunderbolt. Under her feet, the parquet softened. Her legs gave way, and she fell into a heap. With great effort, she managed to keep the phone from tumbling out of her hand. Sitting on the floor with widened eyes, she was unable to utter a word.

A muffled voice from the phone brought her back to her senses.

"Hel...lo...oh. Is there anybody there?"

Regaining her wits, she spoke into the phone. "I asked you how you got my number."

"I found it with the photos."

"Are you taking the piss?"

"I'm telling you, Little Lady...mind you, looking at these photos, not so sure about that. Your number was with the photos."

Leonora closed her eyes for a brief moment. She had to get back into dealing-with-imbeciles mode. "Don't you 'Little Lady' me, you shit. Where did you find the photos? And don't tell me in a rubbish bin."

He cackled. "That's where this vulgar trash belongs. In fact, I found them in an envelope in a plush car. Some prick left the car running, and I happened to pass by. You can guess the rest."

"I suppose the envelope happened to fall into your hands?"

"Hey, you got it."

Struggling to figure out what was going on, it dawned on her that the prick in question was Maxime. He must have put more photos along with an SD card in the car. The caller had stolen them and was now out to blackmail her.

"We're about to do business." His voice held a trace of menace. "I'll keep to the prick's initial price. 5,000 Euros for each photo."

Not again! She clasped the phone tighter, analysing the situation. At least she'd have the satisfaction to tell Maxime to get out of her life. If she had to pay, she'd rather pay this bastard. At least she wouldn't have to sleep with him – she hoped.

A sinister laugh echoed in her ear. "I'll give you until this evening to get the money."

"What if I refuse?"

"Not a good idea. I'll have no other choice but to post them on the web."

Leonora chewed on her thumbnail. She didn't know what he was capable of. He could be a psychopath for all she knew. What if he was an opportunist? Many of them had no morals or restraints. They didn't play by the same book of rules as the rest of society. All that counted was getting what they wanted in whichever way was easiest. Wolves seeking out their prey. She bit the inside of her cheek, cursing the day she'd crossed Maxime's path. The jerk had brought nothing but trouble.

"All okay with you, then?"

Leonora snapped out of her daze. "Er...what?"

"I said, we'll meet in the 18th district in Paris."

With great reluctance, she took a pen and piece of paper to write down the address and directions. A few seconds later, she shrieked. "What! You must be bloody joking. I'm not meeting you in front of some sex shop."

"Why not? Your photos would bring in a bundle."

"I don't think–"

"I don't give a fuck of what you think," his voice snapped down the phone. "You be there this evening at seven-thirty with the money. Or before you know it, you'll be counting the 'likes' of your bare arse on the web."

Screaming, Leonora hurled the phone across the room where it bounced off the wall and shattered on the ground. After whirling round the room like a wild animal, destroying everything in her wake, she sank to the floor. With her head between both hands, she rocked back and forth, wailing like a lost animal.

The late afternoon found Leonora still crouched in a little ball. She swayed unsteadily to her feet and stared at the disaster made in her moment of frustration. Without further ado, she removed the SIM card from her broken phone and left for the appointment with the opportunist, reminding herself to stop off at the bank to draw out money.

***

Leonora approached the small, dark alleyway with hesitant steps.

She paused at the entrance and gazed at the time on her new phone. A little after seven-thirty. The sound of a dog barking somewhere beyond the darkness set her heart thumping. She didn't feel safe.

With a hand over her nose, she put one foot behind the other and moved away from the stench of trash and urine. She jumped when a jingle on her phone broke the silence. Scrambling in her bag, she fished it out.

"I'm at the end of the alley."

Leonora recognised his voice. "Forget it. I'm not coming down that shit-hole."

"This 'shit-hole' is where I live," he hissed.

Leonora took in a deep breath. She'd had enough of this fiasco. "That's your problem."

"Look, Little Lady, we can't all be lucky enough to live in a mini-château."

Leonora gasped. Was he guessing, or did he know where she lived? How much more information did he have? The hairs on her nape tingled.

"If you're unwilling to step into my *hovel*, then I'll have to come to your *castle*, Milady."

Leonora chewed on the side of her thumb. That was out of the question, but she couldn't bring herself to walk down 'Stink-Pot Alley.' Her eyes darted around. She'd plan their meeting when the gardener or the cleaner would be present. Besides, she had her grandfather's gun.

She put on a confident voice. "Fine. I'll give you my ad–"

"I know where you live, Princess."

Christ, she hated his weasel voice.

"I'll have to charge for travel expenses. So it'll be 10,000 Euros per photo."

Leonora's scream echoed at the entrance of the alleyway. "You must be off your fucking rocker!"

"You don't come down the alley? You pay for my inconvenience."

"But–"

His angry voice blasted her eardrum. "No buts. See you Saturday at ten. Can't wait to meet you in person. I'm sure the photos don't do you justice. Maybe you could pose for me. To prove it's you."

Leonora cringed. Neither the cleaner nor the gardener would be around Saturday morning. No way was she going to meet him alone. What if she ended up getting raped? Or killed?

She cleared her throat. "I'm not free Saturday morning. It'll have to be the afternoon."

"You're not in a position to negotiate. Saturday at ten. End of conversation." And without giving her a chance to reply, he hung up.

Leonora moved away from the stench, her wary eyes scrutinising the vicinity as she marched down the road.

10,000 Euros for a bloody photo. How the hell had she gotten into this mess?

***

Maxime entered the living room late the next evening and glared at Leonora. "Why didn't you answer my calls?"

Leonora flicked through the pages of a gossip magazine. "Why should I?"

"If you want us to get along, the next time I ring, you'd better answer."

She closed the magazine with a snap. "Go to hell."

Maxime came to sit beside her. He put a hand out to touch her cheek, ready for a kiss. Leonora shot up in a flash. "Get your hands off me."

He hauled himself off the settee and chuckled. "Don't forget to be nice to Maxou, because Maxou's got that SD card."

Leonora threw her head back, and a high cackle pierced the air. "Believe it or not, *Maxou*, you no longer have that card. Another blackmailing bastard has. Now get out of my life."

Maxime shot her a confident glare. "The card's in a brown manila envelope along with a few other photos in the glove compartment of my car, honey."

"Are you sure?"

She watched him rush outside to his BMW in the driveway, open the passenger door, and lean in.

"Bloody, fucking hell!" he shouted.

Leonora came out of the house and let out a scornful laugh. "When was the last time you checked to see if the photos were there?"

He punched the glove compartment shut before hitting the dashboard. Rushing out of the car, he waved the phone in front of her. "I've still got the photos on my phone."

Leonora stormed up to him, swung a leg back, and nailed him in the crotch. "I hope your testicles explode!"

Maxime staggered back before collapsing to the ground, tears streaming down his cheeks. He dropped the phone and cupped both hands between his legs. Curled up in a foetal position, he cursed the woman with every word that came to mind.

Leonora grabbed Maxime's phone and ran across the garden to her favourite hiding place. Although dark, the moon shed enough light to make out the contours of the trees and bushes.

She sat against an old tree trunk as she'd done so many times during her childhood. It was a place of escape from the rest of the world. A place to forget all her worries. She pulled her arm back and threw

Maxime's phone into the large dark pond. It hit the surface, breaking the reflection of the moon, and disappeared into the murky water.

With a confused sigh, Leonora stared up into the splay of stars. Having escaped from the frying pan, she was now diving head-first into the fire, stuck with another parasite.

Chapter 22

It was time for Jaime and Dante to head to Paris and start their new life. A week had passed since their discussion at the restaurant and Dante had organised everything for the move. They had informed Father Grégoire of their departure and had helped the old man in finding a new housekeeper. Petrus had also been taken back to Luc.

Jaime stared at the patio, fighting back her anxiety. Dante's fingers squeezed her hand in a reassuring grip. Would she become accustomed to the French way of life? Or rather, accustomed to living with this man?

"Ça va?" Dante asked.

Jaime nodded and held a hand out to Father Grégoire. He took her hand in his and shook it gently. She'd grown fond of the old man. Beneath his facade the priest had a heart of gold. Hadn't he taken Dante under his wing?

"Things will be fine," Father Grégoire whispered in her ear. "And if they aren't, you're always welcome here."

Jaime swallowed the lump at the back of her throat and caught a wink in the priest's eye.

"I'm counting on you to take care of her, Dante," the old man said, waving a shaky finger at him.

"I will, monsieur."

Father Grégoire chuckled and gave Dante a friendly tap on the shoulder.

Dante helped Jaime into the car and drove the vehicle off the premises. "Things will be all right, I promise." He interlaced their fingers and kissed her knuckles. "When I make promises, I keep them."

"I hope you can, Dante."

Because this is one hell of a big step to take.

Chapter 23

Thanks to the decent cut Marcel had given him, he'd woken refreshed from a good night's sleep. Ready for the first transaction with Leonora.

He drove Marcel's car up the property's long driveway, taking in the beautiful surroundings. The estate was fabulous. A large pond bordered with bulrushes dominated the grounds. Flower beds lined either side of the weed-free lawn and bloomed with daffodils and colourful primroses. No doubt a full-time gardener. Why couldn't he have been brought up in a rich environment like this? His admiration changed to frustration.

He brought the car to a halt in front of the mansion and jumped out. Jealous eyes flicked around until they fell on Leonora standing on the terrace, glaring down at him.

Arrogant bitch!

"Oh, there you are. Didn't recognise you with your clothes on." He smirked, moving closer. "Shall we go inside?"

Leonora clenched her fists. "We'll stay here."

Without a second thought, he grabbed her upper arm and flung her through the door and into the huge hallway. "We'll see about that."

He hated this woman, talking down to him, dressed in designer clothes and living in a chateau. The more he looked at the rich decor, the more he wanted to lash out. The silly bitch had everything. He had nothing.

"Very nice." His voice was cold.

Leonora rubbed her bruised arm and turned to him. "Where's the photo?"

"Money first."

She reached into her pocket and pulled out twenty 500 Euro notes while he slipped the photo onto the table.

"How do I know you haven't made copies?" she asked.

"You don't. You'll have to trust me." He rubbed his sweaty hands together and guffawed. His luck was in. The silly cow had actually agreed to pay 10,000 Euros.

"Shall we shake hands to conclude our deal?" he asked.

Leonora's features hardened into a disdainful sneer. "Get out of my sight."

"Careful who you're talking to, sweetheart. You might regret it."

His tone cracked sharp.

He pocketed the money and licked his lips. "How about a quick screw? My guess is you like it rough. We could think of it as a bonus. Yeah, I like that idea."

Leonora shuffled back a step or two.

"Let's say it's a guarantee for me *not* to put these pieces of art on the net." A malicious grin plastered his face.

With an icy glare, Leonora grabbed hold of his arm and tried to push him out of the door. Her footsteps came to a sudden standstill when he gripped her by the throat and pulled her onto the tips of her toes. Gasping for air, Leonora clasped his hand, fighting to loosen the grip.

"Don't treat me like that again, you slut." He released her abruptly and snorted.

Leonora fell against the doorframe and dropped to the floor, her eyes flashing horror. He smirked. "I think you've met your match, sweetheart."

He buttoned his jacket and set his hat straight. "See you soon for the next instalment. And be prepared. I'll bring the lube."

***

The grandfather clock in the hallway struck eleven. Leonora snapped out of her trance. Had she been on the floor for almost an hour?

She ran her hand across her throat for the umpteenth time. Was the man sane? Did he honestly believe she would prostitute herself for the damned photos? He was psychotic. She was sure of it now. Perhaps she was better off with Maxime. At least she knew what to expect.

She slipped a hand into her pocket and stroked her grandfather's gun. What she'd give to wipe the bastard's grin away by shoving the weapon up his arse and pulling the trigger.

She'd kill him if was the last thing she did.

***

He arrived home tired and hungry but happy.

Tucking into a camembert sandwich, he sipped a beer and switched on the laptop. All had gone to plan. He was now eager to get on with the next step in his stratagem – the purchase of a car. He'd spoken to Marcel, and his friend had suggested the local garage. The owner was one of a long string of regular clients. Marcel said he'd get a good deal.

He took another long swig and belched. If Marcel was free this afternoon, he'd ask for a lift.

Fumbling for the screwed-up photo in the back pocket of his jeans, he smoothed it out, ignoring the crumbs falling from the sandwich. The photo had been folded and unfolded so many times, crease lines had deformed Jaime's features.

His lips curled upwards. He was one step nearer to tracking her down. One step nearer to deforming her flesh. Might even carve his initials in her.

He kissed the image. *Not long now, Darling.*

***

A swarm of second-hand vehicles lined the forecourt opposite the garage's main building.

"René!" Marcel called.

A short man with dyed-black hair slicked back over his head came to meet them.

"Here's the associate I spoke about." Marcel slapped him on the shoulder.

René's dark brown suit had seen better days. His shoes on the other hand had been polished and shone to a high sheen.

"No problem, mon ami. I'll see your associate gets a fair deal."

Marcel took a few steps forward and grinned. "Everything's okay for next week."

"Great. I appreciate it." René smiled, showing uneven yellow teeth.

"Good. I'll get my associate to do the hand over."

Marcel hurried away, and the two men strolled to the parking lot where René stored the good bargains. "So, how much to you want to pay?"

"As little as possible."

René let out a nervous laugh and rubbed his hand over his chin. He pointed to a navy-blue Renault Twingo parked next to a white Citroen C2. "I suggest one of these two then."

The vehicles seemed to be in good shape. He roamed around the cars, opening and closing the doors, not forgetting to check the boot. No visible rust. He kicked the tyres and grunted in approval.

"Excuse me, René." A young mechanic approached, wiping his greasy hands on an even greasier piece of cloth. "The de Vere's Picasso is ready."

His ears pricked up and his heart missed a beat. Could this be the same de Vere family Jaime was staying with?

René rubbed his hands. "Thank you, Fabien. Have you phoned Mr de Vere?"

"Yeah, he'll be here in about twenty minutes."

Fucking Hell! Have I found her? It's got to be her. Not a lot of de Vere's around.

"Sorry about that," René said when the mechanic stepped away again.

"No worries." He had to stall for time. They'd be here in less than twenty minutes. "You suggested these two cars. Are they both the same price?"

René retrieved a calculator from his jacket pocket and tapped on the tiny numbers. "To be honest with you, the Twingo's a bit more, but I can make it the same price as the Citroen. 6,000 Euros."

"Can I test drive them?" he asked, still debating between the two.

René gave a quick nod and disappeared to fetch the keys.

Watching René return, he saw Fabien drive the de Vere car out of the garage and up to the front of the main building. He needed to get closer.

René held out two sets of keys. "Which one do you want to drive first?"

"Which one do you recommend?"

"The Twingo will give you better satisfaction. Less mileage and the two front tyres are new."

He moved toward the car in question and kicked the tyres again, all the while keeping an eye on the de Vere vehicle. He didn't have time to drive the Twingo. Might miss something interesting. "I won't bother driving it. I'll take your word."

"Are you sure?"

"Of course. You don't want me coming back if I find you've conned me."

René wiped his brow. "Good choice. Let's go to reception and tidy up the paperwork."

They entered the building and sat in an office. A pile of car brochures reposed on one side of a desk, and the Twingo's handbook lay on the other. The garage owner completed form after form, ticking boxes and circling numbers. Now and again, the man stopped to rub his hands, chuckling to himself.

After a while, on hearing a car pull up outside the building, René looked up from the paperwork. "Excuse me a minute," he said and walked out of the office.

From the window, he spotted Mr de Vere shaking René's hand. Nothing to write home about. He eyed up Mrs de Vere as she stepped out of the car. Fuckable, but nothing special either.

"Maman, we want to come with you." A little girl whined from the back of the car.

"You can't, honey. Maman will be driving right behind."

Brawling brat! She needed to be taken for a walk in the woods. Teach her some good manners. Yeah, he quite fancied the idea.

Rubbing his groin, he returned to the desk and pulled out a pocket-knife. If René didn't finish his snivelling act with the family pretty soon, he'd have to show him how to be polite. He clenched both fists. Who the hell did René think he was, leaving one customer to grovel around another? The garage owner needed to get his priorities straight. A quick flick of a knife might do the trick.

"Right," René said, returning into the office.

He looked up from scraping out dirt from under his nails and scowled, fighting back the urge to slice René's pathetic grin. Wipe him off the map. The prat wouldn't even be missed.

"So, that's the de Vere family?" he asked.

"That's right. Luc de Vere, the architect."

A spark flickered in his brain. One of the names on the Pages Blanches. He pocketed the knife and cleared his throat. "Haven't they got an English girl staying with them?"

René scratched the back of his neck. "Not to my knowledge. I did see an English girl with the brother, though. They came when Mr de Vere once brought his old 2CV to be serviced."

"That must be Vadim." The second name he'd jotted down.

Renée stopped scribbling and looked up. "Not at all. Vadim is the father."

He held his breath. There were only two 'de Vere' on the phone list. The third one had to be ex-directory. The bastard. Tracking down Jaime was going to be trickier than he'd imagined.

He snapped out of his musing. "I know the English girl."

René chuckled and handed him the form to sign. "Bit of all right, isn't she?" The garage owner's eyes flicked to the dotted line, desperate for the signature.

"Sure is." He signed the document and took six wads of rolled notes from a black pouch.

René swallowed hard.

"I've been lucky on the horses."

Renée tapped the side of his nose. "Know what you mean, mon ami."

The garage owner counted the money, and they concluded the deal with a handshake.

With the car keys held tightly in his hand, he climbed into the car and grinned. It wouldn't be long before he ferreted Jaime out.

Chapter 24

Dante and Jaime pulled up in front of the flat in Paris. While Dante locked the car, Jaime stood on weary legs and gazed up at the massive stone facade. He handed her two paper bags from the back seat and grabbed her cases.

Dragging her feet, Jaime trailed behind him into the building, glad to stretch her legs. They headed up the flight of stairs to the first floor and walked down a short corridor.

The first thing Jaime saw on entering the flat was the long black and white tiled hallway. Turning right, Dante swung open the doors to a spectacular study. Although masculine with a black swivel chair and green leather top desk, the decor radiated warmth. Modern paintings of abstract design hung on the walls. Contemporary sculptures added to the mellow atmosphere.

"Quick tour?" Dante took Jaime's hand before she had time to answer.

He stopped half way down the hallway to show her the huge living room with its oval merusier table and matching chairs. On the other side of the room, two leather settees faced each other next to the marble fireplace. Jaime imagined herself snuggling up to Dante in front of a roaring fire.

At the far end of the corridor, Jaime glimpsed the well-equipped kitchen on the right with stainless-steel appliances set out on black granite countertops. A delightful place to prepare meals. She placed the two paper bags with their takeaway onto the table.

"And this is our bedroom," Dante said, opening the door on the left.

Jaime kicked off her toe-pinching shoes and treaded carefully on the light beige carpet. Her feet sank into the thick pile as she moved around the king-size bed with its snow-white duvet. The caramel-coloured room led into a dressing room of the same shade. It was spotless. A perfect magazine cover.

Stepping into the en-suite bathroom, Jaime's mouth dropped open at the size of the huge corner bath. Room enough for both of them. On the right, two wash basins sat in front of a huge mirror, covering the whole wall, and an Italian shower unit with multiple adjusting shower heads stood between the washbasins and the bath.

She could see them having fun in there.

Jaime turned and winked at him. "Wow. Can't wait to try that."

Dante grinned. "Like it?"

"J'adore."

Dante bent to kiss her waiting lips. "Good, because this is your home now."

Jaime slipped both arms around his waist and leaned her head against his chest. She was going to like it here. Safe and secure in Dante's flat. The other bastard would never think to look here.

Dante gave her a sweet kiss. "Hungry?"

She fell in step with him to the kitchen. A few minutes later, all was ready, and they sat to eat.

Jaime gazed at Dante across the table in the faint candlelight, watching the shadows dance on his face as he ate. He reached for his glass and lifted it. The candle reflected ruby sparkles off the Châteauneuf-du-Pape.

"To us," he said, holding Jaime's gaze.

Jaime lifted her glass. "To us and a new beginning."

Dante leaned across the table and placed a slow kiss on her lips. Jaime shuddered as the kisses deepened. She'd never get tired of kissing him. The man had a way with his lips that drove her insane.

Chuckling, Dante pulled back, and Jaime recognised the wicked look in his eyes. She guessed the next step of action. He caressed her chest, each stroke more urgent than the one before. A delicious shiver ran over Jaime's body as Dante's eager mouth came down on hers again. She tangled both hands in his hair and groaned.

Without breaking the kiss, Dante lifted Jaime and headed for the bedroom, where he lowered her onto the bed. In two quick pulls, he removed her dress. Dragging his own shirt over his head, he hurled it to the floor before stretching his body over hers.

Jaime's fingers slipped into his belt. "How about getting rid of these jeans?"

"How about I get rid of your panties first?"

Dante slipped Jaime's lacy thong down her legs, his own jeans and underwear following suit.

"I'm yours," he whispered, meeting her lips. "You can ask anything of me. You can have it hard and hot or gentle and slow – all night long."

Jaime bit his lower lip. "I'll have it all."

Dante chuckled and reached for the condom on the bedside table only to have Jaime take hold of his outstretched hand. "I'm on the pill," she said, rolling on top of him.

Her mouth came down on his in a passionate kiss, her head humming in a cloud. She took her time riding up ecstasy hill, eager to enjoy the explosion ready to erupt. With every thrust, the long-awaited summit approached until Jaime reached that blissful point and tumbled over the top. Her cries merged with Dante's as they both climaxed, their taut bodies gradually collapsing into a sated embrace.

Limp and spent, Jaime lay on Dante's chest, her breathing heavy and uneven, their skin damp from the effort. She traced an idle pattern across his chest while Dante grazed her cheek with a light touch before he took her hand and placed it over his heart.

***

Dante woke to the sound of his phone buzzing. Leonora's name glowed on the dark screen.

Shit!

He crept out of bed and tiptoed into the dim hallway, easing the door shut behind him. "Do you know what time it is?" he growled.

"I need your help, Dante."

Dante leaned against the wall, grinding his teeth. "It's not even six-thirty."

"It's urgent!"

Christ Almighty. Why was everything urgent with the woman?

"I'm being blackmailed."

Dante ran a hand through his hair. "I know that."

"No, you don't." Leonora's voice shrieked down the phone. "I'm being blackmailed by someone else."

"What? Look, I can't talk now. I'll ring when I get to the office."

Leonora's persistent voice whistled down the phone. "I need to speak to you *now*!"

"I said I'll speak to you when I get to the office." He flicked off the phone and rubbed a hand over his beard.

Swearing, he turned to find Jaime, eyes narrowed into suspicious slits. Shit, how much had she heard?

He pulled her into his arms and stroked her hair.

Jaime withdrew from his caressing hand. "What does she want this time?"

There was no fooling Jaime. The woman must have a seventh sense. "Nothing that can't wait until later." He scooped her up and stepped back into the bedroom.

***

The smell of fresh coffee floated into the bedroom, making Jaime's stomach grumble. She reached out to find a cold, empty space. The clock on the bedside table showed a little after nine.

Hauling herself out of bed, she wriggled into Dante's shirt and shuffled out of the room. The strong aroma pulled her like a magnet. A few footsteps away from the kitchen, she was stopped by a knock at the door. Noticing Dante's keys on the work surface, she snatched them up and hurried down the hallway, a witty comment on the tip of her tongue.

In one sharp movement, she hauled open the door.

"So you're back?" Leonora stood with hands on hips. "Where is he?"

Jaime stared at Leonora, dressed in a luxurious fur coat with black leather boots. The woman's long auburn hair was styled in tight ringlets, giving an air of Medusa. The contrast between the mass of flamboyant hair against pale skin and flashing blue eyes made Jaime unconsciously look away for fear of being turned to stone.

"If it's Dante you're looking for, he's not here."

Leonora tapped an impatient foot. "Then where is he?"

"At work."

"He's not. I've already phoned."

Leonora was grating on her nerves. "It never crossed your mind that he doesn't want to speak to you?"

"He wouldn't do that to me."

"If you're looking for trouble, Leonora, you've come to the right place. I'm in a perfect mood for a fight. I haven't had my daily dose of caffeine yet."

"You're an ambitious little thing, aren't you, Mademoiselle Housekeeper?" Leonora prodded a hard accusing finger onto Jaime's chest. "Well let me tell you something, Miss Social Climber, it won't work with Dante. He's having a fling with you, as all men do, I hear. He'll end the relationship before you know it. He always does."

While Leonora continued her condescending tirade, Jaime's antennas came to life, adjusting themselves to attack mode. Before she knew it, she raised her hand and slapped Leonora hard on the cheek.

Jaime held onto her stinging hand. Blast! What had come over her? She'd never hit anyone before. Could the smack have been for calling her a housekeeper or a social climber? Perhaps it was just because it was Leonora.

Hand on cheek, Leonora gaped like a fish out of water.

"I think that was your cue to leave," Jaime said.

"You trollop!"

Jaime raised her hand for a second shot. "Get out and keep out of my sight."

Leonora stepped out of the apartment, and Jaime slammed the door. With both hands pressed on her forehead, Jaime leaned back against the door on trembling legs.

"This is nowhere near the end, you whore." Leonora yelled from the other side of the door. "I'll do as I please. So go back to that hole of yours and stay there."

Jaime breathed down uncontrollable rage, both fists clenched tight. Unwilling to hang around to hear the string of swear words ringing after her, she headed straight for the kitchen, desperate for that mug of strong coffee.

Her phone rang from somewhere in the flat. She ignored it, not in the mood to talk. At least not for the moment. She had to calm down.

Realising it could be Dante, she rushed to the singing phone. A photo of Grant smiled on the screen. Her bad mood evaporated.

"Grant!"

"How are you, little sister?"

"Better now I've heard your voice"

Grant chuckled. "Listen, I'm in Paris for business. I thought I could come and see you?"

Jaime's lips pressed flat. "How do you know I'm in Paris? Did mum tell you?"

"Yep, and I'm killing two birds with one stone. I have a new contact with a Parisian bank, and yes Mum is worried about you."

"Wants you to report back on my choice of partner?"

"She cares about you, Jaime. And believe it or not, I'm not lying about my work."

Jaime bit her thumbnail. She'd love to see Grant, and if her mother could be reassured about Dante, that would be the cherry on the icing.

"Are you free this evening?"

***

"I don't care about the new blackmailer!"

Dante removed his jacket and threw it on a chair. He was furious. He'd planned an appointment to see Leonora, but she hadn't been at the mansion when he'd called. He'd wasted precious time.

"I understand."

"No, you bloody well don't understand." The bark of his voice surprised even him. He was going to be late back home and resented Leonora for it. "All I want is to be left alone."

Leonora's eyes widened as Dante carried on yelling.

"I agreed to help with this sticky matter. I now regret it," he said.

"Dante–"

He held up a hand. "I've asked another lawyer to deal with your problems."

Gazing past Leonora, Dante picked up on his reflection in the mirror above the fireplace. His angry profile twitched with rage. He had to calm the burning rage hissing through him. Was it worth letting the volcano in him erupt? This wasn't like him at all.

A heavy atmosphere hit the room. Leonora withdrew to the far end, her gaze never leaving his.

Dante adopted a calmer tone. "Jaime told me you insulted her."

Leonora sniggered. "That's a bit of an exaggeration, isn't it?"

"Jaime is not one for lying or exaggerating. Besides, what were you doing at the flat?"

"I needed to see you."

Dante breathed slowly to calm his anger. "I told you we'd discuss things at the office."

"Did you?" Leonora's lack of innocence betrayed her.

"So why didn't you leave when you discovered I wasn't there?"

"I did."

"But not until you'd insulted Jaime."

Leonora pushed a stray lock of hair away from her face with a trembling hand.

"We were lovers once, Leonora, and I let none of my previous girlfriends trouble our love affair."

"I know," Leonora whispered.

Dante grabbed his jacket from the chair and came to stand in front of her. "So I ask the same of you. Leave. Jaime. Alone."

There was a long silence where only their eyes spoke as they glared at each other.

"Have I made myself clear?" Dante asked.

Leonora gazed at the carpet.

"Have I made myself clear?'

"Yes, Dante."

"And I swear to God, if you upset Jaime again, you'll lose my friendship for good. I won't be as patient as I am today. Got it?"

Dante left the room cracking his knuckles.

No sooner had he slammed the door than Leonora's angry wailing broke through the air.

***

Jaime's stomach swirled. The moment of truth had arrived.

In a few minutes, she'd have her answer. Would her brother accept Dante? Or would she remain morally alone in France?

The doorbell rang, and Jaime hurried to the door.

"Grant!" she shouted, throwing herself into his arms.

Grant twirled his sister round and round, just as he'd done when she was a child. "Sorry I'm late. Had a bit of a problem getting here. Got off at the wrong metro stop."

Jaime giggled and led her brother down the hallway to the living room.

Dante got to his feet. "I'm Dante," he said, smiling.

Her brother shook Dante's extended hand. He was in observation-mode. Narrowed eyes, head slightly tilted to one side, twitching lips. Nothing would go amiss. Bloody hell, what a cold start.

Grant sat opposite Dante at the table. They began with small talk. The weather. Grant's business in France. Followed by meatier subjects like Dante's situation and his intentions for Jaime's new life. Rigid in their posture, both men spoke in an overprotective manner. Were they having a competition? Seeing who could outdo the other?

Jaime bit her nails and listened on. If she didn't get Grant alone in the kitchen soon, she'd have no more to chew. She'd hardly touched the sushi, but kept sipping the chilled koshu white wine. Her head spun, and anxiety cramped her stomach.

"Er...Grant, could you help me in the kitchen?" Jaime asked when she couldn't stand the tension any longer.

Grant turned from Dante and grinned. "Waiting for the verdict?"

Jaime rolled her eyes. Did he have to make it so bloody obvious?

"Well?" she asked once they were alone.

Grant gave Jaime one of his lopsided grins. "You're worried, aren't you?"

"Stop being a mean bastard. Just put me out of my misery."

His laugh blasted around the kitchen, surprising her. Jaime took a few steps down the corridor and peeked into the living room. Dante sat patiently, swirling the wine around his glass, eyes roaming around the room.

"What do you want me to say?" Grant asked when Jaime returned.

"I want you to be honest."

"I like him."

"Are you serious?" Jaime jumped up and down.

Grant grabbed hold of her hands and squeezed them. "He's frank and knows what he wants. If he's sincere, you two could hit it off. He's a man, Jaime. Not like some of the boys you dated in the past."

Jaime's eyes sparkled. "So, I'm right to stay and give it a go?"

"I think so. Dante's capable of looking after you now he knows what you're up against."

Jaime looked away.

"You haven't told him, have you?"

Jaime kept silent.

"The more you share your problem, the less you'll have to deal with on your own. This problem isn't going to go away by you ignoring it. Maybe Dante can help."

Jaime plucked at an imaginary piece of fluff on her sweater.

"The stalker managed to get a note to you. Don't underestimate the swine. You have to confide in someone. I think that person could be Dante." Grant rubbed his hand up and down Jaime's arm. "Let's get back. The food's getting cold, and we need another drink."

Taking hesitant steps behind her brother, Jaime wondered how Dante would react if he knew what she was up against. Would he still want to get into a serious relationship? Would he still want her, full stop?

She couldn't tell him just yet.

Chapter 25

He entered the small restaurant where a waiter showed him to an empty table in the middle of the room.

"I'll sit there." He pointed to a small table not far from the entrance.

"Er..."

He gave the waiter a fake smile, exhibiting nicotine-stained teeth. "I said, I'll sit there. Is that a problem?"

The waiter drew back. "No problem, sir. Can I get you something to drink?"

He pulled out a chair and sat with a perfect view of the door. "A beer."

The waiter returned after a few minutes with the drink and a small dish of peanuts. He took a long sip of the cool beverage, determined eyes fixed on the entrance.

Marcel had told him that René needed an urgent delivery. He was happy to carry out the transaction. There were still a few questions left unanswered. Like where the third de Vere hung out, and if the English girl was living with him.

The next person to enter the restaurant was the garage owner, rubbing his hands. Pathetic prat.

He waved René over and popped some peanuts into his mouth.

"Hello, my friend," René greeted. "No problem getting home with the car?"

"What can I get you to drink?"

René licked his lips. "Oh, I don't know if I should. Can't hold my liquor. Tend to say things I regret later."

"You're safe with me, René. We're two of a kind."

René grinned.

"Champagne to celebrate my new car?" He captured the waiter's attention with a click of the fingers.

"Why not?"

He ordered a bottle of champagne along with a couple of shots of vodka. René raised a glass and finished the champagne in one go. "To your new car."

"To my new car," he repeated, taking tiny sips from his.

René changed glasses and downed the two shots of vodka.

Fucking hell! He'd better get the transaction done before René got too pissed to pay.

He took a brown package out of a pocket and passed it to René under the table. René slid an envelope towards him, making sure not to knock the glasses. Without a word, he scooped up the envelope and glided it into an inside pocket.

"Aren't you going to count the money?" René whispered.

"No need. Marcel knows where to find you."

René downed glass after glass, well on his way to getting sloshed.

"Calm down," he said to the garage owner. He only wanted to loosen the man's tongue, not get the man pissed. The garage owner needed to be slowed down before he became a liability. Didn't the man know how dangerous his job was? He couldn't afford to get caught. He had a trollop to find.

The garage owner wiped his mouth on the back of his hand. "You know when a man needs a drink."

He smiled when René hiccupped. Now was the time to question the man before he got too drunk to talk. Grabbing the bottle chilling in the ice, he filled René's glass once more. "I need your help."

"Whatever you want, mon ami."

"Do you know where Luc de Vere's brother lives?"

René took another long gulp. "Course I do. Why wouldn't I?"

"So, where does he live?" he said, fondling the flick-knife in his trouser pocket. René was getting on his nerves big time. If the prick didn't get to the point, he'd have to use some persuasion.

"Somewhere in Paris, isn't it?" he said.

"That's Dante de Vere the lawyer you're asking about, isn't it?" René said, raising his glass.

Of course it is, you fucking dumbass. "Yeah, that's him." He grabbed René's arm, preventing him from taking another gulp. "What's his address? I'd like to surprise my friend."

René gazed at him through blurred eyes.

"Where does he live?" he asked, slowly getting annoyed.

"Er…in a posh area of Paris."

Might have guessed.

"I'll jot down the address." René took out a pen and struggled to write Dante's address on a paper serviette. After a great deal of puffing and panting, the garage owner handed over a scrawl of letters.

"Thanks for that." He released the knife he was holding in his pocket and grabbed the napkin. "I've got another delivery to make," he lied, turning away from the scent of drink wafting across the table.

"Better make a move then?" René slurred, taking the keys from his pocket.

The garage owner toppled down the two steps leading from the restaurant onto the cobbled pavement. After staggering a few more metres, René doubled over and vomited. Wiping his mouth on his sleeve, he struggled to climb into the car and eventually drove away.

"What a state to get into," he said, shaking his head. With a bit of luck, the prat might even kill himself.

He grinned as he held onto the precious scribbled note, his smirk widening as he bounced down the road. Things were getting exciting. He knew where to find the bitch. Had to keep his nose clean though. Keep his knife out of sight. He couldn't afford to blow off steam just yet.

When the time came, he'd vent out big time.

He'd skin her.

Chapter 26

Dressed in a strict, black-tailored suit and red silk blouse, Jaime paused in front of the office building, ready for her first day at work. She'd let a few weeks pass since her arrival in Paris. Dante had suggested she take her time. They both agreed on her starting work on the second of May, the first being la fête du travail, the French traditional Labour Day.

A little nervous, Jaime filled her lungs with fresh air and stepped inside. She remembered colleagues who worked with their other halves. Continual raised voices with foul language coming through the walls of closed offices. Jaime didn't want any of that.

The bright reception area was welcoming. White cerusé parquet covered the floor, setting off the beautiful acajou reception counter. Antique portraits hung from the white walls.

With bold steps, Jaime strode up to the lifts and pressed the call button. Dante's company had the whole sixth floor. Once inside, Jaime studied the floor location numerals until the lift ground to a halt. She stepped out into another warm reception area.

"Good morning. You must be Miss Sanders?" An eye-catching receptionist in her mid-fifties sat behind the desk. She wore tortoiseshell rimmed glasses and an immaculate white blouse, giving an air of professionalism. Dante had vaguely mentioned the efficient assistant.

Jaime strolled up to the woman. "You must be Francine."

The receptionist nodded. "Not too nervous for your first day?"

"A little."

Francine's face broke into a warm smile as she lifted the phone. "I'll inform Mr. de Vere you're here."

Jaime thanked her.

"He's waiting for you," Francine said, replacing the phone. "His office is at the end of the couloir."

Jaime peered down the wide curved corridor, stretching out in front of her. It disappeared from sight after about ten metres. She hitched her bag higher on her shoulder and headed towards Dante's office, hesitant heels clicking on the old-fashioned parquet.

She found a brass plate with Dante's name to the left of a polished mahogany door. Taking another deep breath, she gave a quiet knock and slid her head round the door. Dante gestured her in, all the while talking on the phone. Judging by the tone, he wasn't happy.

"There are one or two things I would like seen to. And *I* will tell you which files to deal with first. Do I make myself clear?"

Jaime pointed to the door and mouthed, 'Shall I leave'?

Dante shook his head and pointed to the chair in front of the desk.

Bloody Hell! Straight to the point.

She sat on the edge of the chair and listened to him bellow.

"I wasn't asking you. I was *telling* you! If you aren't capable of doing what I ask, I'll have to find someone who is."

Dante's voice softened while he gazed at Jaime. Easing back into the chair, he loosened his tie and continued the conversation. "Good. Now we've agreed on certain things, I want all the information by this time next week."

Dante replaced the phone and put both hands behind his head. "Madame."

"Maitre de Vere," she teased.

Dante chuckled. "Good to have you here. I'll get Francine to show you to your office. Once you're settled, come back and we'll look at your first assignment. I need to check something with a colleague first."

He called the receptionist on the intercom.

Francine arrived and accompanied Jaime into a smart office down the corridor. It overlooked the avenue and was equipped with the usual furniture. A modern rectangular desk was set against the wall to the left of the window with all necessary work equipment. Jaime walked around the desk, running excited fingers over the smooth, polished surface before relaxing in the black leather swivel chair.

Delighted with what she saw, Jaime returned to Dante's office. He made room for her on the round table opposite his desk and they discussed her first assignment.

She poured herself into the document, her pen skimming across the pages, leaving red scribbles to various parts of the text. It would have been quicker to correct the document on the computer, but she guessed Dante wanted her with him. Who was she to complain?

A little before noon, Dante broke the silence. "How's it going?"

Jaime looked up, pleased he'd brought her concentration to an end. She'd read so much, words were merging into one incoherent muddle.

"Time for lunch?' she asked.

"Yes, but you'll have to eat without me."

The corners of Jaime's mouth took a dive.

"Sorry, chérie, I've got have an important business lunch which I can't get out of."

Doing her best to hide her disappointment, Jaime gathered the rest of the assignment, blew him a kiss, and left the office.

***

Shortly after returning from lunch, a succession of melodic notes brought Jaime out of a difficult translation. She grabbed the office phone to have Francine's excited voice chirp into her ear. "You'd better come to reception."

Jaime raised an eyebrow. "Why?"

"Just come quick."

Jaime hurried down the corridor, bizarre thoughts coming to mind. Francine hadn't mentioned anything earlier when Jaime had returned. What could have happened in the meantime?

Stepping into reception, Jaime was welcomed by a beaming Francine, pointing to a beautiful bouquet of red roses. "They're for you."

Jaime brushed hesitant fingers across the delicate buds. "They're lovely."

"Who are they from?" Francine bounced from one foot to the other.

Jaime released the tiny card from the cellophane wrapper, knowing perfectly well the flowers were from Dante. She read the message to the receptionist.

"Guess who?"

Francine grinned while Jaime stooped over the flowers and buried her nose in the sweet velvet petals.

"Aren't you lucky?" Francine said.

She was. Not only did she have a man who loved her, he also made her happy by sending flowers.

"I need a vase, Francine. I'm going to put them in my office. I want to see them every time I look up from my work."

***

With his VIP meeting behind him, Dante stepped out of the building in one of Paris's quieter neighbourhoods, visions of Jaime dancing in his mind. He was eager to get home.

Obscure velvet clouds smothered the light, darkening the early evening. A few drops of rain fell from the overcast sky, and Dante pulled the warm jacket collar higher around his neck. With lowered head, he tried to stop the cool spots of water from dropping on his face. He needed to hurry. It wouldn't be long before the hesitant drops turned into a curtain of water.

From a shop window, Dante glimpsed the reflection of movement on the other side of the road. His muscles tensed. The faint light from a nearby lamp post illuminated the doorway of a building where two medium-height men dressed in black stood watching him.

He swallowed hard and took regular breaths. Something didn't feel right.

To avoid suspicion, he strolled to the end of the road, studying the contents of various shop windows. After a few more long strides, he took a quick peek over his shoulder before he turned into a small alleyway – and broke into a run. Distance was all that mattered.

A good stretch down the passageway, with his back up against the wall, Dante clutched his briefcase against his chest, fighting back the rising panic. Had the Albanians gained ground on him?

Footsteps approached, and Dante's breathing stuttered. The men came into view at the end of the alley. Any second now, one of them would look his way. He had two choices. Stay put and fight or move.

Dante bolted across the alleyway, opened the nearest shop door, and froze. He hadn't been in one of these boutiques for a long time.

"Good evening, sir. Can I be of any assistance?"

Despite his past fright, Dante let out a nervous chuckle. Gathering his wits, he scanned the boutique before pointing to the display unit behind the shop assistant. "I'll have one of those, please."

The assistant reached for the sexy black and red basque corset. "In leather or silk?"

Dante raised an eyebrow. *Is he serious?*

"Silk...and pop in a garter while you're at it."

The young man smiled. "Could I just make a comment on the size of the corset, sir?"

Dante gazed down at his curved palms. "The one on the model looks just right."

"Gift-wrapped?"

"Please."

While the shop assistant wrapped the articles, Dante headed to the door. Pulling back the blinds, he peered out. No one. He let out a deep breath. This unexpected event had brought on a wave of anxiety. He needed something to loosen the tension. The gift for Jaime would help.

Dante paid the young chap and stepped out into the alleyway, raking the surroundings for any suspicious movement. Satisfied he was alone, he regained his composure, anticipating the evening to come. He knew exactly how to unwind.

***

A little after midnight, once all the pent-up steam had evaporated and the corset had taken the place of the shade on the bedside lamp, Dante took Jaime's hand and kissed her palm. He'd been worried to how she'd react to the gift. She hadn't disappointed him.

He lay awake, listening to the rumble of distant thunder and the quiet pitter-patter of rain against the windows. With his mind slowly sliding into sleep, he let out a contented yawn.

Jaime snuggled closer and placed a chaste kiss on his chest. "Thanks for the flowers."

Dante was only half listening as he dropped off to sleep, but he did ask himself a question.

Which flowers is she talking about?

Chapter 27

After a busy day at work, Jaime looked forward to a quiet evening with Suzanne. She needed a rest after the night before. The visions of what she'd got up to in that red, lacy corset still brought heat to her cheeks and fluttering butterflies deep inside her

Luc and Dante were away on a business trip. From time to time, the two brothers worked hand in hand. Luc had landed a contract with one of Paris's general contractors to bring creativity and artistic elements to a building project. Dante had helped draw up the contract.

It had been Dante's idea for Jaime to stay with Suzanne. She didn't know why he'd insisted, but he seemed on edge about something. No doubt work. The business trip meant a night away, but he'd be able to relax. Being with Luc would give him other things to talk about.

Jaime rushed in through the front door, calling Suzanne's name.

"I'm in the kitchen," a voice chirped from the other side of the house.

Jaime gave Suzanne a big hug. "Great to see you again."

"Nice to see you too. How's your new job? Enjoy working with Dante?"

Jaime grabbed a couple of wine glasses from the cupboard. "Yep."

"Did you like the flowers?"

Jaime paused with the glasses in mid-air. "Oh, I assumed they were from Dante. You didn't sign."

"Thought you would," Suzanne said with a cheeky grin. "Need to keep Dante on his toes. We know he can be domineering at times, but he's a good man. He's been through a lot with having to keep a low profile."

Jaime gave a weak smile.

"Right. Let's get the evening going," Suzanne said, bringing the wine and nibbles into the lounge.

Curled up on the sofa, Jaime waited while Suzanne opened the bottle of red Chinon. "The kids are in bed; we're armed with ammunition, and I want to know all about your first day."

Jaime took a sip of the wine and was about to begin when a bubbly jingle rang out of Suzanne's phone. A smile lit up her friend's face. "It's Luc."

Winking, Jaime heaved herself off the settee.

"I'll put that bin bag I saw in the kitchen out to be collected. You'll have time to talk with Luc."

No sooner had she closed the door than her own phone vibrated.

"Dante!"

"Hi there."

"Bored, are you?"

"A little. You?"

Jaime continued down the gravel driveway, swinging the black bag. "Our evening hasn't started yet. Luc's on the phone to Suzanne. I'm taking the rubbish out to the bins at the front gates."

Dante chuckled.

"Will you miss me all alone in your hotel room tonight?" she teased, leaning against the driveway gate. "No one to give you a massage."

"You know I will. Shit! The clients have arrived. I have to go."

Jaime giggled. "Miss you."

"Miss you too."

She tucked her phone into her pocket and hugged herself, breathing in the country fields. Twinkling stars and a half-moon littered the dark sky. The beauty of the night brought a serene touch to Jaime's mood. She closed her eyes and sighed into the cool air.

A muffled snigger made her eyes flash open. The nightlife had silenced. Jaime's happiness turned to anxiety on noticing a movement from across the road. She snapped round towards the trees. Was someone watching? Or was it a trick of the shadows?

"Tu es très contente, n'est-ce pas?"

Not a ruse.

The razor-edged voice sent an eerie chill through her body. Why would anyone ask if she was happy?

"Who's there?" She hoped her voice sounded brave.

Jaime caught the glow of a cigarette on the other side of the road and grasped the unmistakable sweet smell of cannabis. Judging by the movement of the cigarette, the shadow was heading for the gate. Taking a long drag, the silhouette threw the rest onto the ground and crushed it under a heavy foot.

Cold sweat coated Jaime's skin. She stumbled backwards into the driveway, a frantic pulse beating in her ears, blocking out all other sounds.

"Restez," he chortled.

Shaking free of her thoughts, Jaime turned and headed back to the house, wondering who the hell that could have been.

"Suzanne," she called as she walked through the door, his mocking laughter still echoing in the air.

Standing against the wall of the house, Jaime held her head in her hands. Images of the past reappeared. So sharp, so vivid, so real.

His evil amber eyes while he assaulted her friend at a house party. That late-night walk home when she'd heard scuffling and groaning from the other side of the hedge. The split second when he'd stood up from stabbing his victim and their eyes had met. The trauma of bearing witness in court. Not to mention the dead cat sprawled out on the car bonnet.

Why these thoughts now? Was it the stranger's voice? Although he'd spoken in French, there was something about his tone that sounded familiar. Or was she being paranoid again?

Suzanne came out of the house with a sleepy Petrus trotting behind.

"Did you call?" Suzanne asked her.

Jaime chewed on her thumb. How could she explain what was in her head? It was a surging muddle. "I saw someone in the shadows at the bottom of the driveway."

Suzanne peered down to the gates while her hand reached for the button for the electric gates. Silence filled the garden. The only movement was the darkness as it lengthened across the sky, suffocating the last streams of light stretching out from the horizon.

"Let's get back inside to our drinks," Suzanne said, leading Jaime to the settee where Jaime downed her drink in one. The dog tagged along behind them and headed to his basket in the kitchen.

"Wow, Jaime, you must be thirsty. What's up?"

Jaime held out the glass for a refill. "Someone was smoking cannabis on the other side of the road."

"And?"

Jaime shrugged. "Maybe I'm paranoid, imagining danger everywhere. It could be a passer-by."

"Probably is. He no doubt stopped for a smoke and a quick pee."

"But he spoke to me."

"So? Maybe he was being friendly. What are you getting wound up about?"

After a brief moment of hesitation, Jaime told Suzanne the little she'd told Dante. About the stalker in England and the anonymous letters. Suzanne listened without interrupting.

"So every time I see someone who appears a bit suspicious, I lose it," Jaime concluded. "I'm recovering though, thanks to Dante."

Suzanne stroked Jaime's hand. "I'm glad you told me. I feel even more like a friend now."

Jaime reached for the bottle and poured them each another drink, determined to change the subject. Anything to get her mind off the mysterious smoker. Talking about Dante would do the trick. With a forced smile, she turned to Suzanne.

"How about spilling the beans on Dante?"

Suzanne winked and popped a handful of nibbles into her mouth. "We'll need more than one evening. Dante's collected a hell of a lot of beans in his time."

Chapter 28

He jumped into the car and grabbed the vodka from the passenger seat.

Time to celebrate.

Wrapping clammy fingers around the small flask, he downed long gulps, shuddering as the blazing spirit scorched the back of his throat. He couldn't believe his luck. After finding no one at the de Vere flat, he decided to check out the address for Luc de Vere.

And bingo! He'd found the trollop.

No time to deal with the scared kitten now, but her punishment would be sweeter for the waiting. He'd make sure of that.

Taking a last gulp for the road, he tossed the flask onto the back seat and picked up the flick-knife from the dashboard. The corners of his mouth twitched upwards. He'd have fun and games with the bitch. He could see the little lady bleeding already.

The ringing of his phone brought him out of deep euphoria.

"Oui, Marcel."

Marcel's voice boomed. "Where the fuck are you?"

"What's your problem?"

"I've just had Le Marquis bellowing on the phone. You were supposed to make a delivery half an hour ago."

Shit! He'd forgotten. Too busy sniffing out Jaime. He rubbed a hand over his face and gazed at the bag of pills on the passenger seat. "I got stuck in traffic."

"What fucking traffic?"

He pulled the phone away from his deafened ear. Under different circumstances, he would have told Marcel where to shove the pills, but he needed the loot. No point in getting on the wrong side of this associate. He couldn't afford that. Not for the moment. Might still need the prick.

"I got held up in an accident. Tell your client I'll be there in under fifteen."

Marcel let out an exaggerated sigh. "Don't let me down, or you'll regret it."

Before he could say another word, Marcel hung up.

"You'll be the one who'll regret it if you hang up on me again!" he yelled, throwing the phone next to the bag of pills.

Grasping the steering wheel with all his strength, he pulled away, tyres burning on the tarmac. If Marcel pissed him off once more, Jaime wouldn't be the only one on he'd crack down on.

Chapter 29

Dante and Luc had returned from their business trip, and work had taken up a routine. More and more English-speaking clients sought Dante's advice, and Jaime found herself snowed under with translations. Some days, she couldn't even think straight.

Glad this particular day had come to an end, she'd taken advantage of the journey home to relax. It had been an exceptionally busy afternoon. Thank God Dante had decided to call it a day earlier than usual.

Exhaustion had fallen on her like a dead weight. She'd given up trying to keep her eyes open in the car. Dante's voice had become a faraway drone. Before she knew it, they'd arrived at the flat. She'd dozed off for the whole twenty-minute drive.

Jaime entered the apartment and trod on a small white envelope. Seeing her name in bold letters, she retrieved it from the floor and headed to the bedroom, eager to kick off her toe pinching shoes.

On opening the letter, she froze to the spot.

Tu pensais m'échapper?
Tu avais tort!
Même en France tu ne
seras pas à l'abri –
alors tiens-toi prête,
petite garce !

Oh, my God! He really has found me!

The notes never failed to send waves of panic galloping through her. Even after this long. She collapsed onto the bed and read the letter again.

Thought you could get away from me? You're wrong. You're not even safe in France – I'm coming for you, you little bitch!

Jaime put a hand to her mouth and muffled a scream. She'd left England assuming she'd be safe in France. Somehow, he'd managed to turn up on the scene. After only five months.

How did the stalker know where she lived? How did he, or maybe she, get Dante's address? What if it wasn't the same person?

This letter was in French, whereas the others had been in English.

Then again, it said she wasn't even safe in France. So, it had to be the same person. She choked on a sob. What the hell was she going to do?

The sound of Dante's voice brought her back to her senses.

Dante opened the bedroom door. "Jaime?"

"I won't be a minute." She slid the letter in the back pocket of her trousers. "I'm changing my shoes."

"We're going to be late."

"I said, I'll be there in a few minutes." Her snappy tone cut the air like a razorblade slicing paper.

"Hey, what's up?"

Jaime dabbed the corners of both eyes with a paper hanky. "Nothing important."

Dante tilted Jaime's chin to face him. "Want to talk about it?"

Jaime shook her head.

"A problem shared is a problem halved," he said.

Jaime gazed at him through bleary eyes before she eased up onto the tips of her toes. "I'm fine. Just a bit under the weather. Must be that time of month."

She pressed her lips onto Dante's in a deep kiss, promising herself to confide later. He'd only just finished with his own worries. Did he need another? Besides it wouldn't be fair to spoil his evening.

"Let's go. Otherwise we'll be late for Suzanne's birthday," she said, slipping into a pair of red leather flats.

She grabbed Suzanne's present from the bedside table and headed down the corridor to the front door, Dante's footsteps echoing hers.

***

Driving in silence, Dante sneaked a look at Jaime. In a world of her own, it was clear she wasn't going to chat. He sensed something was wrong. What could it be this time?

A horn blasted from behind them, bringing him back to his driving. Dante gave a quick glance into the rearview mirror then back to the road again. He'd been a little slow to pull away from the traffic lights. Was it necessary to make such a fuss?

The drumming of the rain on the car roof made him irritable. Glancing again into the mirror, he frowned. Same car still behind them. Was it tailing them? Or was he imagining things? He'd soon find out. He'd take the next turn on the right.

Without warning, the car dived out from behind, ignoring the speed limits, and rushed past in an angry spray to stop in front of him.

"What the fuck!" Dante slammed on the brakes.

Jaime snapped out of her reverie to see the mad car pull away. It came to a gradual halt at the next set of red traffic lights. "Bloody

French drivers. A fat lot of good that did you, mate. Stupid, dangerous overtaking only to end up in front of us."

Too worried to smile at Jaime's comments, Dante focused on the car's registration plates. Not a number he recognised. Not a person from the region either. Unless they were false plates. Who the hell could this idiot be? Or maybe not an idiot after all. What if this was intentional? A warning? What if it were the Albanians?

The lights turned green, and the road hog took a quick right turn, tyres screeching as the car swayed and torpedoed away.

Dante stared after the car, a deep-rooted fear biting into his gut. A call to Corentin was in order.

***

All was peaceful when they entered the country house a while later. The children were playing in the lounge when they saw Jaime and Dante.

"Tonton!" the twins squealed, running up for a hug.

Once the children had said their hellos, Suzanne took them by the hand. "Time for bed. You have to be up early for school."

The children let out a moan. They gave Jaime a goodnight kiss. Dante and their father received hugs.

"I'll take these two to bed before we start the aperitif. I won't be long. Could you get the verrines out of the fridge, Jaime?"

A quarter of an hour later, Suzanne joined her guests. Leonora had arrived and was speaking in her usual exuberant way. "Happy birthday," she said, kissing Suzanne on both cheeks.

Suzanne returned the embrace. "Thanks for coming. Xavier won't be long. I'm sure he won't mind if we open the champagne."

Luc unwrapped the foil, popped the cork, and filled the waiting glasses. While Dante handed out the drinks, Jaime couldn't overlook the curious way he gazed at Leonora.

"Bonn jure," Xavier said on arriving, imitating Jaime's English accent. "Aaw arr yoo?"

Jaime rolled her eyes. She wasn't in the mood. Not after the letter she'd received, and now with the way Dante eyed Leonora.

"I zee you arr eer," He came up to Jaime for a kiss.

Jaime held up a hand. "Look, Xavier, I hate people imitating my accent, so please stop."

Xavier turned an unbecoming shade of red. "Sorry if I offended you," he said in a low voice.

Suzanne let out a nervous cough. "I'll go up and check on the children."

Realising how abrupt she'd been, Jaime ran after her friend. "I'm sorry, Suzanne. I'm a bit unsettled tonight, and I've taken my bad mood out on Xavier."

Suzanne patted Jaime's arm. "He'll survive, but remember, my door is always open if you need to talk again."

A hard knot formed in Jaime's throat. "Thank you."

Something hot and wet made Jaime pull her hand back.

"He too can feel you're not your usual self." Suzanne nodded at Petrus. "They have this special sense." And she sped up the stairs, leaving Jaime stroking the dog's neck.

Giving herself a few minutes to regain her composure, Jaime turned and froze. Xavier and Leonora were making out in the kitchen.

Christ Almighty! Could this be the cause for Dante's strange looks? Did he know about this?

Suzanne returned to the lounge a few minutes later where she found a pile of presents. Jaime watched her friend while she opened gift after gift. Suzanne's delight brought back memories of a time when Jaime used to be carefree and happy, without a worry in the world. Enjoying life to the full, making the most of her young years.

Would she ever be that same person again?

***

When the time came to leave, they said their goodbyes, and Dante helped Jaime to the car. From the way her legs gave way every couple of steps, he reckoned she'd drunk more than required.

During the homeward journey, he recalled their evening. Thank God Jaime had been in a better mood than when they'd set off. She'd been on edge, worried about something serious.

Could she be holding things back again? He assumed they'd been clear. No more secrets. She obviously hadn't taken him seriously, but there was no point in pushing the woman. Unless Jaime decided to talk, he wouldn't get anything out of her.

He gazed at her sleeping body, the woman's features so much softer in sleep. The creased lines on her brow from earlier had disappeared, replaced by the serene appearance he loved most. The car eased round a sharp bend and Jaime let out a quiet moan before snuggling down again. Dante smiled and observed Jaime's chest rise and fall, tranquillity etched on her face.

He hoped one day, that look would remain forever.

Chapter 30

Dante took a break from reading and peeked at the Roman numeral clock on the office wall. A little after midday. Great, he'd managed to finish the complicated file before lunch and had kept to the mid-May deadline. Mornings after soirées were always a slow start, even more so after Jaime's strange behaviour of the night before.

He ambled down the corridor and popped his head around Jaime's office door.

"Oh, what a nice surprise. When are we going for lunch?" she asked.

"Sorry, I need to get back to the apartment. I'm expecting a letter from the bank." He caught the disappointment in her eyes. "But I'll make it up to you tonight."

Jaime wiggled her eyebrows and continued with her work.

In the pile of letters Dante thumbed through back at the flat, he came across one with no name or address. Nothing special about the texture of the paper. Nothing to indicate where it came from. Weighing it in his open hand, Dante couldn't understand why the letter gave him the creeps.

He slipped the paper-knife under the fold, and in one swift movement, slit the envelope open. Only one piece of paper lay inside. Unfolding it, he read the content.

**Je te trouverai toujours,
peu importe la distance
–petite Salope!**

Dante gaped at the crooked words glaring up at him.

I'll always find you no matter how far you run – little Slut!

Although this note was made from cut-out pieces of paper and not in the same language as the one he'd found in Jaime's room, Dante was persuaded it was from the same bastard.

***

Francine jumped on Jaime the minute she arrived in reception. "Where have you been? Dante's going insane."

Jaime rolled her eyes. "In commanding mode, is he? Am I not

entitled to a lunch break?"

Francine stared at her in silence, and Jaime sighed. She walked past the receptionist and tapped in Dante's extension number. He answered on the second ring.

"Oui!"

Jaime jumped at the curt remark firing through the phone.

"It's me," she said.

"Where the hell have you been?"

"Eating. Is that permitted in this company?"

"Don't test me, Jaime." Heavy tension echoed in his voice.

What stung his arse?

"Come into my office." His voice blocked out all argument.

Jaime headed to Dante's office, racking her brains. She couldn't for the life of her think what he wanted. There had been no cock-ups, and she'd always arrived on time.

Coming to a gradual halt in front of his office, she took a deep breath.

"Sit down," Dante bellowed before she had the chance to close the door.

Jaime perched on the edge of the chair, staring at Dante in his crisp suit. With both elbows propped on the desk, and his two index fingers touching his lips, Jaime waited for the volcano to erupt.

Crossing her arms over her chest, Jaime leaned back, allowing an awkward silence to fall between them. For reasons she didn't understand, he stared at her with a rage she'd never seen before.

Convinced he would make no effort to speak, Jaime broke the ugly hush. "Okay, so what's all this about?"

He shifted on his chair. "You do know there are no secrets that time does not reveal."

Jaime rolled her eyes. "Speaking from experience?"

"You know I am."

Instead of commenting, Jaime sighed with frustration and looked away.

"It's a quote from Jean Racine," he said.

"Never heard of him. An expert is he?" she asked, worried Racine might be right.

Dante took a folder out of his briefcase. "I came across some very unusual mail at the flat."

Jaime rubbed the back of her neck. She didn't like the tone of his voice. Low and authoritative, it sent a shiver up her spine.

Dante unfolded a piece of paper and placed it on the desk. Jaime's stomach lurched, and heat radiated through her body.

"It's a photocopy of a letter I found. The original is with the police."

Jaime took a few seconds to speak. "Where...where did you find the original?"

"At home with the mail, which means the bastard knows where you are."

Jaime fidgeted before lowering her eyes to examine a tiny scratch on the edge of Dante's desk. She lifted a finger and rubbed it.

"Have you had any other letters, Jaime?"

With quivering chin, Jaime looked up.

"Why didn't you come to me?" Hurt seeped through Dante's words. "I feel you're pushing me away."

Jaime returned her gaze to the desk. One second passed. Two seconds. Three. Remorse struck like a drill hammer. She stopped caressing the edge of the desk and looked up. "Perhaps I should have. I was so scared. I didn't know what to do."

A muscle flickered in Dante's cheek. "Scared of me?"

Scared of making a fool of myself.

Dante sucked in a deep breath. "If I shouted at you earlier, it's because my girlfriend is being stalked and won't talk to me. I told you we are a couple, and I meant it."

Jaime bit on her lower lip. The pain in Dante's voice and the way his shoulders drooped, hurt.

"Couples share, Jaime. I may not be much of a talker, but I care for you."

Jaime slipped a hand into her jacket pocket and pulled out the anonymous letter she'd found the evening before. She placed it on the desk next to the other.

Dante's lips twitched at the sight of the crumpled piece of paper. "Talk to me, Jaime. I want to help."

Jaime swallowed past the knot in her throat. "Like I told you, I got letters back in England. Left under the windscreen wipers of my car."

"Why didn't you go to the police?"

"I did, but with no leads, they were unable to find who it was."

Dante slammed a hand on the desk. "Bloody Roast Beefs!"

Jaime jumped at the spurt of anger.

"Sorry, please go on," he said, raking a hand through his hair.

"I couldn't take any more, especially after I found a dead cat sprawled across my car hood."

"The fucking bastard!" Dante pushed his chair back and stood in a rush, startling her.

"I had to get away, and quick. So, I left for France, only to find that the freak has now drawn level with me."

Jaime waited for Dante's reaction. His pained expression and reticence to speak were worse than his shouting. At least when he barked, she knew where she stood. The heavy silence turned Jaime's blood cold, making her doubt. Even more so when Dante put on his poker face.

Dante ran a hand across his beard. "Do you swear you have not received any other letters in France?"

Jaime nodded. "Apart from the one I received in the mail forwarded from my mother, this is the only other."

"Well, we'll need that card too."

"So what happens now?" Jaime asked, chewing a fingernail.

Dante took her note and placed it into the folder. "We're taking this note to the police. They need to know about it."

Jaime fell back into her chair. The tension bottled up over the past months began to melt. Dante knew about her fear and anxiety and was going to help. She felt lighter for coming clean. Happier they had no more secrets. No longer alone with her demons, she hoped this confession and her going to the police would change things. Because that bastard was still at large and gaining ground.

***

Jaime was shown into the inspector's office. Dante followed.

The room was small and plain with a desk and filing cabinet. A window behind the desk gave a view across the backyard of the station where a few police cars were parked. The inspector showed Jaime to the seat in front of the desk. Dante sat on the second chair.

"I'm glad you could come to leave your statement, Miss Sanders." The inspector's voice was gruff but calm. "I'm going to ask you some questions, and I'd like you to answer them as best you can."

Jaime nodded and watched the inspector settle himself in front of his computer.

"Right, so we know from Mr de Vere that you received some menacing letters back in England, and the reason you came to France was to escape them. Is that right?"

"Yes, that's right."

"And since you've been in France, you've received others."

"Yes. I think Mr de Vere gave them to you."

"That's right," the inspector said, taking the two letters and the Christmas card out of a blue folder. He rubbed his chin, his eyes flicking from the card to the letters. "What's puzzling me," he continued, "is that the card you received from England was written in English, and these two letters are written in French."

"As you can see from the notes written in French," Dante said in his lawyer voice, "he said that he'd find her wherever she went. It has to be the same psychopath."

Inspector Durand nodded and turned to Jaime. "Was there any pattern to the arrival of the letters in England?"

Jaime shook her head. "They came in dribs and drabs. Sometimes I'd receive two or three the same week."

"Did you ever see anyone suspicious hanging around the house?"

"Not that I can think of." Jaime let out a deep sigh. "I told everything to the English police."

The inspector nodded and continued with his questioning. Jaime answered politely even though she'd been through the same scenario back in England. Same questions. Same answers. Same end result. Nothing.

"One more thing before we finish," the inspector said, opening a drawer and taking out what looked to be a business card. "Do you know of anyone who may have reason to harm you?"

Jaime shook her head. "The police in England asked me the same questions but they didn't find any leads with regard to my old boyfriends."

Inspector Durand handed Jaime his card. "If you remember anything else that may help, please don't hesitate to contact me. In the meantime, I'll get my men to do extra rounds in your vicinity."

Jaime thanked him and with Dante's comforting arm around her waist, they left the interview room.

Back in the car, she slumped in her seat and picked at the skin around her thumb. "He's coming for me, isn't he?"

Dante leaned over to the passenger seat and put an arm around her shoulders. "We'll find him before he gets to you. I promise."

Jaime buried her face in Dante's chest. "Please don't make promises you can't keep."

"If need be, we'll put up CCTV outside the flat and catch the bastard. He's not going to hurt you." Dante pulled back and lifted her chin. "Do you understand? I won't let him."

Jaime bit her lower lip. The stalker was out there somewhere, waiting to make the final move. Whoever he was. The bastard she'd sent to prison was dead; unless he'd paid someone to carry out his dirty work before he died?

Surely not…

Chapter 31

Stretched out on the bed, he drew in a lungful of smoke, enjoying the pungent taste. Christ, he was ecstatic. Terrifying Jaime and blackmailing Leonora at the same time. The height of happiness. Well, almost.

What he needed was a screw with Miss Hoity-Toity. To show the bitch who was in charge.

He got up and put a hand into the pocket of his coat, hanging on the back of the chair. Pulling out the bottle of lube he'd bought at a sex shop, a sly grin spread across his face.

What if he gave the stuck-up bitch another visit? He hadn't fucked for quite a while. Well, apart from the whores he'd had to pay. This time, a whore would be paying him. How ironic.

Yeah, he quite fancied that. A quick knee-trembler with Leonora.

He flicked through the adult magazine until he came to the page where he kept an old photo of Jaime. His knife had slashed her so many times, it was difficult to make out her features. He ripped the photo into tiny pieces and tossed them in the air.

Time for a new photo. He knew exactly where to go.

Chapter 32

Holding open the car door, Jaime's phone rang for the second time.

"Hello."

Anxious, quick breathing fell into her ear before the caller hung up. Again. She rang the number back. "Mum! Why did you hang up?"

"Oh, hello, darling, I must have pressed the wrong key."

Jaime frowned.

"How are you, honey?"

Something was up. Her mother rarely called her 'honey'. "Great. I'm enjoying my new job, and Dante's a real love."

"I'm glad to hear that."

"What's up, Mum?" Jaime feared the worst. Antonia only got in contact on rare occasions.

"Nothing, darling. You've been in my mind a lot more since you left. I needed to hear your voice. I know I've never been good at communicating."

Jaime bit her lower lip, never at ease talking with her mother. Time to change the subject. "How's Grant?"

"Good, I suppose. He's been away for a few weeks. Some business deals to sign in the States. He should be back within the next couple of days."

A brief silence set in.

"Look, darling, I've got something important to tell you."

"I knew you were ringing about something."

All the noise around Jaime disappeared apart from the drumming in her ears and Antonia's faraway voice.

Her mother only said a couple of sentences before hanging up, but they left Jaime gaping at the phone. The words had landed straight in her gut. Jaime had always known something was not quite right with the way her mother reacted at times. Now she knew why.

If she'd known then what she knew now, would things have been any different between them?

***

"Grant, it's me," Jaime whispered down the phone.

She'd waited a few hours to see if she could come to terms with her mother's incredible news. As with all dreadful announcements, the revelation was so unbelievable, she needed help in accepting it.

"How are you?" Grant asked.

Jaime sniffed loudly before answering. "I don't know. Mum rang, and I found out about…I can't say it, Grant."

"Oh, hell!"

Jaime sucked in a deep breath. "You knew?"

A low groan echoed down the phone. "Yeah, Mum spilt the beans about the insurance letter."

Jaime closed her eyes and leaned back against the car. "This is scary. I assumed everything had been settled at Dad's death? What are we going to do? And why tell us now after all these years?"

Her brother's heavy breathing whistled down the phone. "I don't know. It came as a big shock."

"I tried ringing Mum back after she dropped the bomb, but she ignored my calls. I've been at my wit's end. I wanted to call you, but she said you were in the States. That's when I decided to text."

"You're having a rough time, aren't you, little sister?"

A nervous chuckle escaped Jaime's throat. "You could say that."

"Have you told Dante about Mum's call?"

Jaime remained quiet for a brief moment. "Not yet."

"When are you going to tell him?"

"I've only just told him about the letters."

"Because you've had more?"

"I received a couple here in France. Dante's taken them to the police. He's worried sick about what could happen to me."

"How the bloody hell did the stalker find you?" Grant's voice had risen to a shriek. "If he's in France, Jaime, come back to England."

"Dante's looking after me. Don't worry. I'm in good hands."

Grant let out a deep sigh.

"Do you think I need to bother him with this as well?" Jaime asked.

"You have to tell him, Jaime. To prove you trust him."

Jaime chewed on her thumbnail. "Do you think this is one of the reasons Mum...has been like she has?"

Grant took a sharp intake of breath. "Why should it be?

"Yeah, maybe you're right."

A short silence set in before Grant spoke, "I'm going to see what I can do from my end."

Jaime let out a feeble sigh. "Okay. Keep me posted."

"Sure and look after yourself, little sister. I'm worried about you, and please don't forget to tell Dante."

"Will do," she replied as she got into the car to drive home. *But not just yet.*

***

Dante watched Jaime enter the flat, dragging her feet. She headed straight for the bedroom, undressed without a word, and curled up in a little ball under the duvet. He didn't like the look of her ashen face. He knew what that meant. A migraine.

He went to fetch her medication. If she took the painkillers early enough, she'd avoid nausea and vomiting. By precaution, he put a basin next to the bed and half-closed the shutters. With the bedroom door ajar, he went to prepare himself something to eat. Jaime had spoken to him about her headaches. This was the second strong one she'd had since arriving in France. What was she worried about today?

Three quarters of an hour later, a groggy Jaime emerged from the bedroom with dishevelled hair, squinting as her eyes tried to accustom themselves to the light.

Dante opened his arms, and she settled next to him. "Do you want something to eat?"

Jaime shook her head. "Too soon," she managed to reply.

"Want to tell me what brought on your migraine?"

Jaime shook her head again.

"Later then," he said, kissing the top of her head.

"I think I'll take a shower," she whispered.

"Good idea. It'll release some of the tension."

Jaime smiled and disappeared into the bathroom.

Dante's mind boiled with questions, crying out for answers. She couldn't or wouldn't speak to him, and he feared the worst.

He gazed out the window onto the avenue. The soft streetlights glowed below, throwing the buildings into a mixture of shadow and geometric shapes. Raising his head to the beautiful mid-May sky, he spotted the moon's slim crescent hovering above the dark lines of the rooftops. He envied the peaceful vision. What he'd give to change places with the moon. To swing in the heavens with no worries or cares.

He rubbed a hand over his face and froze.

A black vehicle pulled up on the other side of the road and three strange men jumped out. Big, muscled, dressed from head to toe in black, they peered around before one of them rushed to a semi-lit doorway. The other two made a beeline for Dante's building. This didn't look like a random house to house visit. They knew exactly where they were going. They knew full well who they were after.

Dante headed to the door, grabbing the fire poker on the way. With an eye peeking through the peephole, his heart hammered when a massive form stalked up to the flat and pinned an ear to the wooden panel. Dante propped his back against the door and held his breath. Clammy hands slid down the weapon, but he gripped it tighter.

A loud deep-knuckle bang struck the door, and Dante leapt in the air. *Fucking Hell!*

His heart was about to explode. He put a hand to his chest in an attempt to silence the thumping. What was going on? And who the hell was this stranger?

Another knock echoed in the flat. Shit! He hoped Jaime wouldn't wander out of the bathroom and make a noise.

Rooted to the spot, each second seemed to last forever. He had to avoid making a sound.

When the man's heavy footsteps withdrew down the corridor, Dante let out the breath he'd been holding. He'd had enough. Enough of living in fear. Why had they told him he could come out of hiding? It had been too soon. He should have stayed at Montfort-Le-Gesnois. Hiding as a priest had been a good idea. No one had found him. He'd only been back in the capital for a short while and they were already on his doorstep.

He had to contact Corentin yet again. Tell him the bad buggers were back. Poking their noses where they shouldn't.

Unless Corentin already knew.

Chapter 33

The next few minutes passed in a blur.

With her body bent over the dining room table, Leonora heard him tear open the condom, and observed the wrapper fluttering down next to the photos he'd placed nearby. She grit her teeth. For a quick screw, he'd promised another photo at half price. She wondered now if it was worth it.

Never mind. She'd used her body before to get what she wanted. Once more wouldn't make any difference.

"Holy cow, this is better than any whore," he muttered.

The table legs creaked as he rammed into her from behind. Leonora blocked out the groans and obscene mumbling. She had to focus on her inheritance. If guaranteeing her future meant this sacrifice, she'd comply.

This inheritance was primordial. Besides, the sodding one year clause would be up in June. Next month. Then, no more blackmailers to pay. No more worries about getting found out. Her godfather could go to hell. She never saw much of him anyway. He hardly ever came out of his chateau, hardly spoke to her, but he had eyes everywhere, and they were good at reporting back. Hadn't he known when she'd slept with one of his old friends?

"Right, I'll be off now." He pulled back and tucked his shirt back into his jeans before grabbing the envelope with the money.

Leonora moved uncomfortably as he left the room, fear looping through her mind. This scum wouldn't be easy to deal with. Not like Maxime. She'd have her work cut out with the bastard.

Storming into the bedroom, she stripped off and raced into the shower eager to wash off the bastard's stale odour of nicotine and sweat. Ashamed to have let herself be used like that, she cried into the spraying water.

What was the matter with her? First Maxime, now this bastard.

This was all Maxime's fault. The swine had better not show up again or she'd kill him.

On second thought, she'd kill them both.

***

"Corentin, it's Dante."

Corentin's suave voice sailed down the phone. "How's it going, man?"

Dante opened the door to his building and stepped into the lobby. "Great. I had a road hog hot on my tail the other evening, almost caused an accident, and three men in black turned up for an unexpected home call."

"Shit."

Dante breathed through clenched teeth. "What's going on?"

"No idea, buddy. All's quiet on the Albanian front."

Dante snorted.

"Believe me, Dante. No one's after you."

Dante gripped the phone until his knuckles whitened. "Then what the hell's going on?"

"Wrong address?"

Dante ran a hand through his hair. Professionals never made mistakes. If they weren't after him, they had to be after Jaime. But those men in black were experts. He couldn't imagine them writing those wretched notes. This wasn't their doing.

Someone else was after Jaime. Another thing she hadn't told him? Unless Corentin was lying again. Fear and suspicion settled deep inside him.

"Are you still there, mate?"

Dante held the phone at arm's length. "No need to burst my eardrums."

Corentin chuckled, and let a brief silence fall between them. "You've got nothing to worry about."

Dante closed his eyes and leaned against the glass door. If only he could believe Corentin. They had a close bond because of their past dealings with the Albanians, and Corentin had been his contact during the mission. The one to protect him until the thugs had put him through hell. But now...

"I have to go." Corentin's voice brought Dante out of his reverie. "See you around."

Dante flipped the phone shut and shoved it into his coat pocket. A gasp escaped his throat when he opened the apartment block's letter box. Staring up at him was another envelope similar to the one he'd received before.

Impatient to read the contents, he ripped it open and read the note.

Tu as peur?
Pas encore?
Tu devrais !

Are you scared? Not yet? You should be!

The note had a photo attached. One of Jaime entering the building. The scum had even drawn a dagger in her back.

The threatening words and frightening photo shot out at him, making his muscles cramp. A wave of fury swept through him, and Dante found his fingers crumpling the envelope, destroying part of the evidence. Thank God he still had his leather driving gloves on.

He dropped the envelope and clenched his fist as a substitute. If he mentioned the note to Jaime, it would scare her witless. Not a good idea under the circumstances. Which meant another visit to the police.

He breathed in through clenched teeth. Time had come to settle Jaime in a safer place. The stalker was watching the building. Had even been close enough to take the photo.

Dante stooped and retrieved the envelope. The police would need the evidence. Straightening it out as best he could despite the gloves, Dante contacted the police. If he hurried, he could take the proof to the police station and be back home before Jaime.

Chapter 34

He was on the way home after another delivery, his mind billowing under the weight of his thoughts. All the things he could buy with the money he'd earned.

With an arm hanging out of the car window, he cruised down the avenue, thinking about the meeting with Leonora that morning. He enjoyed fucking the toffee-nosed Madame. Gave him a feeling of superiority. He'd have to get more copies of the prints made up.

The tall, metal lampposts cast a warm glow onto the street, illuminating the pavement's smooth, pale-grey stones. This upper-class part of the city was nothing like his neighbourhood. No graffiti. No beggars. No place for the likes of him. Even the weather seemed better here.

He spat out of the window and muttered a string of insults. One day, he'd live in an area like this with a plush car and designer clothes. First, he had a trollop to deal with. Nothing else mattered. With time to spare before his next appointment, he decided to take another peek at the lawyer's flat. An earlier visit to the architect's house had been a waste of time. Jaime hadn't been there. Where could the bitch be hiding?

Approaching his destination, he switched off the headlights and let the car creep along to the apartment.

Fucking hell! Adrenaline flooded through him. There she was next to her car. He couldn't believe it. The perfect opportunity he'd been waiting for to scare her – injure her even. Make her suffer a little before he played with her.

He slammed his foot down on the accelerator and the car thrust forward, the screech of the tyres capturing Jaime's attention. His heart rate accelerated as his unlit vehicle torpedoed forward. Jaime slammed the door shut, and ran around the car onto the pavement, dropping her parcel in the commotion.

Eager to see the damage done, he slipped a glance in his rear-view mirror.

"Shit, missed her." Disappointment etched into him. Angry with himself for missing his target, he took a longer look.

In a moment of inattention, the car swerved and sideswiped a parked car, ripping away the wing mirror and denting his passenger door. A dull clang echoed in the quiet street as the mirror bounced on the tarmac and landed in the gutter.

"Fuck her!" He slammed both hands on the steering wheel. Tiny bubbles of spittle formed at the corners of his mouth. Not only had he damaged his car, which meant an urgent visit to René, but he'd missed the bitch and had left evidence.

Tyres screeched as he spun onto the next side road, ignoring the 'no entry' sign, and hoping he wouldn't have a head-on collision with an oncoming car. Venomous hatred twisted across his features. He'd underestimated her. She was quick. Not a lucky night.

"Well, at least I scared the shit out of her," he guffawed. He switched the headlights back on and drove out of the side road onto the main boulevard.

***

With her gaze fixed on the ground, Jaime cradled her grazed, shaky knees. She'd fallen hard against the wall, both arms stretched out for the inevitable collision. Her hip had taken the brunt of the shock, and she'd thumped down heavily on the pavement.

She let out a strangled choke and nausea surged up from deep inside, but she focused on keeping it down, scanning the street, worried the mad driver would come back. This had to be another nightmare. She'd wake up in a minute, sweating and panting in bed.

A hand from behind clenched her shoulder.

Jaime's high-pitched scream ripped the air like a siren gone wild. She shook off the heavy hand and scrambled away.

"Jaime!"

Two worried brown eyes gazed down at her.

"Dante!" she shrieked, jumping up.

Panic hung everywhere. Even in Dante's eyes. Jaime couldn't concentrate on anything else apart from the anxiety shown there. Her heart raced and she broke out in a cold sweat. Negative ideas spiralled out of control ready to explode.

"Are you all right?" Dante wrapped his comforting arms around her trembling body. "I heard a car accelerate and you screaming."

Lost in sobbing, Jaime couldn't answer. Dante continued to speak, but she couldn't understand what he said. Her mind was a surge of utter confusion. Dante scooped her into his arms and entered the building.

"The present! The present!" she shouted, pointing to the road.

He propped her against the wall and ran to retrieve the parcel, looking both ways before venturing into the middle of the road.

Jaime cried even louder at the sorry state of the squashed brown package. That parcel could have been her. She'd been lucky. Only a sore hip and grazed hands and knees. How long would her good fortune last?

Back in the flat, Dante sat on the sofa with Jaime on his lap. His warmth seeped through her, shutting out the emotional pain. Every person needed an anchor, a secure attachment of love. Jaime had found her home port in Dante. She soaked up his vibes, calming her inner storm.

When Jaime's frazzled nerves turned into soft, soothing music, she spoke, "Someone tried to run me over."

Dante rocked her in his strong arms, whispering words of reassurance like a father would to a frightened child. After a while, he reached for his phone. "We need to call the doctor."

Jaime grabbed his hand. "It's only a sore hip. I've had worse bruises skiing."

Dante frowned.

"Please, Dante. I'm fine."

"If you're sure."

Jaime gave a weak smile. "I am."

"I'll get onto the police then."

Dante made a quick phone call to the station before pouring them each a strong drink. He returned with the glasses and sat down again.

Jaime took a sip of the liquor and told him about buying the surprise present and hiding it in the car, about creeping down to get it while he was on the phone and about the car speeding with no headlights, hitting another as it drove away.

Dante listened without interrupting. "This whole thing is getting out of hand."

"He tried to kill me, Dante!" Spittle built up at the corners of her mouth and her fidgety hands wouldn't settle. Deep inside, stomach pains came to life.

Dante reached for her hand. "Jaime."

"This isn't the life I want," she sniffed, squeezing his outstretched hand. "I'm not living. I'm surviving one day after the other. I can't plan ahead for fear of *him* putting an end to it all."

Dante pulled her nearer.

"I'm scared, Dante. He's going to get me." Jaime's voice was no more than a sorry whisper.

"He is *not* going to get you. I won't let him."

Jaime lay back on the couch, worn out from crying. Grant hadn't been able to keep her safe. What made Dante think he could? Had he become Superman overnight?

She let out a huge yawn and rubbed her hip. "I'll stay here for a while."

Dante caressed her forehead. "You do that. I'll deal with the police."

***

Dante dashed out of the flat and into the street towards the car that had been hit. He refused to sit around and wait. The vehicle could have been damaged and there might be evidence showing what happened. Thugs from the crime rings did this sort of thing. First a warning, then tougher action.

He lifted his face to the sky and groaned. How the hell was he going to protect her?

Chapter 35

Seated in one of the city's luxury tearooms, Jaime took in the beautiful decor. Crisp damask tablecloths and fresh flowers on the tables added to the charming vintage style. People ate their sweet pastries and sipped bergamot tea from their white porcelain cups. Jaime liked the pleasant atmosphere. The cosy ambiance with distant chatter rising and falling as the other customers commented on the food added a homely touch to the place.

Suzanne had called early that morning and had invited her for afternoon tea.

At first Jaime refused, wondering if she'd be good company after the previous night's trauma. When she explained what had happened, Suzanne persuaded her that a cup of tea away from the flat would do her good. Despite the distraction of the tearoom, Jaime couldn't stop thinking about the maniac car with its crazy driver.

The doorbell jingled and Jaime looked up, recognising her friend. Suzanne greeted Jaime with a quick hug before taking a seat. "It's good to see you again."

Jaime smiled. "I'm glad to be out of the flat. Dante refused to let me work today. Wants to keep me snug and toasty at home. I've had enough of moping around the apartment."

The waitress arrived and they placed their orders. Suzanne ordered a mint tea with a large slice of chocolate gateau. Jaime could only manage the tea.

"Must be hell for you," Suzanne said once the waitress left.

"It is." Jaime fiddled with a silver teaspoon. "The police suggest I disappear for a while. During that time, they're going to do extra rounds in the neighbourhood – especially at night."

Suzanne placed the napkin on her knees. "Where will you go?"

"No idea."

The waitress arrived and placed their order on the table before wishing them bon appétit. Suzanne tucked into the cake while Jaime served the tea, eager to hug the cup and warm her cold fingers.

"Why don't you come and stay in Rambouillet? We'll be away in Deauville for the weekend, leaving this afternoon after school, and Petrus needs a doggy sitter."

For a flash of a moment, there was relief. Suzanne had come to her rescue. Jaime loved the country house. Had even wished she could remain there when she first arrived in France. Looking after the dog wouldn't be a problem. In fact, she'd become quite attached to the mutt.

On the other hand, the house was far in the country. What if the stalker found her? Although the solution didn't bring total relief, it was a start. She should be grateful to Suzanne. Jaime reached for her friend's hand. "Thank you."

Suzanne smiled and picked up the fork for another mouthful of cake. "Have the police come up with anything yet?"

Jaime shook her head. "Dante showed them where I was almost knocked over. A little further down the road, they found a car with its wing mirror smashed off. It had a navy-blue scrape down the side."

"No witnesses, I suppose?"

"I didn't see anyone, and nobody came to help me when I fell."

Suzanne reached across the table and rubbed Jaime's arm in sympathy. "Not much to go on, is it?"

"Not really."

Jaime had racked her brains until it shut down. Dante had questioned her so many times, she was sure she could take on any interrogation and pass with flying colours. She loved the man to bits, but it was nice to get away from the cross-examination. The lawyer in him couldn't help taking over.

After a nice half hour of girls talk, Jaime took a last sip of her tea, and almost choked on seeing a familiar silhouette at the cake counter.

What the hell is he doing here? I thought he was in Montfort-Le-Gesnois.

"Hi, ladies."

Suzanne looked up. "Corentin!" she exclaimed, giving him a quick kiss. "What's brought you to this neck of the woods? I haven't seen you for ages."

So, they know each other.

Corentin took Jaime's hand and brought up it to his lips. "Had some unfinished business to sort out."

The chuckle that rumbled out of his throat transformed his profile to its devilish self, making Jaime wonder what he was up to.

Corentin turned to Suzanne; and held up the patisserie box. "I also fancied some chocolate cake for tonight. We both know they have the best here."

Suzanne giggled, but Jaime wondered if her friend knew about Corentin's connection with Dante's recent need to go into hiding.

"How are Luc and the kids?" he asked.

"Oops, talking of kids," Suzanne squealed, taking a quick peek at her watch, "I have to fetch the twins from school. If there's a lot of traffic on the road back to Rambouillet, I'll be late. Pity we couldn't spend more time together."

Corentin put an arm round Suzanne's shoulder. "We can chat in the car if you give me a lift. My car's in the garage. Had a slight accident. Driving me there would do me a huge favour."

"Sure, but we'll have to leave right now." Suzanne slipped Jaime an apologetic look.

Jaime's skin tingled. Was it a coincidence that Corentin's car had been damaged in an accident? She grabbed her bag and stood. "I have to get back anyway."

While Suzanne paid the bill, Corentin stood deliberately close to Jaime. She'd lost count of the number of times she'd taken steps back. Each time, he shuffled nearer, invading her personal space. If she hadn't known any better, she would have sworn his arm was glued to hers.

Suzanne finished paying, and they all stepped outside into the busy crowd. Jaime watched Suzanne drive away with a happy, boisterous Corentin. Was it a twist of fate that Corentin happened to be in Paris?

Or was he tailing her?

***

Late that afternoon, Jaime packed a small travel bag. She prepared enough clothes for the few days to come, folding them carefully. Her bleary eyes wandered around the cosy bedroom that had become a cocoon. A peaceful retreat. Now she had to leave it because of the stalker. How many more times would she pack cases?

Dante appeared at the doorway. "Do you need any help?"

What help did she need to pack a small night bag? She was only going away for the weekend. Wasn't she? "I think I can manage."

She tugged hard on the zipper and threw the bag onto the soft carpet before slumping onto the bed. Dante came to sit next to her. "It's not for long."

Jaime raised her gaze. Dark shadows circled Dante's eyes. His blank stare travelled through every cell in her body, bringing on an immense sadness. He was having a hard time too. She hated herself for bringing him into this sorry life. They didn't need her dark mood right now.

With a forced smile, she jumped up and grabbed the travel bag. "Come on, let's go."

They strode to the car, gazing up and down the street. Dante drove away in silence, his hands tight on the steering wheel. Jaime was so wrapped up in bleak thoughts; she hardly noticed Dante's presence. Besides, what was there to say? She had to admit, this had been perfect timing. The police couldn't post a gendarme in front of the flat twenty-four hours a day.

Jaime kept her head turned towards the window, hiding fresh tears. "I'm going to be lonely as hell," she whispered.

"I'll be with you every night," Dante said in a confident voice. "I feel better with you out of the firing line."

The anthracite clouds huddled together darkening the afternoon. Where were the beautiful May days the French boasted about? Huge drops of rain thumped on the roof of the car, and Jaime's heart matched the rapid tempo. Beads dribbled down the windows, and the water spraying up from the car wheels made her even more miserable.

The rain fell heavier, thrashing down on the windows, deforming the world outside. Fear of the unknown was overbearing, bringing Jaime to a near depressive state. She had to get a grip on herself or she wouldn't be able to cope.

***

The house appeared behind the rainy windscreen. Hot tears flooded Jaime's eyes, blurring the scenery. Dante kissed her long and hard while she just cried, unable to return the kisses. He pulled her against his chest, allowing her to let out all the fear and frustration.

Jaime buried her face into his neck. "I want you to hold onto me forever."

"I won't let anyone hurt you."

"Can you guarantee that?" she managed to say between sobs.

Dante pursed his lips, and Jaime captured his worried look.

"You're making a habit of soaking my clothes, aren't you?" he said, attempting to lighten the atmosphere.

Jaime choked on a laugh.

"Je t'aime," he said, wiping away a few tears.

Jaime returned to her seat, grabbed her handbag, and ran across the driveway while Dante took their bags from the trunk. Huge raindrops stung Jaime's cheeks while the wind slapped flyaway hair across her face. She was glad it was raining. No one would notice the tears. But then, who was there to see apart from the dog?

Dante brought the bags into the house and set about checking all the windows and doors. "I'll be back as soon as I can."

When Dante rang up an hour later to say something unexpected had cropped up, Jaime sank into nail biting mode. Propelled by anxiety and paranoia, she ran around the place, checking every door and window again before settling down to wait in the silent, empty house.

Chapter 36

Je t'ai loupe !
Mais tu peux
compter sur
moi – *je* ne
te manquerai
pas deux fois !

Missed you this time! Won't miss you twice. You can count on it!

"Shit! Not another note," Dante yelled.

He'd come straight back to the flat. How could the stalker have put together another note in such a short time? Weren't the police supposed to be doing do extra rounds to keep Jaime safe?

Yanking the phone out of his pocket, he called the inspector's number once more.

"What can I do for you, Mr de Vere?" the inspector's familiar voice floated down the phone.

Dante cleared his throat and put on his lawyer tone. "Good day, Inspector Durand. My girlfriend has received another letter."

The inspector let out a long whistle. "Persistent, isn't he?"

"What are you going to do?"

The inspector grunted before speaking. "We need you to come by with the evidence, of course."

Dante perceived the hesitation in the inspector's voice.

"Of course," Dante repeated, knowing the procedure perfectly well.

Annoyed, he rang off and shoved the phone in his coat pocket. Taking the stairs two at a time, he tore up to the flat. A few minutes later, after finding the file he needed, he slammed the door shut and hurried back to the car.

***

He eased the car to the curb and cut the headlights. Curious eyes examined the luxurious building with its elegant façade of massive stone blocks and decorative red bricks. Typical upper class Parisian construction. The place where Jaime now lived. Sleeping around had paid off.

He turned his attention to the building's closed shutters. He knew she wouldn't stay put. Not after the near miss of the night before. Problem was...where the hell had she scampered off to? Angry hands slammed down on the steering wheel. Things weren't going as planned. For the first time in a long while, he was losing control.

Slumping down in the car seat, he dropped his forehead onto the steering wheel. He'd never imagined Jaime would get into bed with a hot-shot lawyer. She'd certainly come up in the world. What a huge kick in the balls. So unfair. But he'd have revenge. He had to be careful, though. No point in letting months of careful scheming go down the drain. Mustn't let the de Vere prick ruin his plans. He had to concentrate on his mission. Rid his mind of unnecessary thoughts.

He raised his head and gazed ahead.

Holy fucking shit!

Prick de Vere was getting into his car and about to drive away.

"Oh, no you don't," he sniggered, excitement coursing through him. "You're not going anywhere without me."

Shoving the courtesy car into first gear, he pulled out of the parking space. Thank God René had lent him a vehicle at such short notice. He only hoped the old banger would keep up with the lawyer's plush road-burner. Bastard.

He settled down comfortably in the car seat, eyes fixed on the vehicle in front. "Take me to her, Lover Boy." His voice boomed out in the confinement of the small car.

Tyres hissed over the rain-washed street as he pressed the accelerator. "Fucking hell, mate, take it easy." If the lawyer carried on at this rate, they'd both get done for speeding. Not what he needed. The last time he'd tailed a guy, the idiot had forced him to race through a set of red traffic lights, meaning three penalty points taken off on his license.

He concentrated on the road. Weaving dangerously around cars and scooters was wearing him out. A couple of traffic lights had turned orange when he'd sailed through them. Was the lawyer in that much of a hurry to get back to the slut? After several more minutes of zigzagging down different avenues, Dante pulled up in front of the police station.

He eased the car up to the curb a short distance away. "Hey, bro," he said to the reflection staring back at him from the rear-view mirror. "The lawyer's shitting his pants. We've got him where we want him. Mr Perfect's all shook up. I told you we'd get our revenge. Didn't Jekyll and Hyde always get what they wanted?"

He slumped back in the seat and pulled out his phone. God knew how long he'd have to wait. He scrolled down a list of photos from a site de rencontre, stopping now and again when a young woman caught his eye. Choosing one was a gamble. The best girlfriends were the quiet ones. Docile. Keen to please. Easy to mould.

Not long after, Dante reappeared and drove away.

Once again, he put the car into first and followed the lawyer.

***

Jaime leaned back on the sofa, stretching her legs. "What shall we have for dinner?"

"Whatever you like, but don't spend hours in the kitchen, sweating over a hot stove. I'd rather have you sweating here on the settee." His fingers inched up from Jaime's waist to her breasts.

Jaime giggled until Dante's smile changed into a worried frown. His hands froze. "I heard a noise."

A heavy thud echoed from the kitchen. Dante curved an arm around Jaime's waist and hauled her down between the settee and coffee table, his heart thumping against her back.

Dante put his mouth to Jaime's ear. "I'm going to take a look."

He gave Jaime's trembling hand a reassuring squeeze before easing himself up and searching around for a weapon. His eyes fell onto the fire irons. He kicked off both shoes and headed over to the fireplace. Who the hell could it be? He hadn't noticed anyone behind him during the drive home.

Dante took a quick look at Jaime. From her position on the floor, trapped between the table and the couch, there was no way she could be seen. Thank God.

"Keep down," he growled as Jaime attempted to gaze up.

Dante crept to the door combat style, straining for noises. One long stride after the other, the irons held tight in hand, Dante took up a position at the door's entrance, his back tight against the wall.

The door eased open, and Dante's eyes focused on the spreading beam of light. He raised an arm, ready to welcome the intruder with the bite of his weapon. Adrenaline raced all over, setting Dante's heart beating at a quicker pace while his muscles tightened.

A clumsy paw emerged in the doorway, followed by a grey body. Petrus paraded into the lounge.

"Merde, Petrus! You scared the shit out of me!" Dante dropped the fire irons and blew out a long breath. The dog sauntered up to Jaime, still on the floor, and licked her forehead.

Jaime let out a nervous giggle. "Licking me's become a habit, hasn't it?"

Dante grabbed the dog by his collar and hauled him to the kitchen. Reluctant to leave, Petrus took his time.

Jaime jumped up and sank into the couch, pulling a cushion to her stomach when Dante returned.

"How did he get in? I'm sure I closed the door after he went out."

Dante needed a drink to calm his nerves. He poured out the Chablis and handed Jaime a glass. "Apparently you didn't."

Jaime's eyes narrowed as she took a large mouthful. "I'm positive I did."

Pensive, Dante pondered over what Jaime had said. If she *had* closed the door, someone was out there. Surely the dog would have growled? Unless he'd made friends on the sly? Petrus was good at that. The number of parishioners he'd charmed in the past with his sorrowful eyes...

Dante shook his head. Who could be out there? The Albanians? Jaime's stalker? Everything was leading up to breaking point. But he refused to sit around and wait for his nerves to give way. Taking a last long sip of the wine, Dante hurried outside to check the grounds.

***

Jaime prepared a simple dinner. Dante devoured the Caesar salad; Jaime nibbled a piece of baguette and sipped the wine, looking around. Dante reached across the table and squeezed her hand. "Everything's fine. No one can get in."

She gave a weak smile and sat patiently until the meal ended.

Dante finished the dessert, licking every last bit of the crème brulé from the spoon. With a satisfied grin, he sat back. "That was great."

Jaime came to stand behind him, both arms cradling his shoulders. "Glad you liked it. I think I'll go up and have a bath."

Dante patted Jaime's hand. "Good idea. Once Petrus takes a last walk, I'll lock up and join you."

Jaime kissed the top of his head, grabbed her sweater, and left the room.

Dante let the dog out into the garden before filling the dishwasher. When all the plates and cutlery had been placed in the machine, he opened the back door and whistled for the dog.

No acknowledgement. Not a bark. Nothing.

Dante grabbed the torch hanging next to the door and frowned. Why hadn't the dog come when he'd whistled? He stepped into the quiet garden, fanning the torch around amongst the bushes, calling the dog's name. Heavy rain clouds, rimmed with fluorescent light from the full moon dominated the dark blue sky, portraying the trees as menacing silhouettes.

"Where the hell is that sodding dog?"

A movement to the right grasped Dante's attention. He spun round, directing the torch to the noise. A smug Petrus stalked up to him, a stick in his mouth.

Irritated, Dante tugged on the dog's collar and led him to the house. He was getting paranoid. And didn't like that. If he let the fear in, he'd lose the ability to push it away and act straight. He had to protect Jaime. But by promising to keep her safe, he wondered if he was biting off more than he could chew.

Back in the house, Petrus settled in his basket, and Dante again checked every door and window. Satisfied all was in order, he climbed the stairs, stripping on the way to the bedroom.

Clothed in boxers, Dante collapsed on the bed. He was pissed off. Since receiving the last menacing letter, he'd been on edge. When the dog had scared him, he'd believed the stalker had found them. Not to mention Petrus ignoring his calls in the garden,

He glanced at the ceiling. If someone *had* tailed him, he hadn't noticed. Creepy ideas surged through his mind. What if he couldn't keep Jaime safe?

Shaking away the suppositions, Dante strode barefoot down the corridor to the bathroom, ready for a hot shower to relieve the tension.

"Jaime, are you done?"

Silence.

Dante's heart missed a beat. "Jaime," he called again. Why didn't she answer? He eased the bathroom door open and gaped in horror. Jaime was submerged in the bath. Eyes shut.

Panic hammered against his ribs and old fears returned.

How did the Albanians get in? Surely not when he'd gone looking for the dog?

Dante's hand shot out and grabbed Jaime's floating hair, tugging her head out of the water.

A loud, ear-splitting scream shot up from the surface of the water as Jaime gasped for air. "What, for Christ's sake, is your game? You scared the shit out of me!"

Dante took a sudden intake of breath and released his grip. He stumbled backward, knocking a heel on the washbasin-stand behind him. "Holy crap! Didn't you hear me come into the bathroom?"

Jaime sat up spluttering. "How could I? I was under the water, you bloody fool."

Dante leaned against the washbasin and rubbed the back of his foot. "When I saw you under the water, I thought…I don't know what I thought," he finished, gaping at her.

Jaime rubbed her sore scalp. "There's something you're hiding from me, isn't there?"

Dante spotted that look of suspicion in Jaime's narrowed eyes.

"Isn't there?" she repeated, raising her voice.

Dante recognised the you're-not-telling-me-the-truth expression.

She wouldn't be easy to convince.

"Of course not."

"So what's with all the strange behaviour?"

Dante scratched the back of his neck. "What strange behaviour? I just need a hot shower to unwind, that's all." He watched Jaime slide under the water again, kicking himself for making the woman suspicious. She didn't know the half of it.

***

Jaime woke with a start. Those damned nightmares. The same ones she'd had back in England. *Him* finding her.

Outside, the faint light of dawn pushed its dull glow through the slits of the wooden shutters. Somewhere a bird chirped, announcing the start of a new day. She inched closer to Dante. He automatically placed a warm arm around her.

"What time is it?" he mumbled.

"Early," she whispered. "Go back to sleep. You were sleeping well."

"Sorry, did I snore?"

"You worked hard last night," she teased.

Dante slid a hand over Jaime's breast. "Wouldn't mind doing a bit of overtime. I know the perfect way to start the day." He kicked away the duvet and pulled Jaime on top of him.

***

A while after, Jaime dragged herself out of bed. She staggered to the bathroom and blinked into the mirror, surprised at the reflection staring back. Lips that had doubled in size, a wild scraggle for hair, she was the spitting image of a woman who'd been screwed within an inch of her life. And she'd loved every minute of it.

Smiling, she stepped into the refreshing shower and welcomed the cool water. Groaning as the spray massaged aching muscles and tender skin, she hoped the strong spray would wash away her negative ideas.

"My first day on my own," she said to the shower unit. "How the hell am I going to stop myself from dying of boredom?" She didn't care much for television, and refused to sit and watch the walls, no matter how beautifully decorated. She needed something to do. The house was worse than a morgue. Could she make it through to the evening before dissolving into tears? It would be the challenge of the day.

A quarter of an hour later, Jaime stepped into the kitchen and up to the coffee percolator. The note wedged under its base, left a sparkle in her eyes.

Will try to get back early - love you.
D.

Jaime drank the hot coffee all the while fondling the note. She was lucky to have Dante. He'd helped a lot, taking a huge weight off her shoulders just by being there. She gazed around the kitchen, wondering how to pass the time. Maybe give the kitchen a thorough clean. Not that it needed it, but it would keep her mind busy. Stop paranoid thoughts. Besides, boredom killed.

***

By lunch time, there was nothing left to scour. Jaime had added extra tasks to the list, and the morning had still dragged.

She ambled over to the window for the umpteenth time. That's all she seemed to do. Look out of the window. Read a book. Look out of the window. Clean the kitchen, and for a change, look out of the window again. She had no one to talk to but the dog.

She was filling the dishwasher after lunch when the phone rang. Dante flashed up on the screen.

"Hey, I'm so happy you called!"

"Figured I'd ring before going for a business lunch. Everything okay?"

Jaime headed for the lounge. "Just a bit lonely."

"The afternoon will fly by. I'll do my best to get away early."

"See you later, then." Jaime rung off and lay on the couch, snuggling under the plaid with a book.

Something moist on her cheek made her jump. Opening one eye after the other, she turned to find Petrus's hanging tongue. She must have dropped off. The time on her phone showed five-twenty. She sat bolt upright. Had she honestly slept for over three hours?

Petrus lapped her hand, panting his doggy breath in loud puffs.

"What is it with you always licking me?" she said, pointing to the kitchen. "Leg it."

The dog didn't budge, apart from plopping a paw on Jaime's knee.

"I said, LEG IT!" To which Petrus snorted, stretched out his forelegs, and fell onto the rug with a dull thud.

Exasperated, Jaime got up and stepped over him. Petrus headed after her with his leash in his mouth and stared up with sorrowful eyes. "Trying to get round me with your please-feel-sorry-for-me face?"

The dog looked up and gave a strangled grunt. Jaime retrieved the leash and clipped it onto his collar. She grabbed her jacket and tied a scarf around her neck. Perhaps a walk would eat up some of the spare time.

"Come on then. Let's go walkies."

Petrus snorted while they marched down the driveway and onto the wet country road. Jaime's springy steps trod on the soggy grass at the sides of the road, soaking the bottoms of her jeans. She'd planned a slow, laidback stroll to unwind. Petrus had other ideas. He bolted forward, pulling on the lead until she was jogging, struggling to pull the dog back.

When they arrived at a quiet lane, and judging there was no danger, Jaime unleashed the dog. No sooner released, Petrus ran around barking and wagging his tail, sniffing out the undergrowth.

They reached a park. Or a so-called park. The place was now an oasis of weeds and shabby greenery. The pathway meandering through the rough land was nothing more than a dirt track edged with clumps of moss.

Jaime strolled with her head hung low. On the sides of the path, weeds drooped under the weight of droplets. She drooped under the weight of frustration. When would all this end? Things were getting worse. Tears welled up and glazed her vision.

"Come on, boy. Time to go back," she called, looking around.

No dog in sight.

"Petrus!"

Still no sign.

She couldn't even hear the familiar rummaging sound the dog made in the undergrowth. Without noticing, she'd wrapped the leash tighter around her hand. The leather bit into her skin, marking her palms with red streaks.

A faraway bark and a succession of high-pitched yelps put an end to the worrying. Far in the distance, a blurred figure stood in the gathering gloom of the fine drizzle. Jaime curled a few strands of hair behind her ear and looked on through wet eyelashes, fearing the worst. Her heart picked up a quicker rhythm. Almost at once, the cigarette man came to mind.

In a frantic voice, she called out to the dog. Petrus came bounding up, sloshing wet grass as he sprinted back.

"Where have you been?" she asked, looking to the far end of the park again. To her amazement and relief, the figure had disappeared.

Unwilling to hang around a moment longer, Jaime grabbed the dog's collar and attached the leash. The mist was curling its way forward from the woodland. Petrus pricked his ears and a guttural growl escaped from its throat. His whole body tensed.

"What is it?"

A tiny frisson ran down the back of Jaime's neck. For an instant, she had the strange impression someone was near. Taking quick steps, she scanned the vicinity. Shadows appeared to be lurking within the darkness of the thicket on the left.

"Let's get back home."

Jaime tried to focus on something else. Anything but being observed. She put a stronger grip onto Petrus's lead and headed home, casting a look over her shoulder now and again.

She stepped into the house and sighed with relief. Pushing her fingers through her hair, she put the leash back in its place and gazed into the camera surveillance screen to be sure the gates were firmly shut.

To keep her paranoid thoughts away from Petrus's protective behaviour and the stranger in the park, Jaime decided to prepare dinner. She set about peeling every single vegetable she could put her hands on, praying Dante liked minestrone.

Tonight he had no other choice.

Chapter 37

Another glance into the rear-view mirror confirmed Dante was being followed. Even half-blinded by the glare of headlights, he knew that same car was right on his tail. To prove his assumptions, it had taken the same side road behind him. Again.

He had to think. And quick.

He eased the car over to the curb and climbed out. Playing it cool, he headed across the street and turned down a dark side road. Disappearing into alleyways had become a habit.

From the sound of approaching footsteps, he guessed the person was alone. Dante hung in the shadows, heart beating hard. Would he be able to grab the stalker before he assaulted him? The tracker's hesitant footsteps echoed down the abandoned alley.

Dante had the advantage of surprise.

Plunging forward, he grabbed the man around the waist and slammed him down to the ground. The man grunted as all the air evacuated his body.

"I've got you, you bastard," Dante shouted with a knee pressed on the man's back.

The stalker made a reach for his pocket.

"Oh no, you don't." Dante seized the man's arm and yanked it behind his back, making him howl.

"Hey, what's your game?"

Dante held him to the ground. "What's yours?"

"You're hurting my arm."

"That's my intention."

The man bashed the ground with his free hand like a wrestler tapping out for submission. "You're making a big mistake."

"Am I now?"

The man wriggled his captured arm. "I'm a good guy."

"And I'm a priest," Dante teased.

"You mean you *were* a priest, Father de Vere."

Dante flinched, and the man smirked. "Didn't Casanova inform you? Or was that another thing he failed to say?"

"Who are you?" Dante questioned.

"Like I said, I'm on your side."

Dante's anger soared. What the hell was Corentin up to? Only the team knew he'd been a priest. Could this man be a new member? He didn't look familiar, but then he didn't know all the staff. A new member could have been appointed to keep him safe.

"Well, for a professional, you're not very discreet, are you? And why would you want to keep an eye on me?"

The man tried to pull his arm free. "Can we have this conversation in a more comfortable position?"

Dante lessened his hold but refused to let go, still uncertain of the man's intentions.

"Look, maître de Vere, what other proof do you need?"

Dante racked his brains for a few seconds. He needed to think of a question. Or a secret that only a person on the squad could answer. A chuckle escaped his throat. "What kind of tattoo does Corentin have and where is it?"

"No tattoo, but a Prince Albert piercing. We go back a long way. I was there when he got it."

Dante released his hold and the man stood, brushing the dust off his clothes. Dante flinched. This person was one of the men in black who had visited the flat a while back.

"Casanova phoned a few days ago saying you were in danger again."

Dante's eyes narrowed. "Did he now?"

"As he couldn't assure your security, he asked the squad to step in."

The raging bull came charging to the surface, waiting to hit the red cloth. The red cloth called Corentin. The swine had lied to the squad, telling them Dante still needed protection, knowing darn well they would keep an eye on him. Corentin also knew how scared he would be. The bastard needed someone to teach him a lesson. Now was his chance to get even. He'd already smashed Corentin's nose. That hadn't deterred him. Apart from killing the man, only one other way remained to get rid of him. He'd had enough of Corentin sniffing around Jaime, not to mention making his own life a misery. One quick phone call would do the trick.

Massaging the back of his neck, Dante fished in his pocket for his phone. He tapped in a number, ready to savour the minutes to come.

***

Dante pulled up in front of Luc's house. He entered the kitchen, smiling, until he saw Jaime's face. "What?"

Jaime rushed into Dante's open arms open. "I'm getting paranoid. A man was watching me when I took Petrus for a walk through the park."

Dante's heart skipped a beat.

"Are you sure?"

Jaime pulled back. "I'm sure he was there. Was he watching me? I don't know."

"Did he follow you?"

"To be honest, I was so scared, I rushed back without looking. Even Petrus behaved in a strange way."

Dante raised an eyebrow. "What do you mean?"

"He kept stopping and growling. Staying close, like he was protecting me. I have to admit, I *did* feel protected."

"You're becoming good friends," Dante joked, placing his chin on the top of Jaime's head.

"Yeah, we're real buddies now."

Dante tried to smile but made a poor show. He wasn't in the mood. Not after what he'd been through. Holding Jaime closer, it dawned on him that he'd been wrong to leave her alone and wouldn't do it again. How the hell could he manage that? No way could he postpone the next day's hearing. Too many people counted on him being in court.

He stroked Jaime's hair and placed a long kiss on her forehead. He had the evening to come up with a solution.

Chapter 38

Another day alone.

Jaime had woken with a terrible feeling. She didn't know why. It was just a hunch, but she'd been on edge and fidgety since breakfast. Something was going to go wrong, and she didn't want to tempt the devil. No walks in the country. Petrus would have to stay in the garden.

She gazed at the clock. Half past ten. Dante had only been gone two hours. It seemed like a lifetime. The day was sure to drag.

Heading across the kitchen, she grabbed the jar of ground coffee. The intercom buzzed, sending her nerves rattling and fresh coffee jumping from the container. Dread crept up from the pit of her stomach. The intercom's loud whirr startled her again.

Pausing in front of the intercom, Jaime peered at the screen, unable to make out the fuzzy blur. *So much for bloody hi-tech.*

Still squinting, she pressed the button, ready to use the not-today-thank-you phrase, when a woman's voice boomed into the room.

"You all right, Jaime? Took you a while to answer."

"Francine! What are you doing here?"

The receptionist grinned into the camera. "Let me in and I'll tell you."

Jaime prodded the second button. No sooner had the vehicle passed the entrance than Jaime pressed the button once again, bringing the gates to a sturdy close.

"What a great surprise," Jaime said, watching Francine haul a heavy briefcase out of the car. "I was about to make coffee. Care for a cup?"

"If that's no bother."

"I'm glad to speak to a human instead of that four-legged hound." Jaime nodded at Petrus. She set about making coffee while Francine hoisted herself up onto one of the bar stools.

"So what brings you here?" Jaime asked once Francine had finished talking about the office news.

"To be honest, I'm here with work from Dante. He imagined you might be bored, and I need help with English. It's killing two birds with one stone, so to speak. I've been meaning to call and see how you were."

"That's so like Dante, thinking of work. But he does have a point. I am bored."

When the percolator puffed its last sigh, Jaime poured the coffee and they stepped into the lounge, ready for work. Both had settled around the dining table, when Jaime's phone purred.

Francine hid a smile. "Bet that's Dante. He said he'd ring."

Jaime grabbed the phone. "You're right."

She mouthed an 'excuse me' and left the room. "Hi, and before you say anything, thanks for organising this work meeting with Francine."

Dante's chuckle warbled down the phone. "I'm glad you approve. I can now plead in court with a clear head."

From somewhere in the background, a door opened, and a loud voice shouted out a list of names. Jaime guessed it was Dante's cue.

"They're calling me," he said. "Enjoy your day, and I'll see you around seven. Before, if I can."

A slow smile appeared while Jaime hugged the phone to her chest. Content, she stepped back into the lounge all geared up to attack the translations.

***

Francine left a few minutes before six-thirty, leaving Jaime with little time to prepare a meal. It would have to be wine and cheese. Now would be the time to taste that strong camembert that stared up at her every time she opened the fridge.

Jaime took a step into the kitchen when something made her check over her shoulder. She glanced nervously down the corridor, a sense of foreboding creeping over her.

"You're being silly," she said out loud, hoping to convince herself. There was no one there, and Dante would be home soon.

Despite the reassuring words, Jaime's skin crawled as the uneasiness in the pit of her stomach began to rise. Uncertainty and anxiety spread their unwelcoming wings and soared even higher.

Maybe Francine should have stayed until Dante arrived.

***

Unable to sleep, Dante heaved off the duvet and rolled onto one side. No matter how hard he tried, he couldn't drop off. His eyes refused to close, and his mind wouldn't rest, buried in worries about Jaime and the man hunting her.

Unwilling to disturb Jaime with his tossing and turning, Dante slipped out of bed. As a rule, he very rarely got up during the night. Tonight was an exception. It promised to be long and sleepless. He stretched a sweater over his head before stepping into jeans and a pair of moccasins.

Downstairs, on hearing Dante approach, Petrus came to welcome him. Dante scratched the dog's neck. "Wanna go out?"

Petrus gazed up with eyes full of hope. Dante chuckled, opened the kitchen door and allowed the dog to trot out. He returned to the lounge and poured himself a whisky. Slouching on the sofa, he mulled over the present problems. A quarter of an hour later, he poured himself another, still miles away.

Sometime later, he looked up at the clock and realised the dog had been gone for over half an hour.

Shit!

He placed the glass on the coffee table and dashed out of the back door.

***

The house lay still and silent. Beautifully submerged in moonlight.

He crept up to the front of the house, careful to avoid kicking the gravel. No point in giving himself away. He meandered between patches of shadow formed by the tall bushes and tried the front door.

Locked.

He crept to the back, knowing the dog had sniffed its way to the bait he'd laid earlier. The way was free.

Slithering up to the house, he was about to seize the door handle when footsteps approaching from inside brought him to a standstill. Stumbling back, he melted into the darkness as Prick de Vere stormed out of the house, calling the dog.

What the fuck was this prat doing up? Anger flared inside like a volcano about to erupt. Time to release some of the tension. With a bit of luck, fleabag would be out for good.

He eased out of the shadows and up to the back door. The moment had come to unchain the monster under the bed. He entered the house and grabbed a knife from the kitchen block, all the while cursing himself for forgetting his own. He weighed the object in his hand. Although smaller than a normal kitchen knife, it was sharp and would do the job.

Clutching the weapon, he climbed the creaking wooden stairs.

***

Jaime's eyes flew open.

This had been one of the rare times she'd slept without those horrible nightmares. What could have woken her? She stretched out a hand and patted Dante's side of the bed.

Empty.

The stairs creaked and Jaime stiffened, all senses alert. Clammy hands clung onto the duvet. The noise was so faint, she almost missed it. "Is that you, Dante?"

No reply. Only the wind rustling through the trees.

Again a noise came from the staircase. The sound became more and more distinct. Footsteps approached. And they weren't Dante's.

As much as she wanted to, Jaime knew she couldn't tug the duvet over her head and wish the noise away. Sliding both legs over the side, she reached for her clothes and padded barefoot across the room. Footsteps resonated in the corridor. Someone was going back downstairs. Straining for noises other than her pounding heart, Jaime left the bedroom.

Nothing seemed out of place when she arrived downstairs. Only the usual sounds of the ticking clock and the soft whirring of the fridge. Yet something wasn't right.

The antique clock on the mantelpiece chimed, and Jaime's heart raced to her mouth. One a.m.

With a hand on her runaway heart, she stepped into the lounge. An empty whisky glass sat on the coffee table. When no Petrus showed up, Jaime assumed Dante had taken the dog outside.

She was about to mount the stairs when a draught from the kitchen sent shivers up her arms. Why had Dante left the door open? The torch hadn't been taken from the hook. So what was that bluish light from the front garden? Returning to the table, she seized one of the kitchen knives from the block and frowned. Another one missing.

"Dante?"

No answer.

The hairs tingled on the back of her neck.

Willing herself to be brave, she stepped into the garden. Taking a strong grip on the knife, she snaked through the darkness to the front of the house, an ugly gnaw stirring deep inside.

"Dante where are you?"

Complete silence.

Why didn't he answer? And where was Petrus? Surely the dog would come bounding up to her? She didn't like the look of this. Had something happened to them?

***

Petrus lay on his side, panting. With eyes half-closed and his tongue hanging loose between his teeth, the dog was a sorry sight.

Frowning, Dante crouched beside the dog, caressing its cheeks. "What's up, buddy?"

Despite being groggy, Petrus managed to sit up.

Steadying himself, Dante's hands fell onto something strange on the ground. He picked up what appeared to be small balls of meat. Raising them to his nose, Dante gathered from the sour smell that they'd been drugged.

"Shit!" he yelled, scrambling to his feet. He'd left the back door open. What if the scumbag who'd tried to poison the dog was in the house and after Jaime?

Dropping a piece of the suspicious meant into his pocket, he raced back to the house all the while phoning the vet helpline for professional advice. Thank God Luc had given him the emergency number.

After a few metres, Petrus caught up with him only to come to an abrupt halt, bearing his teeth and growling.

With one last look over his shoulder, the dog surged forward on trembling legs, barking at the top of his voice, Dante close on his heels.

***

A precise short crunch of a determined footstep on the driveway's gravel brought Jaime to a sudden standstill. With bated breath, she turned towards the sound, gripping the knife tighter. A dark figure in front of the window set Jaime's heart hammering. The silhouette stared down the driveway, tossing something from one hand to the other, blocking access to the house. Jaime glimpsed the light of the moon gleaming off a knife.

Without a second thought, she broke into a dead sprint, dashing down the driveway, dispersing the gravel's loose stones. A long ear-splitting screech startled her before she understood the noise had come from her own throat. Her hysterical screaming filled the silent night. Heavy footsteps sounded close by along with a string of swear words. And at that precise moment, with her tormentor so close, Jaime knew she was capable of anything. Even murder.

A hand pulled Jaime roughly back. Looking round, she came face to face with angry piercing eyes. The rest of his face was covered with a dark balaclava.

"Let go of me!"

Rough hands flew to Jaime's neck. She opened her mouth to scream, but the prowler was quicker. He knocked her jaw shut to stifle the shriek.

Fear sat like a pillow over Jaime's nose and mouth. Only a little air managed to get by, but she did catch a note of something strange. A smell she knew.

Panic increased like an unstoppable snowball, and adrenaline took over and put her in fight mode. Trickles of perspiration rolled down Jaime's back. She kicked out and sunk her teeth into his gloved hand. The bitter taste of leather invaded her mouth.

"You bitch." He whirled Jaime round and punched her cheek.

Jaime fell to the ground, wincing with pain. He seized her hair as she tried to scramble away, and wrenched her scalp so hard, she believed he was going to pull it off. With her face level with his groin, she darted forward to bite his bulge.

Anticipating Jaime's action, another open-handed slap, sent her head spinning and cheekbone drumming. She let out a frightened, pained scream and kicked out, only to receive another slap, splitting her lip.

Use the knife.

She looked at the weapon. She'd never hurt anyone before. Maybe that had to change now.

With a force she didn't know she had, Jaime shot up from the ground and brought a knee up into the man's crotch. He managed to dodge back before smashing a fist onto her nose.

Jaime's head sparked with fire. Her surroundings swayed from the ringing blow as she slipped on the gravel and sank to the ground, hardly feeling the grit ripping into her knees. The last blow had been much stronger than the others. She had to act now before it was too late. Gripping the knife with both hands, Jaime lurched forward, thrusting the blade haphazardly.

Everything happened at full speed. One minute he was hitting her, the next, Jaime felt the blade sink into the top of his leg, puncturing the skin and slicing through several inches of flesh. Blood oozed from the wound and trickled over her fingers. He put a hand over the gash, staring wide-eyed at his leg.

Jaime gaped down at the knife, the tang of blood filling her nose.

"You fucking bitch!" he screamed in English, holding the flesh together. "You bloody, fucking bitch."

Jaime's head buzzed, only just hearing Dante shouting. She did, however, pick up Petrus's barking from the back of the house. With a bit of luck, the dog would stop the attacker from hurting her further. Terrified, she looked up to see amber eyes staring down. They were familiar. Yet, she couldn't pinpoint where she'd seen them.

Furious barking sounded nearby.

"I'll be back," he yelled, clutching his thigh and making another swipe at her.

Jaime kept lashing out at him with her knife, desperate to keep him away.

"You'll be sorry for what you did tonight. I swear, I'll fucking kill you!"

Petrus stumbled forward, releasing a flurry of ferocious barks and snarls. Sensing danger, the dog yelped towards the fence, and remained barking while the assailant managed to climb over.

Dropping the knife, Jaime wiped her bloodstained fingers on her dirty pullover. Her nose and lip were both throbbing in a competition to see which could hurt the most. Both doing a super job. She covered her face and burst into uncontrollable sobs.

"I'm here," Dante said, grabbing hold of Jaime's hands. "What the hell has that bastard done to you?"

Jaime didn't have time to answer. She stooped forward and threw up.

Dante sat and rocked her in his arms. Blood trickled from her swollen nose and cut lip while she shed tears of relief, soaking the front of Dante's shirt. She had so many questions to ask. Where had he been? Why did the dog look off balance? For the moment, all she wanted was a little comfort.

"You're safe now," Dante said, carrying her into the house. Jaime sniffed noisily, and Petrus trotted behind them, whining.

Comfortably settled on the sofa, Jaime gazed at Dante while he tapped a number into the phone. "I'm going to call the police, then the doctor."

Jaime nodded and pulled off her bloodstained sweater. "I can't bear to have all this shit on me."

Dante grabbed a thin quilt and helped Jaime slide down to a lying position.

"It was him," she said, pulling the plaid over her shoulder. "He hit me. I had no choice. I stuck the knife in him."

"You're safe now," Dante repeated.

"He said he's going to kill me."

Petrus shuffled towards them and rested his chin on Jaime's thigh, rolling sad eyes. Dante tickled the spot between the dog's ears "She's all right, buddy. What about you?"

The dog lifted his head and licked Dante's free hand before dragging his feet away.

A murmur escaped Jaime's mouth. Spots formed in front of her eyes. "Dante?" she called.

Then everything went black.

Chapter 39

With a searing burn flaring up his thigh and warm blood trickling over his trembling fingers, he stumbled through the dark bushes to the car. His hand slipped on the car door handle as he tried to pull it open. Fuck! There was blood everywhere. He managed to settle himself in the seat and wrap a grimy scarf around the wound.

Shit! He hadn't given the dog enough sedation. And where the hell had *she* gotten the strength to stab him? He assumed it would have been dead easy to grab the bitch.

Sod her!

He should have sorted the trollop out in the house. With Prick de Vere in the garden with the stupid mutt, he could have got her. He'd even heard her moving about her room. He slammed his fists on the steering wheel, angry with himself for letting panic set in. He'd hesitated, wondering if the two idiots had been the only people in the house. It could have been dangerous taking action if someone else had been there. Besides, he needed a quick getaway.

He shoved the car into first and stepped on the gas, gazing straight ahead, only half-aware of the scenery outside. There was no point dwelling on what he should have done. He had to get away. Distance was all that counted.

Dark spots danced in the inner corners of his eyes and a rush of heat escalated up his body. "I can't pass out. Not now," he shouted, capturing that typical metallic iron tang of blood.

With a quick jerk of the wrist, he swerved the car to a sudden halt at the side of the road. He needed medical help. Marcel had to get him to a hospital for treatment – and quick.

Willing himself to stay conscious, he inhaled deeply, despite an invisible force pulling him down. His hand darted to the side of the car seat, fumbling for the lever to recline the back. Biting the inside of his cheek to stop himself from crying out in pain, he phoned Marcel.

"Marcel?"

"Oui."

"It's me. I'm in trouble, mon ami."

Marcel's voice boomed down the phone. "Don't tell me you got caught with the dope?"

"Nah, nothing like that."

He heard Marcel exhale. "Can't be that bad, then."

Wincing with pain, he explained the problem, avoiding too much detail. Marcel had to come to the rescue. His partner owed him one.

Marcel let out a low whistle. "I'm not far. I'll get my friend to give me a lift. I had some business to finish in the area."

Ten long minutes later, a car crawled to a halt next to his. He rapped his knuckles against the window to catch Marcel's attention. His friend opened the door and stared down at him.

"Took your time," he shouted, readjusting the blood-soaked scarf.

"You're looking peaky, mon ami."

"Of course, I'm fucking peaky. I've just been stabbed in the thigh, you bloody fool."

Marcel cringed on seeing the wound. "Can't take you to hospital. Need to avoid questions."

"Well, what the fuck do you suggest? You'd better not let me bleed to death." He flicked open his knife and poked Marcel's abdomen. "If anything happens to me, you won't be pleasing the demoiselles anymore. I'll slice your balls off!"

With a swift flick of the hand, Marcel grabbed the knife and tossed it into the back seat, beads of perspiration forming on his forehead. "I've got a good friend who's a vet. He can sew you up."

"Fucking hell! I'm not a pig."

"If we do go to the hospital, the pigs *will* be after you." Marcel smirked at his pun.

"Okay." Too weak to protest, he closed his eyes. The wound throbbed and he had to bring his breathing under control without passing out. The adrenaline would soon wear off.

A short while after, they arrived in front of a tall, narrow building. His gaze wandered over the cracked window frames before it came to rest on a brass plate beside the black austere front door. Weeds grew through the crevices of the three steps which led to the door, and the chipped iron railing had seen better days. There was nothing attractive about the place. He only hoped Marcel knew what he was doing.

Marcel helped him hobble inside where a man built like a boxer came to introduce himself. Dressed in green scrubs with jet black hair tied in a ponytail, and a fat neck covered in tattoos, the man looked dodgy. Even more so with holes in his ears for piercings. But then, what did he care? All he wanted was for Hulk to sort out the wound.

With the vet's help, he climbed onto the operating table, and sat, legs stretched in front of him. Hulk sterilised both hands and pulled on a pair of surgical gloves. He peeled off the blood-crusted scarf and dropped it to the floor before ripping the jean material and examining the wound, all movements unhurried and precise.

"You're lucky," the vet said in a thick Russian accent. "The knife could have penetrated deeper or hit a major artery."

She's the one who'll be getting penetrated next, and I won't go easy on her.

The vet's smile transformed into a grim slash as he prodded the wound.

"Holy shit!" he yelled, as pain exploded up his leg. He grabbed the man's arm and pulled it away. "Give me a fucking warning next time."

The vet tugged his sleeve free and reached for a bottle of antiseptic wash. He dabbed the edges of the wound with wet gauze before preparing a hypodermic needle.

"What are you going to do with that weapon?"

"Local anaesthetic. I need to sew you up." The man pressed expert fingers around the swollen wound and inserted the needle.

"Steady on!" Swearing like a trooper, he reached for Marcel's jacket sleeve and gripped the thick woollen fabric. "This is worse than when she stuck the bloody knife in."

The vet took the suture equipment and slowly brought the split flesh together. Once he'd administrated half a dozen stitches, the vet placed a dressing over the wound, and wrapped a clean bandage around his patient's thigh.

Satisfied with his work, the man peeled off his surgical gloves and tossed them into the nearby bin. "Your wound should heal quite quickly."

"It better." He grunted and heaved his leg off the table, searching around for Marcel's support.

"Be careful, though," the vet added, displaying a crooked smile. "And don't overdo it. You should be able to walk short distances without serious pain within a couple of weeks."

"A couple of weeks?" he squealed. "I've got things I need to do."

The vet chuckled and tossed him a small plastic bottle. "Take these, and next time, leave the knife out of your bedroom games."

"Chance would be a fine thing." He seized the painkillers in mid-air and got to his feet, scowling under the pain. With a curt nod, he headed out of the surgery. Marcel remained to settle the bill – or whatever he did under such circumstances.

A few minutes later, Marcel joined him in the car, and they drove away.

"Thanks, mate," he said, after a while.

Harrowed but relieved, he realized how lucky he'd been this time.

Chapter 40

Jaime opened her eyes.

Two dark irises swam forward before drifting apart. A mouth moved. No sound came out. She closed and opened her eyes again. This time, Dante appeared with a bloody Kleenex in one hand. The other pressed a pack of frozen peas wrapped in a tea towel to the bridge of her nose and cheek.

Wincing from the pain, she tried to speak. "What happened?"

"You fainted."

She grabbed his hand. "I came downstairs. You weren't there."

Dante smoothed away a stray hair. "I couldn't sleep, so I came down to get a drink."

A shrill ring echoed in the quiet house, and Jaime's eyes widened as she grabbed Dante's arm.

"Easy, love. Could be the doctor or the police."

Dante returned with Inspector Durand who acknowledged Jaime with a brief nod of the head. A younger officer took photos of her then headed out of the room to examine the scene of the crime.

A sharp knock on the door announced the arrival of the doctor. Dante accompanied a small, roundish man stooping a little under the weight of a brown case. Dressed in dark maroon corduroys, a tweed jacket, and a neck scarf, he looked the typical country G.P. Short smoky-grey hair and a beard of the same colour suited the doctor's weatherworn features.

Jaime peered at the man's arched, pointed nose. It resembled the typical beak-masks healers wore during the Middle Ages to ward off the dangers of catching the plague.

The inspector coughed, bringing Jaime out of her medieval vision. "While the doctor examines you, Miss Sanders, I'll join my colleague securing the crime scene in the garden. When the doctor is done, we'll take your statement."

Jaime gave a weak smile and Inspector Durand left the room.

The doctor peered down at Jaime's blotchy face, split lip, and swollen nose then gazed at Dante. Dry blood had crusted around the base of Jaime's nose and under her fingernails. The doctor busied himself cleaning the blood.

"How do you feel?"

Jaime's eyes screwed shut for a brief moment. "My nose hurts like hell."

He touched the skin around her nose, gently feeling the bridge. Jaime pulled back more from fear of being hurt than of pain.

"A nasty contusion, but nothing's broken."

Jaime's hands shook while the doctor took her wrist. "You're in shock, my dear, and your pulse is a little high. Let me take your blood pressure."

Flashes of what happened came flooding back as Jaime waited for the band to deflate. She'd been in the garden when a man attacked her. He'd blocked access to the house. She'd been terrified. Was still scared now. To top it all off, he said he was coming back.

"That should feel better." The doctor's reassuring voice brought Jaime back to the present. "Here's a prescription for some painkillers."

"Thank you."

"I'll also ask Mr. de Vere to prepare another icepack for your nose. It should return to normal in about a week. Until then, avoid blowing it." The doctor placed the prescription and medical certificate on the nearby table.

While Dante showed the doctor out, Jaime dawdled over to the large mirror overhanging the fireplace. She cringed at her reflection. A boxer after a few rounds in the ring. With gentle fingers, she pressed the bruised cheek, grimacing when her fingers came in contact with her swollen nose. Black spots danced around her eyes.

Pulling the plaid tighter around her shoulders, Jaime stumbled back to the sofa and collapsed onto the cushions. A patter of feet scuffled on the parquet before a concerned Petrus climbed up next to her. He let out a soft whine.

"Not you again," she said, half-crying, half-laughing. With a surge of tenderness, she wrapped an arm around the dog's neck, breathing into his soft coat. The closeness of the dog made her feel secure. Could he guess she needed attention? The dog climbed down when Dante returned. Wagging his tail, Petrus slipped passed him to take comfort in his basket.

Dante sat on the edge of the couch and bent to kiss Jaime's forehead. "How do you feel?"

"Awful." She sniffed and dabbed her nose. "I want him found and put behind bars."

Dante was about to reply when Inspector Durand returned and settled himself on a chair next to the couch. "I can see it's a serious assault, Miss. With the medical certificate from the doctor, we know what charges to bring against your attacker once all investigations have been completed." He pulled out a notebook. "Now, in your own time, please tell me exactly what happened?'

Jaime shook her head, terrified at the idea of having to describe the attack. "I can't do it."

Dante reached for Jaime's hand and squeezed her ice-cold fingers. "You'll be fine. Just tell the inspector what you saw."

Jaime's memory travelled back to the last time she'd given evidence in court. She remembered the day of the trial. How scared she'd been. The murderer's piercing eyes and sadistic features had haunted many dreams.

"I can't remember."

Dante raised an eyebrow. "It only happened a short while ago. You're not in court giving evidence."

At the mention of court, Jaime came over cold. She closed her eyes in an attempt to block out the memory.

"What's up, Jaime?" Dante asked.

Jaime put on a brave smile. Not easy with a throbbing nose and thumping head. Breathing through her mouth, she managed to stop a rush of dizziness.

"Take your time," the inspector said.

With her eyes fixed on something behind the inspector's back, Jaime gave a slow and painstaking narration of what she remembered, making sure not to omit anything. It wasn't easy to think straight.

When her statement drew to an end, the police officer closed the booklet and tapped the pen against his chin. "We'll contact the hospitals. See if anyone has been admitted recently with a stab wound."

Jaime blinked several times and shook the policeman's hand before huddling deeper under the blanket.

"Goodbye, Miss Sanders. Monsieur de Vere."

Safe under the cover, Jaime allowed herself to think back to the attack. Breathing slowly, she tried to put bits and pieces together. How had he found her? How had he managed to get into the house? Something niggled her. Something important. She couldn't quite pinpoint what.

***

Dante accompanied the policeman out of the room. "I'll bring Miss Sanders to the station tomorrow morning. I know she needs to confirm her statement."

The policeman gave a curt nod of the head and Dante came closer. "One more thing, I didn't want to mention this in front of Miss Sanders, but the dog was drugged."

The inspector pulled out his notebook to jot down the last piece of news. "Is the animal all right?"

"Petrus is fine. The vet is coming for him. Just to make sure."

At the mention of his name, Petrus plodded forward and rubbed his head in Dante's hand. Dante smiled. The dog looked a lot better than before.

Outside, an officer taped off the driveway. Another transported Jaime's knife in a sealed plastic bag. Dante shook his head. The garden looked like a scene from a crime movie. How had things got to this?

A van pulled into the driveway and a man jumped out. Dante recognised the vet's logo on the vehicle. The man approached and stroked the dog's head. "You okay, boy?" he asked.

Dante cleared his throat. "I feel guilty about calling you out. Although he's still a bit wobbly on his legs, Petrus seems fine."

The vet smiled. "Like I said over the phone, we'll take him in as a precaution. Could I have the sample of meat you said you'd recovered?"

"Of course." Dante pulled a plastic bag out of his pocket and handed it to the vet. He watched Petrus jump into the back of the vehicle before returning to Jaime's side.

"Let me take you to bed," he said, swinging her up in his arms.

Jaime rested her head against Dante's chest. "I want a quick shower first. Need to wash away all this blood and grime."

Dante carried Jaime upstairs and into the bathroom. He ran a hot shower and helped her undress. Patiently waiting for the running water to stop, he began to put into place the next plan of action.

***

Jaime's restlessness woke Dante. He tried to calm her groaning, only to be pushed away as she bolted upright, panting.

He turned on the bedside lamp and stared at the injured face peering down at him. The attacker hadn't been light-handed. If he ever got his hands on the bastard, Dante would be sure to give him a taste of his own medicine. Even so, a paralysing rage crept over him. With an arm around Jaime's shoulders, he whispered words of comfort.

"Are you all right?" he whispered.

Huge tears dropped from Jaime's cheeks onto the duvet. "Oh, Dante. It was him," she said, shaking.

Dante stared in utter confusion. "Who? Do you know who it is?"

Jaime stared into space.

"Jaime?"

"Yes, Dante, I know who it is. But he's dead."

Dante blinked rapidly. "How can he be dead if you're sure who it is?"

Jaime leaned back against the bed rest, recalling with vivid clearness, the circumstance that had changed her life. "On my way home that night, I heard a groan, or more like a tortured cry coming from the park. I crept nearer and heard someone say, 'Serves you right. You were told to pay up and not sneak off with the dope'. I must have made a noise while peeking through the bushes, because he looked up and saw me.

Jaime kicked the duvet aside and sat bolt upright. "It was awful, Dante. His eyes while he stood over the person with a blood-stained knife, still gives me nightmares now.

Dante took hold of her trembling hand and caressed her knuckles with his thumb.

"I phoned the police. In the second I tapped in the number, he'd vanished. His name was David, David Thibert."

"Why didn't you mention him before?"

Jaime's expression went blank. "Because he's dead. The police in England told me he died in prison."

Dante rubbed his chin. "So they arrested him?"

"Not at first. Only when he tried to rape Cindy."

"Who the hell's Cindy? You're losing me."

Jaime pulled on the paper hanky, shredding the soft tissue. "It's so complicated. I can't think straight, and my nose hurts. The pain's so bad, I can't even talk."

Dante slipped off the bed and grabbed his jeans. "I'll get you a couple of painkillers. That should ease the pain."

Not long after, Dante returned with a glass of water and tablets. Jaime was rocking back and forth, bearing a blank look.

He sat on the bed and held out the painkillers. "Now tell me about Cindy."

Jaime swallowed two tablets and took in a deep breath. "I was invited to her graduation party. When I arrived, it was in full swing. Loud music blared out in the house. So loud, it made my heart beat in time with the bass. I remember seeing someone put an arm around Cindy. Then they were gone."

Dante wiped the tears that trickled onto the duvet. "I think I can guess what happened next."

"On my way to the bathroom, I heard hysterical screaming, so I rushed to the bedroom to find Cindy on the bed, blouse torn open and skirt hitched up. And there he was. The same person I'd seen in the park, standing over Cindy."

Jaime's voice caught in her throat. "I yelled for someone to call the police and ambulance. He panicked and pulled up his trousers, threatening to kill me if I said anything."

"Bastard!" Dante exploded.

Jaime jumped at the vehemence in his voice.

"Sorry, love. Go on."

Jaime blew out softly and stared at the duvet. "When he pushed me aside, I picked up a strange smell. The kind that hits your nose and loiters there. And the strange thing is...he seemed familiar, Dante."

She snapped out of her daze and reached for the glass of water. "A few men at the party stopped him from getting away, and I waited with Cindy for the paramedics to arrive."

"And after?"

"The police took Thibert into custody and asked me to go to the police station the next morning. And the paramedics took Cindy away."

Jaime set down the glass and dabbed the overflowing tears on the back of her hand. "I went to the police station the next day to make another statement, confirming it was the same person I saw in the park holding a knife over a body. They told me I could leave, but I would be called up for a court appearance at a later date."

"Of course," Dante said, handing Jaime a clean paper hanky.

"I don't know how I managed to cope, waiting for the trial," she said, taking the extended Kleenex. "The case even made the front pages. Everyone was relieved the murderer had been caught and sent to jail for life."

Dante caressed the back of Jaime's hand. "How can you be so sure your assailant is this Thibert?"

"His scent. He's got this peculiar smell..." She shook her head.

"What kind of odour, Jaime?"

"It's difficult to explain. All I can say it's a strange scent. Like a clinical odour. A smell you can't forget."

Jaime buried her head in her hands. "I'm going crazy, Dante. I can't think straight. That odour is his, but he died in prison."

Confusion flickered in Dante's eyes.

"Shit! I've just thought of something else," she said.

"What's that?"

"The cigarette man."

Dante's eyes widened. "Who the hell's the cigarette man?"

Jaime bit her bottom lip. "I didn't tell you because I didn't think it was important. There was a man smoking on the other side of the road when Suzanne and I had our girlie evening. Because he spoke to me in French, I didn't think any more of it. He did scare me a little when he crossed the road though."

Dante ran a hand through his hair. "Why didn't you tell me?"

"Please don't shout. I figured I was becoming paranoid."

Dante put an arm around Jaime's shoulder. "I'm sorry, love. Look, you relax and try to sleep. I'll deal with the rest."

***

When Jaime eventually settled down under the cosy duvet, Dante stepped into the corridor and grabbed his phone. He needed to talk to

Inspector Durand. If Jaime was sure it was the same person, why had the English police said he was dead? Had they made a mistake?

He doubted it. And yet...

Inspector Durand needed to do a DNA test from the blood on Jaime's clothes, and through contacts in Europol, compare it to the case in England. Perhaps then, they'd know what was going on.

Either the English police hadn't done their job or Jaime was mistaken.

Chapter 41

A little over a week had passed since he'd been treated by the vet. Being out of action had given him the opportunity to think. Time had come to do some family research. He should have started ages ago but kept putting off the task. Besides, what else could he do now? Almost five months had passed since he'd found his birth certificate. He couldn't believe how quickly time had flown.

Sat in front of the computer with his leg propped on a nearby chair, he surfed onto different websites, hoping to find one that would explain how to search for relatives. He needed guidelines on what to do. Find out who that bastard of his father was.

Frustration and pain made him slam a fist hard on the table. His brain was tied up in knots. He stopped drumming nervous fingers on the table and hobbled to the bedside table where he picked up a packet of painkillers. After downing two with a glass of water, he plodded back to the computer, ready to begin another search. It was going to be long and painstaking. Patience had never been a strong point.

Scrolling down the computer screen, he perked up when he came across what he imagined could be an interesting site.

How to begin a search for your ancestors.

He clicked on the link, only to give up after a few minutes. None of what he'd read made sense. He couldn't figure out what was written. Grabbing a note pad and pencil, he began copying the text, reading the instructions out loud.

1) *Write down what you already know about your family*

   Not a lot. Mother dead. Brother dead. Father dead.

2) *Talk to family and friends*

   Haven't got any.

3) *Look for documents and artefacts in your home, such as letters and documents, to learn of dates and places*

   A birth certificate with father unknown.

4) *Decide which information is missing*
Everything.

5) *Search vital records such as birth, marriage and death records*
Just mother's death certificate.

6) *Evaluate your findings: - did you find what you were looking for?*
No.

7) *Was the information complete?*
No.

8) *Are there glaring inconsistencies?*
???

Fuck!

He snapped the pencil in two and flung the pieces across the room. Maybe he needed to go through his mother's belongings again. He may have overlooked something.

Limping to the bed, he crouched down as best he could and pulled out the small cardboard box. He gazed at his birth certificate.

un enfant du sexe *masculin* né à *Fontainebleau* le *six* de ce mois
aux lieu et maison de ....*polyclinique*.... à *cinq*..... heures du *matin* de
(père inconnu)..
et de ......*Martin Catherine*.............. âgée de *trente huit ans*........
profession de ..*Interprète international*..... et auquel *il* ...a déclaré

Père inconnu. Father unknown.

"What the fuck!" he yelled. Who the bloody hell was this jerk?

Determined to solve the mystery, he searched through the last batch of documents, opening every single paper. Nothing new.

He slammed his fist on the box, swearing. He had to find out who his father was. His brother needed to know too. That's why he kept on talking to him in his head. So many questions left without answers. Why had the man rejected him? Because of his handicap? No one could see it. Well, not until he got intimate.

Even if he did discover what he was looking for, then what? Both his mother and the person who he thought to be his father, were dead.

No one alive to answer questions.

With a flick of the hand, he shoved the box away. Didn't feel like racking his brains. He was in too much pain. Besides, he couldn't stop thinking of Jaime. He was dying to know how she felt after their last encounter.

He lit up a joint, all the while rubbing his leg, wondering when he would be in full swing again. He had a job to do.

Chapter 42

A quiet apartment welcomed Jaime when she arrived home. Too quiet. She stepped into the flat and switched on the lights.

"Dante?"

A deadly hush was the only reply.

She headed down the corridor to the bedroom, panic worming its way through her body. "Dante," she called again.

He said he'd be there. She didn't like this menacing silence.

A noise from beyond the lounge doors set Jaime's heart racing. An uneasy pain gnawed deep inside. Through the door's opaque pane of glass, she glimpsed a shadow moving further back into the room. Who was it? No one apart from her and Dante had a key, and the place hadn't been broken into.

She'd soon find out.

Easing the door open, she slid a hand up and down the sides of the wall, hunting around for the light switch, unsure of what she'd find.

When her finger hit the button, the room lit up with people shouting.

"Surprise!"

"Happy birthday!"

Jaime stepped back, mouth agape. It took a few seconds to register what was going on. With all the past events and agitation, she'd completely forgotten about her birthday. Had she really been in France for six whole months?

She caught sight of Dante beaming between dozens of blown up balloons. *I love you,* she mouthed with a hand on her heart.

Dante approached with two glasses of champagne. "Happy birthday, darling. Je t'aime."

She clinked glasses with him and took a long sip. "I love you too. And thanks for the surprise."

Dante gave her a peck on the cheek. "You deserve a party after this dreadful week."

He was right. Try as she might, she couldn't get the stalker out of her mind. At least for the next couple of hours, she'd have fun.

***

A smirk cracked his face as he gazed up to the fancy apartment on the first floor, a set of binoculars held firmly against his eyes.

This was going to be fun. He loved spying on people. Seeing what the other half were up to.

A car cruised down the quiet road. He took a quick step further back into the doorway, crying out in pain. The quick movement set his leg throbbing again. The Russian vet had been right, blast the bugger. The wound still needed time to heal.

He slumped against the cold stone wall, his eyes observing the scene above. A loud clack of the French windows opening on the balcony brought him out of the shadows.

"Happy thirtieth, Jaime!"

Loud voices escaped from the flat, breaking the silence outside. A growl rumbled in his throat. What a fucking noise. Was it necessary to make such a fuss over a bloody birthday? He spat on the ground.

Jaime took a glass from prick de Vere and gave a charming smile before she wrapped herself around him closer than food wrap. Pulling back, she giggled like a four-year-old. How old was the woman, for fuck's sake? He took a step forward and clenched his fists. What he'd give to slap that stupid smile or even slice it off.

Screams of joy echoed in the background before a small girl ran up to Jaime on the balcony, smoothing her clothes. "Do you like my party dress?" the little girl asked.

"It's lovely. Do they make them in my size?"

"*Do they make them in my size*?" he mimicked before his jaw tightened. How could anyone lower themselves to talk to stupid kids? How bloody ridiculous!

Jaime took a step back into the room and fell into the embrace of an older woman. Her mother. He recognised the old cow. They'd embraced when Jaime had left for France.

"Happy birthday," the woman said, pulling Jaime into an embrace.

The sickening lovey-dovey atmosphere made him want to puke. How pathetic they all were with their airs and graces. Kissing left, right and centre. Making out they loved each other when probably they hated each other's guts. He spat on the ground again.

Jaime hugged the woman back before giving a younger man a quick peck. "I can't believe you two are here," she laughed.

"We wouldn't miss this for the world," the man said.

That jerk had to be Jaime's brother. He remembered seeing him walk her home on several occasions. Especially after she'd received his letters. Absolute works of art.

"Are you all right, darling?" The older woman put a hand to Jaime's cheek.

"Of course."

"Your cheek's still bruised."

He sniggered. At least she had something to remember him by. Pity he hadn't had time to do a bit of sculpting with his knife.

Jaime disappeared into the flat, arms wrapped once again around the big-shit boyfriend, laughing as if she were enjoying herself.

He came out of the doorway and hobbled down the street to his car. "Make the most of your thirtieth, my love, because you won't be celebrating your thirty-first!"

***

Curled next to Dante on the settee, Jaime laid her head on his arm. "What a weekend. Thanks for making it happen."

"It was worth seeing you happy." Dante caressed her cheek.

"It was lovely to see everyone – especially my mother and Grant. Even though I only got to talk to him briefly." She caressed the tiny hairs on the back of Dante's neck. "What on earth were you and Grant doing locked away in the study?"

Dante gave her a peck on the nose but didn't reply.

Jaime let out a huge yawn. "I'm whacked. Not going be good company this evening."

"Why don't you turn in?"

"I think I will." She gave him a quick kiss and left for the bedroom while Dante headed to the study.

Falling into the chair, he stared at the envelope Grant had given him. Opening it, he swallowed hard on reading the contents. It was a copy of the letter Antonia had given her son. The letter she'd kept for over a year.

> *You don't know me, but I know all about you, even though we've never met.*
>
> *I am taking the liberty of writing to you now that John is no longer of this world.*
>
> *I met John a long time ago (almost thirty years) in England. We started dating secretly at work. He was the colleague whose office I shared and who was also in charge of my assignment. So we of course had to work together.*
>
> *I will spare you all the details, but one thing led to another, and we ended up being lovers.*
>
> *On finding I was pregnant, I didn't know if I felt happy or shocked. I was confused and perhaps a little upset. I knew all along he was married. He never hid that, and I knew he'd never leave you.*
>
> *Then came the fatal question. What was I going to do?*
>
> *I didn't want him to accuse me of getting pregnant to trap him, and as my first assignment was coming to an end, I decided to return to France...and not tell him.*
>
> *Being a single mum was something I hadn't envisioned as I was nearing my thirty-eighth birthday. But could I bring his*

child up alone?

A few years later, John got in contact with me again. He came to see me regularly during his business trips over the years, and after a great deal of coaxing, he persuaded me to return to England, where I lived in a small village not far from your home.

When I think back, our children no doubt went to the same school - isn't that bizarre?

At John's sudden death, I was devastated. I never imagined him losing his life like that. He was such a careful driver.

I suppose you're wondering why I'm writing so long after John's death? The truth is, I have a letter John left with me. In this letter he acknowledged his illegitimate son. He was going to write a will to include this son but he was killed before he had the chance.

I have been diagnosed with terminal cancer, and I'm not sure how long I will live. What a huge kick in the guts - John dies in an accident and I find out about my illness not long after. What more bad luck can fall on me?

I have left instructions with my lawyer who will contact you in the near future with all the legal papers as well as the proof of parentage of John's offspring. DNA tests were carried out.

John's son must not be forgotten regarding his estate.

I am sure this letter will come as a shock to you when you realise how little you knew your husband and his secret life.

I assure you, I am only doing this as I have no other choice.

Catherine MARTIN

Dante stared at the words until his vision blurred. What the hell was going on? He couldn't share this with Jaime. Not right now.

He replaced the letter in the envelope and sank back into the swivel chair. Not another head-scratcher. He couldn't think straight this late at night. Tomorrow he'd give Grant a call. See if Jaime's brother had any more information.

Getting up, he left the study and shuffled down the corridor to the bedroom. He had to push negative thoughts to the back of his mind. Make out nothing was wrong.

Jaime needed to be loved. That was exactly what he'd do.

Chapter 43

A few days had passed since Dante read the letter Grant had given him. He still had difficulties coming to terms with the news. He'd phoned Grant as planned, but the man had no more information. Dante had pressed Jaime's brother to ask Antonia. Grant had refused, unwilling to cause more heartache.

Alone in the study, Dante stared into space. The apartment lay quiet in the late evening. With a glass of cognac, he sat back, trying to figure out what the hell was going on. Not only was someone sending letters and attacking Jaime, he now had this incredible piece of news to digest. No matter how hard he tried, he couldn't concentrate on work. Catherine Martin's letter and the long wait for the DNA results from England were getting to him.

Moving uncomfortably in his chair, Dante rubbed his temples. He had to make sure Jaime was safe. That meant sending her away again. Not back to Luc's place though. He could do without that scenario.

Jaime entered the study. "It's late. Why don't you call it a day?"

Leaning back, Dante took in a deep breath. Frustration and anger crept through him. "I can't always stop when I'm tired." His irritable tone grated the quiet atmosphere.

"Can I get you anything?"

"No, thanks."

Jaime's shoulders drooped.

"Go back to bed, Jaime. I need to get on with my work."

"I can keep you company," she said in a whisper.

Dante stared into the glass. "Not in the mood for company right now."

Jaime bent her head and turned to go.

"Jaime." Dante's voice brought her to a standstill. "I'm in a bit of a temper, and I've no right to take it out on you, but I don't feel like talking."

Jaime took a step forward.

Dante held up a hand. "It would be better if you let me calm down on my own."

Jaime turned and left the cold study in complete silence.

***

Jaime woke the next morning to an empty bed. A tide of hurt rolled over her. She hadn't cried herself to sleep in a long time.

She got up and wandered around the empty flat, looking for a clue to where Dante could be. He hadn't even left a note. Returning to the bedroom, worry transformed into anguish. She could handle his commanding moods and bossiness. Not indifference and coldness.

Jaime's uncertainty heightened when her mind began working overtime. Where was he? Why had he been in such a foul mood the night before? Did he know something she didn't? Was he still having problems of his own and wouldn't let on?

The apartment door opened as she prepared the coffee. Dante came in, sweaty, and out of breath, dressed in running clothes. "You're up?" he said.

"And a good morning to you too," she replied without turning.

"I, er…was down in the gym room. Working out on the treadmill."

She peered over her shoulder. "I can see that."

Dante put on a weak smile and turned to leave. "I'm going to take a shower."

Jaime's eyes glazed with a glassy layer of tears and her lower lip quivered while words made their way slowly out. "Look, Dante." She stopped him in his tracks. "You can't avoid me and keep everything to yourself if I'm part of your troubles."

"How can you say that?" Dante's voice was hardly audible. "I've just got a lot on my mind."

"So that means you can dismiss me, not even come to bed with me, run off without a warning, and still not give me an explanation? I am a person, Dante, and I have feelings." She wiped her nose in a paper hanky. "I love you, and I'm prepared to put up with a lot. I know I'm not an easy person to live with. I'm doing my best."

Dante rubbed a trainer over an imaginary stain on the tiles.

Jaime sighed. "You were the one to say that a problem shared is a problem halved. Or does that only apply to others? We could have talked together instead of you fuelling your bad mood all night."

Dante came closer. "I needed to work late and didn't want to disturb you. I'll make it up to you. We'll have a quiet night in. I'll even cook."

Jaime didn't know whether to laugh or cry. He hadn't done all this on purpose, but rejection hurt. Now who was the one who couldn't confide? Had more problems popped up? Ones he couldn't talk about?

Jaime changed tactics, aware of the fact he didn't need more worries. "Is this to make up for your bad behaviour?"

A nervous smile played on Dante's lips.

"So you admit you've been in a bad mood?" she said, cocking her head to one side.

"A little," he grimaced and left the kitchen.

Jaime watched him leave and chewed on her thumbnail. Had she been too quick to criticize and judge? Maybe this had nothing to do with her. It could be work problems after all. Was she getting paranoid to the point of believing that every false move had something do to with her? She had to relax and back off. Not take everything out of context.

Maybe she should take the first step and make up.

She entered the bathroom. Her eyes feasted on the soap and water bouncing off Dante's strong muscled limbs in the shower. She licked her lips and joined him under the hot spray.

"I'm sorry about last night," he breathed into her ear. "Let me love you."

"Yes, please. And I'm sorry I snapped at you."

Dante dragged his tongue from the tender spot behind Jaime's ear down to the middle of her breasts. When he seized her hips and pushed Jaime up against the shower wall, sexy groans drowned out the noise of the dripping water. She clung to his neck, curling both legs around his waist.

The spray ricocheted off her breasts as she rested back against the wall. Moving with him, she cried out as ecstasy rushed to the rendezvous. She jerked again and again, taking Dante with her, both exploding in silent wonder.

Still in each other's arms, they slid down to the shower base, waiting to regain their normal breathing.

Dante broke the tranquil sound of the shower spray. "I've been a bit on edge, but I love you, even if I do act strangely at times."

***

Later that evening, they settled down in the living room with an aperitif.

"I haven't seen Corentin for a while," Jaime commented.

Dante gazed into his glass. "He's been promoted and moved to the south of France."

"That's lucky."

"Very. He deserved it."

Jaime raised an eyebrow, surprised at Dante's curt manner. Why was he so sharp and cold?

"Aren't you going to miss him?" she asked.

"I'll survive."

Jaime jerked her head back. "You and your jealousy."

Dante didn't rise to the bait, and Jaime decided to let things go. She took another sip of the drink. Time to change the subject. "I'm thinking of spending tomorrow evening with Suzanne. I haven't seen her since the party, and then only briefly. We may go out for a meal."

Dante moved uneasily. "Is that wise after what happened?"

Jaime didn't answer.

"I don't want you taking unnecessary risks."

Jaime set the glass down more energetically than expected, spilling the contents. "So what am I supposed to do? Sit at home and wait for the next letter?"

Dante's expression was one of bafflement.

"I haven't received any letters recently." Jaime took on a calmer tone. "Maybe he's seriously injured, lying in a ditch somewhere – or even dead?"

"I doubt it."

Jaime rubbed a hand up and down Dante's arm, feeling tense muscles under her touch. "Please, Dante."

"If you want to have some time with Suzanne, she can come here."

Jaime pulled back her hand. "Not the same."

"I'll even spend the evening with Luc in a bar. I haven't had a brotherly chat for a long while. How does that sound?" He took hold of Jaime's hand and caressed a thumb over her palm. "I'm not doing this to annoy you. Until we have more news back from Inspector Durand, I'd feel better if you stayed at home where you're safe."

Although Jaime had injured the stalker, she knew she had to be cautious. But was being barricaded in the flat a solution?

Chapter 44

Monday morning came all too quick. Busy working on the English version of the company's website, Jaime couldn't concentrate. Her mind kept wandering back to the night before. Although their lovemaking had been fantastic, a sixth sense said Dante was holding something back.

Satisfied with the last line of the translation, Jaime gathered the files and carried them to Dante's office. His swivel chair sat against the wall, no doubt pushed back in a hurry. He'd even forgotten to switch off the desk lamp. A deafening silence hung in the air.

While walking to the filing cabinet, an envelope in the middle of the desk attracted Jaime's eye. She wouldn't have paid much attention if it hadn't been for the name written in Dante's handwriting.

Leonora.

Hovering over the envelope, Jaime chewed on her lower lip while she ran a hesitant finger along its edges. Should she pry into Dante's business?

Just open the damned thing and put your mind at rest.

But would it? What if the contents shattered her world? For half a second, she considered leaving the office. Jaime knew she was playing with fire. No doubt risking Dante's trust.

Concern pulled her toward the envelope like an oversized magnet. What was the saying – curiosity killed the cat?

With a huge intake of breath, she picked it up, all the while checking the door. The envelope lay heavy in her hand. Wasn't even sealed. Besides, with Dante in court all morning, she wouldn't get caught if she took a glance inside.

Without further debate, she flicked the flap open and pulled out the contents. Her heart skipped several beats.

Jesus Christ!

The envelope contained prints of Leonora in the nude, playing with some kind of 'toy' she never imagined existed. Jaime's eyes fixed the prints, mouth gaping like a fish out of water. What the hell was Dante doing with these photos? Was he the one who took them? Could this be the reason he'd been in a foul mood the other night? A reminder of what he'd been missing?

Holding onto the chair, Jaime stared at the photos, anger taking over. Her hand came down with a hard slam on the desk.

Not them!

She shook her head. Was this his kinky, dark side? She couldn't believe it. Dante wasn't like that. Yet she had proof. This time, she slammed both hands down on the desk.

What the f...!

A noise from the corridor brought Jaime's movements to a halt. She wiped away a couple of runaway tears and slipped the prints back into the envelope. Then, rearranging herself into something she hoped looked normal, she left.

Back in her office, she tried to calm the nausea churning deep inside. What was she going to do?

The noise of familiar stiletto heels in the corridor caught her attention. She opened the door and peered at Leonora, a hand raised, ready to knock on Dante's colleague's door.

"Fancy seeing you here."

"Why do you say that, Leonora? You know I work here."

"Of course, you do. Have to work for a living, don't you?"

"Well at least I'm making honest money. Not playing with sex toys for the camera."

Leonora gave her a thumbs-up. "Dante enjoyed our photo sessions. Sorry you had to find out about it this way. He was always a bit of a dark horse."

Jaime stumbled back, steadying herself on the corridor wall. *So the swine did take them.* The volcano in her was about to erupt.

Leonora knocked on the door and took a step into the office. "I should never have trusted Dante. He said it would be our little secret. Men...you can't rely on them."

Jaime held back the well of tears, telling herself this was not the time or place to break down. Dante had deceived her all along. The whole thing was surreal. But those filthy images were for real.

Jaime's fists contracted into small round balls as she imagined ripping into him.

***

Jaime waited in Dante's office, staring at the envelope on the desk. Fear of the forthcoming confrontation escalating with each minute that passed. Not so much the anxiety of questioning him. More of what he might reveal. And the consequences.

Dante entered the office a little before two and found Jaime hunched over the desk, eyes fixed in a blank stare, fingers drumming the table. He placed his jacket on the back of a chair and dropped his briefcase next to the desk.

"What's up?"

Jaime jerked her chin in the direction of the envelope. "You tell me."

Dante turned to the middle of the desk and for a fraction of a second his mouth twitched. "What the hell's that doing there?"

"Yes, Dante, what the hell's this doing here? And what the hell is going on?"

Dante's lips pressed into a thin line. "I suppose you've taken a look inside?"

"Too bloody true I have."

Dante scratched the back of his neck. "I left this file with my colleague."

"Well, it's grown legs and crept from his office onto your desk." Sarcasm edged Jaime's voice.

Dante flashed a scowl in Jaime's direction before moving his gaze back to the envelope. "Calm down. You sound like an angry wasp in a jam jar."

Jaime jumped to her feet, sending the chair scraping across the wooden floor. "Are you going to explain why you're still seeing Leonora for kinky photo sessions?"

"What on earth are you talking about? I have nothing to do with this!"

"That's not what Leonora said. Apparently, you two are still seeing each other."

Dante cast a darkened gaze onto the ground before glancing back up. "Believe me; you've got the wrong end of the stick."

"Are you sure? I know 'love makes you blind'. I assumed I had good eyesight. Plus, Leonora confirmed my suspicions."

Dante swore under his breath. He grabbed the office phone and tapped in an extension number.

"Etienne, could you please come into the office for a second?"

No sooner had Dante replaced the receiver than a knock sounded on the door and a young man entered.

Dante cleared his throat. "Etienne, could you please explain what this file is doing on my desk?"

A flush crept across the young man's cheeks. "That's where it is? I came to leave some papers." He nodded at another pile of files on Dante's desk. "Must have left it behind."

"Thank you, Etienne."

"Is everything all right?" The young man asked before opening the door to leave.

Dante looked Jaime straight in the eye. "Everything's fine."

Jaime stared at the parquet. Long seconds passed. She still kept her head down, swishing her hair forward, trying to hide burning cheeks. Guilt gnawed deep inside.

The door closed behind Etienne and Dante let out a long whistle through his teeth. "I'm going to have another word with Leonora and finish with this mess. She didn't take my last warning seriously. This lie is the last straw. I refuse to have her malice ruin our relationship."

"So what are you going to do?"

"Trust me on this."

Jaime took a step forward. "I'll come with you."

"I'm going alone." His cold voice hinted negotiation was out of the question.

"But..."

Dante raised a hand. "Things may get messy. Leonora has to know that enough is enough."

"Let me come with you. For my peace of mind."

The pleading look she gave him fell onto stony ground. Dante was in lawyer-mode. Eyes set on a point on the wall. No emotion. No point in arguing. He wouldn't succumb to any attempts to convince him.

"The answer is no."

Jaime shrugged and didn't press the matter further, her mind already in full swing with the next stratagem. "When are you going?"

"Later this afternoon. I have an important debriefing in a few minutes." He grabbed his jacket and gave Jaime a quick peck on the cheek.

Jaime watched him leave the office. She'd come up with a plan. That plan meant getting back to the flat and changing into something more comfortable.

***

Dante rushed down the corridor when his phone buzzed. Fishing it out, he stopped in mid stride on seeing the caller's name. "Grant, I'm about to go into a meeting. Can I call you back?"

Uneven breathing echoed down the phone before Grant spoke. "It won't take long. Just give me a minute. It's about our...assumptions."

"Okay, fire away then, but be quick."

It took Grant about fifteen seconds to give the fateful news. Dante's brain formulated no thoughts other than to take in the shock. He closed his mouth and squeezed both eyes shut.

Jesus wept! How was he going to explain this to Jaime?

He let out a deep sigh before speaking. "Are you sure? Grant! Are you there?" He jerked the phone away from his ear and glared at the black screen. Flat battery.

"Fucking mobile crap!"

Raging like a bull, he shoved the phone into his pocket and swung back the door to the meeting room.

***

Back at the apartment, Jaime stepped out of her stilettos and slipped into a pair of flat sandals. Her pleated skirt lay in a heap on the bedroom floor where she'd dropped it in a hurry to pull on a pair of shorts. The weather had finally perked up, and June was proving to be a hottie. With her handbag in one hand and the car keys grasped in the other, she slammed the door to the flat and headed down to the lobby.

About twenty minutes later, pleased on finding a parking space not far from the office, Jaime adjusted the car mirrors and settled down to wait. Tension and anxiety built up while she tapped the steering wheel with nervous fingers. Every muscle was sprung tight, ready for action. Jaime's body screamed to get going, but her mind remained more or less calm, waiting for Dante to appear.

In a world of her own, Jaime jumped when her phone buzzed. A tinge of panic fell onto her chest on seeing Grant's name on the screen.

"Hi. What's up?"

"Er...is Dante with you? I've been trying to get hold of him."

Jaime's face twisted into a frown. "No, he isn't."

Grant's heavy breathing filled her ears. "When you see him, can you get him to call me back? It's important."

Jaime sat bolt upright. "What's important?"

"I'd rather talk to Dante first."

"Hang on, Grant. What's going on?"

Rolling her eyes in exasperation, she spotted Dante rushing out of the office building.

"Shit! I have to go, Grant. Something's cropped up."

Quickly ending the call, Jaime looked at the time and flung the phone onto the passenger seat. Three-thirty. Why was he leaving so early? Did this have anything to do with Grant's phone call?

Dante climbed into his car, eased out of the parking space, and drove away in the opposite direction. Shit! He was going the other way.

Jaime turned on the ignition and swung out of the parking space, almost causing an accident. She thanked her lucky stars and did a quick three-point turn. At the end of the road the traffic lights turned red, giving her the opportunity to get closer. She clutched the steering wheel and smiled.

She was two cars behind. Perfect.

Chapter 45

The afternoon sun wrapped the garden in warmth.

June was Leonora's favourite season. As a child, she'd been allowed to set up a tent on the vast domain. Made a change from the austere atmosphere her grandmother had created in the manoir over the years. She remembered the lake reflecting the magenta sky before going to sleep, the chirping birds waking her early in the morning. All that had long gone.

Her phone rang, and with a sigh, she dragged herself away from the window to answer it.

"Sorry I've been neglecting you, darling."

"Sod off."

"Always happy to hear from me, I see."

Leonora didn't reply.

"I'm coming with another photo. So be prepared. Oh...and I hate to disappoint you, but I won't be able to give you a good ride. I've got a dodgy leg."

Leonora rolled her eyes. "Pity you haven't got a dodgy dick," she hissed.

"Of course, you could always use your mouth."

"Don't hold your breath."

"Now, now...no need to get snarky."

Why shouldn't she be? She felt awful. Being nauseous for the past couple of hours had made her irritable. It could have been the oysters she'd eaten with Xavier the night before. But *he* wasn't ill. Could it be a mild attack of gastric flu?

"I'll be there for my 10,000 in about twenty minutes." His harsh voice brought Leonora back to the conversation.

"What the f–" she began, only to find he'd hung up.

You are not getting another sodding centime. The stipulation has come to an end and so has your money grabbing scheme.

***

"So where's my cash?"

He'd arrived at the estate in a foul mood. It had taken him longer than usual to drive, but no stiff leg was going to get in his way, even if it meant walking like a clockwork soldier.

Leonora stared at him, mouth gaping. "How the hell did you get in?

"I'm full of surprises," he smirked, holding up a lock pick. "Now, give me what's due."

"Sod off."

He couldn't believe his ears. He limped toward her and slapped her across the cheek, sending her staggering against the wall and to the ground in a heap.

"You bastard," she yelped, holding her burning cheek.

A muscle twitched in his right eye. "Where's my money?"

"Up yours!" Leonora thrust her middle finger up at him.

"And that's where I intend to go." He pounced forward and landed on top of her. Leonora's head fell back against the wall, and he heard her cry out in pain as he dug his strong fingers into her knees.

"Want to play games? I'll take my 10,000 from your sweet arse."

Leonora scratched out at him. "Get the hell off me. NOW!"

He pressed his forearm against Leonora's neck to keep her to the ground while the other hand waved the phone at her.

"If you don't give me my money now, I'm going to put a couple of your kinky photos onto the web. All I have to do is press here, and we'll be able to count the 'likes' you'll get for your bare pussy."

Leonora tried to grab the phone, but before she could seize it, he touched the screen, sending the photos onto the web.

Leonora's ear-piercing scream filled the air as she tried to push him away. He gave another sharp slap across her mouth, and she collapsed like a puppet whose strings had just been cut.

Chapter 46

Pensive, Dante slammed the car door shut and stormed up to Leonora's mansion.

A long wail tore through the air like an animal in distress. Dante's eyes widened and his pulse quickened. What the hell was that? With his heart thudding like a jackhammer, he took longer strides.

The shriek came again. Desperate. Human.

Dante's legs pounded up the patio steps and halted for a split second on finding the front door wide open. Surprised but not put off, he hurried in, and slammed it shut behind him.

He strained to listen for more sounds, more hints as to where the cries had come from. Pitiful whimpering came from the living room. Dante turned in the direction of the noise. A hint of blood whirled in the air before he found Leonora's limp body sprawled on the floor, her panties round her ankles.

A sudden pang of pity hit Dante's chest. Regardless of his anger, no one deserved to be treated like this. He rushed over and pulled Leonora's skirt down. Her frightened eyes relaxed on seeing him.

"Dante?" she whispered.

"Yes," he said, gazing down at her disfigured profile and ripped silk blouse. A surge of rage invaded him.

"Go get him, Dante," she managed to say through swollen lips. "He's just left."

"What are you talking about?"

"When I wouldn't give him the money...he raped me and put the photos on the net."

Dante reached for the house phone and called the police. Remaining calm, he gave the address and explained briefly what had happened, also mentioning that the assailant was still in the vicinity.

He switched off the phone and brushed a strand of hair away from Leonora's clammy face. "Help is on its way."

"Run, Dante. If you hurry, you can catch the bastard. He leaves the car on the west side of the property. He can't run. Something happened to his leg. I'll be fine, believe me."

"Are you sure?" Dante's voice was edged with concern.

"Perfectly sure. Stop wasting time and go get him," she shouted, rising slowly to her feet.

Dante rushed outside before pulling to a halt. A thought flashed through him. No, it couldn't be. Shaking his head, he darted across the lawn to the woods.

***

Jaime stared through the entrance of the huge property. Two immense iron gates gaped open on either side of a long driveway. So this was Leonora's home.

She'd parked the car further down the road and had doubled back to the entrance. Standing by the portals, she wondered whether to take a step further. Would she be trespassing? Tough. She needed to know what Dante was up to.

Captivated by the grandiose landscape, Jaime hurried up the long avenue of lime trees leading to the front of the mansion. The fragrance of white jasmine filled the air. Alive with buzzing bees, they sat in well-kept flower beds bordering long stretches of moss-free lawn. Out of the corner of her eye, Jaime caught sight of a beautiful pond mirroring the sky. She took in a deep breath. The property flowed with serenity and class.

Arriving on the patio, she looked around cautiously before reaching for the door handle.

Locked.

She bent to look through one of the panes of glass. No movement. Now what was she going to do?

Jaime spotted a weathercock a short distance away between the trees. It looked to be a summer house. Could Dante be there? She stepped off the patio and strode to the back of the house, taking in the subtle sweet scent of oriental lily and honeysuckle. She cut across the lawn and disappeared into the cool, small woods.

***

Hobbling through the trees, he tucked his shirt into his trousers, grinning at the vision of Leonora sprawled on the floor. Her arse had been so sweet; he hadn't even cared about the pain in his leg.

Wrapped up in his thoughts, he wondered how he was going to get new income. The snap of a twig caught his attention. Turning in the direction of the noise, he spotted her.

The gods were on his side after all.

Chapter 47

Weaving through the trees, Jaime scrutinised the surroundings. She couldn't hear any noises. Birds had stopped chirping, and the breeze teasing the leaves in the trees had ceased. No more distant sound of the woodpecker. That wasn't normal.

She ran across the small clearing, eager to get back into the comforting refuge of the trees when someone dashed out in front of her.

"Hello, darling."

Wide-eyed, Jaime let out a deafening scream. "David Thibert?" Her hand flew to her chest. "But you're dead. The police told me you were killed in prison."

A small smile played on his lips. "I was never inside, you silly slut."

"But I testified against you."

"Of course you did," he grinned. "But I'm not David."

Startled, Jaime couldn't figure out what was going on. One thing she did know: she had to get away. Turning to run, she'd hardly taken a few strides before rough hands pulled her from behind and latched onto her neck. The smell of blood spiraled up Jaime's nose as dirt-stained fingers dug deep into her skin.

Jaime tried to grab for his wrist, but his grip tightened. She gasped for oxygen. If this man wasn't David, then who the hell could he be? He looked like him. Sounded like him. Even smelt like him.

"Who the hell are you?" she managed to ask.

"Why, I'm Eddie. David's twin brother."

Christ Almighty! She definitely had to get the hell out of there. This psycho was capable of anything. Jaime tried to kick back into the man's shins only to have his strong arms stiffen around her, bringing all efforts to a halt.

"That's no way to treat Eddie, is it?" His stale nicotine breath wafted through the air. From his back trouser pocket, he pulled out a sharp flick knife. "This should calm you."

Tears of helplessness and rage trickled down her cheeks. "Get your filthy hands off me." Jaime used all her willpower to stop herself from retching. "I'm not scared of you."

Eddie closed a hand over Jaime's mouth, his lips only inches from her ear. "I bet you were scared shitless when you got my letters."

A little more pressure pushed the knife nearer to Jaime's throat.

The blade was cold on her tender skin, making it hard for her to swallow.

"Mmm, you smell so good," he said, and licked her neck. "Can even taste your fear."

A choking noise sounded in Jaime's throat as his wet tongue raised goosebumps all over her body.

"Thought you could get away from me, didn't you?"

The knife slid between her breasts and Jaime felt his arousal against the top of her thigh.

"Didn't you?" he repeated.

A sharp crack sounded nearby, and the blade glided back to Jaime's throat.

"Come out, whoever you are." Eddie's harsh voice rang in the air as he pulled Jaime into the clearing. "I know you're there."

Jaime gave a startled gasp.

"Come out, now!" he hollered.

Eddie took his hand away from Jaime's mouth, and she cried out in surprise. The sting of the blade cut into her skin. Warm blood slowly trickled between her breasts.

"I said come out, or I'll bleed her like an animal." He pushed harder onto the blade.

Dante stepped into the small clearing, his expression set in a stone mask. "Let her go."

Jaime's heart thumped against her ribcage as she raised her gaze. "Dante!"

Eddie tightened his grip and jerked the knife, drawing more blood. "Shut it!"

An uncontrolled cry escaped Jaime once again.

"Why are you doing this?" Dante demanded.

"You don't know what I've been through. You don't know what it's like to be an outcast and have people sneer at you. I had to work."

"Oh for Christ's sake, grow up, man. Everybody has to work." Dante almost spat out the words.

"Not like everybody. I bet you didn't have to work all hours for a pittance. I even had to work in a slaughter house."

An acrid, bitter odour oozed from Eddie's armpits mingled with that strange, indescribable odour that she'd smelt on his twin. Jaime scrunched her nose. He probably hadn't counted on Dante finding them. Neither had she. But Christ, was she happy. That said, she dreaded Eddie's next plan of action.

Dante glared at them.

"So that means it's okay for you to go around raping women? Is that what you're saying?" Dante's voice was filled with disgust. "Haven't you done enough harm?"

Eddie snorted. "You don't know what it's like to have your long-lost brother sent to prison because this little bitch gave evidence against him in court." He spat on the ground and dug his fingers deeper into Jaime's skin.

"You won't get away with this, Eddie," Dante shouted.

Eddie tightened his elbow around Jaime's neck, making it difficult for her to breathe. "How do you know who I am?"

"I know more than you think."

"Do you now, you pompous prick? Did you know my brother was put behind bars? Imprisonment leaves you alone. All alone with your thoughts."

Eddie threw he head back and laughed into the sky. "It's okay, bro. We've got her. We'll finally have our revenge."

Dante took a step nearer. "And what about, Cindy? Don't you think she was all alone with *her* thoughts?"

Eddie snorted and pulled Jaime towards the edge of the woodland. "David told me Cindy was a cockteaser. She deserved what she got."

The cold metal pinched Jaime's throat with every step they took and the tendons in the back of her neck ached where he pulled her head back, but she grit her teeth.

"You are a nasty piece of shit." Dante scrunched his nose in repulsion. "And what about Leonora who you blackmailed and then raped?"

"Leonora raped?" Jaime whimpered.

"That slag? She wouldn't pay up, so I took what was due to me," Eddie shouted back. "She wasn't a good fuck anyway. She's a whore!"

Dante took another quick step forward. "You deserve to be put away for good."

The knife slid over Jaime's cheekbone before sinking in once more. Warm liquid trickled down her face, and she let out a choked gasp.

"Wanna see the bitch bleed again? Then take a step nearer," he shouted, spittle dropping onto Jaime's hand as she clung onto Eddie's arm around her neck.

Dante remained still. Helpless, he gazed into Jaime's eyes, and she read the torture there.

"I love you," she mouthed, glancing at Dante clenching and unclenching his fists.

"For Christ's sake, let her go! You're ruining your life."

"What's it to you?" A mad laugh escaped Eddie's throat. "My life's been ruined since I was a child. Do you know what it's like to be an only child with a father who was never around, and an unhappy mother because of it?" He gripped Jaime closer to him. "I only knew I had a twin brother when he came looking for me a few years ago. I was so happy even though he didn't want to meet our mother, saying what a bitch she'd been giving him up at birth. But David's dead now. I've got nothing to lose. I've got nobody. No parents. No brothers or sisters. Nobody."

For a moment all turned silent.

"You *do* have family," Dante said, breaking the silence.

"No, I don't. You lying, obnoxious prick. My brother died in prison."

"I wouldn't lie to you. There's too much at stake. Look...your sister's here."

A rustle in the bushes drew Eddie's attention. He gazed around, searching for a face.

***

Through the leaves on the small trees, a silhouette focused on Jaime struggling with the bastard. It felt good holding a gun. A little squeeze of the finger and the jerk would be dead. A difficult decision to make. It had to be done. The swine had brought so much unhappiness and fear to them all. But it would be worth it. Besides, nothing mattered any more. Thank God he was a lot taller than his hostage, but the moment had to be right. If he kept on ducking his head close to Jaime's, the bullet could miss and hit her.

***

Eddie took in quick breaths.

"Jaime's your sister," Dante said in a loud, clear voice.

"Shut your fucking mouth! Lying won't save her." Eddie dug the knife deeper into Jaime's skin.

"She's your *half*-sister."

Jaime gasped. Petrified, she shut her eyes but they shot open when Eddie put a little more pressure onto the blade and moved it dangerously close to her right eye. Walls of darkness closed in, threatening to suffocate her.

Eddie shook his head in disbelief. The sound of sirens wailed in the distance. He moved the knife to slash Jaime's throat.

"Eddie," Dante called, "Eddie, she's your sister for Christ's sake."

"So what? Sister or no sister, she's gonna pay. She put David in prison. Because of her testifying against him, I lost my only family. I hate the bitch, even if she is supposedly my sist–"

A violent crack echoed in the clearing as a bullet shot out from the trees and hit Eddie straight in the temple. The loud noise and whistle of the bullet sailing by her ear made Jaime jump. Eddie's hold loosened, and Jaime realised she was alone. He lay on the ground, the knife still held tightly in his hand.

Holding out trembling hands, Jaime stumbled towards Dante. In a few quick strides, Dante pulled her into his arms. "What has the bastard done to you?" he said, examining the cut marks on Jaime's neck and cheek. "Christ, how I wish he was still alive so I could beat the life out of him."

Jaime's knees buckled and her legs gave way.

"It's all right, mon amour. I've got you."

"I think I'm going to be s...sick," she hiccupped.

"Breathe. Don't think of anything else, just concentrate on breathing."

***

Jaime's eyes fluttered, and Dante wrapped his arms tighter around her, speaking in a low reassuring voice. He couldn't believe it. The person who'd terrified his girlfriend for so long was now on the ground with blood trickling from a neat small hole in the temple. Jesus Christ. If she'd been the same height as Eddie, it could have been *her* lying on the ground.

Dante glimpsed a triumphant Leonora stepping out of the woods. Despite a swollen nose and torn, blood-stained clothes, she headed up to them with a gun held tightly in her hand, and studied Eddie's body with a look of true hatred.

"Good riddance." Leonora spat on Eddie's body and kicked him in the groin before howling with manic laughter.

"You...you saved my life, Leonora," Jaime gulped.

Leonora shot Jaime a quick look. "Don't worry. I'm not getting soft. I didn't do it for you."

"But you could have missed. The bullet could have hit me instead."

"Count your lucky stars I'm a good shot, then."

Loud shouting from the house caught Dante's attention. He released Jaime and darted into the clearing, arms high in the air. "Over here!"

Police and paramedics headed towards the small group while Dante returned to Jaime's side. The woman looked lost. Huge eyes focused on the ground, arms clasped tightly around her body. Was she even aware of her surroundings?

Dante crouched next to Jaime and unfolded her arms. She needed to be hugged. Pulling a few stray hairs away from the blood on her cheek, he placed his arms around her and held her tight.

Leonora stood in a trance with the gun in hand and a hint of a smile pasted on her face, looming over the dead body. Motionless, like a marble statue in a Greek tragedy, she simply stared into the abyss. Unaware of all around her.

"Drop the gun, madame." A policeman's loud voice rang out in the clearing.

Leonora turned, still gripping the weapon. Two police officers approached, firearms drawn, eyes focused on Leonora's gun.

"I said, drop the gun."

The weapon slipped out of Leonora's limp hand before the policemen rushed up to retrieve it. Dante studied the drama before his eyes, unfolding like some sort of detective movie. Only this was reality. The scene couldn't be filmed again if the ending didn't go to plan.

A policeman in his early thirties slipped a pair of handcuffs onto Leonora's wrists before the paramedics took charge of her. Dante hardly recognised the woman. Drooping shoulders, eyes narrowed in confusion, shuffling footsteps...she appeared broken. Not the proud, outspoken Leonora he'd known in the past.

She'd caused heartache to Jaime, yet he felt sorry for her. She had money and came from a bourgeois family, but lacked affection. No love or tenderness as a child. Abandoned by her mother when a toddler. Ignored by her father. Destiny had left her to be brought up in the hands of a cantankerous grandmother.

"The lady's fine to travel," one paramedic called out, closing his medical bag. The hospital will check her out further. She'll need a gynaecological examination."

A policeman guided Leonora to the police car. She took her time, pulling on the handcuffs, moaning under her breath. Before climbing into the vehicle, Leonora caught Dante's eye. A small pout played on her lips along with a slight narrowing of the eyes and a tiny tilt of the head. It was subtle. Dante picked up on it. A sly grin that made him wonder if they hadn't seen the last of the woman. Did Leonora have one last sneaky trick up her sleeve?

"It's your turn now, my dear," the paramedic said to Jaime.

She stared up at the man and Dante released his hold. "I'm fine. More frightened than hurt."

The man smiled and spoke in a gentle voice. "I'll just clean those wounds on your cheek and throat. They don't look deep enough to warrant stitches, but you'll still need to call into the hospital."

Dante stood while the paramedic crouched next to Jaime and attended to the wounds. More people had stepped onto the scene of the crime. Some took photos, others rough sketches. Inspector Durand had arrived, accompanied by the coroner who Dante recognised.

Once Jaime was treated, Dante helped her to stand.

"After your trip to the hospital, Miss Sanders, I'd like you to call into the police station to make a statement," the inspector told her.

The medical examiner inspected Eddie and pronounced him dead. An assistant covered the body with a sheet before it was placed in a body bag and driven to the morgue for autopsy.

“Come on, love. Let’s go home.” Dante pulled Jaime into his arms and held her tight.

She wrapped her arms around his waist and nodded, too devastated to speak.

Chapter 48

Jaime broke the silence that had consumed them in the hours after the long, draining visit to the police station. "I can't get over what you said about Eddie being my brother. I honestly thought you'd made it up to play for time."

"I'm afraid it's true. Eddie is, or rather was, your half-brother."

Jaime slumped down on the settee, a bitter tang in her mouth. She couldn't believe that the person who had stalked and molested her was a member of the family. The thought of his calloused hands and foul, nicotine breath made her skin crawl. Even now.

A cold shiver slid through Jaime's body as her mind replayed what she'd been through in agonizing detail. She pulled the plaid over her legs and took the cup of tea from Dante's outstretched hand before curling into him. "Okay, let me have it."

Dante took a deep breath. "Do you remember the phone call you got from your mother about a month ago?"

Jaime nodded.

"A while back, she received a letter from a Catherine Martin, the woman who'd had an affair with your father."

Sadness flowed through Jaime. What betrayal. How could he have done this to her mother? Had life been so bad at home that he'd sought a secret life? She didn't know the problems between her parents. They'd never shown any form of hatred to one another.

"Are you sure about all this?" she asked.

"Grant was intrigued by the news, so he decided to investigate further by hiring a professional genealogist in France. It appeared that as a result of your father's long-term affair with this woman, who was French by the way, Edouard was born in France."

Jaime raised an eyebrow. "So that's why he had no accent when he spoke French."

"Right. A few months after receiving Catherine's letter, your mother received one from Catherine's lawyer along with DNA test results proving Eddie was your father's illegitimate son. Catherine knew that although your father had left a document with her, acknowledging Eddie as his son, this was not enough."

"Oh my God!" Jaime's skin tingled. "He must have loved this son to include him in the heritage."

Jaime gnawed hard at the cuticle on her thumb, ignoring the

excruciating pain, only just able to take in what Dante was saying. "I wonder if this is the reason for Mum's behaviour since I was a child. She must have had an inkling about Dad's affair."

Her eyes moistened on imagining how devastating it must have been for her mother when she'd learnt the news. Had they tried to patch things up? Obviously so. Her chest ached. Upset because of her father's secret life. She always assumed he'd been away on business trips, when in fact he could have been with this other woman.

Remembering back, though, how could she hate him? The rare times he'd been at home, he'd spent with his children. He'd been a good dad. Maybe there had been a reason for him to have a double life.

"You okay, Jaime?"

Jaime nodded, and set the cup down on the gueridon next to the settee.

"After having been acknowledged by your father as his son, if Eddie had lived, he would have been entitled to part of the inheritance."

Jaime's sigh was audible. "So that's why it was important for Eddie's mother to let us to know about him."

"Yes. She also felt she had done the best for him by coming clean. And maybe find a family, knowing she didn't have long to live."

Jaime fiddled with her pearl necklace. "But why now?"

Dante took hold of his girlfriend's hands. "Being a salesman, and spending a huge amount of his time on the road, your father had signed a special clause in his life insurance. Should he die in a car accident, your mother and his three children would receive equal amounts of the money."

Jaime clasped Dante's fingers.

"When the insurance company contacted your mother, I reckon, she believed it was time to tell her children about Eddie. The news would be better coming from her rather than for you to learn it from them."

"How do you know all this?"

"Grant phoned to clarify that all the information was authentic just before I went to see Leonora."

Jaime closed her eyes and allowed herself to fall loose. Head tilted against Dante's comforting chest, she matched her breathing to his regular heartbeat. The relaxing sound did wonders for frazzled nerves. Her eyes narrowed while she put various pieces together, imagining the different steps Eddie had taken to find her. And he had. Through sheer determination.

She took in a deep breath. "What's all this business about Eddie's twin brother?"

"It seems Catherine gave birth to twins by caesarean. She was told one of them died at birth. In fact, the baby had been taken for adoption."

"But that's illegal." Jaime clamped a hand to her chest.

"I know. The director of the clinic where Catherine gave birth had a small business going with an agency to provide babies for adoption. As Catherine would be a single mother, he believed he was doing her a favour by taking a baby off her hands. And, of course, a reason for him to top up his income."

Jaime gazed at the wall ahead. A pang of sympathy building deep inside for this woman. "So Eddie's brother grew up in France."

Dante reached for Jaime's hand. "That's right. His parents never hid the fact he was adopted. And as most adopted children, he decided to search for his twin. They didn't have much time together because of their problems with the law. And that's where you came into their lives."

"How do you know all this?"

"From your brother and the results he received from the genealogist."

"Why didn't Grant tell me?"

Dante caressed her cheek with the back of his hand. "Maybe he reckoned you had enough on your plate. But I'm sure he'll give you all the details later."

Memories weighed heavily. Part of Jaime felt she'd missed out on something. A brother she never knew existed. Or rather, two brothers. Would the twins' lives have been any different if they'd never been separated? Leading a happy family life without crime?

Flashes of the murder came galloping back. Guttural chokes, the unmistakable metallic smell of blood, and those callous eyes. Jaime's voice caught in her throat. "I saw him stab that man. I actually saw my brother kill someone."

"Your half-brother," Dante specified. "Anyway, David Thibert was apprehended, tried and sentenced for the two offences."

Jaime nodded.

"When I asked Inspector Durand to send your assailant's DNA sample to the police in England to run against their DNA database, a match was made which they couldn't understand as Thibert had died in prison. This meant that the only other person who could have attacked you at Luc's place was Eddie. Being identical twins means identical blood groups and identical DNA profiles."

Jaime's eyes flew wide open, amazed at the news. "They even had the same smell."

Dante acquiesced. "Same smell because same medical problem. A urostomy."

"A what?"

"It's a surgical procedure, diverting the normal flow of urine from the kidneys and ureters into a specially created stoma."

Jaime pulled a puzzled face.

"In other words, a bag for urine."

"Bloody hell."

"There are a number of reasons for a urostomy, all connected to a defect or problem with the urinary system which needs to be removed or bypassed. Babies are sometimes born with a defect of their urinary system."

"That's so sad."

A flash of chagrin drained through Jaime. Some people didn't have much luck in life. Could she consider herself lucky? At present, she didn't even have the energy to answer that question. Her mind too bogged down with confused thoughts. What she'd give to rid her brain of everything. Maybe if she shook her head hard enough, they'd fly away.

She chewed on her bottom lip and went through each event. The stalker's identity. Eddie shot dead. The incredible news that Eddie was in fact her half brother. Not to mention David.

Jaime lowered her knees, and grabbed a cushion. "What about Leonora? I can't get over her shooting Eddie. That said, she did save my life."

"I know, love, but sometimes shame and humiliation can motivate violence to others."

"Like revenge?"

Dante spoke as if in a trance. "Leonora was raped and blackmailed. Humiliated to a point of no return."

Jaime leaned her head against Dante's shoulder. "I'm glad this is all behind us."

"Oui, mon amour, time to forget and move on."

Chapter 49

Curled up on the settee in the warm and cosy lounge, Jaime waited for Dante. Two weeks had passed since Leonora's garde à vue. Dante had kept a close eye on the case. He'd informed Jaime that Leonora had been taken to the 'poste de police' for interrogation regarding the circumstances leading up to Eddie's death.

Leonora admitted to shooting Eddie to save Jaime's life and went straight into remand in prison where she was waiting to appear before the judge.

Dante entered the flat, dropped his briefcase next to the front door and entered the lounge.

"Everything okay?" she asked.

Dante nodded and headed for the kitchen. "How about a drink?" he called over his shoulder.

"Champagne would be nice. We need to celebrate the end of this nightmare. There's no more stalker and I can finally look to the future."

"You're right. I'll get the tall glasses."

He returned to the lounge with a chilled bottle of Bollinger. He eased out the cork and filled the two glasses Jaime held out. The frothy champagne sparkled to life.

Jaime tilted her glass towards Dante's. "This is just what I need."

"To us and a new beginning." Dante took a long gulp.

"So how are things?"

Dante sat next to Jaime. "Leonora admitted to shooting Eddie. The fact that she had been raped and that she wanted to stop Eddie from harming you will be submitted by her defense lawyer at a later stage and will assist the jury."

Jaime nodded.

"In the meantime, she'll remain in custody until the trial, whenever that may be."

Things were looking up.

Could this be the happy-ever-after she'd dreamt of? She knew no one lived in fairytales. Novels had been created to entertain. Perfect worlds woven by words everyone loved to hear. Stories would never become reality. At least, she could hope for a quiet life.

"By the way, you've got mail," Dante said, bringing Jaime out of her daydream. "Apparently it went to the wrong letter box. Monsieur Chevalier from the second floor scribbled a short note to say he was sorry the letter took so long to reach us. He only got back late yesterday from a two week holiday."

Strange. She wasn't expecting post. Maybe a letter from England? She placed her glass on the nearby gueridon and headed into the hallway.

The envelope sat on the small table next to the door. The stamp mark showed Rambouillet. The writing that of a young child. Scrawny irregular letters dotted the envelope, fighting to remain in a straight line. Jaime's lips curved upwards. Had to be from one of the twins, either Sasha or Santine, otherwise Suzanne would have called, or sent a text message.

She'd soon find out.

Taking the small knife next to the mail tray, Jaime slit open the envelope, and pulled out a piece of paper.

Tes chauchemars
viennent juste de
commencer !

Jaime's mouth opened in a silent scream, eyes widening in shock. Perhaps she hadn't read it correctly.

Your nightmares
have just
begun!

"But he's dead!" She yelled to the corridor. "I saw him with a bullet in his head."

Jaime's throat tightened and her mouth dried up as she struggled to breathe. Who the hell was it? The writing and layout of the note weren't the same. Did Eddie work with a friend? Or could it be another member of the family? Or maybe it was never him? Jaime's mind whirled in a carousel of fear, spinning out of control.

Dante came rushing into the hallway. "Jaime?"

"It's starting all over again," she sobbed, collapsing to the parquet.

Dante dropped to his knees beside her. He picked up the piece of paper and read the words written on the note.

"I thought it was all over," she said.

Dante didn't reply. He carried her to the sofa in the lounge where she drained her glass before holding it out for a refill. Dante's eyes widened, but he obliged, pouring more champagne into the outstretched glass.

Jaime hiccupped and put a hand over her mouth. "I need the

bathroom." She stood on wobbly legs and headed out of the room.

***

After a few minutes, Dante's phone rang, bringing him out of his reverie. Did this new fiasco mean another visit to the police station? He strolled to the other side of the room and fished the phone out of his jacket pocket.

"Hi, Dante! Pierre Morel here."

It took a few seconds for Dante to register the caller – Leonora's lawyer.

"Pierre, how are things?"

"Fine. Listen. I'm phoning for a favour."

Dante gazed at Jaime as she entered the lounge. He hoped the favour wouldn't have an impact on Jaime's state of mind. Vulnerable as she was after receiving that note, he didn't want anything further to upset her.

"Fire away, Pierre."

"The prison authorities have granted Leonora permission to have reading material. She wants to finish the books she started before being arrested. They're on the bedside table at the family estate."

Dante listened, guessing the reason for the call.

"Only hitch, I'm too busy right now. Would you mind going? I've settled everything, so you'll have special access to the property. I'll have the keys ready for you to collect."

Dante rubbed a hand over his chin. Could he leave Jaime alone under the present circumstances?

"Please, Dante. It won't take long. Besides, you know the property."

Another gaze over at Jamie slumped on the settee pushed Dante to refuse. But, he couldn't let a fellow lawyer down. Pierre had helped him out on a tricky case in the past. It was time for payback.

He took in a deep breath. "I'll go."

"Thanks, Dante, I appreciate your help." Pierre's grateful tone convinced Dante that he'd taken the right decision. He ended the call and headed to Jaime's side. "I have to go on an errand. A colleague needs a favour."

"Don't leave me on my own, Dante." Jaime's voice came out in a nervous whisper. "Let me come with you." The expression behind those worried eyes was deep, pleading even.

Dante reached for Jaime's hand. Ice cold. Poor girl. What the hell was going on? She didn't need a new stalker on the scene. The bastard even knew where they lived. Best if they both went to Leonora's place. At least, she'd feel reassured. So would he.

***

Jaime stepped out of the car and followed Dante towards the patio. Leonora's property hadn't changed. What had she expected? The place had only been empty since Leonora's arrest a little over two weeks ago.

It had ceased raining a few hours earlier. Drops of water still dripped from the vegetation which accentuated the silence. The shadows of the cedar trees danced upon the lawn. The cool evening air washed over them, clinging to the surface of the lake.

Leonora's property was magnificent, especially with the exuberant vegetation early summer brought. So peaceful. So relaxing. Yet, all was so different in the evening. The outline of the house even more foreboding, the trees more jagged, the hedges thicker.

A feeling of unease crept over Jaime, like a clever spider weaving its web of silk. Glancing around, she held her breath, ears on alert. Dante took hold of Jaime's cold hand.

"It's all right. There's nothing to be scared about."

Jaime wasn't convinced. That last note had left her perplexed. She imagined the worst. Anyone could pop up out of the blue and grab her. Even here.

She squeezed Dante's hand, willing herself forward, stepping carefully to avoid making a noise on the crunching gravel. Afraid she might give their presence away. But then, who was there to hear them?

Dante took out a set of keys and aimed for the lock. The front door creaked when he eased it open. Jaime's hands turned clammy. Why did everything seem worse at night, or in the dark? Noises louder. Gardens spookier. Nerves jumpier.

Jaime scanned the environment one last time and headed after Dante into the hallway. She'd never been in the house. Dante switched on the lights and Jaime was impressed. Beautiful gold decorations adorned both ceiling and walls. The black and white marble floor stretched from the door into an impressive lounge where the room's tall bay windows no doubt looked out over the back garden.

Dante hurried down the hallway and up the large wooden staircase. A pang of jealousy hit her. He knew exactly where to go. He and Leonora had been an item in the past.

They entered an enormous bedroom. It contained a four-poster bed, neatly made, and various pieces of antique furniture. Huge drapery curtains hung at the tall windows. The walls on either side of the mantelpiece were decorated with a small faded tapestry and a couple of sepia prints.

While Dante rummaged through the drawers of Leonora's Louis XIV bedside table, Jaime ambled around the room. A set of antique Russian dolls covered in dust were set on the mantelpiece along with a photo of who Jaime guessed to be Leonora's grandmother.

She walked behind the dresser desk with its large round mirror and sat on the comfortable green leather chair. Framed with golden ivy leaves, the mirror held a cherubic angel at its top. Leaning back, Jaime closed her eyes and compared this life of chateau to the sordid prison cell Leonora was now in. What a huge change

When Jaime opened her eyes, they fell onto the antique vase to one side of the desk. She didn't know why she'd been attracted like that, but the beautiful engravings caught her attention. Jaime took hold of it and traced a finger over the dark writing. It was beautiful.

"Get down, Jaime!" Dante threw the books on the floor and grabbed the candlestick as the bedroom door crashed open.

In Jaime's haste to replace the vase, it toppled over the edge of the desk and crashed to the floor. Jaime covered her mouth with both hands, and gazed from the broken vase to the old man in the doorway holding a shaky shotgun.

Dante replaced the candlestick on the gueridon and let out a huge breath. "Gaspard, put the gun down."

The old man blinked in disbelief. "Master, Dante?"

He gradually lowered the shotgun and sat on a nearby chair, panting and wheezing. "You gave me such a fright."

Jaime recovered from her stupour and drew Dante's attention. *Who is he?* she mouthed. *The Gardener*, Dante mouthed back before turning his full attention to the man.

Jaime gazed down to the ground, slipping out of the conversation between Dante and the shaky-shotgun guardian.

Shit! Leonora's lovely vase was now a shattered mess.

Crouching down, she began to pick up the small pieces of porcelain. Amongst the fragments of fine bone china, she came across pieces of headed paper.

Christ Almighty! The same paper on which she'd just received the last message. Could this fiasco have been Leonora's doing?

"Dante, come here, quick." Jaime's voice came out in a strained whisper.

Dante hurried to her side.

"Look, pieces of torn paper were stuffed into the vase." Jaime couldn't remove her eyes from the fragments.

Dante crouched and retrieved one of the pieces. "It's letter-headed paper with the Saint-Clair family crest."

"It can't have been Leonora all along. Eddie admitted to sending them."

Dante rubbed his thumb over the expensive paper. "Maybe just this one?"

"But how could she get the note to me?"

The gardener cleared his throat and sat higher on the chair. "Excuse me for overhearing your conversation, Master Dante, Miss Leonora asked me to post the letter. She even asked me to write the address, despite my shaky hands. I hope I haven't misspelled the name?"

Dante returned to the old man's side.

"She told me to look after the place during her short absence," he continued, lost in a faraway gaze. "And that's what I'm doing."

"And you're doing a good job, Gaspard."

Jaime felt sorry for the old man. He had no idea his mistress could be away for a while.

The old man wiped away a few stray tears. "No matter what others say about Miss Leonora's sharp tongue, she always treated me right. I was gardener to her grandmother, you know. I saw the little girl grow up. She used to play and potter around with me in the garden. I even made her a tree-house."

Dante put a hand on the old man's shoulder and gave a reassuring squeeze. "I know Gaspard. She often spoke about you."

The old man smiled through watery eyes. "Oh well, if you don't need me for anything, I'll go up to my room. All this commotion has worn me out." He rose on unsteady legs and trudged out of the room, tutting.

Dante retrieved the books he'd flung aside. He smoothed out the damaged pages while Jaime picked the pieces of vase and laid them carefully on the desk.

"I can't believe Leonora would have gone so far with her jealousy," Dante said after a while.

Jaime came to his side. "You probably didn't know her at all. A lot of people are good at putting on a show. Keeping on their best behaviour at all times."

Dante gave a weak smile and tucked Leonora's books under his arm. "Come on, we need to get these to Pierre, and this new evidence to the police."

Jaime gazed at the torn pieces of paper. "Do we need to take this to the police?"

Dante raised an eyebrow

"I mean, what's it going to bring? Leonora has already been arrested."

Dante caressed Jaime's cheek with the back of his hand. "If this is what you really want?"

Jaime had several weak points. Vengeance wasn't one of them. If they went to the police with this proof, what would it change? Hadn't Leonora saved her life by preventing Eddie from slitting her throat?

"I want to close the door on all this, Dante. Let bygones be bygones."

"Then we'll do just that."

***

Dante stood behind Jaime on the balcony of their flat, his strong body cradling hers. Stars lit the peaceful night sky with its familiar pattern, witnesses of the earth since the beginning of time.

A gracious comet trailed its brilliant streak of white across the starry sky, its tail a fine decoration of glitter. Jaime caught her breath. "Look, Dante, a shooting star. Do you think it's a sign to say this whole thing is over?"

Dante raised his head. "Could be."

"Do you realise those stars have been there for thousands of years? How many people have gazed up over the millennia thinking it's the sign of a new dawning?"

Dante kissed the top of Jaime's head, and she snuggled deeper into his body, savouring the moment.

She'd come safely through fear, anxiety, surprises and uncertainty all thanks to this wonderful man.

Perhaps now, she was finally going to begin her life – and live.

About the Authors

A J Saunders is two friends writing under one name. Pat loves reading – Jo loves writing. We met at work and hit it off immediately. Our bond for reading and writing brought us to create our books. Looking for storylines and characteristics we wanted to read, but couldn't find, we decided to write our own.

We both live in the Loire Valley in France where we are English trainers during the week and an author at the weekends.

Thank you for reading *Hyde and Seek*. If you have time to spare, a short review would be greatly appreciated.

You can also e-mail us at adleyjsaunders@gmail.com
We always love to hear from our readers.

Hyde and Seek is our second novel.

The Whispering Magpies (our YA paranormal mystery) was published in 2020.

Printed in Great Britain
by Amazon

79242787R00150